Smooth Fishplate

Matthew Brown

mattbrownwrites@gmail.com

CONTENTS

ACKNOWLEDGMENTS

A huge thank you to my friend Dom, who has been so very generous with his time, patience and help... all of which we both know he'll never be able to get back.

Also the lovely Ruth, who has endured years of me laughing at my own jokes and constant requests for spell checks.

CHAPTER ONE: LOWER DIDSBURY

The mighty class 55 Deltic was approaching the final station run past, delivering its huge load of coal wagons to the Dukes End power station. Colin the driver had only taken delivery of the Deltic in the morning. It had been 'in shed' for weeks, being picked over by Stew, the pedantic maintenance chief. The engine had been renamed 'Hadley's Hope' and was what one could only describe as pristine. Colin had noted with a wry grin that it looked suspiciously like Stew had been polishing the buffers again. The late afternoon sun filtered down from a hazy May sky, the landscape passed smoothly by. Colin knew large groups of people had gathered to watch 'Hadley's Hope' pulling the longest tail on the entire system.

'What the hell' he thought, ignoring Stew's warning to keep within standard operating limits. 'Let's see what this shiny mother can do.'

His hand pushed forward on the chrome power lever. 'Hadley's Hope' imperceptibly at first and then with growing reassurance began to surge forward. The heavy tail of coal wagons stretching out behind jostled and squealed as the train thundered towards Lower Didsbury.

Ex-Group Captain Monty 'The Moustache' Rawlins was standing virtually to attention on the warm concrete of the platform. He was intently watching a small lad on the other side of the line. Monty wasn't quite sure what the pesky little chap was up to, but it looked irritatingly as though he was writing something rude in chalk on the wall of the bicycle rack next to the car park. Monty couldn't quite see what it read. He tried to focus.

'Focus. Focus. Damn this gammy eye,' he muttered bitterly under his breath. That incident over Leipzig when his Lanc 'Lucky Sexpot' had been bounced by Jerry night fighters. He'd managed to nurse the

old girl back to Blighty but never regained his full sight and of course never flew again. So now, nearly 20 years later he found himself in charge of a small provincial railway station, getting cross about some little shit writing what he now thinks is 'dirty knickers' or perhaps 'busty knockers' on his bicycle shed. Monty folded his arms and sighed.

'I miss the war.'

Meanwhile, just up the line from Lower Didsbury, at the road crossing point Dennis idled down his old blue ford tractor. He could just see from his vantage point his prized herd of Jerseys in the field opposite. His favourite cow, his most favourite cow ever, was waiting for him, her head pushed through the bars of the old maple field gate. He smiled affectionately at her and called out:

'Ermintrude oie got a lurvee lit treat afor ye my gal.' Ermintrude stared back, her large bovine lips already chewing on some imaginary delight.

Colin felt invincible. He was in command of the biggest, baddest rig in town. A juggernaut nearly half a mile long. The crowd that had gathered around Lower Didsbury was going to get the performance of the day. If Stew had been around he definitely wouldn't have approved of the sly smile that was spreading dangerously across Colin's face and equally the growing momentum of Hadley's Hope.

Stevo watched his half empty pint of bitter start to jig around on the lichen encrusted table in the garden of the Water Tower and Tender. Ginge grinned at him as his nearly empty glass also started to dance. 'Guess that must be the coal train to Dukes coming through, which also means it's your turn to get 'em in.'

'Alright, alright Ginge. Reckon I might ask those couple of beauties on the bench over there if they want anything too!'

Ginge looked over his shoulder and laughed. 'Good luck mate.'

Colin was just about to sound off the air horn as he approached the station, when a sickening jolt caused the whole front end of Hadley's Hope to bounce up and off the rail. There was a horrendous clattering sound, like a sudden burst of hail on a tin roof as the first bogie of the Deltic hit the ballast at the side of the track, instantly followed by a second fusillade of loose ballast as the second massive bogie dug in. Colin froze. Within a microsecond he had gone from invincible to utterly impotent. He wasn't in charge of anything, least of all his destiny. So Colin did the only thing he could. He put his hands over his eyes and whispered very, very quietly 'Oops!'

The first victim of the Deltic was a disused maintenance hut. It momentarily stuck to the blunt unyielding nose of the engine, like an unwanted pimple before being catapulted away to the rear, where it fell into the trail of coal wagons behind. There was a nauseating clang, followed by a short popping noise and then dozens of wagons, each of nearly 13 tons, flew off at all sorts of random tangents and trajectories.

Ermintrude was dimly aware that something bad was about to happen. A huge green monster came tearing through the hedge at the opposite end of the pasture, its angry eyes momentarily locked with hers before it charged past, tore open the near hedge, sheared across the road and headed towards the railway station. Ermintrude's slow brain desperately tried to make sense of it all but while attempting to keep up with current events she failed to notice a coal truck spinning lazily through the air towards her. Ermintrude's last thought before being severed from all four legs was predictably, how much she was looking forward to seeing that nice man who always had a treat for her. Dennis meanwhile was staring up into the milky sky, his arms fixed in the same position as though driving a tractor. He thought he could feel his legs but they were, in reality, still attached to the old ford. Dennis wasn't. Dennis was lying in a field somewhere else and it wasn't even his field. He felt no pain, just sadness. He was really fond of Ermintrude... and his wife.

Ginge was just about to shout over to Stevo to get some plain crisps when a hundred tons of loco came ploughing through the pub garden. His head would later be found on top of a beech hedge, an expression of bewilderment (his natural condition) painted permanently on.

Janet Butterworth was in the phone box on the south bound station platform. She was trying to disengage from a long phone call to her mother. A somewhat agitated man was standing outside waiting to use the phone. Her subtle hints were far too woolly for her mother, who had just started to explain, for the third time, how the plumber had tripped over the dog and only narrowly avoided chinning himself on the naked statue of Uncle Horace. However, the appearance of a huge loco approaching along the actual platform was enough to end the conversation. The last thing Janet's mum would have heard, had she been listening was 'Oh Jesus Christ' before the line crackled out. Fortuitously for Janet the thick concrete platform sucked out the last of the engine's momentum and it came to a halt, resting precariously against the phone booth's door. After remembering to start breathing again Janet gingerly opened one eye. Her trembling hand reached out to push against the buckled door. It didn't move an atom. 'Oh dear' thought Janet or words to that effect - 'This could take a while' and at this point realized she desperately needed the toilet.

Over the tracks on the northbound platform Monty was still fixed, statue-like, in his pre-crash stance. He had fought an instinct to dive towards the corner of a small brick wall having remembered the conversation between himself and his base commander when he took the controls of 'Lucky Sexpot'.

'Concentrate on breathing because if Jerry's astern, firing shell after shell from his dastardly Hun cannon there is absolutely no point ducking old boy.'

Monty hadn't ducked, flinched or even blinked. He had centred, drawn in a long slow breath and simply let the carnage unfold around him. As the dust settled Monty stood untouched and found to his surprise that he was still staring at the point where the small boy had been. He didn't need to squint to realize that the cheeky chap was probably a little hurt since three coal wagons were now piled up on that exact spot. Monty sighed.

'More bloody paperwork' and in the same breath 'I really miss the war.'

While Hadley's Hope had left a very linear trail of destruction, the coal wagons had bestowed a vicious and random vengeance upon the local community, although not all members of said community had seen that as necessarily a bad thing. Old bent Arthur looked out over the allotments and chuckled. His chief rival's onions lay under an upturned wagon and a satisfying gouge nearly three feet deep marked its arrival via shaky Tom's potentially award-winning artichokes. An evil little thought entered Arthur's mind. Perhaps he could contrive a small accident to befall crooked Ned's show-stopping pumpkins and blame it on current circumstances.

'Yes, yes, yes' he cackled, 'the Lower Didsbury horticultural cup shall be mine this year.'

Spinster Carter, who had struggled through the previous winter unable to afford coal, now had fifty tons of the black gold piled up in her garden. She cunningly decided to start hiding it under the sink lest the relevant authorities attempt to take it back. She would later achieve fleeting notoriety when her house caught fire and required the combined engines of two stations to contain the conflagration.

A deep silence descended upon the devastated landscape.

Deep silence.

Then a huge cheer went up and a few people started clapping in the sort of way that people do when a waiter drops a tray of glasses. A little boy held aloft by his father squealed with delight:

'Again, again, make them do it again!' Nick came running over. He had been winding up a nearby tram appreciation society about the inaccuracy of their actual trams and was just about to point out that one of their prize engines was out of period and also the wrong colour, but had to turn away on hearing the cheer go up. He took one look at the devastation, pulled a dark face at Colin, who was attempting to 'tidy up' if that were possible after a major freight 'incident' and screamed -

'You absolute wanker!' His eyes darted around the model layout seeing this broken bit and that smashed part. 'I spent fucking hours watching cows so that I could pose them naturally Colin. So why did you drive your train through their field Colin? Why? Why? It's not difficult Colin. Look...fast, slow, fast, slow, oh hang on, oh, er stop. It's not fucking difficult. Do you want to know what's difficult? Colin. Shall I tell you?'

Colin looked up and was about to shout 'I don't care Nick' but thought better of it. Nick carried on ranting.

'Shall I tell you what's difficult? Shall I? Can you model an impatient man waiting to use the phone? Can you Colin? Because I can. Where's that fella gone? Oh look, he's looking impatient under a train. Doesn't really work does it?'

Colin knew this rant was far from over. He restrained himself from looking at his watch.

Nick carried on shouting. His wild eyes now alighted upon the devastated pub garden. 'Oh Christ, not the beer garden. I spent hours making all those tables and chairs. I didn't make them out of wood though did I Colin?'

'Did you not?' answered Colin.

'No!' shrieked Nick. 'Because the grain would have looked wrong, so I made them out of very expensive plastic wood and carved the grain in by hand. Do you know how difficult that is Colin?'

'Ooh very difficult' replied Colin.

'Yes, it was difficult Colin. My eyes didn't focus properly for days and what did you say I'd been doing too much of?' Nick looked angrily at Colin. Colin looked him square in the eyes.

'I said that you had been wanking excessively.' Colin stifled a snigger. It didn't help. Nick turned a dangerous shade of crimson. His head looked as though it may start spinning.

'I spent an entire day in Essex sketching an abandoned maintenance hut just to get all the little nuances right.'

'No one should be made to spend a day in Essex' replied Colin. Nick didn't hear him and continued to verbally spew.

'Do you know what a nuance is Colin? I tell you what a nuance is Colin. It's my entire fucking life. It's what I do. My middle name is nuance, I'm fucking mayor of Nuance-on-the-Wold. President of the United States of Nuance. Captain of HMS nu…'

Nick's monologue on nuances within the context of positions of authority was cruelly cut short by a coal wagon hitting him in the face.

'Nick, put a sock in it' barked Pete. He picked up another miniature coal wagon and raised his hand. Nick almost immediately calmed down and stood rubbing his face where the model had hit him. There was something stuck to his cheek, a little piece of plastic or something. He pulled it off and turned it over in his hand. A cow with no legs stared forlornly back at him.

'Oh Ermintrude I'm so sorry' he whispered and slumped to his knees. Pete walked over and put his hand onto Nick's shoulder, giving him a slight 'Don't worry mate we can sort this out' squeeze as he did so.

The public started to move away because once the entertaining swearing and the finger pointing was over, all that remained was a bunch of sad looking blokes and a model railway that looked like someone had tipped a large bucket of coal wagons all over it. The Dewesbury model railway exhibition was nearly over anyway and as the village hall began to clear, Pete Fletcher, president of the Smooth Fishplate model railway club gathered his team about him.

'Look lads it's not a disaster.'

'Er, looks like a disaster to me, Pete. A full-on double-o-disaster' sniped Nick.

'That's not what I meant' continued Pete. 'This wasn't a qualifier, you all know that, we just wanted to get the Deltic tested to see what sort of load it could pull and work out a way of timetabling it to our routine. I mean, Christ, if this had been a competition, well yeah, all over, last one out turn the lights off. Tell you what, let's meet up Wednesday at the pub, work out what happened and take it from there.'

'When you say 'work out what happened' is that your sales speak for 'assign blame'?' ventured Colin, simultaneously glancing over at Nick.

Nick retorted almost instantly 'Driver error, driver error' mimicking a generic Hollywood alarm call.

Pete frowned, he needed to sort this out quick before it all descended into another Nick versus Colin exchange of bollocks.

'Look guys let's get packed up and talk it over with the calming and soothing embrace of beer on Wednesday. Right…Colin?'

'Yes boss?'

'Go home'

'Eh?'

Pete replied quickly before Nick could get involved. 'Me and Nick can pack the boards up and Stew can get the engines and stock together… So get going.'

Colin stole a glance at Nick before walking off. Pete looked Nick directly in the eyes.

'Not a word.'

Nick shrugged his shoulders in resignation, turned round and started to unclip the boards that made up the layout. Stew turned to Pete.

'Very smooth Pete, I believe you've just removed the fuse from the bomb.'

'Well till Wednesday at least' grimaced Pete and in a slightly conspiratorial tone whispered to Stew 'Any idea why 'Hadley's Hope' jumped the track?' Stew rubbed his clean-shaven chin a few times, made a few soft clicking noises with his tongue before letting out a long sigh.

'Well... you know I checked the engine out before we ran it and it was perfect... well as perfect as you can make it.'

Pete looked towards Colin's empty seat or 'cab' as the drivers liked to call it.

'Why did you swap cabs for the last part of the timetable?'

Stew rubbed his bald head. 'Oh Colin wanted to do the Hadley's Hope run.'

'What about Colin then? I wasn't watching him that much today just cos he's normally so good. Was he ok?'

'He was fine Pete, we went through the timetable you drew up... by the way we reckon there are a few moves we can do that will drag in some more points and make the routine a little safer but Colin, he was his usual predictably safe self... only I think he may have got a little bored towards the end.'

'What? Bored like I'm-going-to-crash-a-train-cos-it's-exciting, or bored-and-not-concentrating-leading-to-a-crash?' replied Pete.

'Possibly the latter. It did sound fast from where I was

sitting, the rhythm sounded wrong but Pete, it shouldn't have left the rails. It's easier to derail an engine with no weight behind it and that Deltic had as much weight, I think, as it's possible to have.' Stew took off his specs and gave them a cursory wipe.

Pete looked into some imaginary middle space

'So… possibly not Colin's fault then?'

'Try convincing Nick about that' sighed Stew.

Pete grunted and rubbed his forehead.

'Right, I better help Nick with the boards. If you think of anything let me know.'

Twenty minutes later Stew carefully finished wrapping the last of the locos in cloth and placed them in his special carrying case. He rather liked the discipline of making sure they were all secure and protected. It somehow filled a fatherly need denied to him by a lack of children. He walked slowly past the layout, where Nick was heavily absorbed in sweeping all the detritus of the crash into clear plastic bags. It looked worryingly as though he were involved in some sort of crime investigation. Stew patted Nick on the back and ambled out into the car park. He had just closed the boot of his Montego estate when he clocked Pete on the other side of the car park leaning against the hire van they had used to transport the layout. He was drawing deeply on a Benson and tapping his fingers on the wheel arch. Stew headed over.

'Alright Pete?'

'Yeah… I think? Well that was a somewhat interesting end to the day.' Pete dropped the fag end and ground it out with the toe of his shoe. Stew nodded.

'Well, Nick sees himself as an artist. He takes his work a bit seriously… a little too seriously to be honest.'

'I know… but he's the best. I wouldn't want anyone else to do the model-making. He loves it, absolutely loves it. You heard the story about the last club he was in?'

'Well I've heard a lot of stories about Nick, mostly from Nick himself, especially after he's had a few.'

Pete smirked.

'Yep, he's bloody good value at the pub, but I'm talking about his last club, the 'The Wy-Vale Branch-line.''

Stew frowned slightly.

'Was that the story about him modelling a couple of Daleks robbing the local post office?'

'Well kind of… I guess. You didn't hear the rest of the tale then?

Stew shrugged. Pete cleared his throat.

'So the president of WB sees these Daleks halfway through a run schedule at an exhibition. Suffice to say he doesn't see the funny side. What you might call a bit of a traditionalist. Doesn't seem to understand that the public really loves these little details, especially the kids. I've watched them at exhibitions running from layout to layout, totally ignoring the trains, they just wanted to spot something odd or funny in the layout. Anyway he breaks these Daleks off and places them carefully on the floor, he smiles at Nick and then grinds them to pieces with his shoe. El Presidento then proceeds to lecture him on appropriate detail and the traditional values of the club. And furthermore from now on any new models will have to be personally inspected and passed by him. Well, Nick had put some major love into those little Daleks. I tell you what he's good at, I mean, really good at… he said it himself. He is mister bloody nuance. Those Daleks were so well modelled they actually looked like someone had made them out of old bits of ply and sink plungers. That's what makes his work so amazing.'

'So I'm guessing Nick left the club at that point then?' offered Stew.

'Not quite! No, that would have been far too normal. He was asked to build a new signal box and he set about it with gusto. The detail on the outside was stunning but it was the interior that was really special. Apparently, according to Nick, he built a little inside toilet which you could only see by looking through a certain window to a wall, on which hung a mirror which was angled to show the toilet door, which was itself slightly ajar to reveal the toilet.' Stew sighed and raised his eyebrows.

'This isn't going to have a happy ending is it?'

'Well not for the president of The Wy-Vale Branch-line' giggled Pete. He continued. 'Nick takes the signal box to the president and he loves it. Goes on about what a fitting model it is for a club of their stature and insists that Nick must install the signal box it time for the next exhibition.'

Stew interrupted.

'This exhibition? Wasn't at a school was it?'

'Why yes Stew, a very posh private prep school.'

'Oh dear I heard something about that in the paper.'

'Can I continue?' enquired Pete. 'Thank you. So the head of this school has asked Wy-Vale to set up a day early so all the children can have a look before they go home.' Pete paused and looked absently around the car park. 'Now this is where I've sort of pieced the story together because Nick didn't turn up to the actual exhibition. I heard the rest of the story through a parent, who heard it from a kid, so it may be a little unreliable. What I can tell you for sure, is this:' Pete took a long breath. 'So, Nick fixes the signal box to the layout, only what no one knows is that the signal box is built around a thin steel shell. Absolutely rigid. Doesn't look like it but you could take a hammer to the roof and it wouldn't budge, plus he's only gone and bolted through to the ¾ ply base of the layout. That signal box is going no place in a hurry.'

'Dare I ask why you would want to fix a signal box to a board in such a way?' ventured Stew.

'Do you know what a Swedish stimulator is?' Pete whispered, at the same time raising one inquisitive eye brow.

'Oh, I think my dad used to have one of those for the garden' exclaimed Stew.

'Did it take four batteries?'

'Oh no it ran on… oh. Oh dear' Stew started to redden slightly. There was a reflective pause. 'Is a Swedish stimulator thing a naughty toy for adventurous types?'

'Afraid so. Nick had added a few extra interior details once the signal box had been approved by the El Presidento. Basically, the signal box was now under the control of Mr. Johnson, the signal box operator.'

'He does like to give his creations names doesn't he?' chuckled Stew.

'Indeed! And the naughty Mr. Johnson had invited some equally naughty friends along as well… Basically he had a full orgy going on. Naked women bent over point levers, a large African gentleman operating the Swedish stimulator, someone bound up in ropes and hanging from the ceiling while what looked like an old English sheep dog… in a tutu… licked them. I mean I don't know what goes on in that head of his but it was real Grade-A filth, all perfectly executed in 1/72 scale, although according to Nick the African gentleman had something modelled in 1/32 scale! The day of the exhibition Nick doesn't turn up to help so of course they're a little pushed for time to get everything set up. This of course means no one notices the signal box, especially the president who is busy sucking up to the head master telling him what a beautiful layout they have and how the dear children are really going to enjoy it. Eventually all the boards are connected and the layout is ready. The kids are assembled and the Wy-vale Branch-line go through their standard routine. But still no one has noticed the signal box and then suddenly after ten minutes the model suddenly illuminates.'

'You're kidding!' exclaimed Stew.

'Yep' continued Pete. 'He'd put a timer into the box just to get it some extra attention. Apparently, according to that parent's kid I told you about, the president says straight away that illuminating the signal box was his idea because he felt all the exquisite details needed to be appreciated and he then tells all the children to line up and take it in turns to have a peek.' Stew looked at his feet. Pete continued - 'What really upset the parents though, was for weeks their kids were coming out with stuff like 'Daddy doesn't have silver pants. I wish my friend's mum had gold booby tassels. Mine doesn't look like that, is there something wrong with me?' All the kids developed an irrational fear of dogs and broom handles and apparently one kid started tying up his sister's dolls and licking them.'

'So what happened to the president of the WB?' asked Stew.

'Well according to that kid, the PE teacher had to be brought in to drag the president out of the hall. He had taken his shoe off and was repeatedly smashing it against the signal box while shouting 'You dirty fucker, you dirty little fucker!' The headmaster had collapsed and Mr. Peabody, the old history teacher had simply muttered. 'This all reminds me of Singapore' '

'And then Nick joined us shortly afterwards… no wonder he didn't mention it' said Stew. 'I have to say, given that story, weren't you just a little concerned about letting him in?'

'I knew him through a work contact, well to be honest I

sold him a car but that's another story. Anyway, when I heard he left Wy-Vale it wasn't long before I bumped into him and had a chat about joining us. The thing with Nick is that he needs his space to be creative and I love what he does. If he feels the need to build the interior of the USS Enterprise into someone's front room or have a sniper hidden in a tree about to shoot the milkman or even… or even have a couple having sex somewhere in the layout, so be it!'

'Well I guess' shrugged Stew.

'And by the way Stew' winked Pete, 'all those things I mentioned are in our layout… somewhere!'

'Well where are the sex couple then?'

'The question Stew is not where they are but how many are there?' grinned Pete.

'What?'

'I know of eight and not all are what you might call conventional 'couples."

'I feel a bit unclean' Stew muttered, visibly squirming.

'Anyway better get back to Nick, help him shift them boards. I shall see you Wednesday Mr. Porter.'

Stew drove the short journey home. He kept finding himself looking at windows and down alley ways and wondering what may be going on behind those curtains or in that shed. He pulled up into his driveway and eased himself out of the car.

'Hi love. How did it finish up? Margaret appeared from behind the privet bush in the front garden. A pair of secateurs waved at him.

'Well it was quite exciting actually. Colin had a little crash and wrecked a load of Nick's models.'

'Oh deary me,' exclaimed Margaret, 'that poor boy, he

spends so much time messing around with his models. He should get himself a nice girlfriend.'

'I'm not sure he sees it as messing about. It's pretty much all he thinks about at the moment.' Stew went to the back of the estate and opened the boot.

'I'd offer you a hand with those trains' ventured Margaret.

Stew raised his eyebrows and turned his head slightly.

'Yes I know you don't trust me to not drop them. How about a nice cup of tea?'

Stew went to say something but was immediately cut off by Margaret.

'Yes I'll bring it to your study.'

Stew carefully brought in each carrying case and by the time he was placing the final one in its allocated home Margaret had placed a cup of tea on his desk, a custard cream nestled on the saucer.

'I thought we could have a nice shepherd's pie for supper' Margaret called out as she shuffled to the kitchen humming something vaguely religious.

Stew settled himself into his favourite possession, an old leather swing chair that had come from an ex-GWR station master's office. He sat there a few seconds enjoying the feel and smell of the leather as it flexed and creaked to accommodate his weight. Then he reached for his old toffee tin with a picture of the Flying Scotsman emblazoned on the front. He popped off the lid and reached in for his secret stash of chocolate bourbons, while placing the rejected custard cream in another tin for discrete disposal later. Why he couldn't tell Margaret he didn't like custard creams he had no idea but sometimes there needed to be secrets between man and wife to protect the marriage. Stew started on his second biscuit and his mind began to wander and then somewhat weirdly he got a sudden image of Nick stark naked, his dick out on the model railway while wearing a large LMS porter's hat and making an announcement over a station Tannoy warning passengers that services may be disrupted due to a massive obstruction on the line. Stew looked at the third bourbon he was about to consume and put it timidly back in the tin.

'Must be a sugar rush' he muttered in despair 'or talking about Nick for too long.' He gave himself a little shake, emitted a small cough and decided he better check some of the engines over, especially 'Hadley's Hope' just in case he might have missed something. As second driver, a slightly derisive term he thought, it was his task to maintain and service all locos and rolling stock as well as carry out any mods. He had to admit to being a little worried that 'Hadley's Hope' had jumped the rails due to some sort of wheel defect or perhaps even a broken axle. The thought of Nick blaming him for the death of Ermintrude and a whole host of his imaginary friends was something a man of his age didn't want hanging over him until Wednesday, certainly not with the work load he was going to get at the accounts company this coming week.

'Oh thank God' he exhaled as he examined the wheels of 'Hadley's Hope.' Nothing amiss, in fact the engine ran perfectly on his section of test track and the voltmeter showed a motor in perfect running order. Stew relaxed. 'Well I guess it's down to Colin now, driver error.' He could just hear Nick giving his own summing up at the pub meeting on Wednesday:

'It is the simple conclusion of me that Colin is an actual wanker and should in no circumstances be trusted to drive anything other than a small bicycle with stabilisers on.'

Stew sighed, he had always thought joining a model railway club would be a relaxing little diversion from his often mundane job. Turns out that he often needed his work at the accountancy firm to get away from the stress of the model club. Stew turned to stare at a framed picture of

Winston Churchill. 'Still, why is it I find myself now looking forward to Wednesday? Must be like Pete said, Nick's good value, especially after he's had a few.'

'Food's ready dear' Margaret called from the kitchen.

Colin arrived back at his Victorian terrace having had to park further down the road. Normally not being able to park outside his own house would have been irritating but it had allowed him to approach quietly and hopefully to sneak in without anyone noticing. Raising the house key very slowly, he engaged the lock. There was a satisfying clunk and he tentatively pushed the door forward and then closed it while holding his breath. The hallway was eerily silent, he correctly reasoned that it was far too quiet. He knew exactly what was going to happen next. Suddenly from the top of the stairs came a high-pitched scream followed by a growing crescendo of giggling and laughing and the unmistakable cascade of little people's feet.

'Daddy' screamed Han Solo as he bounced down to the bottom step, before he raised his blaster and let loose a single plastic dart. It arced through the hall and landed on top of Colin's head. Colin mocked a painful injury and raised his fist.

'Curse you Han Solo I may be wounded but I can still chase you all the way to the bedroom!'

Han screamed an unbelievably high pitched 'No!' and tore away back up the stairs. As he watched Han make good his escape he noticed a few steps up, a miniature Darth Vader. Darth Vader stood giggling at him. Colin did a fearsome growl and moved in slow motion up the first step. Vader shouted 'Daddy, daddy, Jabba smelly pants' turned and fled. Colin's wife appeared from the lounge.

'Just warning you, Jabba smelly pants, that they've been building a Death Star all afternoon in Mark's bedroom and

I think you may be required to go and get them.'

'Do I get extra pudding for blowing up the Death Star?' queried Colin.

'No but if you could tidy up before dinner that would be very brave of you especially as you've been playing trains all weekend.' Helen raised an eyebrow.

Colin took a deep breath and shouted upstairs 'I'm getting into my X-Wing. Anyone not in a Death Star will be tickled to death.'

There came a muffled giggling from upstairs.

Forty minutes later, after a successful assault on the Empire's most terrible weapon - a space station the size of a small moon constructed from duvets, cushions, three large cardboard boxes and a lot of imagination - Colin finally got to sit down for some food with Helen.

'So how did it all go today Mr. Train driver?' Helen was staring at him, a huge grin on her face. She loved hearing about the club, it was a constant source of amusement for her.

'Well I - ' Colin paused and smiled a short curt smile at Helen. 'I crashed the new Deltic through a load of Nick's models and he was a little upset.'

Helen burst out laughing. This was comic gold to her. Eventually the laughter subsided and she wiped the tears from her face although her shoulders carried on spasmodically shuddering.

'Any models in particular?' Helen was staring at Colin's mouth waiting for him to speak.

'I think I may have killed Ermintrude.' He said. Helen bit her lip. 'And maybe some other models of emotional importance.'

Helen's shoulders started shaking again.

'How did little Nicky take the death of a plastic cow?' she sniffed.

'He jumped up and down a lot, called me a wanker and wittered on about nuances or something. He was generally not a happy bunny.'

'Will you go to model railway jail?' Helen spluttered, barely able to speak.

'Well, Pete wants us to meet at the pub to talk it over and plan our first competition match. I suspect as the driver I'm going to pick the tab up for the crash.'

Helen put her arm around Colin's shoulders.

'Don't worry, me and the boys will visit you in Dartmoor.'

Inspector Hancock shifted his weight to the left allowing his battered but elegant walking stick to take some of the strain. He always liked to stand still and silent and soak up the crime scene. After a period of a few minutes he slipped his mental clutch and engaged his fearsome detective brain. The crash path was obvious but offered at first glance no explanations for the train wreck unfolded before him. He was standing on a grassy hillock looking east down the line towards Lower Didsbury. The point at which the engine left the track was all too obvious but what wasn't obvious was why? He remembered a similar incident years ago in a marshalling yard not far from here. The cause had turned out to be a failed fishplate that had allowed the rail to kink on a tight bend. The result while not pretty was certainly clear. But this accident at this point in the track was strange. There were no rail joins, no steep gradients or curves. Not even a turnout to blame. Hancock reached into the deep recesses of his long dark overcoat, an odd choice for the sunny weather but he just never seemed able to take it off, and brought out his brass service binoculars. Squinting slightly before adjusting the lenses he proceeded to stare at the railway line. He lost himself momentarily in the regular pattern of sleeper, space, sleeper, space, before noticing just the merest change in the colour of one of the sleepers just up from the

crash site. It looked like a blob of cement or something staining the
wood a slightly different shade.

'Very curious' muttered Nick to himself. He picked up the
tiny model of Inspector Hancock and popped him back
into a small pocket within his wallet. Nick carried Hancock
around at all times, the inspector's calm and analytical
approach to difficult situations often proved most
advantageous. He'd attempted to explain in the past to
various people that Hancock was a physical prop to allow
free flowing mental extension to a given problem. Now he
just kept it to himself.

Pete had popped outside to the car park and he could see
him talking to Stew. Now would be a good time to have a
quiet look at the line and Inspector Hancock had
uncovered a potential clue. Nick looked over the whole
layout, everything in theory was very well glued down
because all the boards were transported in a large rack on
their side. The crash had taken place over a couple of
sections of board so he decided to pick up all the obvious
loose stuff and pop it into a bag. When Pete came back to
help him move the layout they could tip the crash site up
and any loose bits he might have missed would tumble off.
Nick had another look at the section of rail with the
stained sleeper. On running his finger over the sleeper he
noticed the mark had a slightly sharp edge to it, a brittle
edge, almost as though it were the remains of a blob of
superglue. 'Now what would be glued to a railway sleeper?'
Nick thought. Deep inside Nick's wallet a little voice cried
out 'I suspect sabotage!'

Pete re-entered the village hall. It didn't take them long to
break up the layout and move it by pieces into the van.
Pete had been driving a while, the two of them wrapped

up in their own thoughts when Nick broke the silence.

'I don't suppose you know anyone that may have a grudge against our club?'

Pete initially looked a bit nonplussed before replying

'Well probably everyone mate! Don't we have some sort of grudge with about every club we've ever met?'

'Terminus?' ventured Nick.

'Oh don't get me started what a bunch of arrogant, humourless fuckwits. How about 'The Pinewood Flyers'' retorted Pete.

'Bunch of fat fuckers, although I quite like Fat Bob' smiled Nick.

Pete grinned at Nick

'OK what about 'The Shunting Club'?'

'Gay.'

'The LMS appreciation society?'

'The ludicrous monkey shit society.'

'That insult makes no sense' laughed Pete.

'Well neither do they.'

'Swizz Gradient?'

'Sycophantic anal Nazis.'

'Oh, what about Lake Town Exchange?'

'I don't think one person constitutes a club but he's a dick anyway!'

The van drew up at some lights.

'Twin Oaks Narrow Gauge?'

'Simple folk.'

'Guard's Van?'

'Shit van.'

'The Wy-Vale Branch Line?' sniggered Pete.

'Oh fuck right off!'

An angry beep from the Cortina behind reminded Pete the lights had changed and he pulled away.

Pete continued - 'Box Car?'

'Yee ha dick swinging, muscle headed, wanky doodle nob ends.'

'Trams n Trains?'

'Twats n prats.'

'Junkyard Express?'

'I really like Chris and his lads.'

'Thank fuck! So do I' nodded Pete.

'We should arrange a little club to club drink with those boys sometime.'

'Absolutely' agreed Pete. 'So why did you ask if anyone had a grudge against us?'

'Just wondering?' shrugged Nick.

It wasn't long before they got back to Nick's place. Pete reversed the van up the side of the house so they could load everything into the inner-sanctum of Nick's workshop. After a cup of coffee and slagging off some more model clubs, Pete left.

Nick found himself staring again at the boards where the crash had taken place. They had left them out so he could make any necessary repairs. A fair bit of loose detritus had fallen off when they had moved the layout and it was this material that Nick now spread out over his workbench. He knew instinctively what to look for. Something would hopefully have the same specific glue mark on it as the sleeper.

'Time for Inspector Hancock' Nick said slowly and proceeded to place the tiny model on the worktop.

Hancock rubbed his tired eyes and surveyed the scene at hand. His investigation appeared to have led to him to some sort of company warehouse and spread out before him were piles and piles of rubbish. There were bits of hedge, fence posts, smashed wagon couplings, wrecked platform furniture and general detritus. Hancock needed better illumination, this warehouse was a tad dark. Almost immediately a huge arc light clunked on and everything was bathed in a harsh, polarising glare. Initially this proved difficult to work with but did at least create interesting shadows. One shadow in particular caught his attention. It looked like a giant clog.

Nick hovered over inspector Hancock and picked up the tiny clog shaped thing that he had been staring at. Turning it over in his hands Nick immediately noticed a blob of superglue on the underneath. It was a perfect match to the mark on the sleeper. He could feel his heart rate increasing and was experiencing the same sort of thrill he felt as when the finishing touches were put to one of his model creations. With unusually trembling hands, he reached for a tube of superglue, took a crafty little sniff and then fixed the suspect block onto the track where it had previously been. There was a brief pause while Nick rummaged around his spares box until he found a working carriage. He placed the carriage onto the track, inhaled deeply and gave it a push towards the block. The leading wheel hit the shaped block and Nick witnessed at once how it guided the inner rim of the wheel up and over the rail and consequently off the track. Nick sat back in his old office chair and tried to comprehend what had just happened. After a few moments of quiet contemplation the silence was broken by Nick's somewhat stunned brain jolting back into action.

'Un-fucking believable' he cried out followed by a more melodramatic, some might say Hollywood style 'Why!' and then sat there grinning. 'This is actually quite exciting' he thought. Looking towards the bench he could see that Hancock had fainted. He went over and stood him back up. 'Well done old boy! Now we have to work out who dunnit!' he whispered.

CHAPTER TWO: THE WATERTOWER AND TENDER

Pete and Colin were the first to arrive at The Watertower and Tender. They sat down at the usual table in one of the small bays towards the back of the sprawling pub. Pete continued his conversation about model railway calamities which he had started at the bar while waiting for his Guinness to pour.

'So to be honest Col your little train crash was small change really.'

Colin smiled and took a slow sup of bitter. 'I wasn't trying to get on some sort of weird model railway crash billboard. Believe me Pete, if I wanted to do a big old spectacular crash it'd be big and spectacular.'

'No chance' replied Pete, before taking a large gulp of Guinness. 'Just to even get into the top ten it would have to be really, really spectacular or weird or expensive… or violent!'

Colin put his pint down heavily. 'Are you saying there's an actual bloody top ten?'

'Yep' Pete gave him a broad grin.

'What's wrong with you people? These are just models. They occasionally come off the rails. So what?' Colin twisted his pint glass around in his hand. There was a brief silence before Pete tapped his fingers on the sticky table and very deliberately winked at Colin. 'Want to know what sort of crash you need to achieve just to get in at number ten?'

'Go on then. How bad does it have to be?'

Pete smiled, closed his eyes and turned his head upwards as if trying to remember the exact details.

'There was this club in the 70s that spent years developing a layout based on a small Yorkshire line. It was all pretty standard stuff but nicely done. However, the centrepiece was this great big viaduct that carried the line across a deep rocky valley, at the bottom of which was a model town. I mean the model viaduct was just over three foot high and nearly seven foot long. They were in -'

Colin butted in. 'Pete if you're building up to the point at which a train comes off the viaduct and crashes onto the town I'll save you the effort.'

'God you are such a kill joy at times. Can I just finish the bloody story?'

Colin smiled. 'Did a train come off the viaduct?'

Pete folded his arms. 'Yes.'

'Then you may not,' laughed Colin. 'See…it's just another sodding story about a train coming off the track!'

'Can I please finish the story?' Pete raised an exaggerated eyebrow and cocked his head to one side. Something about his calmness impelled Colin to stop laughing and listen.

'Thank you' he said sarcastically. 'As I was saying, this club were in a big show and the climax of their timetable was the appearance of a big old 4-6-2 loco with nearly ten Pullman carriages. Yes Colin, as the loco crossed the viaduct it did indeed come off the rail and plunge onto the sleepy little model town below. The problem was however that the heavy old engine crashed through the roof of the old mill. The old mill had a lovingly modelled water wheel that actually turned. It turned because it was motorised and by sheer bloody bad luck the falling loco sheared through the electrical contacts and created a spark which set light to the mill house. The fire spread very quickly and in case you're imagining a scale fire engulfing a small model think again. Very soon the layout resembled a bonfire and only the quick intervention of the boys on the RAF cadet stand, who threw a fire blanket over the whole valley stopped total disaster.'

Colin let out a heavy sigh. 'Well I guess that makes my crash look a bit crap.'

'Exactly!' exclaimed Pete. 'You really have to have a bad day at the office to get on the list.'

'And that was number ten on the list?'

'Exactly!' laughed Pete.

'I was going to nominate some of the crashes my kids create. Josh has a thing about the 10:30 from Paddington being destroyed by an Imperial cruiser and he recently demonstrated, very seriously, that an Intercity 125 could destroy Optimus Prime if it went fast enough!' Colin sighed again.

'Optimus what?' enquired Pete.

'It's one of those transformer things. Lorry turns into robot, turns into lorry, turns into robot, jams up, something falls off, Josh gets angry, throws it at Mark, who starts screaming and wets himself.'

Pete was chuckling. 'Talking of Imperial cruisers, you know Nick made a model of R2D2 and hid it somewhere on our layout?'

'Well it's not in my area' replied Colin. 'I'm always checking to see if the cheeky bastard has added anything dodgy near my cab. I remember the signal box story!'

'Yeah, I told Stew about that on Sunday. I'm guessing he's going to be looking at things a lot more closely from now on.'

Stew appeared at the table. 'What am I looking more closely at then gents?'

Pete looked up. 'Alright Stew? Just talking about Nick and

his models.'

'Oh please! Since you told me about the signal box I've gone completely paranoid. Margaret caught me looking into all the enclosed engine cabs last night with a torch. I was worried he might have hidden some naughty things in there.'

'Had he?' asked Colin.

'Not that I can see' replied Stew. 'But then I guess he might get off on the fact that he knows he's hidden something weird on the layout that no one else will ever find.'

Colin chipped in. 'Well I'm pretty sure there's something afoot inside the Lower Didsbury goods warehouse. My eye sight's pretty good and yes Stew, I too have on occasion shone a torch into some of the darker areas of our layout and I'm certain that there's a bunch of people playing a game of snooker in there.'

'Well that's not too bad is it?' shrugged Stew.

'Yes it is, because they're all naked and one of them has his cock stuck in one of the corner pockets' sighed Colin.

A long reflective silence descended before everyone present burst out laughing. Pete sat shaking in his chair before heaving himself up and putting his arm around Stew. 'What can I get you Stew?'

'Half a bitter and some nuts thanks.'

'Right ho. Same again Colin?'

'Yep' Colin replied and handed over his empty glass.

Pete suddenly looked across the pub to the front door. 'Ah-ha Nick's arrived' He grabbed his pint and walked over to intercept him. 'Nick. Alright mate? Usual?'

'Sure, is everyone here?' Nick replied.

'Yep I'm just getting a round in, the lads are over there in the bay. You all cool then?'

'Yes mate, never better. Quite fancied winding up Colin a little though' Nick winked at Pete.

'I was hoping to use this meeting as a bit of a team building exercise Nick, so go easy on him.'

Nick merely grunted and strode over to where Stew and Colin were seated.

'How on earth did you manage to get here Colin?' Nick said in a quizzical tone.

'I drove?' said Colin sarcastically.

'That's what I was worried about' Nick sat down. 'Didn't run over any cows on the way here then?'

'Well not any real cows. I might have ploughed through a herd of imaginary ones.' Colin rolled his eyes while shaking his head slowly.

Nick laughed. Stew and Colin flashed each other a worried expression. Nick noticed and immediately said 'Don't stress I'm not going to make a scene in which I accuse Colin of being a useless fat handed twat that managed to make a machine go left when all it's designed to do is go straight. No don't worry I won't say that' Nick folded his arms.

Colin looked him in the eyes. 'Well that's lucky because I was worried that you might do something like that but I can see now that you're not going to call me a fat handed twat.'

Stew remained silent. He wished Pete would hurry up with the round and especially his nuts because he couldn't tell if this was about to kick off or not. Nuts were always good as a spectator food.

'No, no absolutely' retorted Nick. 'If I thought you were, perhaps, a fat handed twat or even a blind fat handed twat, I would absolutely make that point, but don't worry I'm not going to press that matter any further.'

'Good' retorted Colin. 'Then I think we can all agree that I'm not Stevie Wonder in charge of a train and I don't have fat hands and I am, indeed, not a twat.'

Pete turned up at the table with a tray of drinks. 'What's Stevie Wonder done?'

'Well he hasn't crashed a train' Colin informed Pete.

Pete understood immediately. 'Oh! That's good. So, er, we're all ready then?' He passed out the drinks but paused momentarily as he handed over Nick's whisky and coke. Nick flashed him the merest of grins and took the glass. Everyone settled down.

'So,' said Pete, 'we need to work out how we're going to get through this first round of the regionals.'

Colin raised his hand in a mock impression of a child trying to get the attention of the teacher.

'Yes?' asked Pete.

'Sorry' replied Colin. 'I know we did this a couple of years ago but how many rounds to the final? What do we win exactly? And is it hugely important in the long run?'

Pete took a deep breath. 'Right, we compete against three other teams in the first round. Two go forward to round two, where they compete against another three teams. From there two teams go forward to a semi-final and the winner of that goes to the final.'

There was a very confused silence. Colin opened his mouth but Pete stopped him with a quickly raised hand and continued. 'You may also be interested to know that we may compete against some teams twice depending on how the draw goes.' Pete smiled. 'But the winner of the final gets a big shiny cup with the club's name engraved on and a huge cash prize.'

'What!' shrieked Colin and Stew. Nick just raised his

eyebrows.

'Oh! No sorry, no just a shiny cup. And the chance to enter the national final.'

'Oh!' retorted Colin.

'Yes Colin' sighed Pete. 'But if you win the nationals you get an all-expenses paid visit to America to take part in the 'worlds' and that does have a cash prize.'

Colin's ears physically jerked up in response. 'How much would that be then President Pete?'

'Couldn't tell you but I can tell you that no club from Britain has ever won, so don't get too excited. Besides which we're unlikely to win regionals, let alone nationals, so let's just concentrate on round one OK?'

Nick, who had been unusually quiet for a few minutes, stuck his hand up in mock imitation of Colin. 'So anyway I think we need to resolve an issue I have because this issue potentially affects our future success in the competition.'

'Oh, here we go' groaned Colin. 'Could this issue be me by any chance? I thought you were cool.'

'Colin, Colin, Colin, now we all know you were going a little fast and -' Nick was cut short by Colin.

'For fuck's sake, look, I'm sorry OK. Can we move on?'

'Colin, Colin, Colin, hush little one. I was about to say that it wouldn't have mattered how fast you were going, the Deltic was destined to crash whatever.' Nick held up his glass while surveying the blank faces. There was an impressive quiet which Pete eventually broke.

'Er, what do you mean 'destined to crash'?'

Colin added 'Well I read my stars and all they said was Mercury will go retrograde and Uranus will back up so don't move house. I specifically remember it not mentioning avoid trains, especially if you drive them.'

Stew snorted a little.

Nick retained his composure. He was trying to enjoy his reveal even though Colin was inevitably taking the piss. He let out a long sigh and held up his hand in an overly dramatic fashion. He waited till they were all concentrating on him again. 'Gentlemen,' he said in a slow deliberate fashion, 'we have been sabotaged.'

Pete choked on his Guinness. Colin started to say something but merely ended up looking like a goldfish. Stew didn't move, didn't even blink, then slowly started to nod his head. 'Yes. Yes, that makes sense. I don't suppose you found something. Something that shouldn't have been on our layout?'

'What… something like this?' Nick placed a small shaped block onto the pub table. Everyone stared at the bizarre little object and after a few seconds Stew turned to Nick. 'I saw that on one of our boards when I was packing up the engines and rolling stock. Couldn't work out what it was from.'

Pete's jaw was by now hanging down and a slightly moronic outlook had settled over his features.

'This weeny little block' stated Nick. 'Was glued to the track and caused Hadley's Hope to jump the line.'

Colin started shaking his head. 'Computer error, computer error.'

Stew had to talk over him. 'What's it made of Nick?'

'It is made, my inquisitive friend, good question by the way, from a dense polyurethane foam known as plastic wood. Quite expensive to buy. The sort of thing a really serious model-maker would use.'

Colin started to come to his senses. 'Oh get the fuck out of here! Are you seriously saying some sad lonely person, even more sad than you Nick is going to go to all that effort to carve a tiny, tiny block and then somehow fix it to our track without anyone noticing? Why?'

'Why?' responded Nick. 'To cause a crash of course.'

'Yes, but why?' responded Colin.

'Well, and this is just my theory, maybe we're seen as serious competition and someone thought they might see how easy it would be to disrupt us' offered Nick.

'Sad, sad, sad' Colin said, shaking his head.

Stew had been sipping at his bitter. Tiny thoughtful little sips like a mouse licking the morning dew from a blade of grass. He stopped sipping like a girly mouse and opened his mouth. There was a slight pause before any words came out as though his brain was still ticking over. 'What if we're not the competition? What if we're the guinea-pigs?'

Pete pounced on the suggestion. 'Yes Stewy mate, that actually makes more sense. One of the clubs we're up against in round one are the Pinewood Flyers.'

Nick muttered under his breath 'Fat fuckers.'

Pete ignored him. 'They won the regionals a few years ago so perhaps they're the intended target?'

Colin piped up. 'Be quite handy if our main competition was knocked out really.'

'Yes not really in the spirit of things is it Colin?' replied Pete impatiently. 'I think we should keep this to ourselves and see how it pans out' he continued.

Stew had done some more supping and thinking and at his present rate might soon require another half. 'Which other clubs are we up against at Potton next month Pete?'

'Harlington Exchange and Terminus.'

Stew frowned. 'Terminus? They can be a little bit feisty can't they?'

Colin started laughing. 'I suspect that as a club they can't be bargained with or reasoned with. I'm sure they don't feel pity or remorse or even fear and I bet they will absolutely not give up until they win the regionals.'

Nick, who had been smirking away listening to Colin, finally cracked up.

Colin grinned at him because despite their often abrasive relationship he loved to make Nick genuinely laugh. Nick gave him an appreciative nod back. Pete butted in. 'Anyway have you two lovers finished? Right. Good. Yes, Terminus are a tad serious about their hobby but they can be beaten, you just have to remember they're not machines but a bunch of middle aged men with bad jumpers and a tendency to over-plan everything.'

'What about Harlington Exchange then?' Stew asked.

Pete looked nonplussed. 'I don't actually know anything about this lot. I think this might actually be their first outing.'

'Excellent!' exclaimed Nick, rubbing his hands together. 'We can write that lot off then because something always goes wrong and if you haven't been in a competition exhibition before then something will *definitely* go wrong and you will absolutely fuck up.' Nick crossed his arms smugly.

'Like the time you superglued your finger to our type 42 diesel just before it left the fiddle yard' Colin reminded him.

'Yeah and I remedied the problem' replied Nick.

'Yeah and you were lucky the judges didn't spot your skin welded to the roof' smirked Colin.

Stew chipped in. 'That must have smarted.'

'Just taking one for the team dad!' replied Nick.

There was a short pause. Stew spoke quickly before Colin and Nick could start sparring again. 'The saboteur may not actually be from one of those teams though. They could be from any of the teams in the first round. Just a thought.'

Pete now adopted a slightly presidential pose. 'Look I think we're all getting a little ahead of ourselves. Can we start working out a plan for us and stop worrying about everyone else' He looked at Colin. As first driver Colin was meant to come up with some sort of strategy upon which they could plot and scheme.

'Well,' Colin said with the confident air of someone who might have actually prepared for this moment, 'I think we play it safe. We go for maximum traffic. Nothing too fancy, use all our regular stock and go for a solid points win.'

There was a very long and very deliberate silence.

'Oh fuck off' said Colin after the silence had gone on a little too long.

'Well, it does sound like Colin my old friend that you might actually be starting to take this seriously' Pete said, nodding his head in approval.

'Sounds like a solid plan. We can timetable all our tested rolling combinations in and wait for someone to make a schoolboy error' Stew said also nodding his approval.

Everyone looked at Nick.

'It's a little bit sad but as Stew said, I guess we wait for someone to fuck up. Two teams go through. Hopefully us and probably the fat fuckers.' Nick shrugged his shoulders.

'Excellent' smiled Pete. 'Let's work to that plan. Any other ideas to help ease us into the next round let me know.'

CHAPTER THREE: TRACK

Captain Hargraves looked down the long conference table taking in all the faces, some new, others unchanged for decades. He loved these clandestine meetings. It was a chance to reclaim those wartime feelings of purpose and excitement which modern life no longer seemed to offer. Plus he got to immerse himself in the world of model trains with all the best like-minded people in the country. He shut his eyes briefly, took a long draw on his pipe and began to speak.

'Gentlemen I welcome you to the biannual meeting of the model railway standards, techniques and discipline organisation.' He paused, 'Which will now be known as TRACK, not the old name, which I'm told was inappropriate.' There was a ripple of amused acknowledgement. 'As you are all too aware, round one of the regionals are due to take place in a couple of weeks and this presents us with the opportunity to make sure that the very best of British layouts qualify for the nationals.' There was a general murmuring. Captain Hargraves paused, picked up a piece of folded paper to his left and, in front of slightly puzzled faces, began to carefully unfold it. Returning the pipe to his mouth he took a short puff before commencing. 'As you know the USA won the internationals or 'worlds', as they want to call them, last year. This telegram was sent to me shortly after the 'worlds' by my American counterpart. It reads 'Guys, guys, guys. STOP. What the mule kicking son of a bitch are you limeys playing at? STOP. Step it up for 86. STOP. Or just. STOP. PS get a fax. STOP' There was a long silent silence until the south west rep's tea cup slipped from his sweaty hand and clattered back onto its saucer. The sudden noise jerked Captain Hargraves back to the moment. 'I've read and re-read that telegram and while I'm not entirely sure what it all means, it has made me think.' Hargraves took a short drag on his pipe. 'Gentlemen we do need to, er, step it up. For too long we've sent the same old type of layout to the competition. If I see another line based on the GWR with highly detailed hanging baskets as its main attraction I think I may actually get a bit cross. Those yanks at the final had a huge layout. It had factories, the factories had smoke stacks with smoke coming out of them. They had a dockside with huge model cargo ships. The ships were being loaded with actual working cranes. The trains themselves were dirty. Some, gracious me, had graffiti on them. Gentlemen, it was exciting, by jingo I was excited. We need to do this. Our layouts need to be more exciting to watch, especially and I still find this hard to believe, especially if you're not even that bothered about trains. Showmen! Yes! That's what those yanks are, showmen. They know how to entertain. I think we need to stop worrying about using the right scale brass ruddy whistle on the right scale pressure line because most of the public that come to our shows don't really care. I would say, more attention to the detail rather than the detail, if you take my drift and let's get away from this culture of pedantic scale engineering. Last year I had to settle an argument between two clubs who claimed the other was running trains with the wrong scale piston boxes. I told them. I told them I didn't blinking care and they both came back at me and said well you're the chairman of the flipping standards organisation. Yes… Yes, I said, but what is the point of having standards that no one cares about. I mean I like to eat my morning grapefruit with the correct spoon but it still tastes the same, even if I use a different spoon. When I started this organisation, after the war, it was to improve and coordinate the hobby, to get people together, to strive for better. I think our hobby is at a crossroads and we need to think very carefully about which direction to go. Till now we have striven to accurately model the world around us, I think perhaps, gentlemen, we should strive to celebrate it a bit more.'

Hargraves took a reflective draw on his pipe and held the smoke in a little longer before breathing out. He felt strangely relaxed, as though an odd little demon had been excised. He glanced at the faces down the long table. They looked a little puzzled, well he *had* droned on a little longer than intended. Still, best to go with the flow.

'Gentlemen, it's 1984 not 1954, I want a culture change. With this in mind I would like us to discuss an amendment to the points system for the upcoming regionals. Let us reward the clubs that timetable a circus train or a football special with scarves hanging out the windows. Let us not reward the mealy-mouthed clubs who complain that your train is the wrong shade of black or that you have the wrong rivets. Let us see some imagination and if we change now we can at least get ahead of Jerry or even the Nips.'

There was a slight cough from the vice president sitting to the right of Hargraves. Ken Bruce whispered something very quietly in Hargraves' ear. Hargraves clicked his teeth on the stem of his pipe.

'Oh yes, sorry' he said, in a quiet voice. 'Er, can't say that anymore it's not, er, PC is it? Anyway we can get a head start on the Germans, the Japanese, the ey-ties, the er, Italians. I know it's a little late in the day for the regionals but for those clubs that take up the challenge we must be there to reward them.'

Hargraves folded his arms. There was a brief pause before Ken Bruce raised his hands from the table and started to clap, almost immediately followed by the rest of the seated members, who added a random chorus of encouraging mumble. After a suitable time had elapsed Hargraves raised his hand. The clapping petered out to silence again.

'As is traditional' started Hargraves with a twinkle in his eyes. 'I shall tell one of my jokes before we retire to the lounge for informal drinks.' Hargraves took a quick puff on his pipe. 'Right, has anyone heard the one about the three model makers? One was Irish, one was Scottish and –'

Ken Bruce started to cough.

CHAPTER FOUR: PETE'S PLACE

It was Saturday morning. Pete could sense the light as it filtered through the wood blinds and skittered across his bare chest in a shimmering display of alternating horizontal bands. The early, dull noises of the suburbs on a weekend pecked intermittently at the half open window. Somewhere down the street a lawnmower stuttered into life and a moped whined past. He reluctantly opened his eyes, realising that the chance of a long lie in had passed. Pete worked more weekends than he had off, due to the nature of his chosen career, flogging cars. Nearly all car sales took place on a Saturday, something he hadn't fully appreciated when falling into this line of business. Still, at least he could choose which Saturdays to take off and he fully intended to enjoy this one. Rolling over and out of the bed in one smooth movement he grabbed his jeans from the floor, saddled up, put on his old Genesis t-shirt and shuffled down the stairs. At the foot of the stairs he glanced at the front door just before turning to head up the hallway to the kitchen. Something caught his eye. An erect manila envelope watched him in silence. Pete's legs carried on towards the kitchen fuelled by routine but Pete's eyes remained fixed on the letterbox. Doing what Pete thought was a pretty good Jackson shuffle, he did a one eighty and turned to face the door. The crisp manila envelope looked out of place. Pete was more used to a pool of junk-mail sick spreading slowly over the hall mat. This post looked far too classy to roll around on the floor. Pete reached forward and gently pulled the envelope from the respectful embrace of the letterbox. His name and address were crisply hand typed in a most formal manner. He turned over the envelope but could find no clue as to its origin. Pete turned around again and headed to the kitchen, sniffing the envelope absentmindedly as he went. It smelt of indexed files, tradition and cold tea. As the kettle went about its morning ritual Pete sat down at the small pine kitchen table and opened the envelope. Inside was a freshly folded letter with the embossed letterhead of TRACK. His eyes scanned down the words before finishing off with 'your faithful servant Captain Hargraves.' Pete rubbed his chin and stared out of the kitchen window. A cat was tip toeing along the top of the wooden panel fence, sniffing the air as it went. 'Know how you feel' thought Pete before standing up and heading back to the hallway and the small telephone-table to the right of the front door. There was a short pause as he keyed in the numbers, the phone rang a few times before a slightly rough voice answered 'Calling?'

Pete smiled. 'Hey Nick, its Pete. Are you fit?'

'I'm alive.'

'Excellent, get round here as soon as poss.'

There was a very audible groan before the phone clicked off. Pete smiled again and headed back to the kitchen to re-boil the kettle. It wasn't long before Nick's particular rap resonated through the house. Pete could see him yawning through the stained glass panel in the centre of the door. Nick spotted him staring and mouthed something offensive. Pete shook his head and opened the door.

'By God Mr Fletcher, this better be worth it and you better have some breakfast on the go, I'm starving.'

'Good morning Nick, sleep well?' enquired Pete.

'Slept very well, just not long enough' came the reply.

'So what were you up to?'

'Have you heard of team building?'

Pete groaned. 'Yes, my boss keeps threatening it on my sales team.'

They entered the kitchen and Nick sat down heavily at the

kitchen table, supporting his delicate head in his hands. He looked up at Pete, who was leaning against the sink. 'Well, the software company I'm free lancing for decided to try and bond the various writers and coders brought in for the project, at that new conference centre off the motorway.'

'Coffee Nick?'

'Yep, put an extra sugar in mate. Anyway I spent yesterday afternoon doing 'team building' exercises.'

Pete stirred Nick's mug of coffee and placed it on the table in front of his face. 'I'm guessing that was really terrific fun for you Nick!'

'Fucking awful! OK if you were a tree, what sort of tree would you be? And more importantly, how would you represent that in a balletic form?'

Pete sat down and looked blankly at Nick.

'I chose to be a dead redwood and lay on the floor' continued Nick. 'Only, oh no, that's not really taking part in the spirit of things is it, so I had to choose something else.'

'And?' asked Pete.

'Well, I went and got a chair, sat down and started crying' replied Nick.

'Weeping willow' exclaimed Pete.

'See! You get it but apparently I was deemed to be taking the piss and besides it wasn't balletic enough for them, even though I argued it was in the avant-garde Russian style.'

'They must have loved you. Never work with children, animals and Nick' laughed Pete.

'Anyway we did these sort of moronic things most of the afternoon. Including, I kid you not, forming a human circle in which you had to tap the person on the shoulder in front of you and they had to say the first thing that came into their head.'

'Oh dear' muttered Pete.

'Of course, you can't say the first thing that comes into your head if it's offensive.'

'Yes' smiled Pete. 'This is called civil society.'

'Hmm' sighed Nick. 'I think it takes about the third or fourth word in my head before we reach civil society.'

'Or anything approaching comprehension' added Pete.

'Yes!' exclaimed Nick. 'No one knew what a fishplate was.'

'So how did it finish up?'

'Buffet, free bar and taxis laid on' smirked Nick.

'Which answers my next five questions' laughed Pete.

There was a long silence as they both stared across the table, lost in a momentary blankness.

'So why am I here?' enquired Nick.

'Got this letter.' Pete reached over to the toaster, where the manila envelope had taken up a slightly huffy temporary residence. It was clearly expecting to be stored in the pigeon hole of an antique Georgian bureau. Pete handed over the envelope and watched Nick's face intently, as he took out the letter and read the contents. Nick applied his 'thinky' face as he folded the letter back up and replaced it in the envelope.

'I'm guessing every club president has been sent one of these?'

'Definitely' responded Pete.

'Reading between the lines,' Nick paused. 'Reading between the lines I think they want us to appeal to the general public a bit more. Reading between the lines TRACK might finally be waking up to the fact that for the hobby to survive it needs to adapt and this is a small step, a very small step, in the right direction.'

Pete was still staring intently at Nick's face. Nick finally noticed. 'What you staring at Willis?'

'This helps us doesn't it?' said Pete. 'I mean if they're going to award more points for layout creativity at the expense of completed timetables, surely that helps us?' He looked enquiringly at Nick.

Nick sat up right and stretched out his arms. 'Course it bloody helps us. Finally we get a few Brownie points for creative model making and about sodding time.'

'How much is this going to help in the upcoming competition?' ventured Pete.

'Well, there is a lot of space between those lines isn't there?' winked Nick.

'A lot of space indeed.' Pete winked back.

'Now put your knickers on and make some fucking bacon sarnies Pete.'

CHAPTER FIVE: THURSDAY EVENING AT THE WATERTOWER AND TENDER

Thursday evening at the Watertower and Tender came round very quickly. Pete had phoned Stew and Colin on the Sunday evening to let them know of the changed judging criteria and naturally all had concurred that it required an urgent meeting down the pub. Colin and Stew had got there first and bagged a picnic trestle in the beer garden.

'So Pete was telling me about the top ten model crashes last time' said Colin. 'I was sort of hoping he'd just made it all up in his head 'cos it sounds a little weird to me.'

Stew gave him a slightly patronising smile. 'For someone so talented at cab driving you have absolutely no appreciation of the wider folklore of model railways.'

'I have kids' came Colin's curt reply.

'Well yes, but you must talk to other railway club people when we do our shows. Don't you?'

'Not if I can help it, they're all nut-jobs.'

'I do hope dear Colin that you don't think of us as 'nut-jobs' too?'

'Well, obviously Nick is but you and Pete are, er, nice nut-jobs?'

'Hmm.'

'Look' continued Colin. 'I just haven't been sucked into the strange world of model railwayers in the same way that you lot have. Anyway I want to know, is there a top ten?'

'Yes there is Colin, but it's a sort of fluid list.'

'Pete told me about number ten. Do you know number nine?' Colin said at the same time holding up nine fingers, as if to accentuate the question.

'I can give you the version as I know it Colin' Stew nodded sagely. 'This somewhat unpleasant episode happened quite recently at an exhibition in London. A young chap came staggering in, obviously the worse for wear and started looking around at the layouts. They called him something. A yappie or flappie or…'

Colin raised his eyebrows and interrupted. 'Yuppie, Stew, a yuppie.'

'That's the fella, yes a yuppie. Well he eventually stopped at this big layout. I think it was a reproduction of some German marshalling yard. Anyway they had about six trains operating simultaneously. Very impressive, even a man of your talent would have found it a challenge, when suddenly the yuppie fella shouts 'Godzilla!' and jumps up onto the layout and starts stamping on all the trains and buildings.'

Colin started to laugh uncontrollably, which rapidly turned into a coughing fit, just as Pete turned up.

'What's up with Colin?' he asked.

'Crash number nine' replied Stew.

Pete started to do a slow-motion impression of Godzilla picking up buses and ripping out trees.

Colin carried on coughing while Stew attempted some sort of ineffectual patting on his back to try and calm him down. Nick walked up to the trestle table.

'What the fuck is going on? What are you doing Pete? Is this your new strategy? I know this isn't in the new judging criteria.'

Godzilla Pete pretended to pick up a miniature judge and bite his head off before doing a horrifyingly good impression of a chimp dragging its knuckles across the grass towards the bar. Colin finally pulled himself together and sat there wiping his eyes. He turned to Stew. 'So the 'crash' was some drunk twat pissing about then. What happened to him?'

Nick butted in. 'Imagine someone did that to my models at a show.'

Colin closed his eyes and pondered. 'Well death obviously, probably after extensive torture, using little model pliers perhaps?' Colin pretended to use tiny pliers to tweak off Stew's nipples. Stew shuffled away from him along the bench trying to avoid damage to his freshly laundered Millets shirt.

'Well death would just be a cop out' stated Nick.

Stew decided to try and finish his story, he didn't like leaving things half completed. 'Anyway, the yuppie chap got dragged off the layout by some extraordinarily angry model enthusiasts and got a little bit of a slapping before the police turned up to save him.'

'It's not really a crash though is it?' Colin said, slightly disappointed.

Nick butted in again. 'I think you're being a bit pedantic, it's more a list of model railway disasters.'

'Show me the list then' countered Colin.

'Colin, Colin, Colin. You know it's an ethereal collection of model folklore organised into a fluid ranking based on common consensus.'

Silence.

Pete returned to the table, balancing a scuffed metal tray with a fresh round of drinks. 'Alright lads? What we talking about now then?'

Nick whipped his JD and coke off the tray and looking Pete in the eye said 'I think we need to talk about Colin's haircut.'

There was a groan from Colin. 'Oh for fuck's sake I've had this all week at school.'

'Excellent' said Nick rubbing his hands together.

'Well I would put that haircut in at about number seven' quipped Pete.

'Oh come on it's a five all day long' said Nick, still rubbing his hands together. 'What do you think Stew?'

Stew pretended to polish his balding head. 'Not sure I can really comment on matters of a follicle nature.'

Colin all the while was doing a silent 'ha-ha, very funny' jiggle in his seat.

'C'mon Col, get stuck into this.' Pete handed him a pint of bitter and then passed Stew his usual half, before clattering the empty tray onto the table opposite. Stew stopped polishing his head and took a sip.

'OK this is what I've found out about our competition' said Pete in a slightly hushed voice. There was no one else in the pub garden. Everyone hunched forward in what could only be described as a conspiratorial way. 'Right! The Pinewood Flyers.'

'Fat fuckers' whispered Nick.

Pete ignored him. 'I've found out that they've got new control gear which will make their shunting operations a lot smoother and potentially quicker.'

'So they can operate a fuller timetable?' asked Stew.

'Exactly' countered Pete. 'They don't have a new layout as I feared but it has been heavily modified with extra sidings so they could run more traffic, again allowing a fuller timetable. But, apparently they're struggling to concentrate with these new changes because of the increase in traffic. The coordination between the two drivers has to be spot-on otherwise you get a catastrophic overlap.'

Colin raised an eyebrow and pointed his finger at Pete. 'How the hell did you find that out?'

Pete looked evasive. 'I bumped into Fat Bob.'

'Not difficult, he's the size of a fucking iceberg' interrupted Nick.

'And the same shape' added Colin.

'He hasn't sunk any ships though' countered Nick.

Pete attempted to carry on. 'I bumped into him at the Crown. So I bought him a pint and had a chat.'

'Had a chat?' said Stew slowly. 'What did you tell him? I assume it wasn't all one-way traffic?'

'Well I did, er, tell him some things but nothing that's going to help them.'

'What things?' asked Colin.

Pete squirmed visibly in his seat. 'I told Bob that after our last show, you and Nick fell out and had a fight in the car park and are currently refusing to talk to each other. Bob is under the impression that we might not even turn up to the completion.' Pete took a large gulp of his Guinness, while very obviously avoiding eye contact with any one. Colin and Nick stared at each other.

Nick was first in. 'I hope you told Bob that I kicked Colin's arse.'

'Whoa there Chuck Norris?' Colin looked at Pete. 'Pete. Mate. Please tell me that I gave Nick a good slapping in the car park.'

Pete screwed up his face. He looked directly at Colin, then Nick. 'I told Bob that you had a fight, I didn't say who won OK and I think you're missing the point.'

Nick gave Colin a wink. 'Anytime Colin.'

Colin smiled back. 'You wouldn't last two minutes, model boy.'

Pete attempted to carry on. 'So what I'm saying, is, if the Pinewood Flyers don't pay attention and concentrate, they're going home and I think if we turn up looking like a happy loving little team, that might be enough to distract them.'

Nick whispered loudly to Pete 'What if I tell Fat Bob at the show that I kicked Colin's arse and he had to come grovelling back to be let back in the club.'

'Oh for fuck's sake, enough already' Pete said in an unusually irritable voice.

Colin and Nick both chirped in unison 'Ooh Mr Fletcher's getting angry.'

Nick cleared his throat. 'Look, don't worry Pete, I've got a little plan of my own for the fat fuckers.'

Pete looked worryingly back at Nick. 'Please stop calling them that, and what plan?'

'Just a little idea I had if things maybe don't go the way we hope they will.'

Everyone looked at everyone else, before Stew said in a quiet voice 'Promise us all it won't involve a signal box.'

Nick laughed. 'Nothing so complicated. I've got my work cut out coming up with new model ideas to try and scrape us up some more points. Did you guys come up with any ideas about running different traffic combinations?'

Colin and Stew looked at each other. Colin motioned to Stew to explain their ideas.

'Well. Obviously we run big show stoppers like Hadley's Hope coupled to a long coal tail as well as lots of interesting mixed traffic but we wondered about using our spare flatbeds and making up some sort of scrap train.'

Nick liked the idea. 'Yes, fucking yes mate! I've got lots of scrap cars, lorries, vans etc. I could even model some tarps over a few so it looks like they're more precious. Tell you what, we could hide some interesting things under the tarps for people to guess at.'

'Like what?' asked Stew.

'I-n-t-e-r-e-s-t-i-n-g things.'

'Oh OK, well we thought of some other ideas' Stew continued. 'How about a zoo train?'

'Yes, nice, but a lot of work. I don't keep scale monkeys up my arse you know.'

'That's what monkeys say about you Nick' whispered Colin.

'That's what your mum says about you Colin' whispered Nick back.

Pete intervened. 'Let Stew finish lads.'

'What about some sort of James Bond train?'

'Nice.'

'Er, this was more Colin's idea.'

'Go on.'

'Er, some sort of train with cages full of children.'

'A bit like the child catcher in Shitty Shitty Bang Bang. Nice idea Colin.'

Pete interjected. 'No.'

'A military train.'

'Yep a little safe but a definite crowd pleaser. What sort of tanks did they have in the sixties? Centurions?'

Pete answered. 'Centurions, I had an uncle who drove them in the army so I can get some good reference material if you need it.'

'OK that's handy. Airfix do a good kit of it so it would be fairly easy to achieve. Anything else?'

Colin tapped the table gently with his fingers. 'I did have

another idea based on my recent flirtation with train crashes. Could we sort of recreate some sort of disaster?'

'Well with you around mate we don't need to recreate anything.'

'Predictable' responded Colin.

'No, that's a really interesting idea' Pete suddenly came to life. 'The new rules simply state that extra points are available for creativity.' He looked at Nick. 'Remember the spaces between the lines?'

Nick started to grin.

'What the fuck are you talking about?' said Colin, looking confused.

'Colin, me old mucker, what sort of disaster?' said Pete.

'Well, didn't think too much but could we recreate a derailment or an engine fire and actually timetable it in. As long as the judges know it's part of the show we should pick up decent points because we could table in rescue and recovery engines and hopefully it would be considered creative so might get us even more points?'

'I know you weren't actually in that train crash Colin but did you bang your head or something cos that is one fucking brilliant idea' Nick downed the rest of his JD and Coke.

Pete was looking flushed. 'I like it, I like it a lot. Because we not only bag points but the whole exercise might put off or at least give our competitors a false sense that we're going to lose.'

Stew piped up. 'So at the competition, when do we hand in our timetable to the judge?'

'Fifteen minutes before kick-off, our delegated judge takes our timetable, discusses any issues with me and then enters it as our official order of run' stated Pete.

'So, no one else will know our timetable other than us and the judge?'

'No.'

Colin downed the remains of his pint. 'What about the rest of the competitors then Pete?'

'Yeah, got a tad side-tracked there. Well I couldn't find out anything about Harlington Exchange, even Fat Bob hadn't heard of them. As for Terminus you all know about them. I don't think they've made any changes to their layout and they'll go through their timetable with ruthless efficiency, just not much flair. These changes to the points system ain't gonna help them one bit. So just over two weeks to go, it's a case of what can Nick get built by then?'

Everyone looked at Nick. 'Just as well I'm the fucking freelancer, not like you bunch of nine to fivers. Look, I could take at least a week out which would get us some gear, but all that disaster stuff will have to wait for another round.'

'Excellent' said Pete.

CHAPTER SIX: THE FIRST ROUND

The transit van kangarooed into the large carpark outside Potton's grand Victorian civic centre. There could be observed two gentlemen having a heated discussion in the cab. 'For fuck's sake could you drive just a little bit more carefully Pete? I can hear all the boards bouncing up and down.'

Pete crunched the gear stick into first and lurched forward into a space.

'Nick, I got this rental van free for the weekend 'cos I know the guy who runs the firm, so just ease up. All right?'

'Well it needs a new gearbox, or a better driver.'

'It needs a lot of things. Which is why, it's free. Right, shall we unload?'

On his third attempt Nick managed to force open his door and then proceeded to fall out of the transit.

'I hate this van,' he muttered under his breath 'I'm gonna bloody model one of these going into the crusher.' And made a quick mental note of its vital characteristics.

Pete was at the rear doors attempting to get the lock to engage. 'I can't believe they actually rented this thing out to people' He thumped the door, which somehow popped the lock, causing the door to fly open and catch Nick a glancing blow to his ribs. Nick stood there with his eyes closed, sucking in the pain.

'Alright there?' ventured Pete.

Through clenched teeth - 'Just about holding it together mate. Might take the bus home though!'

The two of them were about to start unloading the first board, when an extremely shiny, mud-free range rover pulled up to them. In the front were a couple of expensively dressed parents and in the back three mini versions of the father. 'Good morning my man' bellowed the expensively dressed dad. 'Is this where we unload for the model competition? My boys are taking part.'

'Er, yes' replied Pete. 'Which team are you?' he enquired.

'My boys are The Harlington Exchange, named after my private investor's club.' Mr expensive then proceeded to laugh heartedly, as though it were some kind of joke.

Pete noticed that the boys in the back were all staring. And not at him, but at Nick, who was paying particular attention to the large double axel horsebox, in tow behind the Rover. The boy sat nearest to Pete tapped the window and beckoned him closer. As Pete put his face to the glass the boy wound down the window and whispered 'Is that Nick Compton?'

Not for the first time all Pete could say was 'Er, yes.'

The boys all looked at each other. The middle one nudged the other two and there was a burst of juvenile laughter, before the window was unceremoniously wound up again. Mr expensive grinned at Pete, the light catching his gold fillings. 'Well, up and at 'em I say. See you on the inside.'

Pete watched the Rover pull into a large space reserved for coaches near the entrance. 'Bloody hell, that's Harlington Exchange. Didn't see that one coming. A load of rich kids.' He turned to Nick. 'What do you make of the Hitler Youth team then?'

Nick chuckled. 'They were a bit on the blond side but did you notice that trailer?'

'The horse box? What about it?'

'It's really low on its axles. They must have some pretty serious gear in there.'

'Expensive, serious gear' replied Pete.

'Well, you know what they say about that Pete?'

And together they chanted 'All the gear, no idea.'

Potton civic centre was a magnificent building. Some would say and many often did that it was far too good for Potton. However it was an extremely grand space in which to house a model railway exhibition and somewhat fitting as its construction was funded by wealth brought in by rail from the nearby channel ports. The exhibition was spread over the main cavernous hall with a mezzanine floor running around all four sides, supported by imposing marble pillars. While Nick started to assemble the boards, Pete went up to the wide mezzanine to have a good spy over the floor space. The Pinewood Flyers had been positioned towards the front of the hall, to the left of the main entrance leading to the granite-floored lobby. It wasn't a bad situation and allowed the Flyers a good deal of space plus a clear vision of everyone entering or leaving the exhibition. Harlington Exchange were nestled in the middle of the hall alongside a couple of other club stands and opposite Fishplate across the hall. Pete watched the kids and their parents locking the layout boards together. He had to admit it was tiny in comparison to Smooth Fishplate, probably a quarter the size and he was struggling to see how they could operate a full timetable and move the traffic needed to build a decent points tally. As he was gazing down, the smallest of the three blondies pulled back a cover sheet to reveal a very complex set of sidings and marshalling yards, complete with platforms, loading bays and warehouses.' Ah-ha' thought Pete. 'This lot intend to shunt and shuffle their way through the points. High risk but looking at all that expensive new control gear quite possibly in their reach.'

The hall was really beginning to fill up and while it was still early and the public was not due for a couple of hours, clearly many clubs, even the non-competing ones, had a lot to prove. In the far corner, at the opposite end of the hall, an area had been left for Terminus. The as yet unoccupied space was a perfect fit for the shape of their layout, a huge 'L' section. Pete was about to move along the mezzanine a little, when he spotted Fat Bob coming through the entrance, carrying a large ply box. 'Excellent' thought Pete. 'Let the games begin' and he headed down to greet Bob. By the time Pete had navigated back down the highly polished stone steps, Fat Bob was already in conversation with Nick.

'The layout's looking smart Nick. I see some new buildings and details. Looks really good mate, nice one.' Bob could see Pete approaching. 'Tell me Nick. Are we to see Colin today? Pete said you had a moment with him after your last show.'

Pete finally turned up, looking slightly flushed. Nick smiled at Bob and then turned to smile at Pete before saying 'Bob was just asking if Colin was going to turn up today. I mean after that slapping I gave him in the car park.'

Pete winced. 'Well, er, I hope so Nick. He did say he was coming. Look, I don't want any more trouble between you two. OK? We need to concentrate.' Pete looked Bob in the eyes and raised his eyebrows.

'Well,' said Bob, 'looks like it might be interesting. Good luck anyway!' He smiled at them and plodded off to his station with the ply box. When he was out of view Pete prodded Nick in the chest.

'Oi! What are you doing?'

'Just keeping the story going that you started Pete. Alright?'

Pete carried on poking Nick. 'OK but don't tell Colin, cos he's going to start a fight with you for real just to prove that he could whip your arse.'

'But we all know he couldn't' smirked Nick.

'I...Don't...Bloody...Care' replied Pete. 'Oh Christ here comes Terminus.'

They both turned to watch. Terminus didn't so much walk through the hall as march, their rhythmic steps echoing around the large space. Behind them followed a small caravan of roadies, pulling carts loaded with their boards and controls.

'Terminus on tour eighty-four' whispered Pete, staring hypnotically at the spectacle.

'I wish we had all that help' muttered Nick. 'Be nice to turn up, sit down with a thermos of tea and direct a load of runners to set up for you.'

'Yeah but no-one would set up the boards how you like, Nick, which is why you've ended up getting the gig. Talking of which, shouldn't Col and Stew be here by now?'

'Well, to be honest, I'd prefer to set up the layout without Colin running around touching things and irritating me. So, while I do that, any chance of finding someone doing tea?'

Pete walked off muttering 'I knew there had to be a reason why I'm president of this club.' He decided to head back over to the Pinewood Flyer's stand, since Fat Bob always knew where to find sustenance and, as yet, he hadn't really scoped out their layout. Graham, or 'Massive Gram' as Nick called him, was checking some turnout solenoids, as Pete came over.

'Alright Peter?' Graham said, without looking up from his task. Pete watched him fumbling around with a tiny screwdriver, his massive bulk only just contained by a straining black t-shirt with the club's logo stretched into incomprehension. Pete caught himself thinking that a man of Graham's size would struggle working on a real train let alone something in OO gauge.

'How's tricks?' Pete replied.

'Not so bad Peter. We've got a few sticky points but other than that we're good to go. What about team Fishplate?'

Graham continued prodding a delicate part of the turnout.

'I suppose by that you refer to the ongoing Nick-dash-Colin situation?'

Graham finally heaved himself up. His face already a little blotchy and a small bead of sweat beginning to form on his hairline. 'Dear, dear Nick. Yes. Mr Compton is a constant source of amusement to us. It's got to make your life interesting Peter. So, is Colin going to turn up or are you going to be driver today instead of presiding?'

'Well if he doesn't, I'm a pretty good driver. Not as good as Colin, granted, but I know we'll muddle through.'

Graham smirked. 'Not as good as Colin? That's the understatement of the year. I would love Colin to drive for us. You know at some point you might have to decide whether you want a genius model maker who could wind up Ghandi or perhaps the best driver I've ever seen. Such a shame they want to kill each other.'

Pete sighed. 'Kill each other? Perhaps at the moment it's more maim and disfigure and until it gets any worse, we, my friend are still competing.' Pete turned slightly to face Bob, who had been helping the Flyer's other member Chip load up the fiddle yard with train tails, but who had now come over to join in.

'Is Colin joining the Flyer's then?' taunted Bob.

'In your dreams Bob' countered Pete. 'Now, you're a man that knows. Where do I get a decent tea from?'

'Second floor, there's a small café, should be open by now. Get us a sausage roll if they have any.'

Pete nodded. 'See you chaps in a mo.'

As Pete headed off towards the stairs Chip came over.

'Think he noticed?'

'Not sure' replied Graham.

Bob looked towards their fiddle yard. 'He noticed alright, but what can he do?'

Pete reached the café on the second floor and got a couple of teas in polystyrene cups and a dodgy looking sausage roll, wrapped in a serviette. As he turned to go back down the stairs, he noticed, in the far corner of the café a group of judges huddled together. They were whispering loudly about something but Pete couldn't quite make out the exact words. As he lingered, there was a slight cough and then silence, before one of the judges turned to look at him. Pete smiled, nodded and headed down the stairs. 'Clearly not meant to be listening' he thought. By the time he got back to the layout Nick had finished clipping all the boards together and was busy checking for any damage to the scenery.

'Did you put a couple of sugars in, Pete?'

'Yes mate, don't want you collapsing on us.'

Nick took a slurp of the tea and motioned Pete closer to him. 'Those Exchange kids have got some clever old gear over there. What do you reckon?'

Pete turned his head briefly in their direction, before turning back to Nick. 'I had a look down from the mezzanine. If those lads are good drivers we could face some competition. That, however, is not the main problem.'

Nick looked him up and down. 'And?'

'I had a look at the Pinewood Flyers' fiddle yard.'

'And?'

'They've really extended it and I noticed an extra set of controls. I think they might have a third driver.'

'Well I hope he's thin. It's not like there's a lot of room between Chocolate Chip, Massive Gram and Fat Bob. Are you taking that sausage roll over for one of 'em?'

'Yep' replied Pete.

'Just ask Bob what's his favourite ice cream, or lolly for that matter, but don't make it obvious.'

'Why?'

'Secret plan Pete, secret plan.'

Pete walked off. At this point he decided it might be best to humour Nick and see if he could get any more useful insight into their possible third driver. Nick watched Pete head off to the Flyers. He looked down to his small tool box and the secret weapon hidden within. He couldn't resist emitting a little theatrical evil cackle to himself.

'Yes, see, told you. He's finally flipped.' Colin stood a few metres away pointing at him, while a perplexed Stew stared on.

'Anything we need to know about, Nick?' continued Colin.

'Just warming up Colin, just warming up.'

Stew put down his box of locos. 'Layout looks great Nick. Is it ready to start loading up trains? We need to get things rolling before the public turn up.'

'Yep, everything's good to go.'

'Where's our leader got to?' enquired Colin.

'He's over at the Flyers. You might want to check out Harlington Exchange.' Nick nodded towards their stand.

'Are those children manning the controls?' asked Stew.

'Children of the corn' muttered Colin.

'They're pretty fucking good too' whispered Nick. 'Pressure's on Colin, don't want you to get beaten by some kids.'

Colin smirked, cracked his knuckles and unclipped his box of locos. 'Not on my watch mate.'

Over at the Pinewood Flyer's stand things were beginning to get heated.

'Funny feet?' bellowed Bob. 'It's pink and boring. I'd rather have a Fab, much more sophisticated.'

'Sophisticated?' queried Chip.

'Yeah, because it has bands of flavour and a toffee end with crunchy hundreds and thousands' countered Bob.

Graham started shaking his head. 'Bob, you're confusing bands of colour with flavour. There is nothing, nothing to beat a Strawberry Split. If you want bands of colour get a bloody Zoom.'

'Well I quite like a Black-hole' ventured Chip.

Bob and Graham both stared at him.

'Sorry' said Chip, shrugging his shoulders.

Pete had been standing quietly to one side observing the scene with complete incredulity. What he'd tried to make seem like an off the cuff remark about ice cream had suddenly got out of control. He decided to change the subject. 'So, anyone else joining you today?'

Graham and Bob stopped staring at Chip. They knew exactly what Pete was really asking.

Bob answered. 'Lad called Al, he's helping us with the controls. Taking trains off the main lines and into the fiddle yards and rolling them back out again.'

Pete feigned surprise. 'What? You have a third driver?'

'Yes' replied Graham and Bob in unison.

'When did he join then?'

Bob looked at Graham before replying 'Few weeks ago.'

Pete somehow felt this wasn't quite true but then he wasn't exactly being straight with Bob over the Colin/ Nick thing. There was a slightly awkward silence which Pete quickly broke.

'So when are the judges due?'

'One, I think' replied Bob.

'Well, let's hope Terminus self-terminate.'

They all laughed and Pete headed back towards Smooth Fishplate.

Colin and Stew were busy unpacking locos and rolling stock, while Nick had set up a small workstation next to the fiddle yard. Nick spotted him first. 'Did you find out Pete?'

'They're all bloody bonkers about ice cream, Nick. I think Bob's favourite is a Fab.'

'Excellent' said Nick, rubbing his hands together. Don't suppose he has a second favourite?'

'Well, he mentioned early on about liking or licking hazelnut Cornetto's. Wasn't sure but it certainly riled Graham and Chip and then it all kicked off.'

Colin had been eavesdropping. 'What the hell are you talking about?'

'Nick's secret plan' replied Pete. Colin looked at Nick, stuck his fingers in both ears and started 'la la'-ing.

Pete smirked and looked down at Nick. 'Don't think he wants to know!'

Nick merely cackled and returned to whatever it was he was doing.

Before long all the clubs were up and running. Moving freight and passenger traffic around their layouts, getting ready for the competition to start. The public had been let in and already an exhilarating atmosphere was beginning to build up in the hall. Nick had finished his secret project and had decided to wander off and look at some of the trade stands. One in particular caught his attention because of its quantity of spares and specialist period details. He started to look over a wide display spinner hung with literally hundreds of small clear polythene bags, full of such things as 30s aluminium window frames, gable vents and period rubbish bins. Nick was in true Nick heaven. Time, space and other people seemed to dissolve away as his eyes focused intently on the treasures before him.

'Jesus, look at these sash windows' he whispered reverently under his breath.

'And those drainpipe details.' He stroked a packet full of Victorian cast iron rain hoppers and kneaded a long horizontal bag full of brick effect mats. His probing hand reached around the next side of the spinner to turn a fresh face of excitement his way.

'Hey, hang on I was still looking at this side.'

Nick failed to hear the voice and continued to turn the spinner. A whole new vista of fencing, kissing gates, telegraph poles and municipal planters filled his vision. Nick let out a little moan.

'Are you all right?' A soft voice seemed to permeate through his bubble of concentration. Nick became aware of a figure standing to his left. 'You look a bit confused.'

Nick physically shook his head and turned to see who had broken him from his delectable trance. An attractive girl stood gazing at him. She nodded gently in the direction of the spinner. 'I was looking at that side and you turned it before I could finish.'

'Sorry, really sorry. Er, what were you looking at?' stuttered Nick.

She looked him up and down again and smiled deeply with her eyes. 'I know this sounds stupid, but I need to create a model of a greenhouse.'

Nick was beginning to feel all peculiar. Normally pretty girls and model accessories were two widely spaced commodities and yet somehow they had combined here and were playing havoc with his settings.

'It's a little weird but I'm creating an allotment scene and I noticed how in every allotment is an abandoned greenhouse. Just thought it might be cool to model one.'

Nick wasn't sure if he might just be getting the notion of the start of an erection. Just there in the distance but getting alarmingly closer. 'No' said Nick, which came out a little too loud and urgently for the proximity of the girl and the situation. She backed up a little.

'No.' His voice now back under control. 'No, it's not weird, it's brilliant, it's, er, observationist. Is that a word? I mean you must really take notice of things. That's a talent. I love that. I love this stand. Someone else has bothered to actually look at things and say 'wait' this is the difference between a Victorian park bench and an Edwardian one. I love that. So do you. It's not weird. I'm not weird. We're normal. Everyone else is weird.'

'Righty ho then' smiled the girl.

Nick thought maybe now might be a good time to introduce himself. Either that or run away. 'Hi I'm Nick. Sorry about the spinner thing. I'm trying to model something too and, er, just sort of lost myself for a moment.'

The girl did the slightest of curtseys and held out her hand. 'Well Nick. I'm Justine, nice to meet you.' They held each other's gaze for the merest fraction of a moment.

'So are you with a club or stand or something?' ventured Nick.

'No, just popped in here to scope the place for model stuff. I was thinking of hanging around for the competition though. Are you part of that?'

'Er, yes, I'm with Smooth Fishplate' Nick started to point in the direction of the layout but realised his hand was shaking, so rested it awkwardly against his hip. 'I'm not a driver though. I do all the model making.'

'Yeah, cool. I love model making. It's like being God. My parents think I'm mad. Not for thinking I'm God I mean! They can't understand why a girl would be doing it.'

'Can't say there are many in the scene' said Nick and then a bit shakily 'Not like you anyway.'

'So I can go and have a look at your work then?'

Nick never felt so naked and vulnerable. 'Sure, yes. Look, you go and have a look without me. I know it sounds odd but it would feel like an awkward first date.' The words came spilling out before Nick's brain could check them.

'First date? I was just going to have a look at your models.' Justine paused to reflect and then looked coyly at Nick. 'Well I guess I don't let people look at my models without getting to know them first.'

She breathed her words to Nick, who could feel a dangerous rush of blood, away from his brain.

'I think I need some tea. Yes, a tea. How about you take a gander at my models and y'know, if it's up to your standards, come and join me. Floor two café. I'm the weird looking one in the corner.'

Justine laughed - 'OK, OK. Let's see if you know your downpipes from your drainpipes' and skipped off.

Nick stood there, unsure of what had just happened. He was pretty sure that a lifetime ago he was looking at plastic manhole covers and that, had somehow translated into a hot date.

Mr Greendale alighted from the bottom step into the main hall. It had been a long meeting with the other judges and the new 'points criteria' wasn't exactly clear. He was an ex-guards' van man and a stickler for timing. He didn't like ambiguity and blank space. Greendale tightened his grip on the official issue clipboard and looked towards his designated club. 'Smooth Fishplate' he mouthed to himself. Well, he understood the reference but an odd name none the less. He strode purposefully towards Pete, who was watching Colin and Stew run some of the trains through their paces.

'Afternoon gentlemen. I am Mr Greendale, your judge for the competition. Could I please have your official timetable and talk through any issues you may have.'

'Hi there' said Pete. 'I'm Pete, the president of the club' and offered his hand to Mr Greendale. There was an overly vigorous shaking of hands and Pete handed the timetable over. Mr Greendale read through the listing and Pete followed his eyes, seeing if any reactions could be observed. Mr Greendale snorted.

'A problem?' asked Pete.

'This coal train you intend to run. It has reason to be running and you can show intention and supporting detail?'

'Yes.'

'And you intend to make five trips with 'Hadley's Hope'?'

'That's right. There's a big power station to feed.' Pete grinned cheesily.

Mr Greendale harrumphed slightly and carried on reading. 'Well it all looks to be in order. I will of course be checking for supportive detail.' He pulled a silver pocket watch on a long chain from his pocket. 'You will start your timetable at one thirty sharp. You will have two hours to complete your schedule, to my satisfaction. Any questions?'

'Erm, I was just wondering how much of the points tally will be based on, er, creative detail Mr Greendale… sir?'

'Creative points are at the judge's discretion and I can tell you now I don't like erroneous and tittle-tattle detail.' Mr Greendale slapped his clipboard, turned sharply on his heels and strode to the end of the layout, where he started to prod a tree with the end of a biro. Pete hoped he didn't poke the tree too hard because he was pretty sure that if a World War Two era Japanese sniper fell out he may deem it both erroneous and tittle-tattle, whatever the hell that meant.

Colin and Stew had barely noticed the conversation because of concentrating on their final test run but finally they both got up and approached Pete. Mr Greendale was staring blankly at the back of a goods warehouse, where Nick had modelled someone taking a piss. Stew noticed Pete was looking a little concerned. 'Did that not go well then Pete?'

Pete whispered back 'I don't think this judge is going to like us. I think gentlemen, we might have a struggle on. For God's sake keep to the timetable, OK?'

Colin and Stew both nodded.

Pete looked at his watch. 'Half an hour to go.'

Nick absent-mindedly tapped the side of the mug with his finger. He decided to stir another sugar in. How many was that? Three or four? He scanned the tea room again. The two Terminus drivers were sat in the middle issuing instructions to various minions. A Victorian gentleman in full railway regalia was sat bolt upright, gently waxing his handlebar moustache. Nick started to think about what he could talk to Justine about. What were her opinions on plastic wood? Did she use balsa? OO or HO? God! What if she were an N gauge modeller? Christ, he hadn't thought of that. That would be like trying to talk to his neighbour in Swahili. Hang on, didn't she say her parents didn't understand her model making? Does she still live at home? How old was she? For fuck's sake Nick considering you pride yourself on observation, you failed to notice how old she was? Girls can make themselves look much older than they are these days. Hang on, didn't women try and make themselves look younger? When do they switch from trying to look older to looking younger? Nick could feel his head going fuzzy again. He reached for his wallet and placed inspector Hancock on the Formica table top.

Inspector Hancock rubbed his eyes and surveyed the scene before him. Arranged over his desk were a confused set of photographs, blurry visions of a girl or young woman. Clearly his task was to analyse these images and supply some missing relevant info. Her attire was youthful but not naïve. It was casual but intentionally so. It lacked the confidence of an older woman but had the relaxed attitude of say… someone in their twenties? Her face. These photos were very out of focus. Very softly taken. It was difficult to look for wrinkles but there were definite crow's feet developing around the eyes. Hancock smiled. He had always loved his wife's eyes, she always smiled with them. He considered that the woman in the photos probably did too. Good figure, the slightest hunch to the back, perhaps from bending over a desk for long periods. Hancock looked over a large well-developed picture of the girl's bottom. He tutted. Someone must have stared at that for a while, but you could see why. Very firm, probably a cyclist, possibly couldn't afford a car but could get most places by bike.

Nick looked down at Hancock. 'Anything else?' he enquired.

Hancock remained silent.

'Hancock?'

'Are you talking to that plastic figure?' whispered Justine from behind Nick's back.

Nick closed his eyes. 'Bollocks' he thought loudly to himself, at the same time scooping Hancock from the table and turning to meet Justine looking down at him, a wry smile spreading across her face.

Justine reached into the small satchel slung over one shoulder and pulled out a small plastic figure. She carefully placed a perfect replica of the Metropolis robot onto the table.

'Always good to have someone sensible to talk to.' She sat down next to Nick. 'What's your little fella called then?'

Nick shifted slightly in his chair. He could feel all his blood rushing to the bad part of him again.

Back in the main hall a reverential silence had settled over the exhibition as four stern faced judges checked and rechecked their time pieces. At precisely 1.30pm four stern-faced judges uttered the phrase 'You may begin' and the competition finally got under way.

Pete had positioned himself behind the layout so he could follow the first ten minutes or so of the operations. His plan was then to go and observe how the competition were getting on. He was surprised, although not unexpectedly, that Nick wasn't around, but then Nick, strangely, wasn't that interested in trains 'going in circles' as he called it. Pete settled back to watch Stew and Colin in operational mode, which was, he had to admit, always impressive.

'OK Stew, let's get this show rolling. I'm bringing the Greenvale bound passenger train out the yard… control to you in five, four, three, two…'

'I have control, next stop Lower Didsbury. How's that coal tail forming up?' Stew replied.

'Coupling up nicely. Let me know when passenger one is free of Lower Didsbury so I can bring on mixed freight' Colin fired back.

'Absolutely. Hey Colin, feeling good?'

'Feeling groovy Stew… and the coal train is coupled. 'Hadley's Hope' is good to go. Are you clear of Lower Didsbury?'

Stew adjusted his seat slightly before replying. 'Clearing now, bring on the mixed freight and prepare to take passenger one into Greenvale.'

Pete breathed deeply. Everything was under control and running smoothly. He could see that Terminus had a spotter observing them. In classic Terminus style he made no attempt to conceal or hide himself but simply stood there in his black issue t-shirt and black jeans. He knew that every ten minutes or so a runner would come up, there would be a brief discussion and the runner would go off to update Terminus HQ.

'Sad, sad, sad' muttered Pete. He decided to go over and see how the kids of The Harlington Exchange were doing. In retrospect he wished he hadn't. It was like watching three automatons. They were perfectly in synch and with the minimal of communication. As one kid formed a line of wagons, another took it down the line and the third then shunted it into prepared sidings before assembling another train and sending it back. Meanwhile the first kid had formed up other traffic and was sending it off on other way routes. The judge overlooking them was clearly impressed and the frequent mark making on his clipboard indicated a rapidly building tally of points.

Over at The Pinewood Flyers stand Graham watched his boys do their thing.

'Bringing passenger train bound for Uxminster into

platform two at Kindle. At rest for two and then departing for Chopping' said Fat Bob softly before easing back into his chair for a moment.

'Expect through freight train for Ripping in one minute. How's that local freight to the yard coming on Al?' replied Chip.

New boy Al hesitated before replying 'I'm moving it through the sidings, should be parked at the yard soon. The next batch of main line traffic is ready in fiddle yard west, Chip.' He was beginning to realise that competition mode was way harder than practice.

Fat Bob looked out towards the crowd watching them and then at their judge, who was clearly noting things down on a regular basis. He fired off a little smile, the judge noted his smile and carried on jotting something. 'Humourless twat' thought Bob and eased the Uxminster bound train away from Kindle.

'Uxminster bound passenger leaving platform two at Kindle. Stopping at Chopping. Coming under Chip's control in three, two, one.'

'Uxminster bound passenger under my control, bringing into Chopping. Exit in two minutes for Uxminster. Al, prepare clear siding for train and ready our bauxite tail for a slow through run.'

Graham chomped away on a packet of cheese and onion crisps. 'It's going well lads, keep going. Nice job Al. I'm going to see how everyone else is doing. Anyone want snacks?'

There was a coordinated grunt.

'Was that a yes?'

There was another coordinated grunt. Graham trundled off.

'And that's how I ended up building a model of a model shop' giggled Justine. Nick giggled with her. This might just be the best date he'd ever been on. No. It *was* the best date he'd been on and the date was still ongoing.

Justine took a delicate sip of tea and looked Nick in the eyes. She seemed to be searching him out, looking into him. She smiled again. She smiled a lot. 'So how did you get into model making then? And don't tell me you started with Lego.' She giggled again. Nick grinned, that was exactly what he told everybody, normally, but he felt comfortable revealing more.

'Well,' he started, 'I was getting bullied at school during break times. I was about twelve I think and the teachers weren't doing anything about it, so I ended up hiding in the art department a lot and making things.'

'Things?' queried Justine.

'Well, the only material kind of available, really, was cardboard, paper and paint. So that's what I used. I just sort of made these fantasy buildings and machines and whatever. I wasn't really thinking about what I was doing. It was sort of escapist therapy for me. The main thing was I felt safe and in control.'

'Ah, I see, control' said Justine. 'That's what it's all really about.' She took another sip of tea. 'So how did hiding in the art department work out?'

'Very well actually' beamed Nick. 'Mrs Scrumpton caught me one day as I was finishing off a cardboard model of a steam powered spaceship. She loved it and said would I be interested in joining her brother's model railway club.'

'Sounds dodgy' whispered Justine.

'Well, I guess, but it wasn't. I went to a few meetings and they soon got me making simple things, y'know, sheds, fencing, that sort of stuff. And guess what? I was fucking brilliant at it! Plus one of the guys at the club was vaguely psychotic and when he found out about my school problems he waited outside the gate and then beat the crap out of the problems. So, all in all, everything turned out OK.'

'I would really love to see that steam powered cardboard spaceship.' Justine moved her hand towards Nick's.

Nick reached towards her and squeezed her hand. 'I still have it. Maybe I could show you. How about food round mine some time?'

'Food? I like food!'

'Inbound A5 slowing. Control over C5 crawling. Exit G4 tail outbound and store.'

'Wilco T1, A5 in house. C5 out. G4 in. Exit mixed G5 and terminate. Control to T3.'

'Roger T2. Waiting further instruction. Back to T1.'

Pete had been listening to Terminus for a while and couldn't work out what the hell their command and control language meant. I mean it all seemed to work but quite how, he had no idea. Still, work it did and Terminus were rapidly crunching through their timetable. Even their judge seemed to have acquiesced to their modus operandi and robotically ticked off each train as it completed its scheduled run.

'Alright Pete?' Graham nudged Pete in the ribs. His mouth half full of pasty.

'Alright Graham? How's it going your end?'

'Can't complain mate. This lot seem a bit serious.' A bit of pasty dropped to the floor.

'Yep and they're getting a good points tally.' Graham carried on chomping at the pasty like a cow chewing vacantly on the cud. 'Graham?'

'Sorry, yes mate.'

'Have you seen Nick at all?'

'Yeah, he's upstairs at the café talking to some girl. I waved at him but he didn't notice me.'

In Pete's mind he shouted 'How the hell didn't he notice you, you're the size of a rhino!' but luckily he wasn't like Nick and the thought remained secure in his head. 'OK cheers Graham. I need to talk to him. Catch you later.'

'No probs mate.' A bit more pasty hit the floor.

Pete headed off towards the café, stopping on the way to look down at the exhibition from the mezzanine. It looked a whole lot busier from up here. As he scanned the show he noticed a guy across the hall on the opposite side of the mezzanine.

'For fuck's sake' grumbled Pete. The guy was wearing a black t-shirt and black jeans and was using a pair of binoculars to scan the length of the hall. 'If Terminus put as much thought into their layout as their surveillance they might actually win something.' He waited till the Terminus spook looked his way, flicked him a quick 'v' and carried on to the café. He quickly spied Nick across the general throng of the café and negotiated his way over. 'Nick, hi mate, er, are you coming down to 'help'?'

Nick looked up dreamily. 'Hi Pete. Pete this is Justine.'

A not unattractive girl looked up at Pete, smiled and said 'Hi.'

'Hi there, Justine. Could I borrow Nick? Just for a moment. Team talk stuff. Very boring. Thank you.'

Pete grabbed Nick's arm and pulled him away to one side. 'Nick, this is serious. All our competitors are doing one. No one's fucked up. Colin and Stew are going strong, playing it safe but I don't think we're pulling in enough points.'

Nick focused on Pete's face. 'Justine likes using plastic wood and araldite.'

Pete glanced quickly to either side and then slapped Nick sharply on the cheek. 'Pack it in.' He whispered through clenched teeth. Nick half smiled.

'OK. Look. Give me five minutes but I'm going to need some help.' Nick looked at Justine. Pete looked at Nick. 'What?'

Justine looked at the two of them. 'What?'

Back at Smooth Fishplate.

'Stew, got a problem mate. That short timber train coming your way?'

'Yep.'

'It's too long!'

'Ah!'

'All I can suggest is to back it into the sawmill siding as planned and pray the through express can squeeze past.'

Stew winced. If the express got past without hitting anything and the judge spotted it, they could well lose some points for dangerous practice. If, however, the express wacked the timber train. Well. That would cost them dear. 'OK go for it. No other choice.'

Stew carefully backed the timber train into the sawmill siding as far as it would go. 'Done.'

'The express is on its way Stew' announced Colin. 'Under your control in three, two, one.'

Stew immediately reduced power to the express and brought it in toward the timber train. As the express neared the parallel siding he reduced the power further until it was crawling. The clearance gap between the express engine and the last timber wagon closed alarmingly. Stew breathed in and held his breath as the engine crept past the protruding wagon. It cleared, but only just. The carriages pulled through although there was a noticeable 'kiss and lean' from one of the Pullman coaches. Stew accelerated the express onwards and shot a stealthy glance at the judge. The judge was clearly writing some notes down.

'Bother!' exclaimed Stew.

'What?' retorted Colin.

'I think he spotted that little hiccup.'

'Nothing to be done mate, now get that timber train out the siding and send it on to the Greenvale warehouse, we need to get the timetable back on course.'

Pete and Justine stood gazing at Nick's master plan.

'This is what you've been working on for weeks? This is why you made me go and find out what ice cream Bob likes?'

'Yes mate' Nick smiled at Pete.

'I think its beautiful Nick. What did you make the tyres out of?' purred Justine.

'A softened and tinted polyurethane resin. I've made loads of tyre moulds so it was pretty straight forward.'

Justine looked adoringly at Nick. 'And you filed them down so they look a bit under pressure.'

'Tis the nuance that interests me dear!' tittered Nick.

Pete looked on in horror. 'Nick, you've made a model of an ice cream van. I mean its bloody brilliant and all but…. why?'

Nick folded his arms impatiently. 'Look Pete. You stick this on their layout in front of Bob and at some point he will notice it, think of hazelnut Cornetto' or whatever and inevitably lose concentration.'

'That's it? That's your master plan for the quote unquote fat fuckers?'

'Pretty much' retorted Nick. 'Only -'

'Only what?' Pete stuttered sharply.

'I've sort of grown quite fond of them.'

'What? In the last couple of hours?'

'Well, they're sort of irrevocably tied in with me meeting Justine. I think I might have developed a dangerous case of morality.'

Pete felt like banging his head against one of the many marble pillars. This was just so typical of Nick. Typically unpredictable. 'So what now then?' sighed Pete.

Nick looked at Pete. 'Well, can't say that morality extends to all teams. I would predict that this little ice cream van placed in the correct spot on the Terminus layout might just produce consequences. You know what they're like with their modelling discipline, nothing goes on the layout without at least three bits of paper being signed, if nothing else it might slow 'em up while they fill in some sort of frozen snack form... wankers!'

Pete tilted his head up and thought. A smile slowly crept across his face. 'And how would we place this innocent, sweet little van on their layout?' queried Pete.

Nick looked at Justine. Pete looked at Justine. Justine did a half curtsy. 'At your service.'

Ten minutes later the three of them stood behind a pillar a short distance from the Terminus layout. Pete stuck his head round the pillar and did a quick visual scan of the situation. He turned to Nick. 'OK. I reckon if I walk to the end of their layout, near the tunnel and act sort of inquisitive about something, I reckon that might distract them long enough for Justine to walk to the other end, casual like, and place the 'package' near that level crossing. But! Only do it when there are no trains in that area.'

Nick took a sly look round the pillar. 'OK, good spot for the van. That near driver should clock it when he reduces the power to get a train round that tight curve.' Nick stared at Justine, who was squirming in a black t-shirt that was clearly too tight for her. 'God, small black t-shirts really suit you' sighed Nick.

Justine looked up from attempting to tuck the t-shirt into her jeans, which luckily were black also.

'Where exactly did you get this t-shirt from Nick? It smells a little, er, funky.'

'You really don't need to know Justine.' Nick turned back to Pete. 'Do your inquisitive thing Pete.'

'What?'

'Look inquisitive.' Nick folded his arms.

Pete looked a little embarrassed and then started studying a small chip in the marble pillar.

Nick stared at him. 'Is this your idea of inquisitive?'

'Shush mate, I'm being inquisitive.'

Justine finally finished tucking in her t-shirt and looked up at Pete. 'What's Pete doing Nick?'

Pete started laughing. 'See! It's working.'

'For fuck's sake' muttered Nick under his breath 'OK let's do it but I'm going to loiter just in case Pete isn't inquisitive enough.'

Pete took a deep breath, stepped out from behind the pillar and headed towards the far end of the Terminus layout. He stared ahead and clocked a lone tree that could possibly engage his interest for a while. It was also close to a Terminus driver. Nick watched him go.

'How's he doing?' Justine asked from behind the pillar.

Nick grunted. 'Well for some reason he's now examining a small crap model of a tree as though it was the most interesting thing he'd ever seen.'

Justine smirked. 'Time for me to go then?'

'Just give it a few more seconds. I think a few of the onlookers are looking at Pete to see what's so interesting. Hang on, yes, a few people are bunching round him. OK go, go, go.'

Justine left the cover of the pillar and walked purposefully to the opposite end of the Terminus layout. To anyone not really paying attention she just looked like another Terminus spotter. Pete made a few bizarre twisting movements with his hands as though trying to accomplish some sort of fiendish modelling problem. He then sighed, clicked his tongue and let out a triumphant 'Oh' before sidling off exit right.

A small bunch of curious onlookers pushed forward to see what he had been so interested in. The Terminus driver blinked and shook his head ever so slightly in irritation.

Justine tapped Nick on the shoulder. 'Done, package has been delivered sir!'

'Eh, when? Oh God, I got distracted by Pete. Do not tell him.'

Pete joined them behind the pillar. 'What was that? Tell him what?'

'Tell him, that, the van is in place' stuttered Nick.

'Excellent work. Let's run.'

The three of them walked briskly back to Smooth Fishplate. Colin glanced up at them, while expertly guiding a small 060 shunter through some sidings. He immediately sensed something was up. 'What you been playing at Pete?'

'Helping you guys out. How's it going? Oh, how rude of me, this is Justine. Justine, this is Colin and Stew.' There was a brief murmur of acknowledgement from Colin and Stew as they continued with their schedule.

'So how are the other clubs getting on?' asked Colin as he formed up a mixed freight tale for their old diesel/ electric. He looked up briefly. 'And who is Justine?'

Pete looked at Nick, who looked at Justine. He reached out and touched her lightly on the shoulder. 'I think this is our new co-model maker.'

There followed a silence, broken only by the soft clatter of the Greenvale school run train. The gentle rhythm was abruptly cut short by Colin muttering 'Oh Christ, not another lunatic, I thought one was bad enough.'

Stew diplomatically stepped in. 'So can someone please tell me how the other clubs are doing?'

Terminus operative one (lead):

'In bound A26 and A27. C14 at rest. Status T1 and T2.'

Terminus operative two:

'Wilco, have A26. A27 to stop on red. C11 moving away. Forming up tail for G30.'

Terminus operative three:

'Taking on C11 to end destination. Have G28 in sidings. Slowing C11…'

Terminus operative one:

'T3 do you have exit for C11?'

Terminus operative three:

Silence.

Terminus operative one:

'I repeat. Where is exit for C11?'

Terminus operative three:

Silence.

Terminus operative two looked to his left.

'Oi, what you doing Tony?'

Terminus operative one:

'Please stick to your operating tags T2'

Terminus operative three:

'Ice cream van!'

Terminus operative one:

'What?'

Terminus operative three:

'An ice cream van and it's got hazelnut Cornettos.'

Terminus operative one:

'Christ C11 has just fucking rammed the back of my train, I mean C14. Oh fuck, it's spilled into the sidings.'

Terminus operative two:

'Shit, A27 has just fucked A26 up the arse.'

Terminus operative three:

'You can have raspberry sauce on your 99.'

Terminus operative one:

'What? We haven't reached serial 99. Pull the plug. Pull the fucking plug.'

Terminus operative two:

'Do you mean T1, our leader, to execute a hard shut down?'

Terminus operative one:

'Don't give me the lip you cheeky bastard.'

Terminus operative two:

'How about I give you a slap Terry?'

Back at Fishplate, Pete heard the disturbance coming across the hall from Terminus. 'Stew, in answer to your question I think Terminus may be struggling but Harlington Exchange are looking worryingly good. I may go as far as to say shit hot, in fact.'

Nick, who was showing off the Lower Didsbury allotments to an attentive Justine suddenly piped up. 'Have they got all the juice for their layout connected to one double socket?'

'One sec' quipped Pete, before ambling over the hall to quickly check on Harlington's power set up. Nick and Justine watched him pretend to look interested in a model warehouse, before he bent down to tie his laces and cup a look under the bench to see where their cable led. He returned with a little grin on his face.

'I take it from that crooked little smile that they are indeed just using the one double socket' offered Nick.

'Oh yes and it does smell a bit, er, electrical over there. OK Nick, how long?

Nick licked his finger and held it up to the air. 'Half an hour. All that complicated control gear is getting hot and inefficient and at some point something will give, a badly soldered joint, a loose connection, a jittery fuse, anything not one hundred percent.'

'Well,' exclaimed Pete, 'there's still over an hour to go. Maybe we can get through this.' He looked over at Stew and Colin. 'You guys ok? Need any drink, cake, crisps?' There was a combined murmur in which the barely audible words 'Sugary tea' could be heard, before the usual Colin/

Stew operating chat continued. Pete looked back to Nick. 'Anything?'

'No mate. I think we're going to have a romantic wander through the trade stands.' And with this they shuffled off hand in hand. Pete let out a little harrumph.

'Alone again.'

He checked his pockets for change and headed up the stairs, back to the tea room. As he reached the mezzanine level, Pete noticed or rather fell under the shadow cast by Graham, leaning on the balcony.

'Hey Graham, how are the Flyers doing?'

Graham heaved his momentous bulk from where it had been lodged against the ornate cast railings.

'Alright Peter, alright. I see Terminus has suffered some sort of catastrophe.'

'Er yes, but Terminus always planned for every eventuality except every eventuality!'

'I agree mate, better to make a plan and then forget about it, keeps your mind flexible and all that. How's Fishplate?

'Good. I reckon failing a major fuck up we should see it through.'

Graham rotated back to his leaning position and pointed down towards Harlington. 'What about the wunderkinds though?'

Pete shrugged his shoulders. 'Nick gives their electrics about -' Pete looked at his watch '- Oh, about twenty-five minutes!'

'Really!' exclaimed Graham and gazed intently down at their layout. 'Hmm, think I might stay here a while.'

Pete replied 'Well, I'm on the way to the café, see you in a bit.'

Graham emitted some sort of grunt. He was already

focused on Harlington. Pete smiled and carried on up to the café.

'So, I'm your co-model maker then?' Justine slipped Nick's grasp and nudged him gently in the ribs.

'Why not? You need a focus for your talent, we need your talent and you're way more attractive than the rest of them.'

'I've never been in a club before.'

Nick turned and looked into her eyes. He could see her growing excitement. 'It's not like the Guides or the school book club. We generally spend most of the time bickering in the pub.'

Justine looked over a small display of model trees and sighed. 'Yeah, but I never enjoyed the Guides. What do you think about these?'

Nick moved closer and put his arm around Justine's waist. He pointed at the nearest tree. 'What type of tree is that then?'

Justine gazed at the blobby foliage and the random branches. 'Well, it's quite obviously a madeupus twigus.'

'Exactly' sniggered Nick. 'And that one?'

Justine leant in close and sniffed the model. 'Oh well, that's easy, it's a rubbery lichonus predictus.'

'God, you're good' sighed Nick. 'I guess we really need to find out about each other, if we're to, you know, model together.'

Justine pushed herself up against Nick. 'Absolutely. I mean how many other co-model makers have you had?'

Nick looked a little embarrassed. 'Well, obviously I could have had loads of co-model makers, but, well, it never felt right. I'm not interested in a one show stand. I want a proper relationship not a badly made imitation of a semi-detached with a half-arsed representation of a shed.'

Justine squeezed Nick tightly. 'I've been waiting years to meet someone like you. I just want to let you know that you are my first co-model maker and I will never let you down with a poorly realised semi-detached or half-arsed shed.'

Nick gazed into the beckoning depths of her eyes and felt a gravitational pull that threatened to topple him over.

The owner of the trade stand leant over. 'Oi, mate, you buying a tree or what?'

Pete settled down at an empty table. He needed a quick break with a cup of tea to gather his thoughts. The café was quieter than before but there was still a definite buzz about the place. Pete rubbed his chin, stretched out his arms and cracked his fingers, before settling into a comfortable slump. He was well aware that Fishplate had never got further than the second round but it looked likely they would at least get to the second round this time. The club was looking as strong as it ever had, but he knew that to stand a chance of getting through the next round they realistically needed a third driver. Virtually all their competition had three and very few clubs had ever won with two. To be honest Pete hadn't been that bothered in the past about winning but there was something different this time. A definite *espirit d'corps* had settled upon the club. Pete rubbed the rim of the cup. If we could get a third driver quick, and if Justine was as good as she said she was and if she didn't fall out with Nick, and if these new rules actually got implemented at some point. Well, who knows? Pete sat a while, lost in a strange half vacant, half alert pose, before some mental switch cut in and ordered him to get some sugary polystyrene tea for the troops and see if Harlington had gone up in smoke yet. On his way down he spotted Graham, still gazing down on the hall, but decided to ignore him and head on to Fishplate.

'Hey guys, got your tea. All well?' Pete placed the drinks next to Stew and Colin. Stew looked relaxed and was even smiling.

'Hi Pete, yes, indeed we are well because we have power and Harlington don't.'

Pete looked straight over to Harlington and noticed immediately that nothing was happening. In fact nobody was there.

Colin joined the conversation. 'Yes, it's a little strange isn't it? You would have thought with three kids at the helm that when the power went off there would have been some sort of mega brat tantrum.'

Pete looked puzzled. 'So when did the power go?'

'About five minutes ago' replied Colin.

'And they've all gone?' Pete said quizzically.

'That's right' replied Colin. 'But I see this at school from time to time with the really competitive kids. If they know there's no chance of winning they just lose interest and wander off.'

Pete scratched his head. 'New one on me Colin. So how's the timetable?'

'Over to you, Stew. I've just got to tidy up some sidings with the 060.'

Stew looked over to Pete as he bought a passenger train into Lower Didsbury. 'Bang on schedule Pete. One small error which they probably caught us on but everything else went to plan. We should finish in about twenty minutes.'

Pete drew in a deep breath and exhaled. 'Lads I think we're into the next round.'

'Excellent, so when do we have the post first round pub

meeting?' exclaimed Colin.

'As soon as possible mate. I've got a few, er, minor suggestions to make.'

And so the first round of the regionals at Potton came to an end. It took a while for Pete to get the boards loaded in the van since Nick kept getting distracted by Justine. But eventually, after a long kiss goodbye Nick finally joined Pete in the cab. 'Well Presido, you did it! We must be in the second round. Do this again and it's a new club record!'

Pete gave Nick a sideways glance and muttered 'Sarky bastard' before stirring around in the gearbox. He eventually found a lowish gear and the van pogoed out of the car park and off down the road, towards Nick's place.

'Nick?'

'Yes mate.'

'How good a model maker do you think Justine is?'

Nick looked dead ahead. 'That's a straight up question, no innuendo involved?'

'This isn't a bloody Python sketch. I didn't say, is she good? Does she go? Know what I mean, nudge, nudge, say no more. I just want to know if you think she's any good?'

'As a model maker?' grinned Nick.

'Yes, does she model well? Does she? Eh? Eh? Wink, wink, nudge, nudge.'

Pete and Nick started laughing.

'Look mate, from the conversations I've had with her, she must be pretty good. She says all the right things, knows the right products and has a, er, naughty streak.'

Pete sighed. 'You mean, model of a T Rex in the cow shed, miniature gnome wanking in the garden naughty?'

'What was that last thing?'

Pete sighed again. 'Gnome wanking in the garden.'

'What? Someone wanking off a gnome or a gnome having a wank?'

Pete was in danger of running out of sighs. 'Just asking is she likely to do that sort of model making?'

'Don't worry Pete from what she's told me I think her humour is a little more cerebral. Think little historical figure of Monet painting the village pond.'

Pete slowed to ease the van round a tight corner. 'And how quick do you think she is?'

'Quick? Quick? Eh? Eh? Ooh very quick.'

'God I am so glad you don't meet girls that often' Pete grimaced.

'Oh c'mon Pete. Life is great. We're through and I have a sexy new toy.'

Pete winced. 'Yeah, don't let Justine hear the toy bit.'

'What do you want to know Pete? What are you asking?'

'OK Nick I've had a few thoughts. I think we can go further than the second round but we need more models pronto.'

'OK then. No problem mate. On it like a car bonnet.'

'Also. We need a third driver.'

Nick buried his face in his hands and emitted a long, pained moan.

Pete smiled and drove on through the lengthening shadows of a slow summer evening.

CHAPTER SEVEN: TITTLE-TATTLE

Ken Bruce sighed. It was another clandestine meeting with Captain Hargraves at some dodgy tea room in Rutland. Ahead he could see the silhouette of Hargraves smoking his pipe against a bright sky, his Panama hat giving him an old-fashioned colonial look. Ken walked slowly over and sat down opposite him. Hargraves doffed his hat and carefully removed his pipe.

'Mr Bruce, how delightful to see you old chap.' He paused and smiled congenially at Ken.

Ken knew what to expect.

'Now, Mr Bruce, answer me this. What should I do with the left-handed spigot?'

Ken stared into the distance. These codes were so bloody pointless. He knew what he wanted to do with the left-handed spigot… but that technically wasn't the correct answer.

'Do hurry up Mr Bruce' Hargraves champed on the stem of his pipe.

'You should paint the spigot grey and call it Mary.'

Captain Hargraves smiled. 'Correct Mr Bruce. Would you like a cup of tea? And I can highly recommend the Victoria sponge cake.'

Ken nodded. 'You wanted an informal report on the regionals sir. Anything in particular? I've created a brief situation report summing up the first round.'

Hargraves took a little puff and looked down the hill towards the shore of Rutland water, his eyes focusing on a couple walking their dog. He turned to Ken. 'As you know, the Major has a particular interest in a few select clubs and would like to follow very closely, their progress.

I assume they made it to the second round?'

Ken nodded.

Hargraves nodded back. He took a long drag on his pipe and exhaled slowly. 'Good, good… and our new judging criteria is settling in? I heard there was some trouble with a few judges in the North West.'

'All satisfactorily sorted out sir.'

Hargraves smiled and pushed a blank envelope across the metal table. Ken sighed inwardly and took the envelope.

Hargraves looked him in the eyes. 'New instructions from the Major… and if you have ambition enough to eventually take over from me you will need to follow them… to the letter. We must look to the bigger picture.'

Ken nodded. 'Of course sir.' He paused. 'Will I get to meet the Major at some point?'

'Yes, yes, all in the fullness of time. He's a very busy chap.'

Hargraves rubbed his hands together. 'Now. Let's get you some cake. I say… garcon. Garcon?'

Ken winced and placed the envelope into his small leather satchel.

'So this is where you boys all hang out.' Justine looked up at the crumbling façade of the Water Tower and Tender. 'I should have known. I thought the pub on your layout looked familiar.'

'Well, it's a beautiful example of a badly maintained mid-Victorian building.'

'Oh you say the most romantic things darling.'

'Now, what would be your tipple?' enquired Nick.

'What do you think?' Justine teased back.

Nick stood back and drank in Justine. She was wearing

jeans, rolled up a little to expose a well, worn pair of DMs. Up top, a loose-fitting white lace blouse, over which hung a large faded chequered shirt. Definitely a little 'studenty', a little 'indie' thought Nick. Justine watched him checking her over.

'Are you trying to guess what I drink by the way I dress?' she smiled.

'Erm, possibly?'

'What do I drink then?' Justine did her trademark curtsey.

Nick took a deep breath. 'I'm guessing… something sweet but with a little kick in the tail.'

'Warmish' purred Justine.

'Nick was hoping above all hope it was coke and JD and blurted it out.

'Nope' said Justine. 'A bit more girly.'

'Lemonade and something?' ventured Nick.

'Yep.'

Nick tried to remember what girls had with lemonade. It had been a while since he had to get a round in for a young lady. God! He sounded old. 'Er, how about… sweet Martini and lemonade?' Nick raised his eyebrows and looked expectantly at Justine.

Justine smiled a big beautiful smile. 'Thank you very much Nick. Just a little ice please. I shall be sitting in the beer garden.' And with that she pushed open the sagging double glazed doors of the pub, walked through to the back and sauntered into the garden. Nick sighed aloud to himself. God he fancied her.

By the time the rest of Fishplate arrived Nick had almost forgotten it was meant to be a meeting not a date.

Pete let the team chat a while before taking a long gulp of his Guinness and clanking an empty glass against the ashtray to announce the formal beginning of this informal meeting.

'Well, we got through to the second round. I got the official results through today. It was close though, Harlington probably would have nicked it if their power hadn't shut off. The Pinewood Flyers beat us on traffic points but we beat them on creative points. So looks like TRACK really are bringing in new scoring criteria.'

Colin piped up. 'So the Flyers beat us?'

'Just' replied Pete.

'Is that bad?'

'Doesn't make much difference for us. We compete against a different set of teams to them in the next round and it's not seeded. So, er, no!'

Nick, who had his arm around Justine at one end of the trestle table, put down his JD and coke. 'I thought our judge, what was his name? Greenpale or something?'

'Greendale' corrected Pete.

Nick continued - 'Yeah, Greendick. Anyway, I got the impression that creativity wasn't on his agenda.'

Pete started laughing. 'Well, funny story that. He didn't like some of your creative modelling and made a list of what he considered 'tittle-tattle.'

'Cheeky bastard' muttered Nick.

'Now dear' whispered Justine.

Colin shot a smirk at Nick. 'So what did he do with his 'tittle-tattle' list?'

Pete grinned. 'He phoned the regional rep with the list to seek guidance on points and was told in no uncertain terms to award us not just points but bonus points. I know this because I sold a three year old Cortina to the rep a few months ago and he called me at work to let me know he actually talked to the president about the list. Apparently the old boy wet himself laughing. Turns out Nick's model making might be our new secret weapon!'

Everyone turned to look at Nick, who just grinned and mouthed 'Losers' back.

'So what was on the list?' ventured Stew. 'Anything we could build on?'

Pete winced and shrugged his shoulders. 'Well… he obviously didn't spot that much and remember it was all his personal opinion.'

'Yeah' butted in Colin. 'If he'd really had a look that list would have been obscene, probably illegal and definitely freaky.'

Justine rotated her head slowly and deliberately to look at Nick. Nick looked back. 'I have no idea what he's talking about.'

Justine squinted. 'Hmm.'

'So,' Stew tried to continue, 'what was on the list?'

Pete smiled at Stew. 'He mentioned a few things.'

Colin stood up abruptly, scattering an open packet of cheese and onion crisps. 'Wait, wait, wait, this is an ideal point to guess which aspects of Nick's creative weirdness made it to the list.'

Justine whispered into Nick's ear. 'Does Colin like you?'

Nick whispered back so Colin could hear. 'He's just jealous. Some do, others teach.'

Colin tutted. 'Right, I'm guessing. Back yard garden, small pond, large shark swimming round the fountain.' He looked down at the rest. 'What about you? Stew?'

Stew looked thoughtfully into his small beer glass. A coquettish smile slowly spread over his face. 'Well, I have to say I'm rather fond of the learner driver who's just reversed over a cat. Margaret always refers to it when she finds cat do-da in the herbaceous borders.'

Nick released Justine and leaned forward to give Stew a small embrace. 'Thank you Stewart, I never knew. Thank you, thank you.' Nick sat back and smiled.

'OK, OK. So Nick? What do you think was on that list?' Colin said, still standing like a teacher in the classroom.

Nick settled back to his Justine hugging position. 'Well call me Mr Boring but it has to be the Daleks. You'd have to be blind and stupid... or Colin not to notice them.'

Colin smiled. 'Well I wasn't going to count that 'cos it's so obvious, but anyway... right Pete what was mentioned?' but before Pete could say anything Justine wriggled free and tapped her empty glass.

'Hang on! If I'm going to be part of this club then I get to join in the general stupidity too. I want a guess.'

There was a slightly amused silence before Colin cleared his throat and ventured 'Is Justine in the club? And I won't make the obvious joke.'

Nick shot him a glance before Pete quickly replied 'Yes, as part of the model building effort, definitely.'

'Well OK then' exclaimed Colin in a slightly theatrical way. 'Justine, for today's star prize, your guess is?'

Justine paused for a moment as a faraway smile settled upon her eyes. It felt to all there like some sort of moment. 'I,' she began, 'I love the small faded advert in the window of the corner shop.'

There was a puzzled silence only slightly broken by Nick whispering something into Justine's ear and briefly stroking her hair.

Colin inevitably was first to speak. 'Er, well, I guess by that reaction no one else knows that particular detail which I guess means the judge probably didn't see it either. C'mon

Pete what was on the list?'

Pete closed his eyes and looked up. 'OK on the list. Oh, well he mentioned Daleks of course. Well he mentioned seven of them.'

There was a spluttering from Stew. 'Seven? I've only counted four!'

Nick quickly added 'There's way more than seven anyway.'

Pete continued 'Well maybe a couple is ok but seven is 'tittle-tattle', I have no idea what the new judging criteria is for bloody Daleks. Anyway, what else? Well, there was a lot.'

Pete unfolded a piece of lined A4, focused and took a long breath. 'OK, in no particular order. Napoleon Bonaparte feeding the ducks, a triceratops, Batman, Spiderman and Snoopy. Luckily he didn't spot Wonder Woman. ET, one of the transformer robots, several triffids, various Star Wars characters although, alarmingly he's missed the TIE fighter in for a service at the garage, one flasher, several naked people, an entire shop devoted to the sale of cowboy hats, yes, the shark in the pond. No not the flat cat, lewd graffiti, some school children building a nuclear bomb, a giant sparrow and finally what he described as… a suspicious car park? No idea what he meant by that.'

Everyone was by now chuckling, even Colin.

Pete continued 'Anyway he either didn't spot or didn't mention many, many other modelling details but who cares? It got us points and my feeling is perhaps another judge would give us a whole pile more.'

Stew put down his empty glass. 'Can you tell us anything about the other rounds Pete?'

Pete sniffed. 'As you know there were three other rounds with four clubs in each.' He took a quick sip of Guinness. 'And most of the favourites went through, apart from the red-hot cert in the Mary on the Hill round.'

Stew assumed a shrewd expression. 'What happened?'

'Well,' said Pete 'they had a catastrophic derailment at a critical point and never recovered.'

'That all sounds familiar' retorted Colin.

Nick smiled and whispered to himself 'Wait for it.'

'Hey hang on!' returned Colin. 'You don't think it was a case of sabotage? Red hot favourites don't generally fuck it up that badly.'

'You're right Colin' replied Pete, throwing a smile to Nick. 'I talked to a guy who was there. He didn't witness the crash but did say they were totally on course for an easy points win and check this out. He hung around while the teams started to pack down and he heard them discussing glue or something on the track as well as a few other problems.'

At this point Justine felt she needed to get on board with past events. Pete quickly explained their own little derailment adventure.

'Any idea what the saboteur might look like?' ventured Justine.

Pete shook his head. 'No idea. His…or her identity is a mystery as well as their motives.' He took a quick sip of Guinness.

'I do wonder whether we need a little more man-power to protect our layout.'

'Why can't Nick hang around a bit more then?' queried Colin and was met instantly by Nick.

'Because it would involve watching you blundering around my layout, damaging my models. Besides I need to get out and around the exhibitions to check out the other layouts.'

'You mean check out the other model makers' laughed Colin

Justine grabbed a crumpled up crisp packet and chucked it at Colin. 'He was checking out man-hole covers when I met him' she laughed.

'That's not a dodgy euphemism is it?' retorted Colin.

There was a round of sniggering which Pete ended. 'Well, we definitely need a third driver.'

Stew and Colin looked worryingly at each other.

'Is there room for a third cab?' asked Stew.

'If Colin leaves his ego behind I reckon we could squeeze one in' suggested Nick.

Colin ignored him. 'What would the third driver do exactly?'

Pete closed his eyes briefly and rubbed his forehead. This had to be handled carefully. 'I think we get someone to form up the trains and tails in the fiddle yard. It should be fairly straight forward. Out-going traffic can be quickly checked by you or Stew and it would free you up for more interesting manoeuvres.'

'Interesting manoeuvres?' said Colin, raising his eyebrows.

Nick nudged Justine. 'That's his only impression. It's supposed to be Mr Spock but I haven't the heart to tell him to only raise the one.'

Justine gave Colin a sympathetic smile. 'Maybe it's more of a Roger Moore?'

Colin continued to ignore them. Stew, ever the reliable supporter, chipped in. 'I think it's a splendid idea. Bring some new blood in and make the whole experience a little more relaxing.'

'I was kind of thinking we could run more creative traffic rather than relax the whole experience,' replied Pete.

'Ah!' said Stew. 'Well no rest for the wicked I suppose.'

'You're not wicked, Stew' laughed Nick.

'I might be' retorted Stew.

'No you're not' added Colin.

Stew looked at Pete.

'No.'

Stew muttered something about secret biscuits and looked disapprovingly into his glass.

'I guess this needs to be in place for the next round then?' said Colin.

'Indeed' replied Pete.

'And is that possible?' said Colin, not raising any eyebrows and looking at Nick.

Nick smiled a crooked little smile and raised both eyebrows. 'Easy to wire in a new cab. The problem is finding someone that could put up with Colin.'

'What about myself then?' asked Stew.

'You could get on with Genghis Khan' retorted Nick.

Pete got up. 'Does anyone know anyone suitable? I'm getting another round in. Have a think.'

As Pete disappeared through the open door into the back of the pub. Colin slapped the trestle table top with his palms a few times. 'He's serious about winning isn't he?'

'Well why not?' replied Stew. 'I've known him the longest and I think he feels this is our moment. Our time if you will.'

'Calm down Stew, just good to see El Presidento spark into life.'

Justine raised her hand. 'I might know someone.'

'Yeah, I have a few candidates in mind' said Colin.

'What about my father?' asked Stew.

'No offence Stew, but is he still alive?' queried Nick.

'Yes, yes, he's fighting fit.'

'In that case, er, no.'

'Don't be so mean' Justine jabbed Nick in the ribs.

'You haven't met him' retorted Nick.

Stew sighed. 'Oh dear then, well everyone else I know would find your good selves a, erm, a little racy.'

'A little fucking rude' smiled Nick.

'Yes, that is what I meant' said Stew.

'What about you?' Colin did a 'your country needs you' impression with his hand and pointed to Nick.

Nick gave him a patronising smile. 'As you know, in the past I have been quite clear about my feelings towards the sort of people I work with.'

'They're all wankers?'

'Yes, Colin, they are indeed all wankers. So, actually not sure mate, if I know anyone suitable. Hey, I bet Pete knows loads of victims. He's the best-connected bloke I know.'

'Course he knows loads. He's just seeing if we can save him a little work' winked Colin.

There was a reflective silence. A slight breeze ruffled the feathery ash tree that flanked the beer garden.

'I talked to Margaret about our possible railway saboteur' said Stew out of nowhere. 'I thought perhaps as a devoted Agatha Christie fan she might have a thought or two on the perpetrator.'

'And?' asked Colin.

'She said be wary of doctors, mysterious returning relatives from overseas, anyone foreign and couples in love.'

'Not much help then?' muttered Colin.

'Well, not really but she did talk, at great length I may add, about motive. And how perhaps we should keep a very open mind about what motivates this person, rather than who they are.'

Justine sighed. 'Your wife sounds very intelligent, Stew.'

'Thank you Justine, yes she is.'

'I agree Stew' said Nick. 'They may be a little shit but they're definitely a motivated and probably talented little shit.'

'Without sounding too judgemental,' continued Stew, 'sneaking an ice cream van onto the Terminus layout could, well, should be seen as sabotage. Perhaps they would regard you as a, erm...'

'Go on Stew. You can do it' nudged Colin.

'Yes, as, erm a little shit too.'

Colin laughed but a slightly uneasy mood descended upon the beer table.

Nick felt obliged to explain. 'Well, OK, busted dad. But we didn't physically prevent Terminus from doing anything. They could have ignored the van and carried on. Colin couldn't avoid hitting that glued on block. I think there's a difference.'

'Well it's not sportsman-like behaviour' endeavoured Stew.

'Oh c'mon Stew, Terminus epitomise un-sportsman-like behaviour. They had spies watching everyone else. We just played them at their own game. Just, er, a little more creatively.'

Stew smiled. 'All I'm saying is, I'm a little uncomfortable with this sharp practice, shall we say. I don't think we need to stoop that low. Subject closed.'

'Well, if it's any consolation I was going to park the van next to Fat Bob but I sort of quite like them.'

'What? The fat fuckers?' teased Colin.

'Yes, they're my kind of fat fuckers,' grinned Nick.

'And,' said Justine 'they're part of how we met in the first place.'

'Christ, young love' moaned Colin.

There was a sudden chinking of glasses as Pete tottered out of the pub with a tray of drinks. They watched him advance slowly towards the table before gingerly lowering the tray down. 'Was that Martini and lemonade or sweet Martini and lemonade, Justine?'

'Sweet Martini' replied Justine.

'Bollocks' muttered Pete. 'Is there a big difference? Surely anything mixed with lemonade is by definition sweet?'

'I shall attempt to choke it down Pete' smiled Justine.

'Brave girl. Now any driver candidates? I've had a thought and could probably get half a dozen or so.'

Justine took a quick sip of her 'sweet' drink, winced a little and said 'One candidate possibly.'

Stew muttered that his dad was apparently not acceptable. Nick shook his head and Colin reckoned maybe three at a stretch. Pete remained standing and folded his arms. 'So that would be collectively, exactly four in total then?'

Everyone looked down at their drink.

'OK, well in that case let's arrange an interview at Nick's for the weekend.'

'Do I have to be there?' enquired Nick.

'Seriously?' grimaced Pete.

'Well I could lend you my house keys. Look it's you, Colin and Stew who need to do the interviews. I could set up the boards in the garage and you could see what they're like at driving. Ultimately you're going to have to work with them.'

'Alright, sounds ok to me, I think Helen's taking the kids off somewhere anyway next weekend. What about you Stew?' said Colin.

'No problem, I think. Should we prepare a list of questions?'

Pete unfolded his arms. 'Let's try and keep it relaxed. It's more a case of attitude, common sense and ability. Y'know. Do they have any?'

'So how did Colin get in again?' ventured Nick.

Colin sighed. 'Are we interviewing for security as well?'

Pete rubbed his chin thoughtfully. 'I'm not so sure anymore. If we take on another that would be three new people in as many weeks. Maybe we should gel a bit before taking on anyone else.'

Colin looked towards Nick and asked 'Have you and Justine gelled yet?'

Justine blushed. Nick fired back with 'The only gelling action you get Colin is with your hair.'

Colin smirked.

Pete smiled. 'Colin? Do you fancy hearing another model railway disaster story? I feel it would help your growth as a model railway operator.'

Colin shuffled in his seat. 'I'm not convinced about this. I think you're all winding me up.'

'Ooh, what number?' shrieked Justine. 'I know about number eight. I had an uncle involved.'

'How convenient' mocked Colin. 'That's where we're up to.'

'Hear it or not?' asked Pete.

Colin's head slumped to the table top. 'You're all bloody

mad' he muttered.

'Hear it or not?' repeated Pete.

'Hear it' said Justine excitedly. 'It's a good one.'

'Go on' said Stew.

Nick started chanting 'Hear it, hear it.'

Colin shook his head. 'Yes, OK, alright, tell me please, just stop getting so shouty.'

Pete cleared his throat. 'Justine, if you know the story, do you want to tell it? I'm quite interested to hear your version.'

Everyone looked in Justine's direction.

'Oh, ok then.' She did a little bottom shuffle. 'Gentlemen, our story starts in the hallowed setting of the North Eastern Wool Trading Exchange, near Skipton. My lovely Uncle Benjamin was taking part in a model railway extravaganza to mark the anniversary of something to do with railways and sheep. He was just being, well, lovely and running his scratch-built steam engine around a simple oval circuit when a turnout to a siding got stuck. He didn't notice and his wonderful, wonderful 262, made from the finest quality gauge brass and hand painted over a period of weeks, went flying up this siding. Anastasia, as she was called, overshot the end of the siding and sailed magnificently through the air until she landed with an apparently graceful clank onto the track of the adjacent layout.' Justine paused for effect. Her audience were hanging. 'Now, the adjacent layout was owned by Horace 'Mutton Chops' Beaston, a huge brute of a man, renowned for eating, drinking and experimentation with narrow gauge railway lines.'

'A terrible combination' whispered Stew.

'Indeed' replied Justine. 'Now, when Anastasia alighted upon the rails of Beaston's layout, he was in the middle of demonstrating how his narrow-gauge engine could climb steeper than normal gradients because of its low ratio motor and extra high variable voltage control. Unfortunately he had just wacked the voltage up to max as his beloved 'Empress of the Glen' ascended the steepest gradient of his Scottish themed wonderland. Anastasia, with her scratch-built contacts, sucked up the voltage like a voracious humming bird on nectar and accelerated towards the Monarch as if caught in a suicidal love pact.' Justine took a small breath. 'There was a terrible, terrible, shearing rotating crushing slicing dream ending crash that left both engines utterly ruined. Horace Beaston let out the deepest, saddest bellow as though a mighty beast had been felled by a single spear to the heart and collapsed to his knees.'

There was a mournful silence as though everyone were saying goodbye to Anastasia and the Monarch. If Stew had been wearing a hat he would have doffed it in respect, instead he asked. 'What happened to your Uncle?'

Justine started to giggle. 'He did the only decent, honourable thing a man of his grace and beguiling character could do… legged it didn't he.'

There was a collective intake of breath and a ripple of laughter. Nick clapped his hands together. 'I would like to nominate Justine as future story teller. I bet that version was better than yours Pete.'

Pete stood up and bowed to Justine. 'Much better version, although mine had a small explosion.'

Colin sat there shaking his head again. 'I can't believe a train could jump layouts.'

Pete slapped him gently on the back. 'Colin. You know that if it's theoretically possible then it is possible and that's kind of the point of the story. They're not just a top ten of increasingly chaotic destruction.'

Nick coughed.

'Well, alright, mainly it is but anyway I think it's worthy of a number eight ranking.'

Colin picked his head off the table. 'So how is your Uncle, Justine?'

'He's well and still exhibiting, although it's more static engines rather than rolling.'

Colin nodded. 'I once spent a long, rainy afternoon trying to get a train to jump tracks using Mark's little set but never even came close.'

'Or you didn't try enough times,' added Nick. 'If I spent enough time tossing coins eventually I would flip a hundred tails in a row. That's the nature of chance.'

'Exactly' exclaimed Pete. 'And that's why we have a chance of winning this year!'

Nick smirked. 'So what you're saying Pete, is, while it's basically impossible for us to win, it is at least theoretically achievable.'

'Something like that' grinned Pete.

'Does me' said Nick.

'Well, that was always my viewpoint' teased Colin.

'Well I like being the underdog' said Stew. 'It's very British.'

'Excellent!' exclaimed Pete. 'Forward to theoretical victory!'

CHAPTER EIGHT: THE INTERVIEWS

A few days later Colin was sat at the kitchen table trying to gather his thoughts before Helen dropped him off at Nick's place for the interviews. Helen was fussing around the sink trying to tidy up before she took Josh and Mark out for the day. 'You all seem to be taking this competition a little more seriously than the last disastrous outing, my love.'

Colin looked up. 'Hmm, well the rules appear to have changed a little in our favour and Pete's got up a head of steam about it, hence this thing I'm doing today.'

'Yes,' said Helen, wiping a swathe through some spilt cornflakes. 'This thing isn't going to go on too long? After a day on my own with our beloved offspring I will need, no, I demand, a maximum of fuss and possibly some very dirty fish and chips for supper.'

'Dirty?'

'Y'know, I want to be able to read the newspaper off the chips…and I don't want to be using plates or cutlery.'

Colin smiled at her. 'Still the girl I met at teacher school then.'

Helen dumped the last of the clean cutlery into the appropriate drawer and leant against the kitchen unit observing Colin. 'Do you really want another train driver person in your cosy little social club?'

'Yeah, definitely.'

Helen folded her arms. 'Really?'

Colin sighed. 'OK maybe if you asked me that a couple of months ago, no. But. Well everything seems to have changed. I think I may be getting competitive.'

Helen tilted her head to one side. 'Hey news flash, you've

always been competitive love.'

'No I haven't.'

'Last year at your parents' at Christmas?'

Colin smiled. 'It was just a small victory dance because I won.'

Helen replied quickly. 'Against your arthritic mum, your brother, who was totally wankered, Mark, Josh and Uncle George.'

'Hey, Uncle George had an unfair advantage.'

Helen laughed. 'What? His false leg.'

Colin grinned. 'Twister is an unforgiving game and having a multi rotational leg is a massive advantage.'

Helen tutted. 'So anyway, who did you try and pressgang into your strange little world?'

Colin winced. 'Er, well only two. That new guy at school, who's taken over the wood work class and Andy.'

'What? Andy, Andy?'

Colin pulled a face. 'Yes, Andy, Andy.'

Helen shrugged. 'Do you have to be sober to drive your little trains?'

'It helps.'

Helen picked up a glass and inspected it. 'Have you ever seen him sober?'

There was a long pause. 'Not recently.'

Helen smirked. 'Just asking.'

From upstairs came a high-pitched yelp. Helen swung into automatic mode. 'What's going on up there?' An ever so slightly hysterical 'Josh is licking my Lego' came bouncing back.

Helen rolled her eyes. 'What is wrong with that boy?' and

shouted back 'Josh, leave Mark's Lego alone.'

There was a brief, doomed silence. 'Mum, he's putting the Lego in his pants' followed by further shrieking and what sounded like the Millennium Falcon being chucked at a cupboard. Colin did a shuffle in his chair as though about to get up, but Helen was predictably already halfway up the stairs. He settled back down and stared into his empty mug. He was really worried that he might actually never have seen Andy sober.

Pete got to Nick's house early to make sure there were enough boards set up for a practice. He had persuaded about seven probables to turn up and a couple of maybes. He reckoned with Colin and Justine's candidates they had a chance of actually coming away with a result. Nick had left with Justine in the early morning for a short weekend break. All he would say was that there was romance and model making in the equation. Pete was surprised that romance had made it to first place in Nick's equation. He trotted into the kitchen to see if Nick had left anything in the way of refreshments. Hanging precariously to a cupboard door was a crumpled yellow Post-it. Pete walked over and peeled off the scrappy little note.

'Pete – milk, tea, coffee, sugar in usual place.

In this cupboard – Happy Shopper biscuits for Colin, Sainsbury's for everyone else.

If desperate – Pot Noodles in bottom cupboard. Help yourself to anything else.

Cheers Nick.

PS Don't choose a moron – position already filled!'

Pete shook his head, crumpled up the note and flicked it into the bin. He'd just stuck the kettle on when Stew walked in through the open door. 'Morning Pete. Are we all well and ready?'

'Reckon,' said Pete 'just waiting for Colin. Is that a packed lunch?'

Stew carefully extracted a pale blue tin box from an old plastic Co-op bag. 'Certainly is Pete, and Margaret has baked us some of her famous Viennese fingers.'

Pete raised his eyebrows. 'Lovely. Right then, fancy a brew?' Shortly after making tea the distant thud of car doors announced Colin's arrival. There was a short pause and Colin walked in.

'Morning, milk, one sugar.'

Pete looked at him and then pointed at the kettle. Eventually with the tea made for all and a plate of Viennese fingers sitting happily on the table they could at last discuss the business of the day.

Stew produced a neat little clipboard with an ample supply of lined A4 paper. 'I thought I could record details and observations, which should be a great help in collating the results.'

Colin grinned at Pete and said 'Well, good idea Stew, although I get the impression we're going to know who to pick without the need for any collating.'

Stew looked a little taken aback. 'Well, you never know, it might be close.'

Pete picked up another Viennese finger and bit the chocolate tip off. He looked thoughtfully at the far wall.

Colin observed him. 'What do you think boss?'

Pete finished off the biscuit. 'I have absolutely no idea mate. I know the people I've invited are a mixed bag but I'm pretty sure one of 'em should be good enough. Let's make them a drink, have a chat, see if they can pick up some carriages, form a train and move it, under control, from A to B.'

Colin nodded. 'Sounds like a plan but I think we need

some safety phrases.'

Stew put his tea down. 'What on Earth do you mean by that Colin?'

Colin coughed. 'Well, there are going to be some pretty obvious morons so instead of wasting too much time on them one of us could just say, er, are there any more biscuits?'

'OK,' said Pete, 'and how about 'Has anyone seen my keys? If we think someone's a real prospect?'

'Excellent' said Colin. 'Any idea who we should be expecting first?'

Pete consulted a small scrap of paper. 'Most I told to come between ten and one and the rest between two and four. I didn't want to pressure anyone for time, especially as it's the weekend.'

'What's the time now?' asked Stew

Colin flicked a glance at his Casio. 'Gone ten, anytime now then.'

One very long hour, all the Viennese biscuits and many mugs of tea later there was at last a gentle knock on the front door. Pete rose from the table. 'OK, here we go. Remember we need to like them!' He ambled out the kitchen to the large airy hallway. Colin and Stew looked at each other expectantly. There was a muffled exchange at the door and Pete re-entered the kitchen, followed by a short, balding man, in a tank top and brown cords.

'Gentlemen, this is Thomas. Thomas, this is Colin and Stew.'

There was a nodding of heads. Thomas smiled at them all before nervously laughing 'And don't call me a tank engine!'

Stew started laughing. Colin gave Pete a nervous look.

'So, could I offer you a cup of tea Thomas?' said Pete.

'Yes indeedy' said Thomas and sat down in the spare chair. He looked at Colin and Stew. 'I've always wanted to be a train driver,' he said.

Stew nodded his head. 'Well that's a positive start' and scribbled something on his clipboard. 'What do you do for a living, might I enquire?'

'Oh, I'm an accountant,' replied Thomas.

'Marvellous' retorted Stew, frantically writing. 'I am too. Who do you work for?'

'Lacy and Scott.'

'Oh, I know, local company. Very respected.'

'Well thank you Stew, very nice of you to say. Tell me, who are you in the employ of?' said Thomas

'Bartle and Brown.'

'Really! I know one of your secretaries, Mrs Tangent.'

'Ooh yes,' simpered Stew, 'lovely lady.'

'And,' continued Thomas with a little wink, 'she is not easily distracted!'

Stew let out a little giggle. 'Oh very clever, I see what you mean.'

They both smiled cheerily at each other and in unison turned to look at Pete and Colin. Colin didn't quite remove his 'Oh my God' face quickly enough, while Pete was caught mid 'goldfish.'

An idea suddenly entered Stew's warmly glowing head. 'Colin?'

'Yes Stew.'

'I don't suppose you've seen my keys, have you?'

Colin spluttered. Thomas immediately offered to help find

them, commenting that he was always leaving his calculator in strange places. Pete had to step in quick.

'I'm sure your keys are somewhere nearby Stew but perhaps we should see how Thomas is with the controls first. Yes?'

'Oh, yes, of course. Thomas follow me to the garage if you please.'

Thomas grinned broadly. 'I say. How exciting!'

Colin and Pete hung back.

'What the fuck was that?' whispered Colin.

'I think that might have been Stew's long-lost brother,' replied Pete.

'Pete?'

'Yes Colin.'

'I can't deal with two Stews. I like Stew. I don't like two Stews.'

Pete rubbed his chin. 'Let's just see how he deals with the trains.'

In the garage Stew was carefully explaining how the controls worked while setting up a mixed freight train for Thomas to manoeuvre around the layout. Colin stood by the roller doors and hoped to all that was holy that Thomas was crap at this. Pete was about to join him when a crunch of gravel outside announced the imminent arrival of another candidate. He scurried back out of the garage, pausing briefly to put down the sodding cup of tea that he still hadn't been able to give to Thomas and went back in the kitchen side door and out to the hallway. He was just in time to hear a somewhat aggressive rap to the woodwork. He opened the door. Standing, legs apart and arms tightly folded was a jittery young man, behind whom stood a slightly frail looking girl in faded jeans and a large white shirt tied up in a knot at the front.

'Right mate, this is Justine's mate, Justine.'

'Justine?'

'Yeah, Justine. Her name's Justine. Justine said she could come over and try out for some job or somefing.'

'Hang on. This is Justine's friend?'

The young man scowled and jutted his sharp little chin forward. 'Like wot I said mate.'

'Right,' said Pete 'cup of tea?'

In the garage things weren't quite panning out the way Stew had hoped.

'Oh dear, it's harder than it looks' said Thomas, as the freight train tore round a tight curve.

'No, you're doing fine Thomas. Just ease up on those corners and pull in here. No. There. No. How about another circuit and bring it to a slow stop there... Yes... OK... Good... Slow down a little... No don't stop... A little faster... Too fast... Slower... Slower... Oooh... Er... No... Slower... Stop... Stop... Another circuit perhaps?'

Colin was still leaning against the garage doors but was by now looking smugly relaxed as he watched Thomas steer a nine-wagon train through some sidings and into the back of a water tower. 'Stew?'

'Yes Colin?' muttered Stew.

'Are there any more biscuits?'

Pete finished making Phil and Justine a cup of tea which had taken considerably longer than making a cup of tea should have taken thanks to Phil's propensity to answer simple questions with an aggressive counter question. Colin came in through the side door grinning. 'Are there any more biscuits Pete?'

Pete nodded and smiled. 'Not gone well then?'

'Not really.'

Pete gestured towards Phil and Justine. 'This is Phil and Justine. Justine's a mate of Justine. Come to try out.'

Colin smiled at them. Phil had a puzzled look about him. He twisted in his chair and looked at Pete. 'So have you got any biscuits then mate?'

'Pardon?' said Pete.

'Yer mate asked if you 'ad any biscuits, yeah?'

'Oh right, the biscuits, yes.'

Phil puffed out his chest and breathed in an overly animalistic way. 'Well, 'av you got any?'

'Yes' said Pete.

Phil screwed up his face as he attempted to grapple with the biscuit issue. 'Well, get 'em out.'

Colin interrupted. 'No, just checking that we had some. I don't want any.'

Phil retracted his chin. 'You're all a bit weird if you ask me.'

Thomas walked in, followed by Stew. Thomas looked to Pete. 'Well thank you very much for the opportunity, unfortunately I think I'm rather more suited to timetabling accounts rather than trains. But I've had a lovely chat with Stew and we're going to arrange a time to go out for a drink. We have so much in common, quite incredible really.' Thomas smiled at Stew. 'I have your number Stew so I shall be in contact soon. Pete, I shall let myself out, I can see you're all busy.' Thomas left the room.

There was a slightly weird silence which Phil broke. 'I'd be careful 'bout that one. Looks like a right bender to me mate.'

Stew looked at Pete and cocked his head not very subtly in

Phil's direction. 'Have we got any more biscuits Pete?'

Pete frowned and closed his eyes, waiting for the inevitable.

'Oi! What's your problem with biscuits?' demanded Phil.

Pete sighed, reached into the cupboard, got out the Sainsbury's biscuits, put them on a plate and placed them on the table. Stew furrowed his brow and mouthed to Pete 'I mean, have we got any more biscuits?'

Pete mouthed back 'I know what you fucking mean.'

There was a knock at the door. 'Thank God' thought Pete, with a sense of relief. 'Colin, show Justine to the garage. Stew, have a chat with Phil.' He walked away from the madness and hoped to hell that whoever was behind the door was relatively normal.

Colin showed Justine into the garage and explained the controls. He was hoping she might be as good at driving as the other Justine was at model making, however it was not to be. Colin had always assumed that anyone could 'play at trains' as Helen called it but he was beginning to wonder whether it actually was a real skill. He grimaced as Justine overshot a platform and then wheel spun, while attempting to reverse.

Pete opened the door.

'Hello, you must be Pete. I'm Adrian Peters. I've just started at Colin's school.'

'Ah, yes' said Pete. 'The woodwork teacher.'

'Well, someone has to do it,' replied Adrian.

'Come on in, cup of tea?'

'That's great but first let me show you some stuff I brought along from my old school.'

Pete followed him up the road a few spaces to an old silver

Volvo estate. Adrian opened the boot.

'Bloody hell!' exclaimed Pete. 'They let you have this lot.'

'Yep' replied Adrian. 'All this used to be part of the school railway and there's some good gear. A lot of the parents spent more time working on it than the kids and considerably more money.'

'So how did you end up with it?'

Adrian shook his head. 'A few months before I left, the model room was cleared to make way for a new computer studies centre. Real shame but the kids seem more interested in computers now. Anyway, I stored everything I could at my place but when I left the head essentially demanded I take it with me.' Adrian idly scratched his neck. 'Y'know I'm not so sure he liked the model club. A bit messy.'

Pete looked back at the Volvo. 'Are you wanting anything for it?'

Adrian grinned. 'I'm tempted to say giz a job but you might think of that as a bribe.'

Pete smirked. 'I would consider it a kind donation and hope to hell you're a good driver.'

Adrian put his hands on his hips. 'Well, look. It's no use to me. I need my garage back so just take the lot and if I'm not good enough maybe I could help out some other way.'

Pete nodded his head. 'Sounds like Colin told you we hang out in pubs a lot!'

Adrian cocked his head to one side. 'He might have mentioned it!'

Stew scratched his head and said 'Well, yes, I suppose. That certainly is an interesting opinion. I'm not sure tennis umpires should be issued with truncheons.'

Phil looked angrily into his empty mug. 'All I'm saying is, mate. That if fuckin' McEnroe came into my work and kicked off like wot 'e does on telly, I'd fuckin' bend a pipe round is 'ed.'

Stew looked alarmingly at Phil's knuckles turning white as he involuntarily flexed his fists. 'What line of work are you in Phil?'

'Bending pipes mate.'

'That's not a joke is it? Is it?' Stew was getting out of his depth.

Phil stared at him. 'No mate. I work in a plumbing supplies warehouse.'

'So you do bend pipes?'

'Course I fuckin' do.'

Stew needed someone to rescue him. Happily the side door opened and Colin came in with Justine. Phil looked up. 'How d' it go J?'

Justine smiled thinly. 'I'm not sure Phil. It's harder than it looks. Perhaps we should go now.'

Phil grunted 'OK J.' He looked at Stew. 'Fanks for the tea mate.' Got up. Nodded at Colin and walked Justine out to the hall. After they had exited the house Colin sat down next to Stew and sighed 'Bloody hell! Phil's a bit full on. Who is he exactly?'

Stew puffed out his chest. 'I'm her effing brother ain't I mate.'

Colin laughed. 'I'm sorry you got left with him.'

Stew shrugged. 'Takes all kinds. How was she at driving?'

Colin stared at the wall. 'Average. She could be taught but not in the time we have.'

Just then the front door clanked open and Pete walked in loaded up with a box of train parts followed by Adrian, similarly loaded up. Pete put his box down. Breathed in and smiled. 'This is Adrian. Adrian this is Stew and Colin. Oh yeah, you know Colin.'

Colin and Adrian nodded at each other. Pete continued. 'I saw angry bloke and Justine leave. Any good?'

Colin shrugged. 'She's ok but not good enough for competitions.'

Pete turned to Adrian. 'Well, looks like your turn. Colin, lead on mate.'

Colin hauled himself up from the table. 'Follow me Adrian. Might as well bring that box with you.' They left through the side door. Pete watched them go and turned to Stew. 'Fancy another brew?'

Nick revved the engine of the Triumph Spitfire as he turned into the small, gravel carpark of the Lonely Shepherd bed and breakfast. He loved an arrival almost as much as a dramatic departure. Justine batted her eyelids at him. 'You can be such a poser, sir.'

Nick backed the throbbing car into a space and cut the ignition. There was a satisfying gurgle and the sound of rapidly cooling engine parts. Nick sat in silence, enjoying his beloved car settling down. The gently soothing yet intoxicating smell of oil, two-star petrol and old car settled upon them like a benevolent fog. Justine screwed up her eyes and peered out of the window. 'The Lonely Shepherd? How romantic Nick.'

Nick laughed. 'We're in Yorkshire lass. It was this or tut Slaughtered Lamb.'

Justine giggled and affected a Yorkshire accent. 'You made me giggle. I never giggle.'

Nick smirked. 'C'mon, let's get booked in, I'm starving.'

Half an hour later they were sitting in the garden of the

Bale and Twine. Nick was pondering over the somewhat limited lunch menu. 'Do you like lamb?'

Justine grinned and ran her finger down the various lamb dishes. 'Luckily I do. I'm guessing you're not so keen?'

'It's my mum's fault really. She cooked us lamb roasts of a Sunday, which I quite liked, especially with mint sauce. But then on Monday it was cold lamb with something green. I hate cold lamb, it's too fatty to be eaten cold.'

Justine held him by the hand. 'Such a deprived childhood. Well I'm having lamb chops.'

Nick revisited the menu. 'Might try this Yorkshire stew. Fancy a drink? Please don't ask me to get a sweet martini. Not here.'

Justine put her arm around him. 'How about half a pint of the local bitter?'

Nick made an approving face, kissed her on the cheek and got up to order at the bar.

Colin was hopeful. Adrian had thus far not put a foot wrong. He'd controlled every type of train and combination that had been thrown at him and was extremely competent at shunting (the dark art of the cab driver). He decided to call time on the practical. 'Hey Adrian, I think we're done. I've seen all I need to see.'

Adrian brought the little 060 shunter to a stop. 'Have I made the grade then Colin?'

'Well, put it this way, short of a Jedi Master walking through the door and using the Force to park the 8.30 to Uxminster, I think you're probably in.'

'Excellent!' beamed Adrian.

'I have to have a chat with the boys first, but I guess we need to integrate you in a speedy fashion for the next round. Keep your diary free.'

Adrian snorted, 'I'm what you might call socially challenged at the moment so no worries there.'

They both walked back to the kitchen. Pete and Stew were staring silently into their tea mugs. Colin looked at them. 'Well, I guess the expression 'where the fuck are my car keys?' comes to mind.'

Pete laughed. 'How soon?'

Adrian shrugged his shoulders. 'Whenever. I see Colin everyday anyway, so any practice or team building. I'm in.'

Pete smirked. 'You just want to go to the pub?'

Adrian laughed. 'Team building? Of course.'

Nick wiped the last of the gravy from his bowl with a piece of bread. 'That was some tasty chow.' He drained the remains of his pint and slumped lazily onto the table.

'Well, mine were lamb chops alright, a little rubbery but very tasty.'

Justine dabbed her mouth with the paper serviette. 'So, what are your devilish plans for me now then?' Justine held her hands together and fluttered her eyelids.

Nick remained slumped on the table. 'I thought we could go and have a look at a viaduct.'

'Oh Nick you old rogue, this is really turning me on. Go on, how many arches?'

'Many, many fine brick arches.'

'And what are we to do when we come across these brick arches?'

'We are going to sketch and note how the brick has weathered, my little cherry.'

'Shameless, utterly shameless.' Justine flopped her head

down onto Nick's back.

Back at Nick's house the try outs continued. Mr Drake proved interesting due to a mild condition of Tourette's. Colin said he was actually a pretty good driver but Stew said he couldn't really concentrate with someone shouting 'dirty hole' at random moments.

Dicky Trump was a walking catastrophe both literally and actually.

Kate was lovely. Everyone liked Kate. Stew wrote lots of lovely things on his clipboard about Kate. He may have even doodled something but tore that page out. The problem was, Kate liked Kate as well. She struggled to concentrate driving trains in between hair adjustment, make up and blouse shuffle. Kate would have been very high maintenance. Still, they all liked Kate.

Gareth was a strange one. No one quite knew who knew him. Pete didn't recognise him or even have him on his list. Colin hadn't a clue. Stew said he looked familiar but that was the closest anyone got. Gareth seemed more interested in criticising the interior décor and the quality of doors. In the end they collectively agreed with Stew's clipboard notes, 'odd chap, not quite human.'

By five it seemed pretty clear no one else was going to turn up and it was also pretty clear that Adrian was the chosen one. Colin couldn't fault his driving and both he and Stew agreed they could definitely get on with him socially. So, that was about it. Pete arranged their next pub meeting for Tuesday and with that they all dispersed into the warm summer evening.

A couple of hours later, in a parallel street, at a house with the same number, a slightly surreal conversation took place.

'Hello.'

'Hello, yes, I've come about the -' Pause to balance. '- Yes, I've come about the train driving -' Restrained belch. '- Job.'

'I'm sorry dear?'

A half turn. Inspect shoe. Nearly fall over. Turn back to face confused lady. 'Yes madam. The job to drive small trains.'

'Small trains?'

Hand out to balance on door frame. Hand misses door frame. Man falls sideways into small evergreen bush. A brief conversation to an imaginary friend. Stand up again. Smooth hair back. Attempt to look normal. 'The job.' Long pause as though thinking but clearly not. 'For the model railway club to -' Suddenly distracted by dog barking across road. Strange twitch. Refocus. 'To, to drive.' Emphasise 'drive' again. 'Model trains.' Confident nod. Smile. Bow. Bang head on projecting brickwork. Recover.

'I'm sorry dear but I think you have the wrong address and I think you should go home and sleep it off.'

'Sleep what off?' Stagger. Rebalance.

'All that drink.' Stern look.

Blank face. The last strands of conversation already dissolving in an alcoholic fug. 'Well, tell Col that I popped by and.' Randomly fall sideways into small evergreen bush again. Crawl out. Regain footing. Renewed effort. 'Tell Colin, my dear, that I shall postwith henceforth enquire about the job at a later future date not-with-standing. Thank you, dear lady for your time, verily.' Look to balcony. Accept applause. Bow. Bang head on same projecting brickwork. Fail to notice door already closed. Lady no longer there. Amble up path. Exit front garden. Belch.

Nick looked over Justine's shoulder as she sat sprawled on the grass sketching the viaduct. 'Hey, that's really good. Are you planning to leave it or over colour a bit?'

Justine held out her sketch book in front of her and contemplated. 'Erm, no. I think I like as is. I love the simplicity of these arches though. So elegant.'

Nick sat down next to her and kissed her lightly on the neck.

'What was that for?'

'Where have you been?'

'I've been here all the time. You just couldn't find me.'

Nick looked up into the clear sky and felt the merest of breezes stroke against his skin. 'Christ knows I've looked hard enough in the past' He took hold of her pencil-smudged hand and squeezed gently. 'I always thought deep down I was weird and here you are and… I realise I'm not weird. Everyone else is because you're perfect and not weird.'

Justine slowly closed her eyes and smiled. 'My mum always used to say when I was a kid. Oh one day you'll meet the perfect man and he'll make you happy and you'll know he's the one because you'll think no one else could possibly understand him in the way you do and he will understand you so well that you will think he can actually read your mind and you will never be able to conceive of anyone who can get as close to you as he can. And then you get married and you realise he's not as perfect as you thought and you start noticing all the things that had somehow been invisible before and these things irritate and annoy you in a way that you thought couldn't be possible because he knows how to get to you with a look or a sigh or he has never ever cleaned the bath and leaves his pants on the bannister.' Justine paused. 'I always got that speech after Dad had done something stupid but I always liked the start of it.' She looked into Nick's eyes. Nick looked back into hers. Justine pinched him. 'Thank you for thinking I'm perfect. I'm not you know but it's nice all the same.'

Nick put his arms around her. 'You're my kind of perfect.'

Both of them breathed in heavily and silence hung suspended from the viaduct's arches. Justine sighed softly. 'So, c'mon Nick let's see your sketch then.'

Nick flicked through his well-thumbed hardback. He found the page and presented it to Justine.

'That's beautiful Nick. Really, really beautiful.'

Nick grinned. 'You see, only you could look at pictures of water stained brickwork and say that.'

'But it's so alive. You wouldn't think bricks could have a depth and feeling and beauty like that' Justine stared at the page and ran her finger gently over the image. 'So, is this little trip for something you're planning to model?'

Nick pulled her close and kissed her exposed shoulder. He looked around in an overly dramatic fashion and then whispered in her ear. 'I've got an idea but first we need to do some more fieldwork. What are your feelings on the subject of concrete?' He repeated the word 'Concrete' in a faux overly sexual Barry White kind of a way.

Justine blushed. 'I don't know what you're up to, but it sounds sort of naughty.'

Nick kissed her on the lips and gently held her head in his hands. 'Well, it's certainly dirty.'

'Bad Nick, bad, bad Nick' sniggered Justine.

CHAPTER NINE: TUESDAY EVENING AT THE PUB

Tuesday came around quickly. Pete had got to the Water Tower and Tender early to bags a large table. The weather had turned blustery and wet, a typical British summer and so he wanted to make sure there was enough space for his, by now, rapidly expanding club. He needn't have worried. 'Bit quiet in here mate,' he commented casually as the barman pulled his pint.

The barman shrugged his shoulders. 'Don't know if it is or isn't. I'm the new manager. The brewery sent me in last week.'

Pete recoiled slightly. 'Eh? What happened to old Simpson?'

'Some sort of breakdown. He was carried out cradling a packet of pork scratchings that he claimed was his long-lost sister.'

Pete frowned. 'Poor old boy. So, what's your name then?'

'George,' said George 'and you are?'

'I'm Pete, nice to meet you. Any plans for the old place?'

George looked around blankly, a slightly confused look began to spread across his large face.

Pete watched him with amused interest. 'I guess that means no,' he laughed.

The front door of the pub creaked open and Adrian did that walk that people do when they visit a new pub for the first time.

'Over here,' shouted Pete.

Adrian clocked him and with a clearly relieved face came over to the bar.

'Alright Pete. Like the pub. Sort of faded grandeur.'

George raised an eyebrow, not sure if this was an insult or not. 'What could I get you sir?'

Adrian looked at the beer taps. 'Pint of Old Steamer please.'

Pete took a sip of his Guinness and smiled at Adrian, 'Just to say, things can get lively at these meetings, take Nick with a pinch of salt, he's a good guy under all that stuff.'

Adrian looked confused. 'Stuff?'

Pete rubbed his nose, 'You'll see. C'mon, let's get a good seat.' He nodded to George. 'You'll meet a few of the other regulars soon.' George looked slightly nonplussed.

They'd only been settled for a couple of minutes when there was a sudden loud commotion from outside and the big, old front door crashed open.

'Well that's not what I heard' said Colin in an excited voice.

'No, it's true. Sequel to Alien. Alien Two or whatever. I heard they've got Cameron to direct' retorted Nick.

Justine walked in behind them shaking her head. 'You just want another film to make models off.'

Nick turned round nodding his head vigorously. 'Absolutely and you do too.'

Justine laughed and nodded like a crazy person. Colin got to the bar. 'OK my lovers, usual?'

Nick and Justine carried on nodding stupidly and went to join Pete and Adrian. Colin rolled his eyes, ordered a round, including a half for Stew, who was nearly fifteen minutes late, a possible new record for him.

Pete got up as Nick arrived. 'Hey guys, this is Adrian our new driver and he's also a woodwork teacher, so you might want to put him to use for something Nick.'

Nick studied him briefly as though eyeing up a potentially troublesome dog. 'Woodwork? There could be a job for you building the fiddle yard extension.'

Adrian nodded. 'No problem Nick. I talked over what was needed with Colin and Stew very briefly on Saturday. I love the layout by the way. It was really difficult concentrating on the driving when all I wanted to do was look at the models.'

Nick smiled and cracked his knuckles. 'So you know Colin from school then?'

'Yep.'

Justine batted Nick on the arm. 'Be nice' and sat down next to Adrian. Nick was about to say something but stopped himself. He sat down with Justine.

'Has Colin filled you in about the club?'

Adrian smirked and looked at Pete. 'Sort of. Pete has pretty much got me up to speed on our present situation.'

Nick exhaled loudly and eyed Pete before turning to Adrian. 'So you're alright moving trains around?'

'I guess I'm good enough for what you need.' Adrian took a gulp of bitter.

Nick drummed his fingers on the scuffed table. 'Where's Colin got to with those drinks?'

Pete smiled inwardly. Adrian had just passed Nick's own personal interview although he had no idea that he had. The front door of the pub creaked open and was then gently returned to its closed position.

'Sounds like Stew's arrived' said Pete.

A few seconds later Stew appeared at the table. 'Sorry I'm late everyone. Margaret had a pruning crisis that needed urgent attention.'

'You're still quicker than Colin's round' Nick muttered.

Colin stumbled forward with a tray. 'Yes Nick, calm down, they're here now. Hi Stew, got you a half.'

Stew lifted his glass of bitter off the tray. 'Very kind of you Colin' and sat down next to Nick.

Colin passed the rest of the drinks down and pulled up a chair to complete the enclosure. Pete cleared his throat to centre everyone's attention. 'Well, here we all are. Round two beckons. Let's work out how to get through.'

Colin tapped the table. 'Well, you tell us Pete. Where is round two and who's there?'

Pete grimaced. 'Right, we're going back to a village hall, this one's in Thrumming. Don't know why they need such a large village hall but anyway. OK, we're up against Guards Van, Harbour Town and North Line.'

Pete let the news sink in to see if anyone reacted. Predictably Nick was first to speak. 'Guards Van? Shit Van, how the hell did that lot qualify? Where was their first round?'

Pete quickly looked at his notes. 'Er, oh, St Mary on the Hill.'

'Well how did they even get there? I didn't think any of them could drive.'

Justine frowned. 'Are they very young then?'

'No' laughed Nick. 'They're all utterly incompetent.'

Stew interjected - 'St Mary on the Hill? So that's where the favourites got sabotaged... allegedly.'

'Indeed' said Pete. 'Nick's kind of right in his subtle way. Guards Van wouldn't have qualified if Sideline hadn't been literally sidelined and even then they came in a very low second. The other club in the mix was a filler. They were pressganged in to make the numbers up.'

Adrian thought he better say something. 'So what about

the other two? I know Harbour Town are pretty good.'

Pete sighed. 'Well Harbour Town, are, well, shit-hot to be honest and they're one of the few layouts that have models even close to the quality of Nick's.'

Justine gasped. 'No, tell me it's not true Nick.'

Nick grimaced. 'Yes dear, it's true. There is another.'

Justine looked around. She noticed everyone was avoiding eye contact, apart from Adrian, who simply looked confused. She turned to Nick. 'So who is this model maker guy then?'

Nick picked up his glass. 'He's not a guy. He's a girl.'

Justine hadn't expected this. She was quietly in love with the notion that she was a lone heroic female in a bloke's world. It made her feel special and importantly to her, unique. Even Colin noticed the cloud that passed over the sun of Justine's features. He recognised that veil from occasions with Helen. He dangerously decided to say something, having clearly learnt nothing from those 'occasions' with Helen.

'Hey Justine, if it's any consolation she does actually look like a man.'

'And she dresses like a man' added Pete, wincing as he suddenly noticed that Justine had turned up in her DMs, faded jeans and Fosters t shirt. Like lemmings the rest of the blokes followed suit.

'She's somewhat disagreeable, has issues and I belief still lives with her parents' said Stew.

'She's not as good as Pete thinks she is' offered Nick.

Even Adrian, who clearly had never met or even heard of her felt he had to do something. 'Er, um, well, yeah.' Unfortunately, it was just noise.

Justine forced a little smile. 'No, look, it's ok. I'm not

bothered what she looks like. I just thought, maybe, naively, there weren't any others.'

Nick put his arm round Justine and whispered in her ear. 'There aren't any others like you.'

She began to radiate again. 'Right, well then. I'm just going to have to model her bloody socks off' she beamed at Nick.

'That's my girl' said Nick.

Pete felt the moment had arrived to carry on talking about the competition. 'And on to the North Line, who also are pretty good. They have a layout similar to ours and run their traffic along similar lines. I reckon we focus on beating these fellas because if we do then I think we're through to the next round.'

'Don't North Line think they're a bit hard?' said Colin.

'What? As in a bit handy. Fancy some then?' added Adrian, in a vaguely East End accent.

Nick was grinning. 'Yeah, that's right. Didn't one of them 'barge' you Colin?

Colin frowned. ''Barge'? One of those skinhead muppets gave me a very deliberate shove because he thought I was looking at him strangely.'

'And what did you do about it Col?' said Nick.

Colin gave him an irritable look. 'Well, er, said 'sorry' didn't I. Look, I wasn't staring at him per se. I was staring into space because I had to stay up with two sick kids the night before and while my brain was sleeping clearly my eyes weren't.'

Stew let out a little thoughtful noise. 'Hmm. It is strange how some people react to a stare. I think it's a deep-rooted sense of insecurity.'

'That or thinks he's a dog' quipped Nick.

MATTHEW BROWN

'Well, look. Any fresh ideas? We've still got three weeks before round two.' Pete looked at Nick and Justine.

Nick took his arm away from Justine and took a quick sip of his drink. 'Yeah, we're making a few more models, obviously, but I went through all that stuff Adrian gave us.' Adrian gave Nick a quick nod of acknowledgement. 'And we've got enough gear to create our talked about 'disaster scenario."

Adrian's eyes nearly popped out. "Disaster scenario?' What the hell is that? I like the sound of it, very muchly.'

Colin butted in. 'Another genius idea from me.'

'Alright Colin' said Nick. 'It's all very well coming up with the idea. Bit different to implement it, although you're going to have to do some neat driving to pull it off.'

Stew whimpered slightly.

'Yes and you, Stew' added Nick.

Pete folded his arms. 'So, go on. What does this involve?'

Nick smiled. 'We are going to simulate an engine fire.'

'Not a real one?' gasped Stew. He didn't mean to gasp but he sort of half choked on a crisp.

Nick gave him a patronising look. 'No, not a real fire but we can produce real smoke and Justine's thought of a really clever way to simulate fire.'

Pete rubbed the back of his neck thoughtfully. 'Will this affect the flow of rail traffic too much? I mean are we going to lose points?'

Nick looked at Colin. 'I think if Colin and Stew pull it off we stay evens traffic wise but should score heavily on creativity and I think that's going to be worth increasingly more as we progress.'

'As we 'progress?" mimicked Pete. 'Confidence. I like it.'

Nick rolled his eyes. 'Well, we're going to perform. Just

138

hope everyone else does.'

'OK. Anything else?' asked Pete.

Justine half raised her hand and glanced at Nick. Nick gave her the merest of nods.

'What's up Justine?' asked Pete.

Justine said softly 'We're also working on a big finale project, but it won't be ready for this round.'

'Sounds intriguing. Any chance you're going to tell us?'

Justine smiled and looked sideways. 'No.'

Pete shook his head. 'Right, who hasn't got a round in for a while then?'

Adrian was about to volunteer as new boy but noticed everyone else were looking at Stew.

Stew sighed. 'Well, clearly that will be me then.'

Nick nudged Justine in the ribs and whispered 'Have you seen Stew pay for anything yet?'

Justine looked blank.

Nick continued. 'Ask him about his man purse.'

Justine turned to Stew and took a deep breath. 'Stew?'

'Yes?'

'Nick said to ask you about your man purse.'

Stew affected his indignant face. 'There is nothing wrong with my man purse, I mean my pouch, I mean my wallet. They use them all the time in Scotland.'

'Show Justine how you get the coins out' said Nick.

Stew got out his man purse and unclipped the top. He folded over a flap of leather and slid the coins out.'

Justine sniggered a little as did Colin. Stew looked doubly indignant. 'It's not a purse' he grumped.

Colin patted him on the shoulder. 'It is a little, er, 'pursey' Stew and if not then it's definitely just a little bit gay, shall we say.'

Stew got up, ignoring everyone. 'Same again, I assume?' As he walked away he could be overheard muttering 'They use them in Scotland.'

Adrian sat there grinning.

'Alright Adrian?' asked Pete.

'Very happy Pete. This is way more entertaining than the old school model railway club.'

'I'm guessing it didn't involve pubs then?' said Pete.

'No, just a load of uptight parents and a bunch of kids whose sole intention was to derail everything, literally and actually!'

'I do like that phrase' remarked Nick.

'I'm not sure it's correct English though' said Colin. 'You need to replace one of the words with 'metaphorically' unless you're being deliberately stupid.'

'Excellent, I'll be using it then' said Nick smiling.

Justine suddenly straightened up as though hit by a thought. 'Hey, isn't this about the time someone needles Colin about the old railway disaster stories?'

Nick rubbed his hands together and blew Justine a kiss. 'Well remembered.'

Colin squirmed in his chair. This was becoming dangerously like a pub tradition. The truth was he had no idea whether it was a wind up or not. He made a mental note to ask someone outside of the club about it. He immediately made a mental note to definitely *not* ask someone outside the club about it in case it was a wind up and they found out he'd been asking around. His inner voice told him to play it indifferent.

'Colin.'

'C O L I N' repeated Pete. 'Back with us? Yes? I'm guessing you'd just love to hear the next model railway disaster story?'

Colin downed the last of his pint. 'Oh, go on Pete. Yes, I would love to hear it. Gosh! Where are we again? Please remind me.'

Pete smiled. 'I believe we are at number seven.'

Adrian interrupted - 'Can anyone quickly explain this?'

Nick held up his hand to cut off Pete. 'Quick explanation. Model railway disasters in descending order of ten. Based on style, violence, destruction and improbability' Nick lowered his hand.

Adrian looked unimpressed. 'Bet nothing can compare with some of the catastrophes my kids used to create. One time they -'

Colin butted in. 'Stop, stop. Adrian don't fight it. Listen to the story, however dubious, and then decide if your disaster even comes close.'

'Yes, but one time -' continued Adrian.

Colin stopped him. 'Did it result in a mushroom cloud and the school being closed for a year?'

'Well, no but -'

'Don't bother then.' Colin looked to Pete. 'Pete. Please continue.'

Pete laughed. 'As some of you know, this story becomes very obvious, very quickly.'

Nick snorted. 'Yep, it's way too obvious but it does raise some interesting modelling conundrums.'

'Can you please just get on with it?' said Colin.

Pete tutted. 'OK here we go. Colin have you ever seen a

layout with real water?'

Colin paused. 'You mean instead of 'model' water?'

'Yes.'

Colin wrinkled his face. 'Don't think so. Not at an exhibition anyway.'

Pete looked at Colin as a sage would his pupil. 'Well this is probably because of what happened to this layout.'

'If we ever hear about it' muttered Colin.

Pete ignored him. 'There was this guy in the 70s who was crazy about using water on his layout. In fact, the trains were pretty much second fiddle to the glory of water. The centre of his layout was a reservoir full of the wet stuff. He'd installed a pump that meant that water was continually circulating from the reservoir overflow and around the models. He used it to drive watermills, river boats, a few little waterfalls, an aqueduct. You name it, he had it.'

Colin raised his hand. 'I know I've made this type of mistake before but are we inevitably looking at burst reservoir, water and electricity meeting, screaming, swearing, panic, lessons learnt, wrists slapped etc etc etc?'

Nick and Pete looked at each other.

Pete carried on. 'You are such a bloody kill joy. Well, yes, the water did escape the reservoir but only because a terrier decided to jump in and thrash about. Ha! A dog, didn't predict that did you?'

Nick laughed out loud and slapped the table. Colin attempted to look nonchalant. 'And the rest?'

Pete nodded. 'OK. Well the terrier caused a little tidal wave that, yes, mixed with the power supply, shorted the whole layout and put such a strain on the exhibition hall's breakers that the whole lot fused and everything ground to a halt. Which would have been dramatic had you been able to see it but of course all the lighting failed which plunged the entire place into darkness. So yes, there was screaming and prolific swearing. Lessons were learnt. Water was banned from live railway exhibitions, as were small dogs.'

Colin attempted to stifle a grin. He wasn't sure whether he was supposed to find these 'stories' funny or not.

Justine looked at him curiously. 'What bit do you find funny Colin?'

'Well, apart from the whole thing. I just wondered. What the dog was called?'

Stew tiptoed forward with a loaded-up drinks tray. 'A dog eh? You're talking about the Colchester Hall blackout aren't you?'

Pete raised up his chin and looked at Stew. 'Colchester? Yes that's the one.'

Stew carefully put the drinks down. 'I've still got the newspaper cutting in my scrapbook.'

'So what was the dog called?' said Colin.

Stew chuckled. 'You won't believe me.'

Colin eyed him. 'Go on.'

'Sparky.'

Colin started shaking uncontrollably, followed by a general outbreak of uproar from everyone else. Adrian watched everyone cracking up and felt a happiness unknown to him for a long time. He was beginning to realise that he had probably been quite lonely for a number of years, masked by the fact of being a teacher surrounded by hundreds of people every day.

The laughter slowly died down. Colin took a sip of his fresh pint and looked to Pete. 'Well, you've still got another six stories to make up before this little tradition snuffs itself out.'

Pete put his Guinness down. 'Well strictly speaking Colin, only five.'

'I can count.'

Pete put his finger up to his lips. 'We don't talk about 'the crash.''

Colin put his pint down. 'Hold up Pete, you're not a bard. This isn't Shakespeare. We're not performing 'the Scottish play.''

Pete shrugged his shoulders. 'You either know of the crash or you don't.'

Looking briefly around the table Colin could tell that everyone there except Adrian and probably Justine knew about the crash. In his mind he said 'the crash' in a heavily sarcastic tone and reminded himself that they were involved with model trains and not Formula One cars. Colin shrugged his shoulders back at Pete. 'Well, that's one less daft story to listen to, then' and smiled.

Adrian decided to break the slightly awkward silence that followed. 'Nick you made a comment about modelling conundrums. What did you mean?'

Nick made a contented 'hmm' type noise as though a student had asked a particularly pertinent question. He arranged himself on his seat and cracked his knuckles. 'Well Adrian. Good question. What did I mean? Well, it's all about scale I suppose. As I hope Colin will soon be demonstrating to you, we have to run our trains to a reasonable scale speed to achieve anything close to a realistic operation. You could make even our big old Deltic, 'Hadley's Hope' do a wheel spin and accelerate up the line at a speed that if scaled up would be totally impossible.'

Colin nodded. 'Mark and Josh are always trying to set new world speed records for their Intercity 125. I worked out that if you scaled it up you were looking at about 400 mph.'

Adrian joined in. 'One of my delightful pupils taped a firework to a train once.'

'Little shit' muttered Colin.

'Yeah. The little Einstein figured he could make the train go really fast with rocket assist.'

Nick perked up. 'That's a neat idea, I like it.'

Adrian winced. 'Well, the stupid git taped it on backwards, not that it made a huge difference. When the rocket ignited the train flew off the tracks and through the window before exploding in the playground.'

Nick sat there grinning, his eyes staring upward. Justine had to dig him in the ribs to bring him back to reality. 'Whatever it is you're thinking about. No' she said.

'Bet she says that a lot to you Nick,' quipped Colin.

Justine flicked a peanut at Colin's face. 'Stop being smutty.'

Stew tried to continue the conundrum conversation. 'Pete. How far could you bend the rules on scale speed?'

Pete bit his lower lip and sucked in air. 'Not sure you want to go there. Most clubs try and operate at a low speed to avoid accidents and also so they don't risk picking up penalties for unrealistic operation. I think you would need a very good reason to be moving trains at what looks like an impossible speed.'

Nick reached over and tapped Stew on his arm. 'You know the best scale problem we encounter though?'

Stew looked slightly worried. 'You're not going to get smutty are you?'

Nick looked surprised. 'No. Stew, you old rogue, what were you thinking about?'

Stew stared into his packet of peanuts. 'Oh, nothing. Go

on. You were saying?'

Nick smiled congenially at Stew and continued. 'Gravity. Nothing we can do about it.'

Colin frowned. 'So?'

'Think about it' said Nick. 'If you built a scale model of the Forth railway bridge and pushed a train over the edge. How long would it take to hit the water?'

'Is that real water or model water?' said Colin sarcastically.

Nick gave him a 'sod off' look.

'Second or less' answered Stew.

'And how long would a real train take to fall off the real bridge?'

There was a satisfying silence. Followed by a collective arrival at a revelation. Adrian was first to speak. 'That's surprisingly interesting but how could you scale down gravity? And would it make a difference?'

Nick shrugged his shoulders. 'No idea but it's interesting how people tend to look at models in a kind of one-dimensional reality when it's not just size that needs to be scaled.'

'How did we end up on this topic?' said Colin.

'Conundrums, of course it's really about water' chipped in Pete.

Nick immediately started up again. 'Oh yeah, water! That's what reminded me. That's what needs to be scaled down. A drop of water in OO gauge would be bigger than a sodding beach ball. An umbrella would be fuck all use if you got caught in that.'

Colin laughed and gestured towards Nick. 'You know our hero of dodgy movie effects?'

'The wonderful Doug McClure?' laughed Nick.

'Now, if you really want to see how not to deal with anything in the right scale watch, well, anything he's been in.'

Nick took over. 'Dinosaurs, or rather lizards with fins glued to them. Men in rubber dinosaur suits, cats in dinosaur suits, inflatable dinosaurs, models of ships filmed in sinks.'

Colin waded in. 'Badly carved polystyrene rocks that can not only be heard to squeak but also float and bounce off things, rubber swords, dodgy blue screen effects, God I love it.'

'Warlords of Atlantis, The Land Time Forgot' added Nick.

'At The Earth's Core. Oh wait, The People Time Forgot' countered Colin.

Nick grinned. 'Oh yeah, forgot that one!'

The meeting gradually degraded into what most people would consider a normal night out at the pub.

But while they continued to bicker about subjects as diverse as Pete's favourite canned fruit (peaches) or why the American war of Independence should have been renamed the first American Civil War (not concluded), strange things were afoot at Lower Didsbury.

CHAPTER TEN: STRANGE THINGS AFOOT AT LOWER DIDSBURY

The night duty officer at Greenvale police station was seriously thinking of hanging up the phone. It had been going continuously for the last half hour and all the calls were about the same thing. Strange lights over Lower Didsbury. The phone rang again.

'Police, yes, hello. I would like to report low flying lights to the east of Lower Didsbury railway station.'

Fat Frank Fullerton put his pudgy hand to his forehead, closed his eyes and attempted to remain professional. 'Can you see them now sir?'

'Affirmative. Two lights moving in a curious bobbing motion towards Greenvale. I would say approximately 40 to 50 knots.'

Frank licked the tip of his regulation 2H pencil. This chap sounded more professional than all the other nutters. It might even be worth a report. 'Could you tell me your name, sir, and contact details?'

'It's Monty Rawlinson, station master at Lower Didsbury.'

'I believe we've met sir.'

'Yes, I do believe we have. Well those lights remind me of the foo fighters we used to see over Germany. Move in the same curious fashion, not as quick though. If I had my tail gunner here I'd get him to give them a short burst, see if that didn't speed 'em up, eh?'

'Well, precisely sir. Thank you kindly for this information. I shall let you know if anything, pardon the pun sir, comes to light.'

Morning came to Lower Didsbury and with it a growing list of concerns for the locals.

Dennis was up early, as usual, to check on his herd of Jerseys. His legs still ached from 'the incident' and Ermintrude had never been quite the same since that awful day. He idled down his new, old Ford tractor, paid for by the insurance company. The upper field was curiously silent. Dennis looked to the spot where Ermintrude normally stood awaiting him. Something was very wrong. He spotted a crumpled form lying close to the old water trough. Dennis bent double before screaming 'Mootila-en, cow mootila-en.'

Old Ned walked slowly through the allotment. He had never fully believed that his prized pumpkins had been destroyed in 'the incident.' There had been too many boot prints and not enough coal truck parts to have caused the apparent carnage. Ever since he had decided to take security much more seriously. As he neared his pumpkins he was forced to stop dead in his tracks. Old Ned drew in as much breath as his tar filled lungs could cope with, before releasing it in the form of a low whistle. Old bent Arthur's shed lay reduced to a crushed pile of splinters under a huge and very shiny apple. Ned could think of only one thing, well two actually. It was either aliens, or, and he chuckled at this, the God of Karma, making a triumphant return in the form of a giant fruit.

News of strange happenings continued to spread throughout the day and not just in Lower Didsbury but perhaps the most troubling and completely baffling incident concerned the Water Tower and Tender. It wasn't there anymore.

CHAPTER ELEVEN: INVESTIGATIONS AND REVELATIONS

A drizzly, damp Saturday morning in the suburbs. 'Nick, can you just slow down. What do you mean it's gone?' Pete rubbed the sleep from his eyes.

'The Water Tower and Tender. It's gone. Someone's nicked it.'

Pete looked hazily around his entrance hall and made a mental note to level the mirror near the foot of the stairs. 'Hang on Nick. Sorry. Are we talking about model railways here?'

'Of course we fucking are you stupid twat. What did you think I meant?'

Pete tried to wake himself up by pinching his inner thigh, a task made difficult by trying to keep the phone receiver to his ear while Nick ranted on. 'OK, OK' said Pete. 'Ease up. What's the time?'

'Six thirtyish.'

'Oh fucking great. I have to go to work in a couple of hours, thanks Nick.'

'A couple of hours. Excellent. That gives you time to get your arse over here.'

Precisely twenty minutes later there was an irritated rap on Nick's front door. Nick opened the door slightly and thrust a very hot, sugary mug of tea through the gap. There was a slurping noise and a sigh.

'Better?' said Nick through the gap.

'No.'

'But you're not going to hit me?'

'Not with a mug of tea in my hand you prat.'

Nick opened the door. Pete gave him a scowl and walked in. 'So, right, c'mon show me what all the fuss is about.'

Nick led him to the garage. Spread across the layout were various notes, sketches, drawings and random measuring instruments.

'Bloody hell' said Pete. 'Is this necessary?'

Nick stared at him. 'Well, is this necessary?' and pointed to the ground shadow left by the departed model pub. Pete squinted and ran his finger along the exposed base.

'And this?' Nick picked up a crushed model of a cow. Pete stared at the cow before recognising the markings. 'Oh dear, is that Ermintrude?'

Nick raised his eyebrows.

Pete hesitated. 'And they didn't mutilate any other cows?'

Nick raised his eyebrows.

'Shit' muttered Pete. 'That's bad. Anything else?'

Nick pointed to the cars. Pete studied them and thought how neatly they had been nailed to the road, like a Victorian entomologist's insect collection.

'What do you think it means?' Pete looked up at Nick.

Nick gave him an exasperated look. 'Well Clouseau, let's see. Someone here has had his first model of a cow, a very dear cow to him, almost a small cow son, mutilated to hell. No other cows, just that one. Someone else here sells cars for a living. Hang on, oh look, a row of vandalised cars.'

Pete attempted to say something but was immediately cut off by Nick. 'And the symbolic HQ of Smooth Fishplate has been stolen.'

'What about Stew and Colin then?' ventured Pete, beginning to become a little alarmed.

Nick pointed to the red smear of paint across the layout's accountant's office in Greenvale.

'Oh dear' whispered Pete. 'And Colin?'

Nick gestured at the small beautifully modelled infant school towards the back of Greenvale. Pete leant over to have a closer look. 'Can't see anything obvious.'

'Look again, especially at the roof' said Nick.

Pete squinted. 'Oh yeah, you're right, looks a bit, er, bulgy?'

'Yes' sighed Nick. 'and you see that hole at the base, near the main door?'

Pete adjusted his eyesight. 'Oh yeah, got it.'

'Well,' continued Nick, 'that little fucker injected expanding foam through that hole.'

Pete crouched lower to look at the large window that oversaw the playground. He could just make out small desks and models of little children compressed against the glass by a wall of beige foam. He suppressed a dangerous urge to laugh and stood up.

'I hate to say this but it's like there's a Nick in a parallel world who is set to destruct rather than construct.'

Nick stared at Pete. 'Point is Pete, he's not in a parallel world, he's in my world and he's made it personal.' There followed a burst of expletives and a short list of glues that could be used to close certain holes associated with the human body, before Nick slumped into his old office chair.

Pete rubbed his neck and looked down at his trainers. 'Are you going to tell Justine?'

Nick blew out a short breath. 'Yep, we're going to need her to help repair the damage but don't tell the others, let's keep it under wraps.'

'OK' said Pete. 'I need to go and flog some motors. Keep me in the loop mate.'

'Sure thing Pete.'

Pete turned to go and then paused. 'What was the apple in the allotment about?'

Nick closed his eyes. 'I think not being an obvious clue it may well be the most important one.'

After Pete left, Nick decided to get another cup of tea, but before disappearing to the kitchen he placed Inspector Hancock in the allotment next to the apple.

Inspector Hancock blinked and rubbed his eyes. He had been fully briefed on the latest case. The series of strange events across Lower Didsbury and Greenvale with their apparent link to Fishplate and the appearance of a giant apple in the allotments was as yet unexplained. Hancock mistrusted allotments. Too many places to hide bodies, too much disturbed earth and rotting compost. He pulled up the collar of his overcoat and sniffed the air. Apart from the obvious reek of a twenty-foot apple there was also a subtle addition, the faintest whiff of modelling enamel. He noted this down and was about to return the pad to his pocket when from the corner of his eye he caught sight of three white lines, that had been painted onto the nearby telegraph pole. Hancock stared at them a while. He had a faint notion of seeing them somewhere but couldn't quite put them into context.

Nick picked up Hancock, blew some dust from him and replaced him into his wallet. He plopped back down into his chair and took a gulp of tea. This whole situation was getting weird. Why is someone trying to disrupt us? If you've made the effort to break into someone's property, why not just smash the place up? That would ensure our exit from the competition. It seemed to Nick that there must be a bigger agenda or perhaps they were simply dealing with some sort of psychotic. He smiled. To be brutally honest this guy was not doing anything he wouldn't contemplate if he had a strong enough motive. He thought back to the signal box incident, years ago. I suppose seen from the other side I might have appeared a tad psychotic myself then. He chuckled. Still, my psychotic behaviour was constructive. This guy likes breaking things in symbolic and interesting ways. He's made it personal with us, was it personal with the other club he derailed from the competition. Nick finished his tea. Justine was due over at lunchtime, so he decided to start on the 'fire train' project as it had been dubbed.

Before long he heard the gentle tap on the garage door. He quickly opened the small front door let into the main door itself. Justine stood there backlit by the mid-July sun.

'You look very gorgeous today' he said and reached out to grab her.

Justine closed her eyes as Nick hugged her tightly.

'I brought a few extra clothes with me this time' she whispered into Nick's ear.

'Really' Nick relaxed his arms and kissed her. 'Anything outrageous?'

Justine squeezed his hand. 'Not those type of clothes' she laughed. 'I just thought as I spend a lot of time here it might be useful to have a few more things stored here. Y'know?'

Nick stood back slightly. 'Are you trying to move in, sock by sock?' he teased.

Justine frowned. 'I was hoping you might give me a couple of drawers to call my own.'

Nick frowned back and put his finger to his mouth as though thinking. 'Well, let's see then. How about we go out and buy you a whole sodding chest of drawers?'

Justine squealed and did a little dance. 'That was a 'I love my boyfriend dance" she laughed.

Nick grabbed her bag and put it inside the garage. As he turned back to hold open the door he could see Justine looking intently at him.

'What's up?'

'I'm afraid that we've reached a certain stage in our beautiful, blossoming relationship, my dear Nick.'

Nick did a comedy gulp. 'I'm not ready for kids yet,' he confessed.

Justine looked down at her scuffed baseball boots. 'I'm afraid it's far worse than that Nick. I think it's time you met my parents.'

Nick jumped back in the garage and closed the door.

Justine shouted 'You can't hide. You know he's a locksmith.'

Pete looked Mr Dunn in the eyes. 'As I say, two very careful owners. Low mileage. Fully serviced. It's a good honest car sir.'

Mr Dunn looked back at the Vauxhall Cavalier. He made a little clicking noise with his tongue and folded his arms. Folding arms was not a good sign, although it meant to Pete that he was at least serious and not just wasting his time. Mr Dunn's feet however were pointed at the car. That was a very good sign. It meant he wasn't positioned to walk away. Pete felt negotiations were probably imminent.

'How much MOT is left?' asked Mr Dunn.

'About five months' replied Pete.

'What about the road tax?'

'Same again' replied Pete.

Mr Dunn sniffed and stared at the car in silence. Pete felt he ought to throw in a sweetener. 'We'll give it a full valet before you come and pick it up sir.'

Mr Dunn smiled and nodded his head. 'I'd expect that as standard. Can you do a bit better on price? Fifteen hundred seems a bit steep. I saw one down the road for thirteen.'

Pete let out a little dignified laugh. 'Yeah, I know the one but its two years older and has an extra thirty-three thousand on the clock.'

Mr Dunn clicked his tongue again. He knew the price was about right and he did like it. He decided to go for the tried and trusted extra. 'How about some new floor mats then John?'

Pete laughed silently and inwardly. That old chestnut. Well, better show willing. He held out his hand. 'Shake there sir, you've got yourself a deal.'

Mr Dunn paused before shaking Pete's hand.

'If you could follow me to the office we can fill all that tedious paperwork in.' Pete ushered Mr Dunn forward, as a shepherd would a reluctant lamb or perhaps a stockman would a pig to the abattoir. He'd just shuffled the last piece of paper and was coaxing Mr Dunn to sign it when his office phone rang. Reluctantly Pete picked up the receiver.

'Ace car sales, Peter speaking.'

'Pete, listen she's asked me to meet her parents. What the fuck do I do?'

'Could I phone you back, sir, about the Cavalier?'

'Oh fuck, you've got a customer there?'

'Yes sir. It is a good price.'

'Tell him it's got a leaky window seal and a damaged sill, you dodgy old dealer.'

'Thank you for your enquiry sir.'

Mr Dunn looked at Pete. Pete looked at Mr Dunn. Mr Dunn signed.

It was a while before Pete got a chance to call back but his timing was randomly perfect.

'Well done Pete, she just popped out for some more tea bags. So, what the fuck? I've never had to meet parents before. What do you do? What happens?'

Pete sighed. Quite why he had to act as Nick's go-to on everything he had no idea. 'Well… I… guess… you meet her parents.'

'Yeah, I don't need sarcastic advice. Have you met parents before?'

Pete rolled his eyes up and rubbed the back of the phone with his thumb. 'A long time ago, my ex-wife's parents.'

'So how does it go down?'

Pete smiled, remembering the anxiety and dress code stress. 'They just want to check you out Nick. Make sure you're not some sort of psychotic' Pete paused.

Nick laughed. 'Oh cheers mate.'

'Look, just try and be a tuned-down version of your normal self. Wear something safe, don't talk bollocks or act overly sexually towards Justine. I guess what I'm trying to say is let them know you're her best friend. That's what they want you to be. All parents mentally block out the sex bit.'

'And what do you talk about?'

'Make an effort to talk about her parents, what they do, what they've done. Be very attentive and interested. Intimate what a good job they've done bringing up Justine. Let them know you have a future, that's really important. They do not want Justine going out with a loser' Pete paused.

'Ha-ha' said Nick slowly.

'Don't suppose you've any more ideas on our psychotic friend?' enquired Pete.

'I have a starting point in mind but that's all at the mo.'

Pete grunted. 'Well, that's positive. Tell you what, why don't we have a pint during the week, just the two of us and talk a little off-the-record strategy?'

'Sure' said Nick. 'Best keep the other simpletons out of the picture for the moment.'

Monday came. Nick decided to, on a hunch and a whim to head off to the big model shop in nearby Stotsford. It wasn't really his sort of thing. He generally used specialist and commercial suppliers for his modelling needs. This place was a little too much Hornby and Airfix jet fighters for his liking but that whiff of enamel paint had him thinking. He pushed open the glass doors of 'Jackson's Model Emporium' and walked in. A balding man in his late fifties gave him a nod from the far counter before looking back down at some sort of catalogue. Nick surveyed the premises, it took a few seconds to spot the corner where the rack of Humbrol enamel paints was located. He ambled over and took a deep breath. 'Yes' there it was, that unmistakable whiff of Humbrol. Whoever had vandalized their layout was definitely a user. Nick sniffed around a little more, he actually quite liked the smell although in reality he used water colour and blended emulsion for his models.

'You alright there sir?' came a slightly worried question from the counter.

Nick looked up. Maybe he'd been enjoying the paint a little too much. He blurted out an answer. 'Yes mate. Just wondering if you, er, had, any more grey paint?' Nick winced at the stupidity of the question, he actually didn't give a flying buttress.

'Not at the moment sir. It's all those AFV modelers. I think they drink the blooming stuff.'

Nick was momentarily caught off guard. 'AFVs?'

'Yeah, armoured fighting vehicles. There's a massive war-gaming scene at the moment.'

Nick took a mental step backwards. 'Bloody war-gamers' he thought. He had naturally assumed the 'psychotic' as he was now called was a train modeller. 'So what sort of AFVs do they mostly go for?' he asked, walking towards the guy at the counter. As Nick reached him the balding man held up the catalogue he'd been absorbed in.

'They mostly go for World War Two, especially mid to late stuff.'

Nick scanned the catalogue. It was full of illustrations of tanks, self-propelled guns, half-tracks, jeeps and a wide range of soft skinned vehicles and ancillary equipment. Something caught his attention and a little voice from his wallet shouted *'Bingo!'*

'Where are these kits displayed?' he asked.

'Just there sir -' the guy pointed to the middle aisle.

Nick walked over and started looking. They were mostly 1/72 scale kits and it didn't take long before he spotted the kit he was after. He took the ESCI model of the Mk1 Tiger tank down and smiled.

'Very popular that one sir' exclaimed the counter guy. 'The old AFV modelers love to personalise them for their war-gaming. All fancy themselves as a bit of a Wittman.'

Nick knew the reference to the wartime panzer ace but it was the gun barrel of the beautifully illustrated Tiger that really interested him. He remembered what the old tank aces did when they scored a kill. They painted a white band onto the gun barrel.

It was Tuesday, early evening and Colin was sat at the kitchen table helping Josh build some sort of Lego model. Helen was busy chopping vegetables into a boiling pan of water.

'How was school today then?'

Colin placed a small yellow brick onto the 'wing' of whatever it was he was helping Josh with.

'Usual barely contained anarchy. That little sh…er, brat Stanley decided to spend most of the afternoon lesson flicking chew balls around the place. He managed to get one to stick to a map of Iceland, which I can tell you now will be the summit of his academic career.'

Helen reduced an onion to a diced oblivion.

'I bet you miss the days when a rolled-up newspaper to the back of the head was acceptable.'

Colin scoffed as he watched Josh remove his yellow brick with a slow and deliberate scorn and replace it with a red one.

'I miss the days when you could chain the buggers up and put 'em on a one-way trip to Australia.'

Helen laughed. 'Talking of children. What's the latest from your toy club?'

Colin frowned. 'Well, the next round is at Thrumming and we need to integrate Adrian in A.S.A.P to stand a chance of winning.'

Josh made an irritated squeak because Colin had stopped helping. Colin randomly stuck a white block to the 'engine.'

'And how is Nick and his girlfriend?' smiled Helen.

'Justine and Nick are strangely still together.'

Helen's knife hovered over a carrot. 'Does he behave any differently?'

Colin watched Josh remove his white brick and replace it with a yellow one. 'He's not so extreme I suppose, but he's still basically Nick.'

Helen smiled and shook her head. 'I hope he doesn't change too much. It won't be as entertaining.'

Colin sneered. 'I don't think there's any chance of that.'

Josh squeaked and passed Colin a Lego wheel. Colin put it in his mouth and pulled a face.

'Alright Pete?'

Nick sat down at the small table near the bar where Pete had secreted himself.

'Alright mate, what's that?'

Nick dropped a thin paperback onto the table. 'It's a general book about Tiger tanks and their crews. It's sort of an anorak's guide. All the AFV war-gamers use them.'

Pete nodded. 'AFV?'

'Armoured fighting vehicles' replied Nick.

'Yep of course, and why?'

'What? Why they use them or why bring this into the pub?'

Pete smiled. 'The latter.'

Nick tucked his chair in tighter and looked to both sides before lowering his voice.

'Apparently during the war, especially so on the Eastern front you got these tank aces that built up big scores of Russian tanks. Here's the thing. The Tigers would dig themselves into a commanding battlefield position and wait for the hordes of T34s to come rolling along. Then they would pick them off at long range with their 88s. It was so easy the crews used to call it apple picking.'

Pete felt this was supposed to be important but couldn't quite work out why. He stuck out his lip and gestured with his hands.

Nick took this as a 'more clues please' sign.

'Well Pete, after a successful engagement, the Tiger crews would paint a white stripe on their gun barrel for every kill.'

'Oh I know that' exclaimed Pete. 'My Uncle joined up towards the end of the war and they were forever coming up against Tigers covered in white kill marks.'

Nick gently banged his head on the table.

'What was that for?' queried Pete.

'I just realised. You didn't know about the three white rings on the telegraph pole.'

The penny finally dropped. Nick let the knowledge hang between them for a few seconds.

Pete attempted to sum up the new situation. 'So, hang on. We have some sort of psychotic war-gamer coming after us and he clearly has a thing about Tiger tanks?'

Nick laughed. 'I'm guessing that's not a sentence you thought would crop up in conversation tonight, eh?'

Pete snorted. 'These sentences only tend to come out when I talk with you. So what now?'

Nick rapped the table gently with his knuckles. 'Well, we find out where these war-gamers hang out and then work out who's behind it all.'

Pete looked into his Guinness. 'OK. So you go to one of their meets or whatever they do. Could you tell who it might be just from looking at their models?'

Nick snorted. 'Easy. C'mon we worked out from three white circles and an apple that this guy likes Tiger tanks and I bet you I could spot his work a mile off. This guy is going to be good at war-gaming. He can plan and execute. He's got a large pair of balls, isn't risk averse. He is clearly talented in many different materials, has way too much spare time and has a massive plank of wood on his left shoulder.'

Pete scrutinised Nick's excited features. 'You bloody like him, don't you?'

Nick closed his eyes and stuck his chin up indignantly. 'How can I explain this to you in easy terms?'

Pete laughed. 'I'm waiting.'

Nick looked Pete in the eyes. 'He's like Darth Vader and I'm like Luke Skywalker. We're both strong with the Force. I mean we're talented fuckers and we know it. Only difference is I don't intend to turn him from the dark side. I intend to punish him in a way only I could.'

Pete looked blankly back at Nick, before a smile slowly spread across his face. 'So you do like him? Be funny if he turned out to be your dad.'

The few remaining weeks before round two at Thrumming were quickly eaten up by intensive model making, drinking, operating practice, planning, un-planning and thankfully for Nick, as yet no arrangement to see Justine's parents.

CHAPTER TWELVE: THRUMMING VILLAGE HALL

Pete eased the Leyland Sherpa van to a halt. Nick had spent most of the journey getting ready to grab Justine, expecting something to go clang or at the very least fall off and was vaguely unsettled that it hadn't.

'This is…quite a good van Pete.'

Pete jerked up the handbrake and turned the ignition off. 'I know Nick. Came in as a part exchange on a deal. I'm thinking it could be a new club member if someone with a large drive were to embrace it.'

Nick ignored him. 'So where are we then?'

'According to the plan, right at the arse-end of the hall. Still, does have some advantages.'

Nick raised his eyebrows. Pete unclipped his seatbelt. 'At least it's near the toilets.'

Thrumming village hall was a white elephant. Paid for by a philanthropic villager at the turn of the century after a successful life in diamond mining, it had proved a financially ruinous legacy for the small village and had only remained standing because, one, it was very well built and two, the Parish Council couldn't afford to demolish it.

Nick looked down its receding length and shook his head. 'What a ridiculous building. C'mon, let's get unloaded.'

It didn't take long for them to get the boards levelled and clipped, a task made much easier with access to a nearby fire exit. Stew turned up shortly and they helped him move the precious plywood cases of engines and rolling stock. Within an hour everyone was there and Smooth Fishplate was ready to roll. Pete decided a little team talk might be in order. He beckoned everyone to huddle around the layout.

'OK guys, here we are. Second round. We've got a great chance of qualifying, probably better than in the first round. So please, let's just concentrate. Everyone know their job?'

Justine put up her hand.

Pete smiled and checked behind him before whispering 'You and Nick are going to wander off and observe. See if there's any sort of weakness we could exploit or at least need to know about.'

'And get us some tea' added Colin with a smile.

'I think that's Pete's job' said Nick.

Pete stood up. 'Hang on. Why have I suddenly become the tea-wallah?'

Colin and Stew looked at each other before Colin turned to Pete. 'So what is your task today?'

Pete stumbled. 'To er, facilitate the execution of our timetable.'

Colin grinned. 'Interesting, interesting. Could you facilitate three teas? Sugar Adrian?'

Adrian nodded.

Pete raised his eyes skywards and muttered something. 'Right. Good. Well I need to check out the other teams anyway' and he wandered off down the long hall towards the temporary tea bar.

'Right' said Colin. 'Let's get some trains moving. How long before the competition starts?'

Stew consulted his little clipboard. 'Time tables in at thirteen-thirty hundred hours. Competition starts fourteen hundred hours.'

Colin turned to Adrian. 'How you feeling Adrian?'

Adrian looked over the layout. 'Bit nervous, bit nervous. Some warming up required and tea.'

Stew gave him a pat on the shoulder. 'You'll be fine.'

'And if you're not, don't even think about coming to the pub again' added Nick.

Justine pulled Nick away. 'C'mon, let the drivers get settled. I want to check out Harbour Town.'

Harbour Town had in fact just located the last of their boards and the completed layout sat majestically within its setting below a run of low windows. The July light spilled through the old glass and helped to animate the tiny figures and buildings. Even the carefully moulded breaking waves seemed to be actually moving. Justine sighed. 'This is gorgeous. Look at the beach. Those little models of windbreaks and sandcastles.'

Nick was busy checking out the seaside town to see if any new buildings had been added. He was about to prod the door of a rather well rendered garage when he received a gentle poke to the back. Nick turned around.

Angie stood staring at him from under a blue denim cap.

'Hey there Angie. How's things?'

She remained staring, while rotating a small screwdriver in her hand. 'What you up to Nick?'

'Just seeing if you had any new models. You know I'm a big fan.'

Angie half smirked and squinted her eyes. 'You better not be thinking of adding anything to my layout, you git.'

Nick shrugged innocently.

Angie looked into the distance. 'I've heard of things happening to other layouts. Strange derailments, ice cream vans, secret plans... peculiar noises.'

Justine sidled up to Nick.

'Angie, this is Justine, she's helping us with model making.'

Angie screwed up both eyes as she observed the new

arrival. Justine tried to look briefly back at her but couldn't be sure what she'd seen. This woman was closed off, secretive and suspicious. Justine smirked. To be honest, she was utterly normal for this past-time.

'What's funny?' said Angie, retaining eye lock with Justine. 'What's funny?' she repeated.

Nick butted in. 'C'mon Angie, be nice. Justine was saying what a great job you've done. She's never seen Harbour Town before.'

Angie shifted her gaze back to Nick and adjusted her cap slightly. She slid the screwdriver back into the side pocket of her dungarees and turned. 'No funny business' she muttered.

Justine squeezed Nick's arm. 'I'm a little scared' she whispered.

Nick waited until Angie had shuffled back behind the far end of the layout. 'Don't worry about Angie. She has what you might say are slow processes. You'll see her think 'I'm going to hit you' before she actually does. Nothing to be scared of, just don't make any sudden moves, it makes her twitchy.'

'Great modeller though' quipped Justine.

'One of the best, one of the best' sighed Nick. 'C'mon, let's see how those plonkers at Guard's Van are doing.'

Pete looked around the impromptu tea room that had been created from a smorgasbord of different vintage chairs and fold-up utility tables going back eighty years or so. He had to confess he quite liked the effect and unlike Potton they were at least serving tea in proper cups. He was diligently adding sugar to two of the team teas when a large presence hove to.

'Look ooh it is. Mister Fishplate 'imself.'

Pete glanced up. A bulky red-faced bloke leered down at him.

'You an' yer little boys come out t'play then?'

Pete tried to stand as tall as his five-ten frame would allow. 'Mr North Line. Hello there. How's tricks?'

North Line looked Pete up and down. 'Fuckin' alright mate, s'long as you and yer boys don't get in the fucking way.'

'Right, ok, well we're up the far end, so no problem mate' replied Pete in a quavering voice that annoyingly decided to go squeaky at the end.

North Line scowled. 'Up somefing's end, you bender' and turned away.

Pete watched him walk deliberately away before he picked up the drinks tray and scuttled back to Fishplate.

Silent tears were rolling down Nick's cheeks as he watched Guard's Van attempt to put their layout together.

'Geoffrey. Look. The clip goes here dear friend.'

Geoffrey looked affronted. 'Francis, if you say that one more time my dear fellow I shall become really quite peeved.'

'But Geoffrey, where else would it go?' As if to accentuate his point Francis took his hands away from the board to make a grand theatrical sweep. The unsupported board started to list slightly before rapidly heaving to one side. Geoffrey and Francis both made a dive to catch the falling section, which they successfully halted. But as they crouched there congratulating themselves there was a 'crump' and a low groan as the other board sheared away from its stand and slammed into the floor.

'Oh for goodness sake Geoffrey did you not clamp down

your end?'

Geoffrey raised his eyebrows. 'My dear Francis, I was too busy trying to manipulate your end'

As they glared at each other a short chap in comfortable brogues wobbled towards them, carrying a large leather suitcase in front of him. Geoffrey and Francis cried out in tandem. 'Henry dear boy, stop.'

Henry didn't stop. There was a filmic wail from Geoffrey and Francis as Henry's comfortable brogues caught the edge of the stricken board and launched him forwards.

'Oh dear mother!' cried Henry as he involuntarily jettisoned the suitcase and crashed onto the wooden floor, one leg left entangled in the layout. Geoffrey and Francis quickly re-clipped their board and fussed over to him.

'Oh you poor, poor boy' said Francis. 'A cup of chamomile from the tea rooms quickly.' Geoffrey hurried off.

Justine had to drag a heaving Nick away.

Pete distributed the tea out at Fishplate.

'Anything going on?' said Colin, taking a slurp of tea and coupling up a freight train.

Pete hissed. 'Your mate from North Line is here.'

Colin put his tea down. 'I think the big fella's name was Ray.'

'Yeah, well, Ray is not very friendly. I think you all need to stay up here for your own safety.'

Colin picked up his tea and took a gulp. He looked at Pete. 'Trouble is Pete, Ray's the friendly one.'

Pete had a sudden wild thought. 'Fuck, where's Nick?'

Over at North Line.

'You alright there mate?'

Nick stood up. 'Yeah, just having a butchers at all that valve and pipework. You do that?'

The well-built operator leant back in his cab and smiled. At least Nick thought it looked like a smile. The smile didn't seem reflected in any other part of his face, which remained impassive. It spoke.

'You part of the competition then, John?'

Nick attempted to look surprised. 'Competition? Oh that thing, no mate, I'm, we're helping a friend out on a trade stand.'

Justine sidled up and did her cheesy 'honest' grin. She was becoming a willing accomplice in what-ever Nick decided to embark upon these days.

There was a grunt from the operator.

Nick smiled. 'Yeah, tell us your name and we'll see if we can get you some discount or something.'

The operator rubbed his hand over the top of his shaved head before jutting out his chin slightly.

'Yeah, alright mate. Name's Vince.'

A shadow fell across Nick and Justine. They turned to see a mountainous slab of meat packed into a straining t-shirt.

'Yeah, and this is Ray, ain't it Ray?'

'Fuckin' too right mate' said Ray, staring at Nick.

Ray continued to stare at Nick for the next twenty seconds amid an increasingly alarming silence. Eventually the situation got even a bit weird for Vince.

'Oi, Ray, wot you staring at mate?'

Ray moved his jaw. 'I fink 'e was talking to that Fishplate lot.'

Vince eased himself up from the cab in a dangerous manner and stood next to Ray. He was worryingly not much smaller. He moved his face close to Nick's.

'Were you talking to that bunch of wankers?'

Nick moved his puzzled face back slightly. 'Yeah.'

Justine closed imperceptibly nearer to Nick and gripped his shirt.

Vince folded his arms, which given the size of his biceps was surprisingly difficult. He lowered his voice to a soft growl. 'Now listen 'ere mate. That bunch are as fuckin' gay as the hills. Don't go near 'em. I 'eard all sorts of stories 'bout them. Their model maker. Wots is name Roy? Roy?'

The third member of North Line turned his shaven head as a JCB would rotate and blinked into life. 'Wot mate?'

'That Fishplate bunch. Wot's their model maker called?'

'Nick, I fink' He thought a second. 'Ee's not bad I hear.'

Vince snarled. Roy lowered his head in submission.

Ray muttered through clenched teeth 'I eard 'e's a no-good faggot that 'angs round kiddies playgrounds and such.' Ray added a snarl at the end for Vince.

Vince snorted in appreciation. 'Yeah.' He dropped a heavy paw onto Nick's shoulder. 'You steer clear of 'em mate if you know wot's good for you. Might catch somefing if you know wot I mean?'

Through a small gap between Vince and Ray, Nick suddenly saw Pete coming towards them. He looked like he wanted to speak.

Vince's meaty hand remained clamped to his shoulder. Nick looked up to Vince. 'That's a shame. I did hear he was the best but if you gentlemen insist.'

Vince gave the merest of nods.

Pete was almost upon them.

'Didn't catch yer name mate' said Vince looking inquisitively at his face.

Justine crashed in. 'Bob, he's Bob and I'm... Nicole.'

Pete was making eye contact.

Vince removed his paw.

Justine shrieked 'What's that?' and pointed in the opposite direction of Pete.

Vince, Ray and Roy turned in perfect unison.

Nick shot Pete the 'fuck off sign.' Pete twigged immediately and veered off to the right, bent down and pretended to tie his shoe lace. Meanwhile Vince had turned back to Justine.

'Wot the fuck wos that about?'

Justine attempted to look flustered. It wasn't difficult. 'A squirrel.'

'Fuckin' wot?' said Vince.

Ray's ears visibly perked up.

'Shit' said Vince. 'Ray, calm down mate. There ain't no squirrel.'

Ray started twitching and a large vein swelled into existence on his vertical forehead.

Justine did a little curtsey, turned to look at Vince and smiled. Vince tried to raise his hands to stop her, but Justine was too quick. She said in a loud voice 'I saw a squirrel just there' and pointed to the opposite wall.

Ray was off, dragging Vince behind him, rapidly followed by Roy, who appeared to be scrabbling for some sort of medication.

Nick observed the pandemonium unfolding. 'Squirrel?'

'First thing I could think of' said Justine.

'Bob?'

'First thing I could think of' she laughed. 'Hey do you really hang around kiddies playgrounds and such?'

'Course I do. How else would you make a model of them? Anyway we're all as gay as the hills', Nick snorted. 'Where do these people come from. Let's get back to Fishplate but let's not look like we are.'

As they passed Pete, still pretending to tie a lace, Nick whispered 'Pete, I'm Bob. Justine is Nicole and we don't know you. OK?'

Pete suppressed an urge to get out to the van and go home.

As they walked off Nick winked at Justine. 'Just wondering Justine. When we get back tonight. Would you like to be Nicole?'

Over an hour away at Ribbington Town Hall, Fat Bob looked with satisfaction over the Pinewood Flyer's layout. Everything was tip top, the warm up schedule had passed perfectly and now they were just waiting for Graham to get back with the tea and buns, for the traditional team talk. Opposite them, the Junkyard Express team were finishing off their test runs. While Bob wasn't so keen on their layout, a sort of strange American semi-desert landscape, he did like their trains. Junkyard Express didn't really take competitions that seriously and in previous years were always penalised for running inaccurate models. However, the recent rule changes had clearly helped them and running the two-thirty Mad Max special always got a little cheer from the spectators. Fat Bob especially liked their massive 'Big Boy' locos that pulled enormous loads across the desert landscape. The real crowd pleaser involved doubled up locos pulling a tail that stretched the entire length of the boards. They called it the 'log jammer' and while it was a dangerous stunt to pull in a competition it did have the benefit of racking up massive points. Bob smiled, this was going to be a really tough round. A panting noise made him turn. Graham wheezed up with a tray of teas and iced fingers.

'Going to get rough today lads' said Graham as he demolished a first finger.

The rest of the boys joined Graham and Bob and they settled down for a team talk that looked akin to what-ever the collective term for a group of space hoppers was.

'OK' said Bob, 'you know the other teams are Junkyard, Mind The Gap and Wayward Ho.'

There was a general nodding. 'I think Junkyard are the ones to beat and luckily they're opposite so we can keep an eye on them. Mind The Gap are good but I don't see them putting out enough traffic and as for Wayward Ho…'

'Wayward Ha Ha, more like' added Chip.

'Exactly' said Bob. 'Now, this information remains strictly between us.'

There was a puzzled murmur.

'I got a call from Pete at Fishplate. He said we need to watch out for a potential saboteur.'

Chip was first to react. 'Oh come on Bob. It's just Pete playing games, trying to put us off.'

Bob nodded. 'I know, I know but I think there's something to it.' There was a general grunt. 'He said that the saboteur would almost certainly strike in the second round and he reckoned as a contender we should be wary. It is Pete's opinion this guy is not wasting time on losers.'

Graham laughed. 'That almost sounded like a compliment.'

Bob smirked. 'Well, we know Pete can be tricksy. Don't

buy a car off him and all that, but let's just stay alert. If you think anything's been added to our layout, just stop operations and check. I would rather lose a couple of minutes than risk a crash. We can make up time but not a derailment.'

Chip nodded. 'Sure, sure. Do you think Pete told you everything?'

'Course not' said Bob. 'But the fact that he's told me this much means it has to be serious.'

Back at Thrumming the judges had appeared at exactly thirteen-thirty hundred hours to discuss each team's timetable. Some aspects of the Smooth Fishplate schedule were proving tricky for Mr Smyth-Watson to understand.

Pete took a deep breath and centred himself. 'Yes, we intend to schedule a train on fire.'

'I am so sorry Mr Fletcher. Could you just explain the 'fire' scenario again?'

'At a given time, we bring on a train that appears to be on fire.' Pete paused.

'Yes. I understand. But why exactly?'

Pete frowned. 'Well, it's part of the entertainment of our display.'

'I see and how does one resolve a train on fire within your timetable?'

'Well, as you can see. We bring on a fire, a rescue train puts out the fire and then a recovery train tows it away.'

Mr Smyth-Watson ran his finger down the sheet. 'Yes, I see. Now this is all done to a strict time table?'

'Exactly' said Pete. 'But we want it to appear as though it were an unexpected event.'

A wrinkle formed across Mr Smyth-Watson's forehead. It

looked dangerously as though understanding was penetrating. 'Oh, oh, I see. Yes. Quite. Gosh, yes. Well really, that's very clever. Very clever indeed. I'm sure the spectators will find that most entertaining.' And then he winked and put a finger to his nose.

'Well I shall take a good look at your layout and study your timetable a little more. So, don't leave the country I say.' He guffawed and started to write things on his clipboard.

Pete turned to look at the drivers. They all shrugged their shoulders. Pete rubbed his forehead. 'Why can't we just have a normal judge for once?'

At fourteen-hundred hours there was a shrill whistle and round two began. Nick had borrowed a chair from the café area and had seated himself down in front of Guard's Van. Justine stood behind him resting her elbows on his shoulders.

'Nick, stop laughing.'

'I can't help it my love. The anticipation is overwhelming.'

'It's very rude.'

'But it's going to be very funny' he retorted. 'Just watch.'

Justine settled her head on top of Nick's and put her arms around him.

The first ten minutes of the Guard's Van timetable passed without incident and Nick was beginning to think that he'd misjudged them when there was a high-pitched wail from Francis.

'Whatever's the matter dear?' said Geoffrey, as he brought a goods train to rest in a siding.

'I've spilt Harvey's on the track.'

'Oh Francis. I thought we talked about you drinking and driving?'

'It was just a medicinal sherry' said Francis, trying to soak up the sticky liquid with a handkerchief simultaneously guiding a passenger train past a long platform.

Geoffrey tutted. 'And where have you ejected this sticky liquid?'

'All over Norman Cross' said Francis, frantically dabbing at a level crossing.

Geoffrey called to Henry 'Henry dear. Can you delay the through express until Francis has cleared up his mess?'

Francis brought the passenger train to a stop and began to use both hands to clean the track. Geoffrey powered down his goods train and got up to help Francis. 'Henry? Hello dear. Did you hear me?'

Nick squeezed Justine's hand. 'Here we go.'

Francis was aware of a miniature rumbling coming from the tunnel very close to Norman's cross.

'Henry, my deary. You have ceased and desisted have you not?'

The through express came flying out of the tunnel and sliced into Francis's fingers. He screamed and jerked back his hand, inadvertently whacking Geoffrey in the crotch. Geoffrey groaned and fell forward, nutting himself on the nearby southbound platform. They ended up sprawled on the floor behind the layout.

Justine felt perhaps they should help but judging by the way Nick's body was shaking violently, she guessed it might be a futile gesture.

At this point the lovely Henry stood up from behind his cab at the far end of the layout. He looked around trying to discern where Geoffrey and Francis were. He removed the Walkman head set. 'Francis, Geoffrey?'

There was a pitiful cry from the floor. Henry walked forward and peered down behind the boards. 'Gracious mother! What are you doing?'

Geoffrey wailed back. 'Disaster has befallen us my lovely. We have been undone by an afternoon sherry.'

Justine helped Nick to his feet and ushered him away, sobbing quietly to himself. The judge took note of the time and sighed. He made a few marks on his clipboard and wandered off for a cup of tea.

The saboteur had parked his aging Marina a short distance from the venue and sat meticulously going through his kit. On every new mission the ante was upped and he was pretty sure several of the clubs would by now be expecting trouble. It had taken a while to perfect his latest weapon but the idea had come to him after working on a building site. He referred back to his list and smiled, then checked his small rucksack again and reached for his disguise, a hat. This time he was going for a worn-out baseball cap. Everyone remembered a hat but never the face. Much easier to keep changing the hat.

Pete checked his watch and started towards Fishplate. Colin, Stew and Adrian were by now in a steady working rhythm and were moving traffic efficiently and by the numbers. He watched Smyth as another mixed freight train reached its destination. Smyth remained motionless. Pete waited for him to tick the move off on his clipboard. Nothing happened. A minute later a passenger through-express completed its run. Pete watched Smyth as he seemed to jolt back to the present. A slight look of panic momentarily came over him, before he ticked off the movement. 'Christ' thought Pete and made soft contact with Adrian.

'Adrian, have you been observing the judge at all?'

Adrian carried on forming up a bulky scrap train. 'On and

off Pete. I wanted to tell you I don't think he's recording everything. Looks like, well looks like he keeps nodding off or something.'

'Crap' said Pete under his breath. He looked at his watch.

'Colin?' he whispered loudly.

Colin flicked his eyes up momentarily. 'One sec' and delicately shunted a small row of empty wagons onto a side line before moving off a large diesel with coal wagons in tow. 'What's up?'

'You about to do the fire train?'

'Yep, about four more movements and then we start. How the other teams doing?'

Pete exhaled. 'Harbour Town haven't put a foot wrong. Guard's Van are already out and I have no idea about North Line because I'm shit scared to go near them.'

Stew tutted and brought a Pullman into Lower Didsbury.

Pete ignored him. 'Right I'm going to hang around for the fire train and then get back to Harbour Town. Anyone seen Nick or Justine?'

Nick and Justine were at the present moment in a small room that backed off the gents toilets. Nick had been standing at the urinal doing his thing when his wandering eyes had alighted upon a small door set into the far wall. 'Odd place for a door' he'd thought and tried the handle to see if it was unlocked. It was, and after a quick peek he'd gone back and ushered Justine past the urinals and into the odd room. The first couple of square meters were stacked with mops and cleaning products but beyond this the small space rapidly gave way to stacks and piles and abandonments of stuff. A dirty light struggled to penetrate the one small window set high into the boarded wall and made the room somewhat ethereal. Along the entire length of one wall was set a substantial high shelf supported on a series of cast metal brackets upon which was a motley collection of stuffed creatures. Some in cases, others wedged in the space between.

'Don't shout at me but I quite like all this taxidermy stuff' said Nick, his eyes jumping from one sad specimen to another.

Justine giggled quietly. 'I have a barn owl called Prof in my room. Mum hates it. Actually, I could bring him back with me next time. He'd look great in the kitchen.'

Nick bit his lip. A few months ago this sort of request might have worried him. No way would he have been prepared to commit to joint custody of a stuffed owl, but Justine was turning into one of those 'chance in a million' encounters. He gave her a gentle hug.

'What's that for?' teased Justine.

'Just because.' Nick held onto her for a while longer. 'Hey, why don't we do a model of a pet shop?'

'Ooh yes' cried Justine. 'I want a Labrador.'

'A model Labrador?'

'Um, yeah, a model, of course.'

Nick was beginning to think a stuffed barn owl was now looking comparatively sensible. 'Maybe I could model Colin in a fish tank?'

Justine laughed. 'Hey, what time is it?'

Nick flicked a glance at his watch. 'Bugger, the fire train.'

The saboteur moved through the entrance to the exhibition. It was an hour into the competition and there was a good mix of spectators shuffling between the different layouts, ideal cover. He decided to stand a little way off his target and casually observe them, get into their rhythm and pattern. The target seemed to be concentrating hard on the task in hand. He got the definite impression they were building towards something. This would be the ideal strike time. He pulled his cap down and slowly lowered his back-pack to the floor.

A pall of dense smoke hung over Lower Didsbury. Monty had immediately called the fire brigade the minute the 1530 diesel/electric hauling a timber tail had gone up in smoke. He stood rooted to the main platform cursing his luck, the recent series of disasters that had afflicted his small domain were bound to be sending some sort of alarm messages to his superiors.

Dennis idled down his new, old blue ford tractor and watched the flames take hold of the train.

'Bover. I 'ope thart dun go an' set a light to moi pastur. Ermintrude, you stay 'way gal'

Ermintrude's large bovine eyes moved from Dennis to the flaming train. She dimly remembered being crushed and mutilated in the recent past and didn't fancy being immolated. She was about to move away when she remembered he always had a tasty treat for her. She turned back to stare at Dennis, her brain awash with the thought of turnip.

Ginge gripped his pint in the new beer garden at the very recently refurbished Water Tower and Tender. He could see the smoke rising from behind the trees bordering the line. He rubbed his neck nervously and wondered whether he should contemplate finding a new, less dangerous local.

'Good show' announced Monty to no one as the emergency fire tender drew up close to the timber train. Within minutes several thousand litres of foam had expelled the flames and the fire tender was withdrawing as a huge recovery diesel slowly powered down and clamped onto the smouldering train. Monty had been told by the fire chief that none other than Colin Baker himself was at the controls of the recovery engine 'Indefatigable.' He couldn't resist a salute as the

mighty 6000HP monolith rumbled slowly past, shaking several panes of glass loose in the newly painted waiting room. Monty looked enviously on, reminded of his time at the controls of his beloved Lancaster.

The saboteur took a long intake of breath. He started to walk towards the layout, the foam bomb felt hot against his cupped hand. He stopped momentarily and focused on his target, a small tunnel entrance at one end of the layout. Another breath. One, two, three, train enters at opposite end, four, five, walk, six, seven, pull safety, eight, walk, flick bomb into tunnel, nine, ten, exit to tea room. There was no explosion, no fireworks but just inside the tunnel a huge sticky expanding mass of insulating foam was going about its deadly task.

Bob instinctively looked up from his cab towards Junkyard. You get used to the rhythm and noise of other team's layouts and something acoustically alien had alerted him to an incident. It had been a sort of a 'flump' noise. He squinted. Chris was flapping around one end of the layout. It looked like one of their so called 'log jammers' had jammed. Bob made a small satisfied 'tut' and concentrated on the shunter he was backing into an engine shed.

Back at Fishplate, Pete was trying to have a crisis team meeting with forty-five minutes of timetable still left to run. It was made all the more difficult by trying to keep the conversation from Smyth.

'Look, guys we're in trouble, that twat hasn't been marking down all our points.'

Stew brought his passenger train to a halt. 'Surely we can appeal Pete. It all seems terribly unfair.'

Pete crouched in nearer to Stew. 'I don't think it works

that way Stew. I think we may be buggered.'

Colin coupled up some spare wagons and started to shunt them into siding number four, all the while talking. 'Can we still win? I mean we are kicking big serious arse at the moment. Through express over to you, Stew. Adrian decouple car transporter tail and form up mixed freight for Deltic. I mean if he's missed, say, ten percent I bet we could still win.'

Adrian joined in. 'Not sure guys. I've been watching him. I think he's failed to log in at least a quarter of our traffic.'

There was a collective moan of despair.

'Anyone considered an intervention?' Nick's voice drifted up from behind the layout, where he and Justine were hidden.

'An intervention?' repeated Pete

'Well, I'm sure those wonderful human specimens on North Line could be persuaded to quit.'

There was a muffled giggling from behind the boards.

Colin grinned as he sent another express through train to Stew. 'Are you naughty bunnies up to something?'

There was a slight cough and Nick's disembodied voice continued. 'Look, Ray has threatened Pete. Vince has previously assaulted Colin.'

'Barged.'

'That's right Colin, assaulted. Vince also wishes violence upon me, even though he has no idea what I look like and both Ray and Vince, oh and -'

There was a short, whispered conversation.

'And even Roy think that Stew is a raving queer.'

There was a spluttering from Stew. 'I am not queer' he said a tad too loudly.

Smyth caught his eye before returning to writing some notes. He appeared to have missed the through express that had just completed its run.

Pete calmed Stew down. 'Look, look. OK. Personally, I would have no moral objection to an 'intervention.''

'Fuck 'em' whispered Colin.

'Ditto' added Adrian.

The weight of expectation shifted to Stew, who wriggled uncomfortably in his cab. He sighed. 'Alright, just this once as they are clearly socially unfit for this competition.'

There was a collective 'Ooh.'

Justine's soft voice rose up into the air. 'Thank you Stew. I won't think any the less of you. You are still the compassionate moral compass of this team.'

Stew coughed and reversed a timber train up the line. 'Thank you', he said. 'That actually means a lot to me.'

Pete clapped his hands together. 'Go, go, go!'

Junkyard Express had ceased operations and were in the process of trying to extract gunged up rolling stock from the tunnel. The disaster had been noted by the Pinewood Flyers and Fat Bob was urging everyone to stay calm and complete their timetable out. Graham eased up next to Bob. He lowered his voice. 'Sabotage Bob?'

Bob raised his eyes momentarily. 'Christ, yes.'

There was a brief silence before they both whispered 'Pete was right.'

Nick and Justine were back in the odd room off the gents. They were gazing intently at the taxidermy collection.

Nick nudged Justine in the ribs gently. 'Stop giggling.

Now. Which one?'

'Well I think we should start with Mr Badger.' Justine pointed to a really badly stuffed, moth eaten specimen, crouched high on the wide shelf.

Nick nodded in approval. 'Yes, Brian the Badger as an entrée. I like it.'

Justine pulled up a cardboard box of floor cleaner and timidly stepped up so she could get a better view. 'Oh look. How about that one?'

Nick peered into the gloomy corner. 'What is it?'

'I think it's a beaver, but its tail has dropped off.'

'Freaky' laughed Nick. 'Boris?'

'Oh no. It needs to be something like…Bumble.'

'Bumble? Bumble the crippled Beaver. OK.'

They both had to take a short laughing break.

'Right, so we start with Brian, then Bumble and then?'

Justine wiped her eyes. 'And then' she reached out and took down a stuffed grey squirrel. It had the look of an animal caught in a moment of sheer surprise. She cleaned its dark beady eyes and fluffed its mangy tail. A bit fell off. 'Then Sheila' she stuttered. Making Sheila do a little dance around the shelf.

Nick nearly choked. 'Ray's going to love that.'

The saboteur sat down with his mug of tea, a safe distance from the unfolding carnage. He removed his cap and tucked it into his rucksack. He took out a sun faded Aussie hat and slid it firmly onto his head. He looked around, no one was paying him the slightest attention. Good. He unfolded his hit list and put a line through Junkyard. He sat back and smiled. His employers would be most fucking satisfied.

Ray was concentrating. You knew this because it looked a lot like he was sitting on the toilet trying to squeeze one out. Vince had kept Ray and Roy under strict control and their timetable, simple as it was, had nevertheless gone smoothly. Ray was straining to bring in a sooty old coal train and park it into a siding when a 'tappity tap' at the nearby window and something furry briefly scooting past distracted him. He stared at the clear glass, not sure of what he'd seen before settling back to focus on the train. He slowly backed it towards the buffers, pulling alongside some grubby hoppers. There was that tapping noise again. He looked up. A badger appeared to skip across the outside window ledge. Ray could feel his heart rate begin to increase and the static. The static filling his ears. That smothering static. There was a gentle bump as the rear coal wagon ran into the buffers and the couplings along the length of the train compressed. Ray jerked back to reality, he shut the power off and decoupled the engine.

'Awright there mate?' muttered Vince.

'Yeah, yeah mate' replied Ray, rubbing his eyes and scratching his ears to try and rid himself of the static.

There was a 'tappity tap' at the window. A strange mottled beast with huge teeth slowly raised itself into view. Between its teeth was a section of track. It shook the track angrily and head banged the glass. Ray was transfixed. His heart was deafening. The static. The blinding static. It was filling his ears. It had to stop.

'Ray, wots rong, wots rong?' pleaded Vince.

'Roy, more tabs quick mate.'

Roy fumbled with a plastic pill bottle, his large hands struggling with the child-proof top.

There was a tappity tap at the window. A squirrel twirled and pranced across the space ending in a little pirouette.

186

The static escaped Ray's ears, entered his brain and blew every main circuit. He stood up squealed like a demonic pig and tumble rolled over the layout before jumping to his feet and charging towards the window. Justine and Nick were already legging it. By the time an enraged Ray had prized off the window locks with his teeth, and bundled through they were half way down the road.

Nick and Justine had been settled in the Ploughman's Rest for a couple of hours before a sweaty and stressed looking Pete popped his head through the door and spotted them hunkered down in a little alcove.

'There you are. Thought the nearest pub would be a good starting point.'

Nick looked up from his drink, his fourth, and smiled crookedly. 'Welcome Pete, my friend, do join us.'

Justine looked Pete up and down. 'You look…tired Pete, sit down. Pint of Guinness?'

Pete closed his eyes and nodded. He pulled up a nearby chair and sat down heavily, letting out a groan as he did so. Nick observed him in silence, rubbing the side of his glass. 'They do an excellent local bitter.'

Pete tapped the table and attempted a smile. 'Well, after that performance at least we're through to the next round but Christ, I'm not sure I could go through all that again.'

Nick smiled congenially. 'So tell me dear friend what happened after our hasty departure?'

Pete shuffled in his chair and rested his elbows on the small oak table. 'Well, obviously there was a bit of a rumpus what with Ray breaking through a window. Anyway, one of the Neanderthals got some drugs in him and he calmed down, but the judge disqualified them on the spot. Guard's Van had already given up and spent their time arguing about curtain samples and colour swatches or something. All I know is Francis likes Autumn Plum while Geoffrey errs toward Backroom Grey. I hope they're redecorating?'

Justine turned up with Pete's pint. Pete took a long slow gulp and exhaled deeply. 'That's much better.'

Justine patted him gently on the back and sat down next to Nick.

Pete continued 'Anyway, I can only assume that ourselves and Harbour Town are through.' Pete grinned. 'We've never made it past this round before.'

'I know, I know' said Nick softly.

'So… no need to be stressed dear Pete' cooed Justine.

Pete placed his head in his hands. 'Yeah? You two missed the finale.'

Nick sat upright. 'Go on.'

'Well guess who turns up near the end of the competition?'

There were blank expressions. 'Helen. Helen turned up. Left the kids with a friend and decided to come and make sure North Line didn't try anything on with Colin.'

'And did they?' asked Justine.

'Oh yes. That lunk Vince came over as we were packing down and started jabbing his thick finger at Colin, saying what a ponce he was and getting right up in his face. Before any of us could react, Helen pushed him to one side, kneed him in the balls and then did some sort of Judo-Karate thing that left him bleeding on the floor. She then jabbed her finger in his face and told him that if he came near Colin again she would make absolutely sure the only thing he could ever fuck again would be a thimble.'

'Fucking hell' cried Nick. 'Bollocks. I missed all the action.'

Justine was clearly agitated. 'Kick arse bitch! Is she some sort of black belt or something?'

Pete took another gulp of Guinness and wiped his mouth. 'No. God no. She's way past that. Some other colour with attachments or something.'

'So what happened after that?' laughed Nick.

'Roy or whatever his name is came over and helped Vince back up. He actually apologised on Vince's behalf. Well… that was pretty much that. I said we should all meet up week after next when I know the results from the other round. What did you do with the stuffed things by the way?'

Justine started to giggle. 'Well Brian is living wild and free in a hedge. Bumble is stuck in the branches of that oak tree out there and as for our star -' Justine reached under the table and brought up a shabby looking squirrel. Pete instinctively recoiled as the squirrel's glassy eyes locked with his.

'Jesus. No wonder Ray went batshit.'

Justine danced the squirrel around the table which set her and Nick off in a laughing fit. She recovered herself. 'Actually, I'm keeping Sheila. I think Prof needs someone to talk to.'

Pete had no idea what she was talking about and let it wash over him. He looked at Nick and sighed 'We did it mate!'

CHAPTER THIRTEEN: THE SABOTEUR NAMED

The next day on a cloudy Monday Pete was sat at his desk staring into space. The phone rang.

'Hello, Ace car sales.'

'Hi Pete, can you talk?'

'Hold on Bob. One second.' Pete put the receiver down and stuck his head out of the window that overlooked the large expanse of forecourt. 'Sam!' Louder. 'Sam!'

Sam looked up from the Golf he was attempting to stick some large red plastic price numbers to. Pete winced. 'Sam, you've got the nines upside down. It should be 1999 not 1666.'

Sam took a delicate step back. He gave Pete a simple grin and started to remove them, again.

Pete put his head back in the office and picked the phone back up. 'Hi Bob. Don't need any help up your place do you? I've got a real star here. Brilliant with figures.'

Bob chuckled. 'No mate. Listen. You won't have heard the results. We got through and so did Mind The Gap.'

Pete snorted in surprise. 'How. What happened to Junkyard? Oh!'

'Oh indeed!' replied Bob. 'It was like you predicted Pete. Sabotage. They got hit about an hour in. All over for them.'

Pete clicked his tongue. 'That's sad. Do you know how?'

'Expanding foam in the tunnel' replied Bob.

'Ouch, no one needs that.'

'I guess so' said Bob.

A couple of days later Pete met up with Nick for a clandestine chat.

'See you managed to get out without Justine then.'

'Yeah, she's back over her parents' for a few days.'

'She's spending more and more time with you though Nick.'

Nick stared at his JD and coke. 'Hmm. I think the moving in permanently scenario is fast approaching.'

Pete smirked. 'Still haven't met the parents then?'

Nick slumped. 'No. I guess that needs to be done.'

'You might like them.'

'And I might not.'

'So, I've got a little bit of info for you.'

Nick sipped his drink. 'Go on.'

'There's a war-gaming exhibition coming up this weekend. From what I hear it's mostly AFVs.'

'He's going to be there then' said Nick.

'Exactly' Pete lifted his pint.

Nick glanced around the pub. 'I reckon I probably know him. I mean to say that I will probably recognise him from somewhere. I was trying to think of anyone who I might have fallen out with in the past.'

Pete pretended to choke.

'Yeah, yeah. I know you think that's everyone I've ever met but I must have really pissed this one off.'

Pete raised a finger. 'Hey, maybe it's me. Maybe I've sold them a dodgy car in the past.'

Nick gave him a patronising smile. 'He's not out there persecuting second-hand car salesmen though, is he?'

'OK. So did you think of anyone?'

Nick wriggled slightly in his seat and pinched his nose.

'C'mon Nick. Confess.' Pete cradled his pint. 'C'mon you can tell Uncle Pete.'

Nick frowned. 'Look. I was young, easily influenced. I didn't have much of a social life.'

'Oh no, you didn't?'

'I did.'

'Which club?'

'Spearpoint.'

Pete spluttered into his pint. 'Spearpoint?'

'Yep. They were a bunch of quite young, shall we say, feisty modelers. But quite sociable. They had a clubhouse and everything.'

'So what did they do?'

'Oh took part in general model exhibitions. It was all sorts of stuff. Dinosaur dioramas to the QE2 to a MIG jet. Anything really. Then this guy turned up and started getting a lot of them into war gaming and the atmosphere changed. He was really aggressive and divisive. Eventually it got to the point where unless you were into military modelling and by this I pretty much mean 20th century, then you weren't welcome at the club.'

'So, go on. How did you piss him off?'

Nick closed his eyes and snorted. 'Well it was the last exhibition of the year and he'd made this blooming great big model of a panther tank. He loved his dioramas, so he modelled it half in and half out of a wrecked building. It was pretty good. Actually, what this guy did really well, that no one else managed, was to get the tracks looking right. I mean they had weight and weather and mud. For a total and utter arse-munch he was a really good modeler.'

Pete looked slightly puzzled. 'What sort of models were you making then?'

'Oh buildings. I was in my architecture phase. That little building society model in Greenvale. That's basically one I made while at the club. I changed it a bit for our layout but it's pretty much the same.'

Nick could see Pete straining to picture it.

'Oh gee thanks Pete. Memorable then?'

'Did you enter a model at this exhibition then?'

Nick twitched slightly. 'Well, I wanted to enter a model of a corner shop.'

Pete shook his head. 'Christ you were weird. What was wrong with entering a jet fighter or something?'

'Because everyone was doing it. No one was doing my kind of stuff.'

'Did he like your corner shop?'

Nick squinted. 'Not really. Well to be precise he said I could enter it if I made it look like it had been bombed.'

Pete tutted. 'Nice!'

'Yeah' said Nick. 'Stupid cock wasn't even in charge but got his war gaming mates to pressure me out.'

Pete sighed and took another slurp of Guinness. 'Go on then, what did you do?'

'Well, he modelled this Panther tank with the crew at ease. The commander was half in the turret talking to an officer on the ground. The driver had his head sticking out of a hatch and the loader was lying on the rear of the tank reading a book.'

Pete was pretty sure where this story was going.

Nick took a sip. 'Right, I made an alternative crew for his tank and swapped them over just before the judges arrived to inspect the entrees.'

'Alternatives?' winced Pete.

Nick rubbed his hands together. 'Well, it was his fault, he should have glued his tank crew in place not left them easily available for, er, removing.'

'Nicking.'

'Sensitive relocation Pete. Now just imagine this guy is like the tax man. He has absolutely no sense of humour.'

'OK.'

'I swapped the Nazi tank commander for Julie Andrews, circa sound of music.'

Pete started to shake.

'The driver's head was replaced by a pantomime donkey head and the loader reading a book -' Nick stuttered.

Pete's shoulders were shaking. 'Go on.'

Nick clenched his teeth. 'Yeah. The loader I replaced with a nude replica of this guy wanking off to a gay magazine. The centrefold of which was a picture of himself.'

Pete stopped shaking abruptly and closed his eyes. 'Jesus, you don't take any prisoners.'

Nick shrugged. 'At the time I thought it just deserts. This guy really loved himself but maybe… with the wisdom of age I might have been a bit harsh.'

'Harsh would be one word for it. What did the judges think?'

Nick grinned. 'No idea mate. Never went back and that must have been nearly thirteen, fourteen years ago. But I can't help feeling this might be our guy.'

Pete stared into his pint. 'Great, so we've got some sort of psychotic lunatical Nazi model maker on a revenge spree. This deal just keeps on getting better.'

He took another gulp of Guinness. 'Don't suppose you can remember his name?'

Nick looked up into the heavens. 'Sure, it was Gary. Graham. No. Wait. No. It was Gareth.'

Pete went white and held his hand up to his forehead.

'What?' said Nick. 'You know him?'

CHAPTER FOURTEEN: BACK TO THE PUB

The week after at the Water tower and Tender was a humid late July meeting and the talk was inevitably about Helen.

'Well, I at least understand where your fragility around women stems from' teased Nick.

'Oh sod off,' exclaimed Colin, 'she's only beaten up five men to the best of my knowledge.'

'What, really?' exclaimed Stew.

'No, Stew. Not really' replied Colin sarcastically.

Justine laughed. 'Where did she learn that self-defence then?'

Colin thought a second. 'Well, she's been taking lessons for years. Most Mondays at the Sherrington sports hall.'

'Is it just for women then?' enquired Justine.

'That class is. There's a men's version too, but if you're thinking about Nick joining, best start him off with the girls.'

Justine smirked. 'Nick's all man to me. Besides he can run very fast when he needs to.'

'And while carrying a stuffed beaver' added Nick.

'It's not to be sniffed at' said Justine.

Colin shook his head. 'You two are just getting weirder. Pete? What's happening next? C'mon we're all waiting.'

Pete grinned. 'There's good news and bad news. We're through to the semi-final and we're up against Mind The Gap which is terrifically brilliant because they're not that good. So, and I can hardly bring myself to say this... But. I think we're going to get to the final.'

Stew coughed. 'And the bad?'

'Well…we're being stalked by a psychotic, revenge-seeking war gamer called Gareth.'

Colin raised his hand. 'Excuse me. When did the distant threat of some crap saboteur turn into an actual person called Gareth? Anyway, can't we just send my wife round his house to beat the shit out of him?'

Stew started to scrabble through some papers. 'Hang on, hang on' He pulled out the interview list. 'We talked to a chap called Gareth.'

Pete tapped the trestle table. 'Yes indeedy. Remember much about him?'

Stew looked at his clipboard notes and shrugged. 'We dismissed him as a bit weird. Not socially compatible.'

Pete interrupted - 'Can you remember what he looked like? What about you Colin?'

'He had a hat. A baseball cap. Blue?' Colin pulled a face.

Stew scratched his head. 'I think he had a bag with him, but I cannot recall anything specific.'

Colin squinted his eyes and faced Pete. 'OK. I get the feeling that some of us know more about stuff going on than they've previously admitted. Over to you Pete.'

Pete cleared his throat. 'Yes. Well I thought as president maybe it might be better to let the drivers concentrate on driving.'

Colin snorted in the direction of Stew and Adrian. 'Go on then. What haven't you told us gentle wallflowers?'

Pete inhaled deeply. 'Don't interrupt me. OK. Shortly after the interviews someone broke into Nick's and sabotaged the layout. It was basically a calling card. The damage was very specific. Some of you may have noticed the new model pub. He nicked the old one. We worked out from clues that he was probably a war gamer and then in round two Junkyard Express were sabotaged and went out. As far as we can tell, he alternates attacks between us and someone else. Nick made a connection to a guy he pissed off in the Stone Age, who was a war gamer and… his name was Gareth. Seems a bit too coincidental.'

There was an amused silence broken by Adrian. 'I just had no idea this model railway stuff was so serious.'

Colin sniffed. 'I think the word you're looking for is sad.'

Stew looked perplexed. 'It doesn't make any sense to me. Why would this Gareth chap leave a calling card and use his actual name?'

'Because he's a complete psychotic twat' muttered Nick. 'He's so in love with himself and arrogant that the thought of not getting recognition for his work gets him all in a bind.'

'He's not some sort of long-lost brother is he Nick?' said Colin crossing his arms and smiling.

Pete started to laugh. 'Nick thinks he's Darth Vader to his Luke Skywalker.'

Nick grinned at Pete. 'If I went evil that's what it might look like. I'm just saying in some ways we're very similar.'

Stew politely butted in. 'You're sure it's this chap Gareth then?'

'Pretty sure' said Pete.

'So, why don't we call the police?'

Everyone stared at Stew.

Colin patted him on the back. 'What exactly do we charge him with? Model-o-cide?'

Stew screwed up his face. 'Well it seems jolly unfair. It's hard enough competing without this idiot making it stressful.'

Nick held out his hands. 'Look. Guys. I think I can stop him but it's going to take me to a dark place… and I can't take you lot with me.' He put an arm around Justine. 'Not even you my lover.'

'What the fuck are you talking about Nick?' cried Colin. 'Can we all get some real-life perspective.'

Adrian stuck up his hand. 'Can I come with you? I promise I won't touch anything.'

'What?' said Nick.

'Wherever you're going.'

'It's a course of action not a destination' sighed Nick.

'But you'll probably end up going somewhere' joked Colin

'Can I please just say one dramatic fucking statement and be left alone?'

'Are you going to pack a lightsabre for the journey?' asked Colin.

'Fuck off' said Nick.

'Are you going to try and hire a blockade runner in the town market? You know, one who's done the A28 in less than twelve minutes.'

'Fuck off' said Nick, trying not to laugh.

Justine whispered into Nick's ear. 'As long as you come back and rescue me. You're my only hope.'

Pete raised his pint. 'Well, here's to Nick. And if you get into trouble I've never heard of you.'

'I'll drink to that' said Colin and raised his glass.

There was a general good-humoured cheer.

Gareth walked casually down the quiet cul-de-sac. The late evening sun was low in the sky and cast lazy deep shadows across the manicured lawns of the sprawling chalet bungalows. He checked his watch. 8.30. A full hour before anyone was likely to return. He glanced about. The stillness felt exhilarating to him. Why was he about to break into someone's house? Was this escalation worth it? He dug up the heavily repressed memory of the Panther incident. Yes, this was going to be worth it. The scales would be balanced and no one would mess with him again. Another furtive glance behind him and he darted up the drive, keeping to the shadow line formed by the boundary. Gareth reached his first objective. He gave the glossy grey plank door between the bungalow and garage a good shake. It rattled defiantly. Good, it wouldn't collapse on him when he shimmied over. Gareth slipped his rucksack off and smoothly dropped it on the other side of the barrier. He retreated back into the shadows. A car slowly wound its way down the meandering road and parked further up. There was a sound of heavy doors slamming and voices. Gareth jumped up at the gate, his fingers hooked over the top and he heaved himself over and down the other side. He composed himself, checked his rucksack and surveyed the new situation. There was a side-door just ahead. It was basically one pane of grotesquely patterned glass set into a thick frame. He tried the handle. The door moved slightly but was clearly locked. He applied more force but there was no more give and he was about to turn the corner and see if any windows were open at the back, when he noticed an odd collection of garden ornaments in a side border. One in particular caught his attention. It was a large concrete snail. The top of the shell looked cleaner, less lichen encrusted, than the rest of the body.

'No way' he muttered and lifted the shell up. Located inside, like a precious egg was a bright, metallic key. 'Idiots' he whispered. Within seconds he was inside the bungalow and quickly found the prize he sought. Gareth slowly widened the neck of the rucksack and carefully removed several bubble-wrapped packages. He chuckled quietly to himself. 'The batter is ready, the batter is ready.' He still had 45 minutes. Plenty of time.

'Well, why would anyone attempt to couple up so many locos?' shrugged Colin.

Pete was getting irritated. 'Stop interrupting Colin, they're American. Remember? Right. The only way to feed the engines with enough power was to juice up the current being supplied to the track. This all worked really well and they did a few huge circuits pulling around three hundred box cars.'

'And it's a record that still holds. The 'Arkansas box pull' it's called' added Stew.

'Thank you Stew,' continued Pete, 'then someone decided to switch the train to a larger parallel track. I think the idea was to add even more box cars. Anyway, they had a circuit breaker between the two parallel tracks and as the lead train crossed the breaker it naturally became, temporarily, the only electric motor on a massively juiced up current. The motor rapidly heated up and ignited. The thing was that as more locos crossed the breaker they evened out the current at the front of the train but the locos pushing at the back were now beginning to heat up as more engines crossed the breaker leaving those still on the other side dealing with a sharply increasing electrical load. Does any of this make sense Colin?'

'Yes Pete, I understand. So what you're saying is the first and last engines across the breaker essentially had their motors burnt out. And?'

Pete applied his 'well done face'. 'And the plastic motor housing melted, followed by parts of the body, before the lead loco created so much debris from failing parts that it derailed and essentially guided three hundred wagons and about thirty locos off the track.'

'Wow' cried Adrian. 'My school kids would have loved that.'

Stew raised his hand. 'It's a record derail too. The 'Arkansas box car' derailment.'

'Really Stew. Really?' Colin frowned.

Pete grinned. 'Nearly there Colin. Just a few more disasters to go and you'll be a fully clued up driver.'

'Right. OK. But it sure as hell won't make me a better driver. Will it?'

Pete tutted. 'Might do!'

CHAPTER FIFTEEN: THINGS GET SERIOUS

'What are you going to wear for this secret mission then?' Justine gazed up at Nick from the kitchen table.

Nick carried on spreading butter across his toast and was very particular to make sure that all the corners were covered. He sat down at the table with his breakfast and took a bite. Justine watched him. She loved the way she could tell when Nick was thinking. She especially loved the particular way he liked to think when eating toast. Nick wiped some crumbs from his mouth. 'Well, I thought about wearing some sort of hat.'

'A what?' said Justine. 'That's rubbish. I thought we were talking about a beard and sunglasses or a false nose or something. Anything more exciting than a hat.'

Nick tipped his head to one side. 'Yeah. I know it's boring but that's the point really. All I need to be is invisible. Nothing shouts disguise more than a comedy beard and sunglasses.' He took another mouthful of toast and drummed his fingers on the smooth melamine tabletop. 'Yes, a hat and… a bag.'

'Whoa there, spymaster Nick. A bag?' Justine laughed.

'Yep, that's all I need. Now can I leave you to get on with 'Operation Finale' while I'm gone?'

Justine batted her eyelids. 'I suppose. I mean I was thinking of washing my hair but if you insist on me creating model concrete pillars then I shall have to obey.'

Nick winked at her. 'You love it. Go on. Admit it!'

Justine smiled and turned her head away. 'No sir, I shall not' and blew him a kiss.

The drive to Hythe took nearly an hour and Nick was careful to park several side streets away from the exhibition venue. He hadn't really thought through any sort of plan. He guessed Gareth would be an exhibitor and therefore would probably need to pack his gear down at the end of the show. He figured he would follow his car or van back to his home and then go from there. Quite where 'go from there' would lead him was another question. Maybe he should have packed a lightsabre. He donned his disguise and ambled towards the main entrance of the exhibition. The late Victorian building looked like an old town hall, quite grand with two impressive Corinthian columns flanking the large double oak doors. He sauntered through, casual like, rucksack at the ready should he suddenly need to hide his face behind it. The Hythe War Gaming and Model Exhibition was spread over the large ground floor and Nick decided to head straight towards a centrally located trade stand to get his bearings. The stand looked suspiciously similar to the one he'd met Justine at and he found himself being instantly transfixed. He ran his hand down a spinner full of 1/72 scale military accessories ranging from a packet of jerry cans to a selection of entrenching tools. He turned the spinner to the next section. Here was a beautifully arranged selection of blasted items. Broken windows, bullet riddled doors, wrecked house furniture. A rather macabre clear packet had some improvised grave markers. Nick left a hand on the spinner and craftily looked out into the main exhibition space. There were large trestle tables displaying all manner of military inspired models and towards one end he could hear the unmistakable chatter of war gamers. The sound of dice and the rustling of paper charts, broken by the occasional exclamation, wafted around the hall. Nick was about to move closer to the action when he felt a light tap on his shoulder.

'That you Nick?'

He turned slowly around, rucksack at the ready. A shortish bloke in camo trousers and a t-shirt proclaiming 'War gamers like it dirty' stood before him.

'It is you. Fuck. Like the hat by the way! Where have you been then?'

Nick racked his brain which was still toying with the idea of making a run for it. 'Andy?'

The shortish bloke smiled. 'Ta dah.'

'Bloody hell, how are you? You part of this?'

Andy took a step back and looked Nick up and down. 'Alright mate. In a club called 'Firefight'' He pointed vaguely back towards the main entrance. 'We specialize in Vietnam re-enactment. Got a really ace gaming table set up. I have to say mate I'm surprised to see you here.'

Nick feigned surprise. 'Why's that?'

'Gareth.'

'Gareth?'

'Yeah Gareth. Gay Panther Gareth.' Andy smiled.

Nick shrugged. 'That was a lifetime ago. I've moved on.'

Andy smiled or leered. Nick wasn't sure which. 'Well Gareth ain't moved on. In fact he's just over there.'

Nick looked lazily over there. 'Might pop over and see him then.'

'Woah there. Bad idea, if you want to live. When you didn't return to Spearpoint he went mental and vowed 'eternal' revenge or whatever.'

'Bit dramatic' ventured Nick.

'Well you knew him. The humourless twat.'

'So what happened?' asked Nick.

'After the 'Panther' incident he created a new club just for

AVF modelers and broke up Spearpoint.'

'What did you do?'

'Joined another club. One with a more relaxed attitude and then got into Vietnam war gaming a few years ago. What about you?'

'Oh you know me. I was more into buildings at the time so I've ended up getting into model railways.'

Andy smirked. 'Fucking hell, model railways? Looks too boring. Prefer the buzz of a good game. You around a while?'

'From what you say, it might be dangerous.'

Andy smirked and put his hands on his hips. 'Don't worry mate, when old Gareth gets into his war gaming he don't have eyes for anything else and they're re-staging the Battle of the Bulge or something. Gareth reckons he could win it.'

'Idiot' muttered Nick.

'Yep' said Andy. 'Anyway mate, got to get back to me boys. Nice to see you, drop by in another fifteen years.'

Nick smiled.

Andy started to walk off and then stopped and turned round. 'Hey, if you fancy a laugh go and have a look at his house, it's only a couple of streets away. Turner Street.'

'Which number?' Nick asked.

'No idea. But you can't miss it. Oh, and don't sweat it. I haven't seen you, alright?' Andy grinned, gave him a wink and walked off.

Nick needed to assimilate this new information into his overly stressed brain. He furtively looked around for some sort of refreshment. In the far corner on a sort of raised stage area was a small tea station. Nick headed there keeping to the recesses and side stands. He managed to get a small table overlooking the hall and pulling his hat further down his face he settled back to observe. What became at first alarmingly apparent and then bizarrely comforting was the presence of Gareth and his club just meters away. Luckily the thick cast iron rails at the edge of the stage provided a relatively good barrier and by slumping in his chair and tilting his hat he could watch them from an angle. Gareth was definitely still Gareth. That same cocksure stance and unwavering confidence in his own ability. Christ, he wanted to walk up to him, say 'Hello Gareth' and punch him in the face. Nick calmed himself down. What was that Klingon saying? Revenge is a dish best served cold. He decided to watch and learn. After studying him play at war gaming for half an hour Nick began to realise how dangerous he might be. Nick had briefly tried war gaming, a long time ago, and had quickly realised it was very much like playing a highly complicated game of chess. And Gareth was good. Nick watched, how time and time again, he teased and probed and niggled his opponents. Jockeying them into a position until he could unleash his deadly Tiger tank force and crush them. The worry was this guy thought ahead. Not just a few moves but seemingly far into the future. But. He had a weakness. Nick was sure of it. He liked his model Tiger tanks too much. Everything seemed to plot around them. They were like his children and when one was destroyed during play he took it very personally. How might he react if one were destroyed physically? The phrase 'both actually and literally' filtered down from his brain and he acknowledged the thought with a sly smile. Nick had seen enough but he still needed to locate Gareth's house and the tantalising thought that he had probably parked in the same street filled him with an excited energy. He carefully extracted himself from the exhibition and headed back to his car. Once there he looked ahead to where the street curved. The only possible place left for his house must lie around that corner. Sure enough, after a brief walk, Nick came across what could only be Gareth's house. To all intents and purposes it was your classic 1930s semi-detached. A generous plot and a garage to the right-hand side. What perhaps marked it out as a little odd was the garden. Nick had seen topiary before but not in the form of tanks. Naturally the biggest box sculpture was in the form of a Tiger tank, the barrel not quite fully grown but pretty close. Scattered around was a Sherman, a T34, a Mk IV Panzer, a Churchill and some sort of self-propelled gun. Nick couldn't help feeling just a little admiration for the skill, patience and dedication this would have involved. A dirty, evil, malignant thought came to him. He resisted the thought for a few seconds and then gave in. Funny how a Tiger tank could make you very, very vulnerable. He mentally noted down the security of the location, especially the garage, as he suspected that's where his prime interest would be and returned to his car.

Justine was just finishing off a crucial part of 'Project Finale' when she heard the Spitfire backing into the drive. She came out to meet him. 'That was a long adventure.'

Nick eased himself out of the car and gave her a hug. 'I know' he smiled, 'but worth it.'

Justine wriggled from his arms. 'Would Mr Skywalker be interested in a cold glass of beer?'

'God yes but first I just need to make a quick phone call.'

Justine skipped off and Nick headed for the phone table.

'Hey Chris, is that you?'

'Yep mate. Who's this…? Hang on. Is that you Nick?'

'Yep.'

'How you doing mate? You heard what happened to us?'

'That's what I'm calling about. You still undertake landscape contracts?'

'What's that got to do with it?'

'I know where the fucker lives that put you guys out.'

CHAPTER SIXTEEN: STEW AND MARGARET

'Where did you say the next round of your competition is dear?'

Stew finished eating a mouthful of fisherman's pie. 'Pring.'

'Oh they have some wonderful galleries there. If you get the time you should visit some.'

Stew chased a piece of fish and pastry around his plate. 'I'm not sure there will be any spare time dear. These competitions are pretty hectic.'

'Oh I know dear, I know. Is there any more news on this Gareth character? He sounds like he needs a good talking to with a therapist.'

Stew smiled and remembered why he never invited Margaret to their pub meetings, not that she would want to go anyway. 'Well I think Nick said he might try and arrange something.'

'I do like Nick. I'm so glad he's courting that girl Justine. He really needs something else to concentrate on. There's more to life than silly model making.'

Stew was about to finish off his meal when he remembered the thing that had been slightly bothering him.

'Margaret?'

'Yes dear?'

'I don't suppose you 'tidied' up my study a little, did you?'

Margaret pulled a puzzled face. 'Of course not. I know you men and your 'studies.' Goodness, I make it domestic policy to let you stew in your own juices.' She smiled at her pun. 'Why do you ask dear?'

He rubbed his forehead. 'Oh I don't know. I swore I left one of my train cleaning brushes next to my lamp and the other day it was back in my tool box.'

Margaret gave him a pitying look. 'You're such a creature of habit aren't you dear?'

Stew clicked his tongue. 'It's the accountant in me. I like to know where things are. I don't like objects in places they shouldn't be.'

Margaret started to tidy up the plates. 'Well, I would have thought a little brush should live in a tool box.'

Stew sighed. 'Yes, but this one always lived by the lamp and only, only goes in the tool box when I go to an exhibition.'

'Oh Stuart. Is it really important?'

He handed her the empty bowl of veg. 'Not important, just... niggly.'

Margaret started to walk off. 'I'm sure Poirot could solve the mystery of the missing brush.' She started humming the theme tune and walked off to the kitchen.

Stew watched her go and muttered under his breath 'It's not missing dear. It's in the wrong place.'

There was a clattering from the kitchen as Margaret served up pudding. She stuck her head around the corner. 'Nick wouldn't do anything silly would he? I do worry about this Gareth chap. Would you like custard?'

CHAPTER SEVENTEEN: BIG CHRIS

'Excellent. He's bang on time.' Nick said to himself as he watched Chris pull up outside Gareth's house with his Landy and trailer. He walked over and tapped the window. Chris slid it back and stared at the front garden, before staring at Nick. 'Morning Nick. A phrase you might enjoy. We're going to need a bigger trailer.'

'Oh c'mon Chris we can get that Tiger in the trailer.'

Chris coughed. 'Not if you want to keep it alive. I mean I couldn't give a flying fuck. I've got a chainsaw if you really want it in the trailer.'

Nick looked back at the Tiger shrub. He could see what Chris meant. To get it out with a big enough root ball would be tricky, especially as the mini digger had to fit back in the trailer.

'How about we nick the Sherman' suggested Chris helpfully.

Nick deflated slightly. He wasn't so sure it would have quite the effect on Gareth that he wanted but they needed to crack on. 'OK. Operation Tiger is cancelled. Operation Sherman is a go.'

Chris looked at him while shaking his head. 'Why I couldn't just beat the shit out of him with a shovel I'll never know. It'd be a lot quicker and easier…and fun.'

Nick patted him on his broad shoulders. 'Listen Chris. By the time I've finished with him he'll wish you did just that. Remember some things hurt more than mere ground working tools.'

Chris shrugged his shoulders. 'OK then. I'll put up a screen and get digging. The bolt cutters are in the back if you want to pinch out that padlock… but wait till I put the screen up.'

Within the next ten minutes Chris had effectively blocked off a large chunk of the garden with an impervious tarp that read 'Electrical Cable Repair. Ground Works' He fired up the digger and got to work excavating around the Sherman box sculpture. Nick cut the garage padlock and slipped in with his rucksack. He immediately brushed against a light cord and tugged it on. Four double strip lights blinked, stuttered and came on.

'So this is what Darth Vader's workshop looks like.'

Down one entire wall was an immaculate melamine-topped bench above which were racks and racks of tools. Each tool had its own clip and silhouette to show where it lived. A couple of wall mounted lamps were located towards the middle section. Against the opposite wall was a huge galvanized shelving system housing all manner of boxes, crates and modelling supplies. And running down the centre of the garage was a large sturdy wooden bench, upon which was a main section of Gareth's gaming board. This was the treasure he sought. Nick cracked his knuckles, breathed deeply and removed his rucksack.

It took just over an hour for Chris to dig out the root ball, tarp it up and dump it in the trailer. By the time the screen was down Nick had finished his business and relocked the garage with a new padlock. He may have broken in, but he didn't want anyone else to. He popped the key into an envelope and posted it through the door. Chris had been watching him. 'You Nick are weirder than I first imagined. What the fuck have you been up to in the garage?'

Nick tightened up the straps on his rucksack. 'Gareth likes to play people. I'm just playing him back.'

Chris grinned. 'It's like payback but with added psychosis.'

'Something like that' said Nick. 'Fancy a drink out of town?'

'OK. Go on then. When's fuck face due back?'

'Not for a couple of days.'

Chris squinted at Nick. 'How do you know this?'

'Just do' Nick looked at the large hole, most would say crater. 'Looks a tad unsafe.'

'Yep' said Chris. 'I'm hoping he falls in and breaks something.'

CHAPTER EIGHTEEN: MONTY GOES TO WAR

Monty 'The Moustache' Rawlins was back in the hot seat. His mighty Avro Lancaster pulled hard on full throttle as it sought operational altitude. This was the big one. The mission to end all missions and if he pulled it off, perhaps the war. Even though it was close to midnight the cockpit was saturated with moonlight and Clive, the flight engineer could tell Monty was grinning manically. He tried to ignore him, there was an air of excitement sitting to his left that made him nervous. Clive tapped a sticky gauge and looked through the plexiglass. A clear crisp night and a bright moon, not a great invitation to tangle with the Reich's air defence network. Cold sweat began to pool in the small of his back and his neck stiffened with tension. The intercom crackled.

'Tail end Charlie. Are we good for weapons test Monty?'

Monty picked up his intercom and turned to Clive. Clive nodded in the half light.

'Roger, Charlie. Test the hydraulics and a short burst if you please. Confirm please Tim.'

There was a slight pause before Tim in the dorsal turret answered.

'Roger, Monty. Dorsal turret confirmed.'

Monty felt the subtle change in aero dynamics of 'Lucky Sexpot' as two Thompson Frazer Nash hydraulically operated turrets went into full traverse and fired off a two second burst. The relentless drone of the four Merlin engines quickly returned as the guns fell silent.

'All good. Charlie out.'

'All good. Tim out.'

Monty could sense that Martin the bomb aimer wanted to test fire the twin Lewis guns in the front turret. In practice he rarely got to use them as the German night fighters nearly always attacked from the rear. Monty clicked on his intercom. 'Monty here. Go on Martin. I *know you want to.'*

'Brilliant… Roger.'

A lengthy delay followed as Martin scrambled forward past his bomb controls to the gun turret. There was an excessively long burst of fire from the twin guns before 'Nice, er, all good… Martin out.'

Monty leaned over and man-punched Clive in the shoulder. His crew were definitely up for it.

The intercom crackled. 'Navigator here. French coast coming up. Forty minutes from target.'

After Monty, the navigator was the only crew member to know the true nature of the mission. He had been added at the last minute when Geoff, the regular navigator, had mysteriously come down with flu.

'Monty here. Eyes peeled everyone. Charlie, watch your six. There are no friendlies here. I repeat no friendlies. Any shadows, open fire. Monty out.'

Clive nervously scanned the instruments. The oil pressure in number three engine was a little low but ok. Everything else seemed to be running fine. He squinted at the overhead moon. A huge forbidding cloudbank stretched away to port but ahead all was clear.

'Tim here. Check to port. Thought I saw a shadow. Out.'

Every available eye in Sexpot opened wide and scanned the night sky. Any unnatural movement, a flicker of exhaust fire, an approaching shadow. Anything.

Charlie the tail gunner lived in his own strange world with literally no human contact for hours, just his imagination, the moon and the intercom for company. He also lived with the knowledge that he was the primary target for the sharks. He craned his head to peer down to his right. The thick cloud bank was getting closer and darker. The darkness moved… too quickly. He swung the turret as far as it would traverse. Nothing. The clouds returned to an impenetrable dense mass. Charlie swung the turret back to rear ahead. His gloved thumb hovered above the fire button.

'Navigator. Thirty minutes to target.'

Tim rubbed a couple of the panels in his dorsal turret. It made little difference. He pushed his head up close. He briefly saw a texture, a movement and was about to drop back onto his canvas seat when he realised it was his partial reflection. He stroked the fur lined collar of his flying jacket and tried to control his breathing. His breath hung momentarily, suspended like his reactions.

Monty's initial excitement was starting to give way to a nervous determination to succeed at whatever cost but he was sensing imminent danger. It had been too quiet. They were a lone bomber over occupied France. The Germans must know where they were. He could almost hear the chatter of coms between radar stations and fighter dispatchers directing death onto their bearing. They were out there... waiting.

'Navigator. Twenty minutes.'

'Monty to crew. I'm going to start jinking a little.'

'Lucky Sexpot' started to bank left and then right. Martin moved up to the forward guns.

Tim had his eyes fixed again on the cloud bank. It had thinned slightly in the last minute and the merest of colour variations could be detected separating the dense lower half from the thinner top. It created a sort of line, a division. The division seemed to be moving. He blinked and focused. The division was getting thicker, like a wedge cleaving the cloud apart. He spun the turret to bear. The wedge shape thinned and lengthened and separated. Two distinct shadows were moving in quickly.

'Bandits, bandits, 9 o'clock.'

Monty threw the stick over and 'Sexpot' veered to starboard. A stream of tracer from one of the shadows arched out and fell towards the rear of the Lancaster, just missing the tail arrangement. Charlie frantically swung his turret and fired a burst downwards as the two shadows raced below his turret.

'110s, two of them' he shrieked into the intercom.

Monty cursed. They had a chance against one but two was going to get nasty. He put 'Sexpot' into a slight dive to gain speed and angled the rudder to give the gunners a better field of fire. Seconds later the intercom erupted again.

'Bandit 3 o'clock!' The dorsal turret opened fire.

'Bandit 9 o'clock!' Charlie tried to engage but couldn't get the traverse. The 110s were attacking in a scissors manoeuvre, splitting the defence. Monty heaved back on the stick and 'Sexpot' nosed violently upwards. Tracer fire streaked across the top of the Lancaster, punching holes in the frame and narrowly missing Tim in the dorsal turret.

'That was ruddy close, it's getting hot up here. Tim out.'

Monty's climb had just allowed Charlie to squeeze a burst off at a 110 as it banked away from its attack run. He watched his tracer follow the slender body of the Messerschmitt and connect with a rudder. There was a satisfying series of flashes as the 110 wheeled out of sight.

'A hit, a hit. Got the blighter in the arse. Charlie out.'

Monty levelled off 'Sexpot.'

'Monty to navigator. How far?'

'Hang on, hang on, ten minutes, give or take.'

Monty grimaced. So close, so close.

A sudden series of small explosions ripped through the front fuselage. The bomb aimer's dome shattered and a savage wind started to howl through the cockpit. The dorsal turret opened up and Monty watched, fascinated, as tracer chased a 110 as it veered to starboard, so close now he could see the markings.

'Bandit astern, bandit astern.' Charlie engaged from the rear turret. 'Sexpot' began to vibrate from the relentless chatter of the quadruple guns. Tracer flicked past the cockpit and raked across the port wing, before connecting with an engine. Number two Merlin flashed and died. Thick smoke streamed out.

Monty pushed full throttle on the remaining engines. The rudder wasn't reacting properly. He jinked to port. Immediately the dorsal turret opened fire again.

'Gotcha, you Jerry swine!' screamed Tim.

A 110 slewed in front of 'Sexpot', one engine bleeding fire. Martin opened up from the forward turret. Tracer glanced and skidded off the rear of the Messerschmitt. The tail section folded and it plunged immediately downwards, the port wing detaching under the murderous fire from Martin.

'Monty here, good shooting, good shooting. Status please. Charlie over.'

The intercom threw back static.

'Charlie. Status.' Silence.

'Tim. Status.'

'I'm ok, ok. Over.'

'Martin. Status.'

'Blinking cold. Over.'

'Navigation. Status.'

'OK. Shall I send Andy off to check on Charlie? Over.'

Before Monty could reply Tim was returning fire as the remaining 110 came hurling towards Sexpot in a power dive. Its 20mm cannon thumped away and bracketed the Lancaster across the dorsal turret towards the cockpit. Tim ceased returning fire. Monty wrapped his hands around the stick and plunged 'Sexpot' into a dive.

'Navigator? Where are we?'

Static.

'Navigator?'

Clive looked to Monty and started to unbuckle.

'OK. I'm ok. Navigator ok. We should be above target somewhere. Look for red marker flares. Andy dead. Out.'

Monty removed his mask and shouting above the screaming wind, turned to Clive. 'This crate has to keep flying. We have to reach the target. Do what you can. We're not returning home.'

Clive somehow knew it. This whole operation had been weird from the beginning. He started to dump any spare fuel. Engine two had completely shut off and stopped burning thanks to the steep dive.

Finally Monty caught a small break. The dive had thrown off the last 110 and it remained at altitude looking for the stricken Lancaster.

'Monty to bomb aimer. How are we?'

There was a sarcastic laugh. 'Alive. Christ knows how the bomb sight's still working… but it is. Over.'

Monty exhaled. He could still complete the mission. The sacrifice had to be worth something.

'Monty to bomb aimer. Lower doors and sight on first red flare. Over.'

'Roger that.'

Monty levelled 'Sexpot' off and looked to the horizon. Below and off to starboard he could make out a faint red glow. As Sexpot limped closer further red flares became apparent. He lined them up and commenced the bomb run.

'Monty to surviving crew. We're going in.'

She came in low, the three surviving Merlins straining at the leash. Six one-thousand pound HE bombs whistled to their target followed by a cluster of smaller incendiary devices. Monty pulled 'Sexpot' up into a shallow climb and turned to circle back around for a second run.

'Monty to Martin. The last one needs to be spot on the target area. Get this right and we can end the war.'

'Roger Monty. Just keep her steady as she goes.'

'Sexpot' came thundering in again. Lazy ack-ack fire came up to meet them but was way off target. Martin released the final payload and a small dark canister tumbled from the bomb bay, before a drag

chute deployed and a larger parachute spilled open.

'Sexpot' climbed again and began to gain altitude.

'Monty to surviving crew. Prepare to bail out.'

Captain Von Rutinger had other ideas. He'd spotted the bomb explosions and more importantly sighted 'Sexpot' illuminated by the ground fires. Rutinger had put his damaged 110 into a long, angled bank and come up behind the struggling Lancaster as it fought for altitude. He methodically began chewing up the plane with his twin Reinmetal cannon. 'Sexpot' was spent. Her starboard wing sheared off and she spiralled down in a death dive. Von Rutinger saw only two chutes escape the stricken plane as he flipped the 110 over and headed for base.

Gareth returned home late. It was dusk and the last two days had been spent dealing with some irritating commercial insurance people. At this point he just wanted to eat something and fall asleep in front of the telly. He managed to get a space outside his house and fumbled for his house keys as he walked up the garden path. The silhouette of the Tiger box stood guard in the failing light and he paused momentarily to study the form. Yes, a little pruning to the rear, sharpen up those exhaust points. He opened the front door and immediately felt the drag of junk mail trying to resist his entry. Finally, he closed the door to the world and reached for the hall light switch. He let out a tired sigh, dumped his briefcase next to the telephone table and made his way to the kitchen. It was only halfway through boiling the kettle that he shouted 'Shit' and ran back outside, where he almost broke his arm falling into a large hole in the lawn.

Monty slowly opened his eyes. He was lying in an open stretch of field, illuminated by harsh moonlight. Just ahead was the mangled wreckage of 'Sexpot.' In the distance he could make out the silhouettes of destroyed tanks. Had that been their target? The red flares had long burned out. He gritted his teeth and attempted to raise himself off the ground. It was a surprisingly pain free experience, apart from a gash to his right leg, he appeared to have survived the final onslaught with few injuries although his air force uniform was in tatters and his flying jacket nowhere to be seen. He limped towards 'Sexpot' and started to scramble among the remains for any survivors. It became rapidly apparent that there would be none, so with a heavy and guilty heart he stumbled away into the darkness, unsure of where to go or what to do.

Gareth sat on the grass rubbing his sore arm and staring into the dark void that had once been a beautifully clipped Sherman topiary. He was just beginning to get an awful sense that he had been severely done over. He hauled himself up and hobbled to the garage door. The lock was still intact. That was good. Wait. That wasn't his padlock. Shit. His heart rate started to increase. He stood a short while thinking before heading back to the house and going through the junk mail. There it was. A small plain envelope with 'key' written on. Gareth closed his eyes and tried to rein in his emotions. His heart wobbled and he coughed in response. 'C'mon, get a grip you idiot' he muttered and ripped the envelope asunder. He walked slowly back towards the garage. The padlock popped and he tentatively opened the door and reached for the light cord.

Monty stumbled on aimlessly until he clanged bodily into a dark metallic canister. He ran his fingers along its smooth curved surface until he felt a catch. He sprung it open and groped inside. There was a fresh uniform, even a cap, which he gratefully put on to fight the chilly night air. Rummaging further he found some sort of long rolled up tube, like an oversize roll of wall paper and a stick. He picked up the stick and held it up to try and see what was on the end. There was an enormous crackle and a fearsome searchlight came on, freezing him to the spot.

Gareth stood-stock still as his eyes adjusted to the light. He was expecting to find something weird in his workshop but at first glance it all looked… fine. Tools hung in their correct places. Everywhere was tidy but. But something was off. The collection of planes hanging from the ceiling looked thinner, yes, there were a couple missing. His wandering eyes fixed on to the gaming board and stopped. The scene before him confirmed the nagging thought that Nick had finally caught up with him. A line of realistically modelled bomb craters wandered crazily up the middle of the board. A formation of Tiger tanks had been caught in the carnage. Their remains lay rent and scattered among the craters. Gareth could feel his fingers clenching and his eyes begin to moisten. He moved in closer to examine the destruction. Turrets lay detached from hulls, tracks were strewn about like confetti and spread around like deformed jelly babies were the panzer crews.

So, this was what it felt like to get fucked over by an angry model maker. However, the more he surveyed the scene the more he realized these were not his models. Nick had obviously spent time creating all this. Gareth felt both relief and profound fear counter-tug at his emotions. Despite the cool air he could feel sweat forcing its way out onto his forehead and down the bridge of his nose. He walked to the other end of the board to examine what looked like a crashed plane. A fuselage lay burst open like a bloated whale. He could just make out a name painted on the side, 'Lucky Sexpot.' After the name was an illustration of a flying can-opener. Leading away from the crash site were some tiny painted footprints which very clearly led to the conclusion of this dramatic scene. Gareth craned his neck and squinted. Right at the edge of the board was an odd cylindrical canister with a parachute attached and standing next to it waving a stick with a white flag on the end was what appeared to be a railway station master.

Gareth picked up the little canister. Inside was a rolled-up piece of paper. He took it out and unrolled it.

Greetings Gareth,

I've sent my representative, Monty, to hand deliver this message. I hope you treat him as a prisoner of war and award him all the relevant courtesies.

As is obvious, we know all about you as indeed you of us. We are both highly skilled model makers and both a little bit mental. I suppose what ultimately separates us is the lengths to which we are prepared to go. On that matter don't worry about the Sherman topiary. It's safe for the time being. You should realise I don't believe in negative destruction, only constructive destruction. Which is the greater force? Perhaps we shall find out Gareth my friend.

I propose a meeting on the day of the third round in a neutral pub to discuss our differences in a gentlemanly manner.

Yours in hope of a creative solution and an end to hostilities,

Nick

Gareth rolled up the paper and placed it back in the canister. He could feel a certain sense of reality beginning to assert itself. What the fuck had he been doing for the last few months? How did he think it was going to end? Why was he so fucking cocky about leaving clues behind? This wasn't a war gaming exhibition. This was real life. The questions, the counter questions, the doubts, the shock and the loss of some shrubbery crowded his mind and began to make him very, very tired. He wandered back to the house in a daze and re-boiled the kettle.

CHAPTER NINETEEN: MEETING THE PARENTS

Justine was secretly watching Nick trying to put together an outfit. It was a very sweet entertainment and at least gave her the warm and fuzzy feeling that he was making an effort, which must mean he was taking 'them' seriously. Right? She sneaked back from her vantage point and crept downstairs to wait for him in the kitchen. Eventually and still on time Nick entered the room dressed in his 'meeting the in-laws for the first time' outfit. Justine looked him slowly up and down. She found it amusing that he looked genuinely worried and, unusually, vulnerable. She dragged out her verdict.

'Yes, like, hmm. Not sure. Maybe. Good. Oh, and that. OK. If you think.'

Nick looked a little crestfallen. Justine got up and gave him a gentle squeeze.

'You look gorgeous my love. Thank you.'

Nick relaxed. 'Thank God. I was worried it looked a little casual sailor.'

'Not at all, not at all. So where do you moor the motor yacht?'

Nick kissed her. 'To the car woman and let's get this over with.'

As they approached Justine's parent's house Nick ran over a few pointers again.

'So Stephen is a locksmith and years of dealing with stressed people has left him a little emotionally tired.'

'Correct.'

'And I shouldn't mention roller-bearing hinges?'

'Correct.'

'Why?'

'Ask him and find out.'

'OK and mum Jean works in a job centre and has been left a little emotionally tired after years of dealing with stressed people.'

'Correct.'

'Excellent. A good night was had by all.'

'Nearly here. Turn left there.'

Nick pulled into Pear Tree Close and parked up outside number twelve. As they stood outside waiting for the door to open Nick suddenly felt more nervous than he'd been anticipating. He needed this to go well. A tall blurred figure loomed up the other side of the door. Nick squeezed Justine's hand. She smiled. The door opened.

'Hi dad. Here he is. Nick this is Stephen. Dad, Nick.'

Stephen nodded and gestured them in.

'Your mother's been busy fussing around all day preparing this dinner. Do not mention the trifle base.'

They walked through the entrance hall, past the open tread stairs into the sitting room. Jean got up from the sofa.

'Hello Nick, nice to meet you.'

She gave him a hug and ushered him to sit down on the faux leather sofa. Justine quickly sat next to him.

'Could I get you a drink Nick? Beer, wine, something soft?' Stephen asked.

Nick looked up from the sofa.

'A beer please.'

'Very good. Justine?'

'Usual dad.'

Stephen nodded and looked at Jean.

'I'll stick to my orange juice dear.'

She looked slightly sadly at a half-drunk tumbler sitting on the smoked glass coffee table. On the bottom shelf was a selection of magazines; Woman, Woman and Home, Home and Woman, Woman and Horses, Garden Women and Locking Mechanisms Bi-monthly. She sat down next to Justine and squeezed her leg.

'God it's been busy at work this week.'

Nick felt he should join in.

'Justine says you work at the job centre. Must be interesting.'

Jean sighed.

'Nick. Interesting? I suppose, sometimes. Mostly it's too many desperados chasing too few jobs. Honestly, some of them come in with no qualifications or experience and expect me to find them a job at NASA or something.' She reached for the orange juice.

Stephen walked in with a small tray of drinks.

'Oh Stephen! Don't use the tea tray for drinks.'

Stephen looked puzzled as though the sentence made no sense and placed it down on the coffee table. He took his glass of beer and settled down in the big chair.

'So Nick, Justine tells me you're a computer programmer.'

'That's right, although we call ourselves software engineers.'

'Engineers? Really? Must use very little tools' he smirked. Nick smiled.

'And do you work for a company?' Stephen added.

Nick took a polite sip of beer.

'No. I'm a freelance.' Nick paused. 'A gun for hire if you

227

will.'

'And are you busy?'

'Well, I tend to be very busy for short periods of time. It's all deadline stuff but I've got plenty of contracts to pick and choose from.'

Stephen shuffled slightly in his chair.

'Well paid?'

'Daddy!' gasped Justine.

'I was just asking.'

'Very well paid, Stephen. There aren't many of us around and it's a massively growing sector.'

'Well that at least explains how you can look after Justine and do your model thing.'

Justine gave her dad some sort of Paddington stare. Stephen settled back into his chair. He'd done his duty. At least Nick wasn't a waster.

Jean got up.

'Excuse me one moment. Just got to check on the dinner.'

Nick had another polite sip of beer.

'Justine told me you're a locksmith.'

'That's right. Over thirty years. Self-employed for the last twenty.'

Nick grinned. 'And do you use tiny tools?'

Stephen laughed.

'Sometimes. Other times I just use ruddy big lumps of metal to, as we say, gain entry.'

'So what could you gain entry to? How about a safe or something?'

'Not planning an unauthorized withdrawal, are you?'

'Just interested how secure a safe really is.'

Stephen started to perk up. He'd thought that a 'software engineer' interested in models might be a boring night in, but perhaps not.

'Well, contrary to the international cat burglar myth where some la-de-da caresses a supposedly uncrackable safe open, the best way is with the right key or combination. Failing that it's a blooming big angle grinder or explosives.'

There was a loud clang from the kitchen and the merest hint of burning. Stephen looked towards the kitchen.

'Talking of explosives, I better check your mother's alright.'

Nick watched him leave and turned to Justine.

'Is this going well? Do they like me?'

Justine put her arm around him.

'I think so. Dad was at least engaged with you. He once stared at one of my boyfriends for ten minutes… in silence. Anyway it makes no difference to me if they like you or not.'

Nick smiled.

'Yeah, but it makes things easier if they do.'

Stephen stuck his head into the room.

'Dinner is served' and in a whisper, 'Don't ask about the gravy unless you have a chisel to hand.'

They filed through to the dining room, a small boxy space with a serving hatch in one wall through to the kitchen. Nick and Justine sat in their allotted seats while Stephen passed dishes of food through from the hatch.

'Nick, could you open the wine? It's in the sideboard along with the corkscrew.'

Finally, after much shuffling and re-arranging of plates

they settled down to eat. Nick tucked into his plate of roast beef with some of the trimmings. Many hadn't made it. Jean looked on nervously. Nick smiled.

'Lovely dinner, Jean. Been looking forward to this all day.'

Jean visibly relaxed and had a dainty drink of wine.

'Oh, thank you Nick. Do you cook at all?'

Nick hesitated. He'd never been asked that before. He looked to Justine for an answer. Justine took the hint.

'He's not bad mum, for a bloke. He knows the right end of a whisk.'

'He has a whisk?' sniggered Stephen.

'Yes' said Justine a little indignantly.

Stephen snorted as though at a private joke. Nick finished off a mouthful of barely roasted carrots and cocked his head to one side.

'I mainly use the whisk for mixing plaster' and winked at Stephen.

Justine gave Nick an angry look.

'Hey, I use that for doing the omelettes.'

Nick shrugged.

'I always clean it thoroughly.'

Stephen gave Jean a very deliberate smile. She beamed back.

'So… Justine. You heard about your sister?'

Justine looked up and raised her eyebrows. 'She is with child again?'

'Yes,' said Jean, 'due in February, oh I hope it's a girl. And David has had a promotion. He's now a vice executive manager.'

Justine closed her eyes and wrinkled her face.

Nick looked perplexed.

'What's a vice executive manager?'

Jean beamed.

'Well, it's a very important position within the company.'

'So what does he do?'

Stephen butted in.

'We're not sure what he does. Something to do with electrical cables and their connecting bits.'

Justine sighed and raised an eyebrow.

'Have you heard anything from Brian then? What's he up to?'

Jean frowned at Stephen who inhaled deeply and took a large gulp of wine.

'God knows. He popped by a week ago, said he had some contract work on nearby and was staying with a mate.'

'He asked after you, wanted to know if you were still seeing Nick' Jean added. She grinned feebly. 'I try to keep him up to date with everything. Oh I just wish he was more like David, I don't know, he just doesn't seem to settle.'

'What was he doing here then? What did he want?' said Justine.

'Well, he rummaged around in his old room a while and buzzed off.' Stephen shrugged.

Justine frowned. 'He didn't go in my room did he?'

Stephen looked sheepish.

'Dad!'

Jean took another sip of wine and delicately turned to her daughter.

'Have you had any further thoughts about your future

Justine?'

'Yes.'

There was silence.

Stephen gave her a stare.

'And are you going to share those thoughts?'

'Dad!'

'Dad what?'

'I don't know. I'm thinking about writing. Articles, short stories, a novel, I'm not sure yet.'

Jean looked to Nick.

'What do you think Nick?'

Nick wasn't sure he'd drunk enough for this. He had a go anyway.

'Justine's a very talented model maker, she's precise and creative… thoughtful. I think she has lots of options. Writing? Why not? Give it a go and see what happens.'

Jean pursed her lips.

'Yes, I'm not sure about all this model making business. I've never seen anything to do with it at the job centre. It's really more a little hobby isn't it?'

Nick smiled graciously and clenched his fist under the table.

'A hobby?'

'Well it's not that important. I mean no-one ever made a career from playing trains.'

Nick could feel his eye twitching. Stephen felt the subtle shift in mood and attempted to lighten the atmosphere.

'Hey, did you hear about the guy who had his garden vandalized. Apparently someone dug up one of his bushes that he'd clipped in the shape of a tank or something. I mean who does topiary tanks?'

Justine bored a hole into Nick's head with her eyes.

'I didn't hear about that dad. When was it?'

'About a week ago. It was in the local paper. There's a reward for the return of the shrub. I think it was a Sherman.'

'What's a Sherman bush?' asked Jean. 'Would it look good in our garden?'

Stephen sighed.

'The bush was shaped like a Sherman tank.'

'Oh' said Jean, with no hint of understanding.

Nick tutted.

'People will steal anything these days. What on earth are they going to do with it?'

Justine raised an eyebrow and smiled.

'What are you… what would you do with it Nick?'

Nick half choked.

'Might be funny to re-prune it to the shape of something else.' He was going to suggest a giant cock but checked himself.

'Like a bunny or something… er, peaceful.'

Stephen laughed.

'Maybe I should prune something into the shape of a key for the front garden. Might be a good advert.'

'Be ironic if that got nicked, eh Nick?' said Justine.

'Indeed it would' he laughed and put his cutlery to one side of the plate.

'That was lovely Jean. What have we got for desert?'

'Oh Christ' muttered Stephen.

Jean finished off her wine and grinned maniacally.

'Trifle surprise.'

'Intriguing' said Nick.

Justine and Stephen exchanged knowing glances.

After desert they all retired to the lounge with coffee and a large box of Milk Tray, supplied by Nick.

Jean was studying the chocolate illustrations, trying to decide what to have. Stephen sat watching her. He winked at Nick.

'This is the big difference between men and women. Women look at the options and make an informed choice. Men just pick the biggest.'

Nick chuckled.

'Not in everything, I hope.'

Jean glared at Stephen.

'No, no, you're right. But we still never look at the instructions.'

Nick laughed.

'Well it would be handy if women came with instructions.'

'Yeah, true, but we'd still not read them' snorted Stephen.

Nick paused and blew Justine a kiss.

'But it would be useful to have them there, as a reference or for an emergency.'

Stephen tried not to smile. Jean tapped her coffee cup.

'You might want to look up the bit about not leaving your pants on the bannister.'

'Mum!'

Stephen put his cup down.

'So, what are you up to next week Nick?'

Nick thought.

'I've got a couple of days coding to do, oh! And my Spitfire goes in for a major service.'

Stephen sat up.

'Spitfire eh? You didn't say Nick had a Spitfire, Justine.'

'Yes I did' muttered Justine.

'I've always thought about getting a TR6 when I retire. Something to keep me busy.'

'Nice' said Nick. 'What are you up to next week then?'

Stephen sighed and shrugged.

'Oh usual, a couple of house repossessions, upgrading locks on a few shops. No doubt helping some poor sod repair their door after a break in.'

He looked to Jean who mouthed a sympathetic kiss.

On the drive back to Nick's, Justine was unusually quiet. After a long silence he asked what was up.

'Oh, it's mum, asking me about 'my future."

'What of it?' Nick replied.

'I don't know what I'm going to do.'

'Does it matter?'

'I can't keep freeloading off you.'

Nick didn't really know how to respond. He knew he loved Justine and wanted to be with her. Beyond that… it was a bit of a blank.

'What about the book idea?' he suggested.

'Maybe.'

'Do you have any ideas?'

'Maybe.'

'Justine!'

'OK. Promise not to laugh?'

'No.'

Justine bit her lip and stared ahead.

'I thought… about… maybe… writing a short story based on the model railway scene.'

Nick remained silent.

'Well at least you're not laughing' responded Justine.

'You're going to make it a little more exciting. Right?'

'Yeah. But it's a great backdrop for some character writing.'

Nick pulled a face.

'Names of real people have been changed to protect their identity… yes?'

'Maybe.'

'And where would you submit it to?'

'No idea.'

Nick smiled.

'Sounds like a brilliant plan.'

Half an hour later they were sitting in the kitchen discussing the week ahead, when the phone rang. Nick heaved himself up slowly and walked through to the hall.

'Hello.'

'Nick, its Pete. Just phoning everyone to see if they're free for a meet up. Thought Wednesday, usual time, usual place.'

'Yeah, no problem mate, see you' and then in a whisper, 'I've done it. I've met the parents.'

'What was that? Speak up.'

'I've… met… the… parents.'

'What? Speak up.'

'I've… met… oh fuck off you wind-up merchant.'

Pete laughed. 'See you Wednesday.'

Nick put the receiver down. It was only then that he noticed a small brown envelope hanging from the back of the letter box. He reached out and released it from the door's embrace. There was no address or stamp, just Nick's name neatly stencilled on. He knew immediately the identity of the sender and held the envelope in his hand a few moments before shouting.

'Stick the kettle on. We've got a live one.'

CHAPTER TWENTY: PRE-PRING PUB

By the time everyone had assembled at the pub the mid-August sun was beginning to set and the Water Tower and Tender was bathed in a soft harvest pink.

Stew had been gazing through the window and turned to Pete.

'Well, Autumn's not far away.'

Colin overheard him.

'Christ, there's always one. I bet after the summer equinox you walk around telling everyone the nights are drawing in.'

'Well they are,' retorted Stew, 'and I go and check all the radiators.'

Pete looked amused.

'This is why Stew's in charge of engine and rolling stock servicing. A thorough man with a thorough mind.'

Colin scoffed.

'Well just don't appoint him to head of light entertainment.'

Stew sipped his little beer.

'I don't suppose you bother to check your radiators then Colin?'

Colin rolled his eyes.

'A, its summer and B, I have kids. The radiators are either all on or all off, depending on which meddler fiddled with them last.'

Pete shook his head.

'All this central heating talk is way too racy for a Wednesday evening. Can we please discuss the very imminent next round at Pring.'

'I notice you've called it the next round. It's the semis by any other definition' teased Colin.

Pete nodded.

'True and if we get through this round we get to the next one.'

'Called the final' exclaimed Colin and added 'Am I the only one excited?'

Pete smiled.

'Yes, yes, yes. Just don't want to jinx it.'

Colin looked to Nick and Justine.

'You two have been a bit quiet so far. Everything ok?'

Justine looked to Nick, who coughed, breathed in deeply and folded his arms.

'I'm afraid I won't be able to make the next round.'

'The semis' butted in Colin.

'The next round,' repeated Nick carefully, 'because I shall be at a rendezvous with Gareth.'

Everyone, apart from Justine, pulled a shocked face. Adrian's was the best.

'Will you be safe?' asked Stew

Nick laughed.

'I'm not sure, after what I did to him.'

Adrian gabbled excitedly.

'So you *did* go on a dark quest.'

Colin smirked.

'I bet you didn't pack a light sabre like I told you.'

Nick raised his eyebrows and grinned.

'Used something far more dangerous than a light sabre.'

'What, what?' cried Adrian.

'A 320JM SIX TREAD digger.'

'Oh Christ,' said Pete 'what did you do?'

'I took part of his garden hostage.'

Colin laughed.

'Please tell us that local news story wasn't you.'

Nick shrugged and looked to one side. Justine held his hand.

'I figured if I had something to bargain with it might be easier to deal with him. Plus by having the meeting on the day of the next round I can guarantee no sabotage nonsense will befall us or anyone else.'

Colin shook his head.

'At least no one can say you're not committed to the cause… although many would say you should be committed.'

Pete screwed up his face.

'Well it works for me.'

Colin interrupted.

'I possibly wouldn't say that in court.'

Pete chuckled.

'As I've said before, if it comes to that… Nick who?'

Colin nodded.

'Well, the plan works for me, especially the bit where you're not there. Easier to concentrate on driving rather than worrying about what you and Justine are up to'

'Hey!' cried Justine. 'If it hadn't been for us and the taxidermy show we wouldn't be talking about the next round.'

Colin smirked at Justine.

'I bet you kept one of the little critters, didn't you?'

'Might have' grinned Justine.

Stew let out a very large 'tut'

'You stole someone's garden?'

'Borrowed, Stew.'

'But, but you can't just steal someone else's property.'

'Borrowed, Stew.'

'But, you can't, it's not right.'

'He'll get it back.'

'Well I hope you're taking good care of his property. You can't bargain with him if whatever you 'borrowed' has died.'

Nick frowned. He hadn't actually checked with Chris if the Sherman tank was still alive.

'I can always paint it green and do a runner.'

Stew's face became serious. It was his 'I've made my point' look.

Pete took up the slack.

'No, it's good, it's good. All we have to do is turn up and run a normal timetable and we'll get through. Mind the Gap are way off the pace. If Nick can guarantee us a sabotage free run, then... excellent.'

He took a long draw on his pint of Guinness and then looked back at Nick.

'Have you and Justine generated any more models? Anything we might need to know?'

Justine stuck her hand up.

'I've been working on the allotment. Making it a bit more interesting.'

She turned to Nick quickly and whispered.

'And I found that dead Colin model buried in a compost heap.'

She returned to Pete.

'What else have I done? Oh yeah! I've redone one of the shops.'

'Not the cowboy hat store' said Adrian.

'No, God no. I've turned the curtain shop in Greenvale into a pet shop. Thought it might be a little more entertaining.'

'Yeah!' said Colin, pointing at Nick. 'Why did you model a curtain shop? Not exactly exciting.'

Nick held his glass close to his face and looked Colin in the eye.

'Depends on whether you bothered to look through the curtains.'

Colin looked at Justine. Justine smiled.

'Well at least it's one less brothel on the layout. I'll work my way round to the rest… eventually.'

Colin put his hand to his forehead and smiled.

'And what sort of pets are they selling?'

Justine waved her hands breezily.

'Oh, you know. Regular pets.'

She tried not to laugh.

Stew gave Colin a knowing look.

'Well, it's your side of the layout Colin.'

Colin simply rolled his eyes.

'Oh!' said Nick suddenly. 'Sorry Stew, but Monty is missing.'

'Lower Didsbury's station master? Why?'

'It's a long story. I'll replace him with someone else, hopefully only temporarily.'

Stew looked a little sad.

'I always have a quiet word with Monty at the start of a show. I like to tell him what we're going to do.'

Pete looked to Colin. Colin rolled his eyes for about the twentieth time.

'Yes, he does.'

'What about new rolling stock?' Pete queried.

Nick put his hands on the pub table and rapped the sticky surface.

'Not much for this round. I'm keeping back the best stuff for the final round.'

'The final' butted in Colin.

'Yes, the final round. I've created a couple of complete trains. Sounds a bit boring but I've got a brick tail for that old diesel type 42 to pull. You never use it enough and also a car transporter. About five long wagons with two tiers.'

'Like the sound of that' said Pete.

'Yeah and my cars are about the same standard as the sort of cars you sell Pete' retorted Nick sarcastically.

'Should be good then' replied Pete equally sarcastically. 'Anyway, whose round is it?'

Adrian stuck his hand up. The evening wound happily on, more so for Colin, as he realised no one was going to mention a top ten of railway disasters on this outing. Discussions included Colin's taste in music (dubious), the best filling for a sandwich (unresolved) and a healthy debate on the alternative method to destroy the death star without using small thermal exhaust ports (inconclusive, but not according to Nick).

CHAPTER TWENTY-ONE: PRING

Stew met up with Pete at Pring's civic centre car park to help put the layout together. It was a hot, cloudless, late August day and all felt well with the world. Pete was merrily whistling away as they manhandled the boards up the shallow granite steps and into the large vaulted main room that served as a general space for the town's various needs. The stress of the previous rounds had vanished and he was actually looking forward to the day's competition. Several other clubs went around getting organised and he quickly spotted their competition for the day setting up in a corner location. He motioned Stew over to take a look.

'What do you reckon Stew? Doesn't look like Mind the Gap have made any changes.'

Stew scanned the boards. It all looked together but something wasn't quite right. One end of a board looked like it needed another attaching, like an incomplete jigsaw.

'I'm not so sure Pete. Those two tracks there. They should terminate, but they don't. I think they're going to clip in some more boards.'

Pete looked again and back to Stew. The happy whistling in his head ceased and he felt the onrush of uncertainty and doubt.

'Bollocks. What sort of time table did you and Colin draw up?'

Stew closed his eyes and clicked his tongue.

'Let's see, well, a pretty standard one really. We thought about completing a solid points tally with a minimum of risk.'

Pete rubbed his chin.

'OK. Could you revise it before the judges arrive to give us a higher points margin?'

'If Colin gets here soon it shouldn't be a problem.'

'Right. OK Stew. Let's get the last board in and the rest of the rolling stock.'

Nick swung the Spitfire into the tree lined corner and accelerated. He felt the tyres grip and the sideways motion as the car fought the camber and the simmering tarmac. There was a satisfying squeal as the rear wheels slipped a little. Nick eased off the power and brought the Spitfire safely out of the bend. There were only a few more miles of open countryside before he reached the Coach and Horses, overlooking the village green of Hopston. Nick had agreed the location because it was at least an hour from Pring and therefore kept Fishplate at a safe distance from Gareth. Nick also intended to be a little late for the meeting and to keep him engaged for as long as possible.

By quarter past eleven Nick was reversing across the large gravel car park. He decided to park in the shade of a large beech hedge, with a clear view of the exit. He cut the ignition and scanned the immediate vicinity. There were several cars parked randomly around but none that he assumed might belong to Gareth. It dawned on Nick that he was the only one who recognised him and here he was sat in a pub car park, miles from Pring with no way of communicating with the other guys. He hoped Gareth wasn't going to use this as a diversionary opportunity. He looked at his watch and then hauled himself out of the Triumph. The Coach and Horses was a big old traditional inn. A stone lower story with a black timbered top half and a large mop of thatch. He paused at the doorway and admired the worn granite slabs leading into a large porch. The cool darkness of the pub seemed to flow out past the imposing studded oak door and the smell of floor cleaner, beer and old conversation was carried along by the intoxicating current. Nick comically stuck his head through the archway and had a good stare. There were a few groups of people sat around quietly discussing and supping on still full pint glasses. An old couple near the bar, ignoring their tea and each other. A fat bloke reading a large broadsheet near the dart board. No sign of Gareth. Nick turned round to look into the garden and straight into the face of Gareth.

'Morning Nick.'

'Fuck! How long have you been there?'

Gareth looked up at the sky.

'Nice day for it.'

Nick had to take a step back and collect himself.

'Yes, sorry. Well, morning Gareth.' He paused. 'Christ this is weird.'

Gareth shrugged and muttered.

'SNAFU.'

'Right' said Nick. 'Could I offer you a drink, a fight in the car park or a term in jail?'

Gareth reached into his back pocket. Nick took another step back and raised his hands in self-defence. Gareth took out a handkerchief and blew his nose. He looked at Nick's ridiculous stance and laughed.

'Summer cold.'

Nick collected himself - again.

'That wasn't an option.'

Gareth sighed.

'OK Nick, obviously a drink. After you.'

Nick walked into the pub and pointed to a secluded corner. Gareth nodded and muttered. 'Let the games begin.'

Justine had got a lift to Pring with Colin and was now fully engaged in trying to calm Pete down.

'But have you seen their layout? They've added three new boards. That's like…'

'A lot' said Justine.

'Yes, bloody hell yes. It's a lot. I hadn't factored that in.'

'Do you want me to go and get a certain stuffed rodent?'

'What? No! Er, well…'

'Calm down Pete. We'll be fine.'

Colin ambled up to them.

'OK we're good to start a warm up run. We've beefed up the timetable, just hope it's enough.' Colin looked Pete up and down. 'I was going to suggest you go get us some tea, but it looks like you're about to go pop. Pete, c'mon mate, we've got this covered. Just imagine what Nick would say.'

Justine gave him a look.

'And what would that be then?'

Colin grinned at her.

'Something daft, like… new boards, new fuck ups.'

Justine shrugged.

'Yeah, that's probably what he'd say.'

Colin slapped Pete on the back.

'See. They'll bugger it up yet, especially when they clock the numbers we're going to run.'

Pete seemed to rally.

'Yeah. Yeah, no, you're right, sorry, just got it into my head this was going to be a walk in the park.'

Colin put his arm on Pete's shoulder.

'I mean if you do fancy taking a real walk in the park, there's a lovely little café there. Two sugars for me, one for Stew and Adrian. Cheers.'

'Normal service has been resumed' muttered Pete and walked off.

Gareth and Nick faced each other across a small, round, heavily varnished table. Both had placed drinks mats under their glasses and positioned the glass in a considered and, probably in their mind, strategic location. Like gunslingers they waited for the other to twitch first. Nick thought perhaps he should take the initiative. It was after all his idea but then he'd seen Gareth wargame. Gareth never made the first move. He waited. Gareth was watching him, an air of indifference shrouded his face and made him difficult to read. Nick was going to have to lead. This situation needed resolving. Sitting here in silence was weird. Nick raised a finger, was about to say something and then stopped himself. Gareth responded by taking a sip of bitter and wiping the thin film of foam from his mouth. There was a slight bristling noise as his fingers caught the three-day-old stubble. 'Stubble' thought Nick. Strange. Gareth was the sort of person who shaved every day. Come to think of it, he looked a little dishevelled. Did he have a psychological edge here? Was Gareth in some sort of crisis? He squinted at Gareth anew. Gareth sighed and closed his eyes.

'Well you set up this meeting Nick. If you want to play a game of 'first to talk loses' then congratulations, you win.'

'Damn' thought Nick. 'Knew I should have spoken first.' He attempted a relaxed laugh.

'Where do we start then?'

Gareth smiled.

'We could start with where the fuck's my fucking Sherman?'

There was a peculiar silence in which both parties tried not to laugh at the absurdity of the question. Nick cocked his head to one side.

'All I can say for the moment is it's safe and well and enjoying the sunshine.'

'Not too much though, what with being ripped from the ground and losing half its roots' countered Gareth.

'Safe and well. Safe and well' repeated Nick, although he'd still not contacted Chris. For all he knew Chris could have stuffed it through his massive German shredder and danced naked on the remains. In fact, that might be the one of the sanest things Chris might have done to it. He secretly bit his tongue and stared at Gareth.

'So, why Gareth? What's with all this sabotage nonsense? And remember, you started it.'

Gareth slowly shook his head.

'I do remember, and if you want to be strictly accurate, you started it.'

Nick wanted to reply 'No you started it' but thought better.

'Are you referring to that thing with the Panther tank in the last Bronze age?'

'What? The gay Panther? The pink Panther? The pink Panther strikes again? Gayfang? A pound of Panther mince? Panzer Mark V gay edition? Ooh what a big barrel you have…' Gareth tailed off and stared back at Nick while taking a gulp of bitter.

Nick looked across the pub to the bar. The old couple were still there ignoring each other. How to deal with Gareth? This was an old wound.

'Do you understand why I did it?'

Gareth looked down, there was the merest shrug of the shoulders.

'Tell me Gareth. How did you get into model making?'

Gareth took a deep breath and exhaled very slowly. Nick felt there was more than just air escaping from lungs. Was Gareth's soul actually leaking out a little?

'My dad bought me an Airfix kit for Christmas. I must have been six or seven.'

Nick smiled.

'Do you remember what it was?'

Could he detect a slight moisture to Gareth's eyes? Was it really a summer cold or deeply held memories?

'A Spitfire.'

Nick nodded in approval.

'Yes. Nice. Did you make it yourself or did dad help?'

Gareth developed a far-off wistful smile.

'Nope. I glued most of that kit to my hand, got very frustrated with the instructions and ended up crying.'

Nick nodded knowingly.

'It's a rite of passage.'

Gareth picked up his pint and took a long draw, then clunked it back down on the table.

'Still, I saved up for the exact same kit and built it again a few months later. Did quite a good job. From then on, I was in. Same for you?'

'No, not really Gareth. I got into model making because it was nicer than having my shins repeatedly kicked until they bled into my school socks.'

Gareth looked down again. Nick carried his emotional

advantage.

'When you turned up at Spearpoint it just felt like being at school again, having my shins smashed to shit.'

Gareth closed his eyes and thought back. It wasn't his finest moment. To be fair, at the time he hadn't thought about anything other than model making, not even girls. Was that emotionally immature? Probably.

'Why didn't you say something?'

Nick raised an eyebrow.

'There was so much testosterone swilling around that club I doubt, at the time, you would have listened, especially as you hung out with your little male gang all the time. Still, I got your attention in the end.'

Gareth shook his head.

'And that's what you want? Isn't it? Attention?'

He studied Nick's face, looking for some sign of guilt or acquiescence, some admission. Anything to make him feel less bad than he already did. Gareth was having to let something go. Something that could have cost him dear in the last few weeks. He saw it, sitting here opposite Nick. Well. Life moves on. People forget... mostly. He didn't need the anger or the shame. The teasing that had nearly pushed him to a bad decision. That burning, stupid need for revenge, for control. Control... that's what it was all about. He needed to control everything. Why? He knew why and tried to mask it, to contain it all the time. But there was no masking it any more. He was gay.

'What? said Nick. 'Did you just say you were gay?'

Pete watched the judge look through the Smooth Fishplate timetable. This guy at least looked and sounded professional, not like the last muppet.

'Well Mr Fletcher, all looks in order. I have to say though, it's a very ambitious schedule. Do you think you can really achieve it? You will incur a large penalty for not completing your published table.'

Pete nodded positively.

'Absolutely. We're all professionals here.'

There was a sniggering from Colin, who was in earshot of the conversation. He turned to face Stew across the layout and whispered loudly.

'Hey, Stew, when are The Professionals turning up?'

'The professionals are turning up?'

'No. When are The Professionals turning up?'

'What, I don't know. What do you mean?'

Colin grinned at him.

'Never mind. You ready? Feeling good?'

Stew saluted. Colin eyeballed Adrian.

'Ready? Any nerves this time?'

Adrian grinned back.

'No nerves. Not like Thrumming. I might actually enjoy this.'

Colin laughed.

'That's the spirit.'

Nick couldn't help feeling a little like he'd won something, not a goldfish or a weekend at Butlins but a definite advantage. Gareth was wide open, vulnerable… beaten? Thing was, he felt sympathy, concern and a truck-load of guilt, well, some guilt… a little guilt. Gareth didn't look broken, perhaps more human, reborn. Nick needed to say something, anything to ease the delicate situation.

'So, Gareth? Watch much of the Olympics?'

Gareth remained staring at his pint, then slowly moved his hand up to his forehead and massaged his skin with trembling fingers. A crooked smile started to grow. His shoulders began to shake and he laughed. He laughed until the laugh became a cough and he ceased to catch his breath. Then he spoke.

'Nick, I'm sorry. Sorry, sorry, sorry. La, la, la. Could we start again? Forget the past… forgive the past and just… talk normally. I'm tired of the act.'

'OK. Alright, but I need you to do one thing for me. It's sort of pathetic and juvenile but I can't stand draws. I don't like losing. Any chance you could just say something like 'Nick I'm sorry. You win'?'

Gareth frowned and stared at him.

'You really don't know when to stop do you?'

Nick shrugged.

'No. And you're right about the 'attention' thing. I do need attention. Yes, I am flawed but I'm also a simple man at heart. I just need you to say 'I've won."

'I've won.'

No, no. 'You've won."

'Thanks, thought I would.'

Nick laughed.

'OK. Just say 'Nick you have won."

Gareth took a long heavy breath and bowed his head. He reached into his pocket and pulled out the white handkerchief.

'Nick you have won.'

'And I'm sorry.'

'For fuck's sake Nick. I'm sorry and you have won.'

Nick raised his arms.

'Yeah!'

He put his arms down.

'Same again?'

The whistle went.

'OK Stew, hold onto your hat, here we go. Greenvale-bound mixed freight coming out of the yard. To you in five, four, three, two -'

'I have control, taking it for a slow run past LD and onto Greenvale' said Stew.

'Commuter train ready Stew, sending it towards you in thirty seconds. Colin, I've got a small mixed tail of freight for the yards. Ready when you are.'

Colin clenched his fist.

'Excellent guys. We're up and running. Adrian, hook up Hadley's. Let's get those points.'

Justine smiled at Pete.

'C'mon Pete, let's go and check out Mind the Gap.'

Nick placed Gareth's pint carefully in front of him and sat down.

'You know in Scooby Doo when the villain confesses everything and then blames the pesky kids?'

Gareth could see where this was going.

'Yes Nick.'

'Well, how did you get that little block to stick on our line?'

'Just before I tell you. Can I confirm you think I'm the villain and you're the pesky kid?'

'Yep.'

'OK, well, I definitely agree with the second bit.'

Nick laughed.

'Go on, how'd you do it?'

'Lick and stick.'

'Explain.'

'I used a tiny bit of low tack double-sided to stick the block to my finger tip. I then put a blob of superglue on the exposed part of the block and -'

Nick interrupted.

'You licked the end of a finger on your other hand, touched the sleeper and then stuck the block on the wet patch.'

'Exactly. Superglue sets on contact with moisture.'

Nick nodded.

'That's how you could do it so quickly.'

'In and out' shrugged Gareth.

Nick snorted and rolled his head.

'You didn't hang around for the consequences?'

'No chance. Why?'

'I lost it and called Colin some bad things.'

'Colin's a teacher, right? I'm sure he's heard worse.'

Nick smirked.

'Maybe. So how did you break into my garage?'

'A lot more creatively than you broke into mine.'

Nick laughed.

'We have so much in common. C'mon, how?'

Gareth took a quick gulp of bitter.

'I went to the audition for a new driver and when Colin went to get a cup of tea, I took an impression of the garage key that was still in the lock.'

'What! And you did a cast from the impression?'

'Yeah, it's easy. That's basically how I make tank treads for my bigger models.'

Nick cocked his head.

'Have you still got the key?'

Gareth reached into his pocket and placed the copy onto the table. Nick picked up the key and slowly turned it over, examining the surface texture and detail with one finger tip.

'Bloody hell that's good. You cast that at home?'

Gareth seemed to perk up a little.

'Sure.'

Nick turned the key over again.

'Another question for you Gareth. How did you know I wouldn't be at the interviews?'

Gareth smiled. 'Let's just say that we sort of have a mutual friend.'

Nick raised his eyebrows. 'And?'

'And that's all I'm saying for now.'

Nick took a deep breath. 'Ok ok. Well, maybe, at some point, we could team up on the odd project.'

Gareth beamed.

'OK.'

'And you know I'm not gay.'

'Yes' said Gareth shaking his head.

'Definitely not gay' repeated Nick.

'OK then.'

'How's that box van train coming along?' said Colin, as he shunted a line of ballast wagons into a siding.

Adrian paused.

'I'm coupling them up now. Did you make any mods to them, Stew?'

Stew brought a small shuttle train to a halt and glanced at Adrian.

'No, why? Moving the timber train out of the sidings Colin.'

'It just seems a little heavier than it should.'

Colin coughed.

'Could you cease with the coffee morning and get that ballast train out to me Adrian?'

'No problem.'

'And start forming up a Pullman for the express through run… thank you.'

After observing Mind the Gap, Justine turned to Pete.

'They look alright, don't they?'

Pete frowned.

'They're certainly making use of those extra boards.'

'Not that inspiring though, is it?'

'No. No, you're right, but they're putting a load of traffic through them.'

Justine rolled her eyes and patted Pete on the back.

'If we continue as we are, we'll win, Pete. That much I can see. C'mon, be a bit more chipper.'

Pete shrugged and forced a smile.

'I'm trying.'

The sun had moved round to the side of The Coach and Horses, optimistic sunshine attempted to penetrate the small thick windows and illuminate the fuggy atmosphere. Nick was crouched over a piece of paper explaining how to build convincing model windows. Apparently, Gareth struggled to recreate glass, especially broken glass. They were beginning to get along as though no history existed between them, but Nick was still aware there were a few more questions to be answered and also a feeling Gareth had something yet to confess.

Nick put his pencil down and looked up to Gareth.

'Why now, after all this time, why now?'

There was a reflective sigh followed by a brief period of staring into space. Nick waited patiently.

'It always niggled me, like that feeling of having left the fridge door open when you go on holiday, the forgotten utility bill, er, the unsent Christmas card.'

'Nope, too easy an answer.'

'That feeling you get when you outflank your opponent and have attained the perfect cut off and you suddenly realize you might have deployed a Volksturm unit as a blocking detachment instead of your Panzer Grenadier point unit.'

'Gareth! You filthy beast. C'mon, express in some sort of way I would understand… bearing in mind my social simplicity.'

Gareth shook his head, took a thoughtful sip and leant back.

'I had a massive gay crisis and went berserk.' He smiled at Nick.

'Ok, that works for me. And might I add you sub-consciously wanted to be caught in the same way you sub consciously wanted to come out. Which, by the way, you were and have just done.'

Gareth chuckled. 'Not bad.'

Nick closed his eyes and tapped the table.

'Just one other thing. Pete picked up on it and if Pete picks up on it, then it's sort of obvious.'

'Go on' said Gareth 'as long as it doesn't involve any more gay stuff.'

'Right! Why did you sabotage the other railway clubs?'

'What're you talking about?'

'Side Line, at St Mary on the Hill and Junkyard, at Ribbington. Why them?'

'I didn't.'

Nick, for once, was utterly speechless. It would be kind to say that for a long moment, he looked like a gas boiler waiting to come on. The pilot flame flickering away but no other signs of life.

Gareth gave him a puzzled stare.

'I only went after you Nick, well your team I suppose. No one else. Why would I?'

The pilot light flickered.

'Nick?'

Ignition.

'Oh Jesus Christ there are two saboteurs!'

Gareth couldn't help a cynical smile escaping.

'My, you model rail buffs are popular.'

Nick glared at him.

'I get you. I understand why you did it. What the fuck's

this other fucker up to?'

'Is that what you called me?'

Nick snorted.

'God, the stuff we called you.' He paused.

'What do you think Gareth? What's this other bugger up to? Give me the saboteur's perspective.'

Gareth put his hands together and nodded sagely.

'Hmm. I bet you it's political… or another club desperate to win. Presumably if it's another club they must still be in. I'm guessing it's not a rogue element in Fishplate?'

Nick held out his hands.

'I'm the only rogue element in Fishplate. The rest couldn't sabotage themselves out of a wet paper bag. The only clubs left are Mind the Gap, Harbour Town and Pinewood Flyers. Can't see any of them getting frisky.'

'What about Justine?' said Gareth.

'What about Justine?'

Gareth shrugged. 'Just a thought.'

Nick ignored him. 'What did you mean about political?'

Gareth downed the rest of his pint.

'Well, you know, infighting at whoever organizes your competitions. Could be about anything though, that's the trouble with political.'

Nick sighed.

'Bet war gaming doesn't get like this?'

'Course it is. War is the ultimate extension of politics.'

'And it's a game you're very good at.'

'Good? Fucking brilliant.'

'So, what was your next move against us going to be?'

Gareth slumped back in his chair and took a deep breath. He bit his lip and smiled at Nick.

'OK, I'm going to tell you. I think we're getting along. I trust you. I'm sorry for what I've done. Please try and remember that. OK. Right. Well. I broke into Stewart's house and put time bombs in five long box wagons.'

Nick turned back into a gas boiler.

'Nick?'

The pilot light dimmed, nearly went out and then brightened. Ignition.

'Jesus Christ!'

A few people on the other tables momentarily turned and looked in their direction.

Nick turned himself down.

'Time bombs? What the fucking fuck?'

Gareth smiled.

'Don't worry, it's just foam. At approximately half past three this afternoon, parts A and B will mix and expand ten times their volume.'

Nick rubbed his chin.

'Oh good. That's fine, as long as you're not blowing the roof off Pring civic centre.'

'If you set off now you should have plenty of time to remove the wagons' said Gareth, with a slightly mischievous grin.

'And when were you going to inform me of this?'

Gareth frowned.

'It's not the sort of thing easily slipped into conversation.'

'You broke into Stew's house?'

'Well, he left a spare key out… so technically not.'

Nick shook his head.

'I don't know where to start.'

'Sorry' said Gareth again.

Nick rapped the table.

'OK. Look. What's done is done. I have to admit I thought you might be a few moves ahead. Would have been sort of disappointed if you weren't. Gareth, we shall meet again.'

Nick got up and started for the door.

'Nick?'

'Yes?'

'I still get the Sherman back, right?'

Nick paused, smiled and walked out to the car park.

Back at Pring the competition was reaching the critical half-way point and Colin was struggling with a type 47 diesel.

'God dammit, the motor's jumpy on this thing Stew. Know of any problems with old Daisy?'

'Hold on' Stew brought a timber train out of the siding and onto the main line. 'Adrian, timber train inbound. Get the school special ready to re-join the circuit. Sorry Colin. Yes, Daisy. She's got worn brushes, but I thought they were ok.'

Colin had to keep rapidly altering the voltage to try and smooth out the juddering diesel.

'She's a' crackling Stew. Adrian, when I pull the old girl into the fiddle yard, can you replace her with the big old 44?'

'No problem' said Adrian. 'What shall I couple the car transporter tail to?'

'Hold on. Stew, control of the cement train over to you in five, four, three. Go. Crap, we're running out of spare engines. Use the old 2 6 0 tank engine. Should work fine.'

The time bombs sat in the long box wagons, digitally counting down to half three. Well, four of them were. One, due to a minor fault with the battery, was running a little faster.

Car-park gravel scattered in all directions as Nick wheel-span from the pub onto the road. In theory there was plenty of time, but it was late August in the countryside and late August in the countryside meant… harvest time. Two miles from Hopston, Nick ran into the back of a queue. It didn't look like the type of queue that was moving any time soon. He got out the Spitfire and with a growing sense of panic, walked a short way down the line of cars. All had their engines turned off. Around a slight bend he discovered the blockage. An old boy stood scratching his head and working out how he was going to re-load the three tons of straw bales that had tipped off his trailer. A youth in an Escort shouted 'Stupid wanker' and helpfully bibbed his horn.

'Fuckity hell' muttered Nick and jogged back to the car.

There were already another four cars stuck behind him. He got back in and quickly consulted his map. The faded and yellowed AA road atlas indicated a very minor road that would circumnavigate this mess, a couple of hundred meters back. Nick fired up the Spit and did a tidy three-point turn, before howling off back down the road. The detour road rapidly came into sight, Nick braked hard, eased into second, dumped the clutch and accelerated round the tight bend. High grassy banks, full of tall, dry summer browns and yellows brushed past the speeding Triumph as Nick took the racing line along the narrow country lane. After a mile the lane constricted and went into a long shallow bend. Nick gunned the engine and braked gently down into third, before holding the line and easing away. As he cleared the bend, the back of a car came rapidly closer. Nick braked and dropped back into third. Before him, an old green Moggy meandered haphazardly along. Nick could just observe some sort of flowery hat, set low down in the driver's seat. On the passenger side a faded, chequered cap seemed to be nodding… slowly. Nick eased off and kept far enough back to be able to spot an overtaking opportunity.

An ancient wood lapped barn appeared to the left. The Moggy slowed still further and two hats turned in its direction. The Moggy drifted across the middle of the road, before correcting and jerking back again. A small thatched cottage appeared to the right. The Moggy slowed further and careered drunkenly across the road again.

'Bloody Saturday early afternoon drivers' shouted Nick to a cow as he slowly drove past.

A lichen encrusted sign announced a turning, coming up in half a mile.

'Turn left, turn left, turn left, fucking turn left' Nick repeated as the junction drew nearer. The Moggy didn't turn left. Its speed had dropped to twenty. The road straightened out and in the distance, a line of poplars by the edge indicated a widening of the situation. Nick hung back a little further, ready to do the pedal shuffle. Finally, a distant church spire caught the attention of the hats and they turned in unison, the Moggy veered dangerously to one edge of the road. Nick took his chance and stamped down on the accelerator, the Spit leaped past the Moggy and hit the open road again. After a hair-raising but incident-free few miles, he was able to re-join the main road towards Pring. Only the small market town of Stump Cross could foil his plans now.

'Adrian, could you get those long box wagons ready to roll. I need to shunt them into siding eleven.'

'No probs Colin. The second coal run's lined up ready.'

Stew looked over from his cab.

'Wonder how Nick's getting on with that meeting?'

Colin laughed as he cleared an empty line of flat beds from siding four to siding five.

'He's either chickened out, had a fight, or bored him to death.'

Stew sighed.

'I hope they're sorting things out. I don't like the uncertainty. Pullman leaving LD bound for Greenvale.'

Colin huffed.

'I bet he's outside a pub having a pint.'

Nick sat fuming in the Spitfire. It'd taken twenty agonising minutes to crawl to the front of the queue at the road-works and now he was stuck, staring at the moron holding the stop/go sign.

Large bent work boots, saggy jeans hanging off an arse that threatened to expose itself at any moment. A stained blue t-shirt and a faded, by now low viz jacket that had bonded together in the day's heat. A fag lingering from a slack jaw and eyes that projected an utter disinterest in anything.

Nick called out from the open window.

'Oi mate! Are we moving soon or what?'

The body remained utterly motionless, the head revolved agonisingly slowly. The fag stuck to the bottom lip, a slight trail of drool seeping from the mouth.

'You wot?'

'Are we going to be moving soon?'

It regarded Nick with an indifferent squint of one eye.

'Maybe.'

'Is it clear?'

'It'll be clear when you shut yer trap.'

Nick took the hint. It made him wait another two minutes which was just long enough for it to satisfy some sort of primordial need. It rotated the sign to 'Go.' Nick snapped the handbrake off and floored it. Finally he cleared the gravitational pull of Stump Cross and belted headlong for Pring. It was rapidly approaching three but he could still make it with time to spare if the centre was clear.

'I've got sticky points' declared Stew.

'I wasn't going to say anything' laughed Colin. 'Where?'

'The spare siding at Lower Didsbury.'

'Shouldn't be too much of a problem. What's going in there?'

Stew quickly looked at the timetable.

'You're sending down a line of mineral wagons in about half an hour.'

'Well, just watch the long carriages using the main line. Take it easy.'

'Nearly there, nearly there.' Nick moved slowly forward down the one-way road. Just another street to cross and he'd be into the centre. The old Maxi in front of him came to an abrupt halt, its one working brake light flickering alarmingly. An officious looking steward walked across the mouth of the junction and placed a couple of battered cones down. He strode over to the Maxi and engaged with the driver. There was much gesticulating until the Steward pointed back up the street. The Maxi driver leant out of his window and followed the steward's arm. With a rising feeling of panic déjà vu, Nick did the same.

Partially obscured by a tree trunk was a floppy cardboard sign, almost bent in half, announcing the annual Pring summer parade.

'Fuck, fuck, fucking fuck... treble double fuck... fuck squared, rooted and fucking fucked.'

The Maxi's engine turned off, pinked, tried to restart and then died. A transit van had pulled up behind Nick and the driver had already got his Sun paper out. Nick gently banged his head on the steering wheel. A few spectators began to assemble at the junction, awaiting the arrival of the floats. The steward stood authoritatively the other side of the cones, holding a large walkie-talkie. Nick studied him and decided he looked like a knob, but he had no other choice. He slowly got out the Spitfire and casually walked toward the steward, attempting to remain as calm and friendly as possible.

'Alright mate. Nice day for it.'

The steward smiled. 'Yes indeed it is.'

'How long do you think they're going to be?'

There was an organised fumbling in the top left breast pocket. An unfolding of paper in a precise and nimble manner.

'Let me see now. This is Hunter's Corner. Ah yes. First float due fifteen hundred hours. Last float due fifteen thirty hundred hours. A little later than last year, I believe.'

'I don't suppose there would be any chance of just letting me slip across very quickly. I would be very grateful.'

Nick got his wallet out and absentmindedly sorted through its contents. The steward watched him with an air of disappointment.

'More than my job's worth… sir.'

'How much is your job worth?' asked Nick.

'I'm a volunteer, sir, for the civic pride of Pring.'

Nick closed his eyes and sighed.

'Very good, carry on' and walked back to his car.

He got wearily in and drummed his fingers on the dash. It was almost three. At half past three, the foam bombs would go off and engulf everything within a six-inch radius in gloopy, sticky shit. He imagined Pete having some sort of mental episode, stripping off his 'Genesis on tour' t-shirt and running around squeaking like a little guinea-pig. He couldn't let that happen. The public had to be protected.

The first float started to move slowly past. It was bedecked in some sort of tropical foliage, a small troupe of Hawaiian dancers attempted to hula, while throwing paper flowers into the thin line of spectators.

Nick groaned, trapped by a crap carnival. Was this to be the undoing of Fishplate? A second float juddered past, more of a pick-up really, with a few children waving odd looking masonic flags around and generally looking maniacally cheerful.

'Jesus, what next? A car with a couple of balloons attached to it?'

Two kids walked by holding a balloon each.

'Hey kids, where did you get those from?'

The older one stopped and pointed vaguely in a direction.

'Thanks.'

Nick got out and headed in the vague direction indicated. He was just about to give up and thought momentarily about mugging the kids - '*I mean, how hard could it be?*' -

when he saw a clown standing next to a bottle of helium.

'Excellent' he cackled.

It took about five minutes to adorn his car all over with the balloons, much to the amusement of the transit driver, who shouted out a few helpful tips. They weren't.

Nick ambled over to the steward.

'I guess someone told you about the breakdown… just up the road?'

The steward looked hurtfully at his walkie-talkie. Nick continued. 'Yeah, they're looking for any available volunteers to help.'

The steward stiffened up.

'I know my duty. That way you say?'

'Indeed.'

Nick waited a micro-second before kicking the cones out the way and rushing back to his car. He edged the ridiculous looking Spitfire into the road and quickly tucked in behind a flatbed, carrying a tractor. Worzel Gummidge was busy dancing around with a bucket, throwing carrots at the crowd.

'Idiot' mouthed Nick.

His one-way exit quickly appeared on the right. Another steward stood guarding his cones. Nick waved him over.

'Hi there, got a little problem with the oil pressure. Any chance I could pull over and have a tinker?'

'Yes sir. I'll just move those cones.'

The moment there was a big enough gap, Nick engaged second and roared off down the empty road, leaving a puzzled civic volunteer and a few balloons drifting randomly in his wake.

Pete looked at his watch and smiled, he was pretty sure that failing an utter balls-up, the competition would be in the bag… their bag. Mind the Gap had been pushing but hadn't really taken advantage of their extra boards and standing here, watching Colin, Stew and Adrian running their time table, he could feel a shroud of smugness begin to envelope him. He winked at Justine and started to whistle a happy, tuneless little number. It was at this precise moment that he caught sight, out of the corner of his eye, Nick stumble through the exhibition entrance, look wildly around, clock him and come running over.

The judge looked up from his clipboard and flashed the sweating Nick a certain look. Nick took the hint and ushered Pete to one side. Justine tucked in behind him.

'What the hell's happening?' said Pete in as quiet a whisper as was reasonable under the circumstances. Nick glanced at his watch.

'Listen, don't interrupt, Gareth has placed foam time bombs in the long box wagons. They go off in seven minutes. We need to get them in a bag, away from the layout. I do not want to be spending any more time chiselling things out of insulating foam.'

'Hang on' said Pete and walked calmly over to Colin. There was a tense whispered exchange, Stew briefly ducked and then sat up again. Pete walked smoothly back, smiling and nodding at the judge. He got tight up to Nick.

'Colin says the box wagons are in a remote siding and aren't due to be cleared from the layout for another… wait for it… six minutes.'

Nick shrugged. 'Sod that, just lift them off the layout with your hands.'

Pete shook his head violently.

'No fucking way. We'd lose too many points. That's a total no-no.'

Nick glanced over towards Mind the Gap.

'Can we take a big points hit and still win?'

Pete pinched his nose.

'Fuck knows, to be honest I'd rather we get them off the layout via our timetable.'

Nick stared towards the layout.

'Think Colin and Stew can do it?'

Pete rubbed his forehead violently.

'This is where Colin has to live up to his reputation.'

Colin was already taking charge.

'OK lads, we've got to move those wagons quick and maintain the timetable. Stew?'

'Yes Colin.'

'You're going to have to run traffic over those sticky points, faster, not slower. We have to speed up this section of the schedule. Adrian?'

'Yep boss.'

'We've got three more full trains to run from your fiddle yard. Reduce each down by a quarter, we'll lose a few points but it should cut the risk by a margin.'

'OK boss.'

'And Adrian…'

'Yep?'

'Get a bag or something ready. The second those box wagons enter the fiddle yard, in the bag. Bag to Nick. Nick runs screaming out the hall.'

'Got it.'

'OK, I'm going to start shunting those box wagons up to the main line. Soon as the Pullman clears, I'll bring them down the line with our class 20 diesel. Stew?'

'Colin?'

'Think you can handle the class 20 when I transfer it to you?'

'Well, I'll certainly do my best.'

'No Stew. You will be a mother fucking tyrannosaurus rex… and own it.'

There was a puzzled silence.

'Stew?'

'A what?'

'Just do it.'

Pete unstrapped his watch and held it up.

'When do you reckon Nick?'

'Gareth said three thirty.'

'Fuck!'

'What?'

'Can't remember if my watch is fast or slow. What does yours say?'

'Three twenty-six.'

'Mine says three twenty-five' Pete groaned. 'Is yours fast or slow?'

'No idea mate' laughed Nick.

'It's not funny Nick.'

Nick closed his eyes and patted Pete on the shoulder.

'The lads know what time it is, they're running to a tight schedule. The real problem is, what time do Gareth's bombs think it is?'

Colin edged his little 060 shunter up to the box wagons. He flicked the speed up and immediately hit reverse. The shunter jumped forward, delicately coupled up with the wagons and started to back up. He could sense a little more resistance than normal. Adrian was right, they were heavier but at least this made them slightly smoother to move. He could feel the tense eyes of Pete, Nick and Justine watching his hand movement. Colin flicked a couple of point switches. Little solenoid motors whirred and the turnouts redirected the small train on to a secondary line.

'OK. I'm disconnecting the shunter and bringing the type 20 in. The deliberately dirty looking type 20, known as 'Pinky' rattled towards the line of wagons. Colin had to be careful. Pinky was heavy, studiously so. He'd instructed Stew a couple of years back to at least double its weight, to help with traction and now every spare nook and cranny, within the model, was packed with lead ballast. He couldn't afford a sudden jolt while coupling up but thanks to a relaxing evening (for Stew) spent cleaning all the electrical contacts, Pinky was happy to be gently finessed by Colin.

Stew looked over his shoulder briefly.

'Colin, I'm sending the Pullman up the line from Lower Didsbury. When it passes, you have a clear route.'

'Excellent Stew. When you take control you're going to have to run it over those sticky points at speed. Do not slow down. Pinky needs the momentum.'

'OK, if you think so.'

'Trust me Stew.'

Pete's eyes were transfixed on the roofs of the box wagons. He was trying to detect any movement, any bulge that indicated a detonation. He peered at his outstretched watch. 3.28.

Nick had ushered Justine to one side and was having what appeared to be a slightly undignified 'domestic'. Pete shook his head and mouthed. 'Unbelievable.'

The Pullman cleared the main line.

'OK Stew. I'm bringing Pinky on. When she transfers to your circuit -'

Stew butted in. 'Fast.'

'Grease lightning Stew, grease lightning.'

'I've got the bag ready' whispered Adrian.

Pinky began to accelerate towards the tunnel entrance. When she next re-emerged, it would be under Stew's control.

Pete thought he saw one end of the roof lift on wagon three. Yes it was. The roof was beginning to tilt. He hissed at Nick.

'Number three's gone off!'

Nick gave him the merest of nods and turned back to Justine. He put his hands together in mock prayer, his eyes wide open, imploring, screaming silently at her. Justine closed her eyes momentarily, and then suddenly walked towards the judge, dismantling something under her t-shirt.

Pinky emerged from the tunnel. The third wagon had lost its roof and what looked like a loaf of bread was expanding slowly upwards. The judge looked up from his clipboard. Justine blocked his view, raised her t-shirt and gave him an entirely new vista to evaluate.

Stew pushed the power lever to max as he watched the foam expanding ever higher. It was also starting to billow over one side. Pinky hit the sticky points, there was a judder that rippled along the length of the train. The roofs on wagons two and four began to rise, little specks of foam began to escape.

Justine snapped her t-shirt down and ran off, quickly followed by Nick.

The judge briefly followed her flight before shaking his head and turning back to observe Fishplate.

Pinky disappeared into the tunnel that would take it to the fiddle yard and the waiting bag. A smear of foam above the tunnel entrance the only clue as to what just happened.

Pete's eyes had nearly burst. Foam, trains, tits, judges, winning, losing. He tried to concentrate on something. Adrian was waving a rapidly expanding bag at him.

'Shit!'

He walked over, grabbed the bulging package and ran off.

Colin spoke.

'OK. OK. We've done it. But there's another half hour to go. Everyone ok? Stew?'

'Goodness that was exciting, my hands are shaking.'

Colin laughed.

'I know, I know, mine too, but now we have to keep going. Adrian? OK?'

'Yes. The foam's all clear, I'll just tidy up the tunnel entrance and nothing will have occurred.'

Colin looked tentatively towards the judge.

'Adrian, did the judge see anything?'

'Unlikely Colin.'

'Why?'

'Justine flashed her tits at him.'

Colin failed to stop a line of carriages quickly enough and they smacked into a buffer stop.

There was a 'tut' from the recovered judge and a small reduction of points.

Colin refocused.

'D'you think we'll get extra points for a quick flash?'

'Two points definitely' sniggered Adrian.

Outside, on the expansive granite steps, Justine sat enveloped in Nick's arms. She was deeply upset, more so because Nick had meant her to just flash her bra… not that that was much more honourable. She sobbed quietly into her folded arms, cocooning herself against the outside world and trying to understand what she'd done. Nick tried to console her.

'I'm so, so, sorry. I couldn't think of any other distraction in two minutes that would have worked.'

Justine wiped her eyes.

'I feel… dirty… and used.'

'What can I do?'

'I don't know. This competition stuff… it's all getting out of hand. I'm not sure I want to be part of it.'

'Justine?'

She pushed his arms away.

'I want to go home. I want to go back to Pear Tree.'

Nick felt sick. None of this was worth losing Justine over.

'What can I do? How can I make it better?'

Justine stood up.

'Just… take… me… home.'

Nick backed up.

'OK. OK. The car's this way.'

The journey to Pear Tree was made in silence, apart from the inappropriate squeaking of helium balloons.

CHAPTER TWENTY-TWO: NICK, JUSTINE AND PETE TOO

Helen couldn't believe it.

'She did what? Why?'

Colin hadn't realised this revelation would elicit quite the reaction it had.

'To distract the judge.'

'Oh poor girl, how humiliating. That had to be Nick's idea, right?'

'I guess so. They left without saying anything.'

Helen added a sugar to her tea and stirred it in.

'Ooh, that's bad. That's deadly serious.'

Colin scratched his head.

'What, break up bad?'

Helen looked at him.

'If you tried to make me strip off for the sake of toy train land...'

Colin flinched and put both hands up to protect his face. Helen laughed.

'Exactly.'

'Well, on the plus side, I bet we've got through to the final.'

Helen gave him a long pitying look.

'You know I love hearing about your sad exploits and boy-oh-boy, has this campaign trumped all the others, but, really, is the breakup of a relationship worth it?'

Colin shrugged. 'We don't know if they have.'

Helen sipped her tea.

'Y'know I like Nick doing mad things, but I was feeling really happy about him finding someone. God knows he needs it.'

'Look, I'm sure they'll be alright.'

Colin paused and looked into the lounge.

'Could I just ask what that thing is next to the sofa?'

Helen raised an eyebrow.

'That, daddy, is your reward for playing trains all day.'

Colin looked again.

'A badly sellotaped cardboard donkey?'

Helen folded her arms and tutted.

'Oh no! No, no, no. That is a state-of-the-art AT-AT. You know jolly well who spent all day building it.'

Colin started to creep away.

'And they expect you to finish it. In other words, your job is to make it look like an AT-AT, not an ass.'

Colin stopped sneaking away and turned to look at Helen. She was wearing a very shapely charcoal grey shirt, over the top of which, hung seductively, an open cardigan.

'Tell you what, show us your tits and it's a deal.'

Luckily he had a head start.

A couple of evenings later Pete dropped in on Nick.

'Hey Nick, how's everything?'

Pete stepped into the hall and closed the door. Nick looked rough, unshaven, still wearing the same clothes from Pring on Sunday. He led Pete to the kitchen and flopped down onto a chair.

'She hasn't called then?'

Nick lifted his hand pathetically off the table surface and back.

'Cup of tea then?'

Nick shrugged.

Pete filled the kettle and attempted to find two serviceable mugs from the carnage that used to be the sink.

'Look, you need to buck up. We've got to get a plan together for the next round.'

Nick frowned. Pete watched him as the kettle boiled.

'I don't know officially but I'm dead sure we're in the final round and… this is going to blow your mind.'

Pete stopped talking. Nick was staring at a stuffed owl.

'Nick, c'mon.'

Pete placed a mug of tea in front of him and sat down.

'I talked to Fat Bob to see how they got on and he said it was a disaster.'

Nick continued to stare at the owl.

'Said they had three derailments and are almost certain they're out.'

Nick sniffed.

Pete took a gulp of tea and stared at Nick. This wasn't looking promising. How to repair a broken heart in, well, a week max? He really needed Nick, Justine less so, but Nick… he definitely needed Justine. Pete took another gulp of tea and patted Nick on the shoulder.

'OK. Nice talking to you, I'll let myself out.' Pete got up and left Nick tracing circles of sugar on the table top.

The next morning Pete was sat in his office staring at the wall, an untouched mug of instant coffee by his side. He tapped his fingers continually on the edge of the veneered desk as if following a looping soundtrack. There was a knock at his door. Mike popped his head through.

'Hey Pete, guy interested in that Princess we've had parked on the back lot for... six months? Seems keen.'

Pete looked at Mike and stopped tapping.

'What? Princess. OK.'

He picked up his mug of coffee, took a sip, pulled a face and put it down again.

'You ok Pete?'

'Yeah, bit distracted.'

Pete walked out to meet the customer, who was kicking the front offside tyre.

'Morning sir, I hear you're interested in this... car?'

'Yes.'

'Why?'

'What?'

'It's a Princess.'

'Well... yes... that's why I want to buy it.'

Pete wanted to be professional, he really did, but he also wanted to win the final. They were close, so close. To be honest he couldn't really raise much enthusiasm for this deal. Bollocks to professionalism. He needed Nick back. That was his priority. This guy was just in the way.

'So you want to buy it?' said Pete.

'Well, I'm not sure about the price.'

'So you don't want to buy it?'

'Yes, but could we do a little better on the price?'

'No.'

'But the paintwork's a little bubbly, especially on the nearside front quarter panel.'

Pete took a scornful look.

'Yeah, that's pretty standard for this model.'

'Well, the vinyl roof needs a bit of re-sticking and the window seals are a little, er, mossy.'

'Mossy?' said Pete.

'Well, very green… look… there's some moss here' he picked out a little green sludge and flicked it away, before smiling at Pete.

How was he going to get Nick back? Obviously he had to get Justine back to him. Where did her parents live? He had it written down somewhere. He took his wallet out and started to rummage.

'Excuse me.'

Pete looked up from his wallet.

'The Princess?'

'What about it?'

'Can you do a deal?'

Pete found the address on the back of an old receipt. Excellent, maybe he should go round. Hang on, not while her parents were in. They both worked though, didn't they?

'Hey!'

'Oh sorry. Yeah. Right.' Pete took a step back and waived his arm expansively at the car.

'You see what we have here is a crap green Austin Princess 750 HL. You won't find another like it as they've all rusted away or been crushed because they're so unbelievably shit. We've had it standing here for half a year with zero interest, which is why it's 'mossy.' I have no idea if it will even start. It's done quite a high mileage, which is frankly surprising, given how bad they are but if you still want to buy it then fine. Am I going to do a deal? No, because as far as I'm concerned this is the last Austin Princess 750 HL left in the world and scarcity makes it valuable. If you want a deal, find someone else with the bollocks to have one of these eyesores on his car lot and haggle with them.'

Pete turned on his heels and started to walk away.

'OK. Alright, keep your hair on. I'll take it.'

Pete stopped and shouted to Mike across the yard.

'Hey Mike, this genius wants to buy the Princess, sort out the paperwork will you. I've got to pop out for the rest of the day.'

It took a while to find Pear Tree Close and as Pete pulled up outside the house he began to feel sick with nerves. It had occurred to him while driving over that turning up with no plan might possibly make things worse. He just needed to get them together again. It was obvious Nick couldn't function any more without her, he was pretty sure she wasn't too far behind. He was about to find out. Pete slapped himself.

'Jesus. This is ridiculous. I'm nearly fifty and I'm buggering around passing notes in the playground.'

He got out the car and walked up the short path to the door. He hesitated, almost turned back, scolded himself and knocked on the glass panel of the door. The noise reverberated deep into the house. Silence. A blackbird took to the air, releasing an alarm call. He knocked again, a little slower and cocked his head to one side like an alert dog.

Nothing.

'Pete?'

He whipped round. Justine stood next to his car, holding a small bag of shopping.

'Justine… how are you?'

She regarded him while slowly swinging the plastic bag.

'OK Pete. Can't imagine what you're here about. Cup of tea?'

Pete sighed in relief.

'Yes, that would be lovely, thanks Justine.'

Justine curled up into the sofa while Pete perched on the edge of an armchair. He put his mug of tea down carefully on the smoked glass coffee table. He didn't quite know how to start.

'I… went to see Nick yesterday evening. He's not in a happy place. To be honest, he looked awful.'

Justine absorbed the information but remained impassive. She stared into her mug of tea.

Pete looked round the room and back to his clasped hands.

'I was hoping you might agree to meet with him.'

Justine made the slightest of head movements. Pete couldn't tell if this was good or bad, or worse, indifferent.

'I could drive you over.'

There was the merest release of exhaled air before Justine took a thoughtful sip of tea and her eyes fixed on something in front of her feet.

'Pete?' she said softly. 'Do you think he's using me?'

He frowned.

'I don't really know what you mean. I suppose I've used you for your model making talents, if that's what you mean. I don't think Nick looks at you in that way.'

Pete paused to reflect.

'He's never involved anyone else in his world. You're the first... if he has used you, it's a compliment, believe me. You know how tolerant he is of others' abilities.'

Justine sniffed softly.

'But he did use me. He put pressure on me, unfairly. He used the situation at Pring to force me into doing something stupid. I mean, I get caught up in the events too. I know what this competition means... to you all. I want to help, to be part of it, but...'

Pete gestured.

'Go on.'

'Would he have asked you to do something like that?'

Pete smiled.

'Oh Christ yes, he just makes it up as he goes along, reacts to the situation at hand.'

'But it's different for me. What if I'd said no?'

Pete winced.

'Well knowing Nick he'd have done something even more stupid. He was just looking for a way to win.'

Justine stared into her mug.

'What if he does something like that again?'

'He won't.'

'How do you know?'

'I know. Since he's been with you, he's changed, become way more...'

'More what?'

'More adult, certainly about you. And he needs to carry on learning about being an adult and dealing with the consequences of his actions.'

Justine smiled for the first time.

'Yeah, he really is a big kid.'

'Exactly. He just forgets now and then what should pass as adult behaviour but Justine, please believe me, the Nick I saw yesterday was broken. I've never seen him like that before… and he's been dumped at least four times since I've known him.'

'Four?'

'Yep, and to be honest you'd never have known. He'd just say stupid things like, 'plenty more Lego in the box' or 'sniffs in the glue tube'. Yesterday he didn't say a word. Not a thing.'

Pete thought he saw just the merest flicker of concern in Justine's features. He continued.

'The kitchen was a dump. He hadn't shaved. There was post still on the floor. I mean, you know how he likes an ordered house.'

Justine was definitely looking concerned. Pete noticed this and motored on.

'I told him all about the goings on with Fat Bob, all the stuff he needed to do. Not bothered, just sat there staring at a stuffed owl.'

'Prof.'

'Eh?'

'The owl's called Prof.'

'Right. Well. Point is, I've never known anyone mean more to him than you. You need to see him.'

Justine uncurled her legs and put the tea down.

'So, in summary Pete. Nick's broken down and I'm the only spanner in town that'll fix him. You need Nick to help you win the competition and in that regard I'm invaluable. Right?'

Pete dipped his head.

'True… and yes I am using you for my own ends, but I don't love you Justine. Nick does. And the fact that Fishplate gets Nick back is, let's just say, a happy bonus.'

'But you are using me.'

'Yes.'

'OK. Let's go.'

Pete could feel the tension in his stomach ease. Things looked they were going in the right direction again and with a positive outlook restored, he led Justine to his car. He dropped her at Nick's and got the hell out. He'd done all he could. The note had been passed on in the playground and it was up to them now.

Justine thought about letting herself in but decided, perhaps, it might be better to knock. She rapped a slightly slower version of their special 'tune'. The door was opening before she'd finished. Nick stood there, trembling.

'Are you coming back?'

'Promise never to put me through anything like that again.'

'Promise.'

'I'll come back then.'

Nick flung himself out and wrapped his shaking arms around her, lifting Justine bodily from the step. They remained motionless for a while, bound together. Nick breathed in and whispered to the nape of her neck.

'I was beginning to forget what you smelt like.' Justine could feel his tears against her skin.

'Talking of which, you could do with a shower Nick.'

He released her slowly and smiled.

'Come and live with me. Please? I can't function without

you.'

Justine kissed him lightly on the lips.

'OK, I'd like that.' She held him by the hand. 'And we can discuss terms over dinner tonight.'

Nick stuttered. 'I might have to clean the kitchen a little first.'

Justine shook her head.

'Discuss terms over dinner in a very nice restaurant.'

'Yes, I need to book a restaurant.' He put his hands on her hips. 'I love you so much.'

Justine beamed.

'I love you too, sailor.'

CHAPTER TWENTY-THREE: MR MOUNCEY

Mr. Mouncey was the chief of Greenvale's transport and traffic integration department. In other words, he was their only traffic warden. Such was his reputation that when a car owner found a place to park, that is, a legal place to park, they tended to stay there. Indeed, many never moved again.

Mr. Mouncey was currently standing in the main Greenvale station car park, next to an old Ford Anglia that appeared to be parked slightly over the delineation of the official space. He had whipped out his tape measure, noted a few precise measurements in his beloved navy, regulation department pad and had been about to write a number three parking offence docket, when a rather odd thing occurred. The cast iron drain cover, just to his right, started to rattle and vibrate. He had instinctively put his big standard issue boot on the cover to see if it stopped… which it did. But the moment he removed his boot, the rattling continued. Mr. Mouncey looked around the car park and its environs, there appeared to be no building works that he could observe that might account for this. It was a most bizarre thing. He noted it down. In truth this wasn't the first strange occurrence in relation to Greenvale station car park. Two weeks ago, a thin subsidence line had appeared around the entire perimeter and only last week it had been reported to him by a few worried owners that their cars were apparently changing spaces overnight.

Mr. Mouncey put his department pen and pad into a deep pocket and pulled out his official contemplation pen. It didn't work, in the sense that it had no ink, but it did work as a thinking aid, especially if lightly chewed and accompanied by a hummed rendition of Moon River. Mr. Mouncey prided himself on his ability to spot things in places they shouldn't be. It was why he was so good at his job and he'd had a disquieting feeling in the last few days that something in the car park wasn't quite where it should be. He gave the site his full and unqualified attention. The inclement weather shelter or shed, was as it should be. He mentally noted it could do with a new layer of roofing felt. A pile of parking cones was neatly stacked next to it. All the potted planters were in their exact location, apart from one, which the widow Margaret Spencer had accidently bumped into the other day. Every single fence post was correctly aligned and the small stand of birch trees in the far corner, planted in memory of the late Mayor, was as it always was. He stopped chewing the pen and blinked. The soft rendition of Moon River ceased. His brain did a little unexpected somersault and didn't quite land right. By jingo, he could see what was out of place. It wasn't that things in the car park were misaligned, it was the rather puzzling fact that the entire car park was out of place. It had moved several meters towards the railway line.

CHAPTER TWENTY-FOUR: BACK TO THE PUB

Precisely one week later, the last meeting of Fishplate before the final round took place at the Water Tower and Tender. It was a murky September evening, a night for conspiracy, plans and revelations.

Pete looked round the table as he sipped his Guinness. Everyone looked, at least for the moment, relaxed and chilled but he knew the next round was going to be the toughest yet. There would be nowhere to hide and to be so close to winning would really test their nerves.

'So Pete, what the hell happened at Pring? No one has fully explained that incident with the exploding wagons' Colin folded his arms and lowered his head towards Pete.

Pete nodded in acknowledgement. He wondered if he could get away with the small matter of the break-in at Stew's, which he hadn't quite got round to mentioning to Stew yet.

'Well, if I could perhaps speak on behalf of Nick on this one.' Pete glanced at Nick, who smiled and faintly nodded. Pete took a long breath.

'The exploding wagons were a present from our friendly neighbourhood saboteur, Gareth.'

Colin nodded.

'Yes, we get that. My question is how?'

'How they exploded?' said Pete, expressing a hopeful face.

'No Pete, we know how they exploded. We were there, trying to deal with it, remember? We want to know, how were they booby trapped?'

Pete stole a glance at Stew, who was happily munching on some nuts and enjoying the warm social atmosphere. Pete felt like a deer stalker, watching a gentle little doe-eyed deer sipping at a small woodland pond, just before he blew its brains out.

'OK. Gareth sort of got into Stew's home and sabotaged them there.'

Everyone looked at Stew. He stopped nut munching as a pitifully hurt expression slowly descended over his features.

'He broke into my home, into my… my inner sanctum?'

Nick stifled a double entendre. Pete tried on his best calm face.

'I wouldn't say 'broke in' as such. I believe he used a key that you kindly left supplied in a concrete frog, or was it a snail?'

Stew squirmed uncomfortably in his seat and muttered something indecipherable about garden centres. Nick felt he needed to help the old boy out.

'Stew mate, Gareth's as mad as a bag of hammers. Nothing you could have done, or not done, would have stopped him. At least leaving a key out saved you a few repair bills. He's a professional nut job, well up to my standards.'

Nick winked at Colin. Colin took the prompt.

'Glad you said it, saved me the effort.'

Stew looked back at his nuts.

'I should have known something was up.'

'Whys that?' said Pete.

'My little cleaning brush was in the wrong place. I remember feeling unsettled about it.'

Nick chipped in. 'He's a very thorough madman, and gay too. Probably why he tidied up afterwards.'

Colin put his head in his hands.

'How do you know all this stuff? I remember when we just used to go and exhibit trains. Now we're up against a psychotic war gamer called Gareth, who is now additionally gay. What next? He's also from Saturn?'

Nick shrugged.

'To bring you bang up to date, Gareth has been disarmed. He is genuinely sorry for all that has occurred and hence forth will not be a problem. And I... er... actually got on with him quite well.'

'I knew it. I bloody knew it!' shrieked Colin.

'Yeah, yeah, yeah' replied Nick.

Colin calmed down.

'So Luke Skywalker and Darth Vader got on like a house on fire?'

'Yes, although Darth Vader turned out to be gay' said Nick.

Colin smirked.

'Well, you just had to look at his outfit.'

Stew looked confused.

'Gareth or Darth Vader?'

'Darth Vader' shouted Nick and Colin in unison. Everyone but Stew laughed.

Pete nodded.

'So in terms of the final round we don't have to worry about any more sabotage nonsense?'

Nick raised his hands up and slowly put them together.

'Here we go' announced Adrian. 'I recognise all the signs of an imminent revelation.' He prodded Stew and smiled. Stew started to eat his nuts again. Nick closed his eyes.

'Sorry Pete. I thought I'd keep this latest, revelation,

thanks Adrian, 'till now.'

'Well, lucky me' muttered Pete. Nick continued.

'Gareth only sabotaged us.' He let the news sink in. Pete and Stew looked confused. Adrian grinned maniacally. Colin managed to look both angry and confused.

'Hang on, so there's some other loon out there going around derailing shit for whatever reason. Does this situation strike anyone else as a little mental? Isn't life hard enough that we can't even bloody play trains without someone having some stupid idiotic agenda to mess it all up? Honestly, you'd think the model railway scene would be the one place of relative sanity.' Colin slowly looked around the table. 'OK. Alright, the scene's full of strange people but c'mon, I mean!' Colin ran out of words and threw his hands up in frustration. Pete took over.

'Any idea who this other lunatic might be?' Nick assumed his pondering face.

'Well I was talking to Justine about this and she surprised me by suddenly producing this.' Nick reached under the table and brought out a dog-eared newspaper. He carefully unfolded it and turned to the middle page. Colin leant over and read the main headline.

'Courgettes are easy to grow and full of vitamin C.'

'What relevance has that to anything?' enquired Pete.

Stew looked pleased. 'Well it's about time someone stood up for courgettes, they're a most under-rated vegetable. Margaret grows loads of them.'

'What's a courgette?' Asked Adrian. 'Is it like a marrow?'

Stew was about to answer but was prevented by Nick roughly placing a hand in front of his face.

'Ok, enough. For fucks sake could I just tell you about the small article below the fucking courgette story?' Nick grabbed the paper and folded it up again.

'It's all about South Korean betting syndicates.'

Colin smirked. 'Guess the weight of the courgette?'

Nick laughed. 'Actually that may be nearer the truth than you think. Apparently there are these really wealthy businessmen in Asia who have way too much money and love to blow it by gambling on bizarre competitions.' He paused to let everyone catch up. 'And when I say bizarre I mean stuff like 'best kept village in Somerset' and the winning club in the 'Norfolk over 60s bowling league.' Justine wondered if this second saboteur might be trying to fix the outcome of the regionals for some betting scam or something.'

Pete pushed out his lower lip. 'I guess that might make some sort of sense. But South Korean betting syndicates, really?'

Nick shrugged. 'Well, it was just a suggestion.'

'How about this for an idea then?' Colin tapped the table for attention. 'Let's say, for arguments sake, that a bunch of idle, rich, bored Asian business men have put down obscene amounts of money on the outcome of a model railway competition. What if, they've bet money on us winning? It would mean that the saboteur would, in effect, be helping us to win.'

There was a collective 'Ah' and sage-like nodding.

Stew was disapproving. 'Well I don't think that's a very sporting way to win.'

Nick took a short sip of JD. 'No need to worry about sticking to the Queen's rules Stew because I can absolutely guarantee that if there is a large sum of money at stake, it won't be placed on us to win.'

Stew finished his nuts and carefully folded up the empty packet and placed it into the plastic Fosters ash tray.

'Has anyone thought about talking to our regional rep

about all these goings on?'

Pete shook his head slowly.

'Our rep is hopeless, he doesn't even live in the South East. Besides, if there is some sort of betting conspiracy, I'd rather keep it to ourselves. I don't want 'them' knowing that we know.'

'But we don't really know anything' said Stew.

Pete grinned.

'Yeah, but they don't know that.'

Colin smirked.

'But we don't know that they don't know that we might know.'

Pete folded his arms.

'There's a big difference between assuming someone knows or perhaps doesn't.'

'No there isn't' said Stew.

Adrian butted in.

'I'll get the next round in, it's all getting a bit surreal for me.'

'Anyway,' said Pete, 'we have to proceed on the basis that we may or may not be sabotaged in the final.'

'Excellent plan' mocked Colin. 'So on that basis, what sort of time table are we going for?'

Pete slowly got to his feet and spread his arms.

'My friends… we are going all out.'

Adrian watched George, as he pulled the various pints and placed them down, like errant kittens, onto the battered drinks tray. Finally, with a wheezy sigh, George fulfilled the order. He turned to Adrian.

'What you discussing tonight then mate? Tension in the Middle East? Liverpool to win the cup? Interesting Attenborough documentary?'

'Model trains' replied Adrian matter-of-factly.

'Model trains you say. Crickey, same as last time then.'

'Yep' nodded Adrian.

'And the time before.'

'Yep.'

'Do you ever talk about anything else?'

Adrian rolled his eyes upwards and thought. George observed him with humourless eyes.

'I think… we might have talked about Star Wars.' Adrian smiled again and handed over the right cash. He picked up the tray and carefully headed back over to the table.

George wiped the bar top with the towel that hung permanently over his shoulder and shook his head sadly.

'I need normal people in here. Normal God-fearing, telly-watching, football-loving normal people.' He sighed again and looked over to the small window table. 'Pigs alright Dave?'

Colin nodded in agreement.

'I know it's a tight squeeze but if we could extend the fiddle yard or… hey, how about making it sort of two storey?'

Adrian frowned.

'Two tiers? I know I'm relatively new to all this but wouldn't that require a lot of practice?'

Colin frowned.

'No, you're right, we need to keep it simple. Just some sort of further extension then, so we can load up more trains and bang 'em out quicker.'

'OK. OK. On it.' Adrian pumped his fist.

Pete turned to Nick.

'Now, what about this 'finale' you and Justine have been teasing us about for weeks?'

Everyone drew up closer around the table and Nick tried to let the anticipation grow a little more. It didn't last long.

'Wait, you've made a silent train or is it invisible?' Colin said sarcastically.

Nick flashed him a patronising smile. 'Gentlemen, what If I were to say to you… nuclear missile attack?'

There was a general perplexion of heads.

Pete raised his hand.

'We would probably say… what the fuck are you talking about?'

Nick continued.

'I've installed some speakers in Greenvale that can act as sirens and I've also built a secret underground bunker. Well, me and Justine have. She did a lot of the concrete work.'

Colin coughed relatively politely.

'At the risk of being Mr. Obvious…'

Nick rolled his eyes.

'Yes?'

'If it's underground, how do we see your beautiful concrete bunker?'

'Well, obviously, it's a rising bunker, concealed below the railway station carpark. When the sirens go off it slowly raises itself out of the ground and a large steel door opens to allow the special nuclear survival carriage to be shunted in. The bunker then disappears back under the carpark.'

Colin turned to Stew.

'Obviously.'

Pete sat mouth agape. George started to wander over, to pick up the empties. Pete recovered.

'You've built a nuclear bunker under the carpark?'

George stopped, turned round and quietly headed back to the safety of his bar. Pete couldn't help himself and repeated his last statement.

'You've built... a nuclear bunker... under the carpark?'

'Yes.'

'Excellent, I was worried it might be something weird.'

Stew looked refreshingly interested.

'I think it's a very unusual idea Nick. This nuclear survival carriage? I imagine it would contain all the vital people needed to ensure the survival of civilization after such an attack?'

Nick smiled.

'Kind of... hey, I wasn't going to tell you... but... what the hell... I've modelled the Fishplate team inside. And we've got years of beer, crisps and chocolate in there too.'

Adrian cheered.

'I like chocolate and beer!'

Colin rubbed his eyes.

'So, after nuclear Armageddon, the world devastated, who pops up to help with the reconstruction... a bunch of model railway enthusiasts.'

'Hey,' winked Nick, 'it's the new Utopia.'

'You just want to be God, don't you?' laughed Colin.

Nick reached over and placed his hand gently on Colin's shoulder.

'And you shall be my first disciple, son.'

'Enough of the profanity' said Colin, brushing Nick's hand away. 'This 'finale' will need a little practice, won't it?'

'Of course.'

'OK. Well me and Stew can sort that out, anything else you're doing that might involve the drivers?'

Nick folded his arms. 'Nope, me and Justine are just going to concentrate on getting a few more interesting models in. She seems determined to stamp her mark on something.'

'Other than you' joked Colin.

Nick smiled slowly. 'Hey Pete?'

Pete finished his Guinness and nodded. 'I know what you're thinking.'

Colin looked at them both and started to get up. 'My round I believe?'

Pete motioned him to sit down. 'No Colin, I think we forgot to tell you a certain story last time.'

Adrian adjusted his chair with a slight squeak. 'Jackanory, here we go.'

Nick got up. 'I'll get the next round in.'

Pete nodded at him. 'Which number in the top ten have we reached?'

Colin interrupted. 'It's number five of your made-up stories.'

Pete folded his arms. 'Oh yes, know it well.'

Nick walked off towards the bar. He always wondered how a disaster like story number five would have felt like to the models. He grinned to himself and caught George's eye at the bar.

'I bet George would love to hear that story' he whispered to himself. George attempted a feeble attempt to hide under the counter.

Shaun McBowen, head of Moulding Solutions Incorporated, looked down from his office window onto the factory floor. Production was barely keeping up. The building industry couldn't get enough of his new product. Cheaper than concrete, stronger then concrete, lighter than concrete and quicker setting than concrete… Moldo-crete. He was selling it by the bucket load, barrow load and truck load. Every house on the new estate had been made from it, the re-built bus station and the railway station, even all the sleepers for the new branch line. He rubbed his hands together and looked down at the new advertising samples.

'If you can think of it, we can mould it, with new Moldo-crete.'

'Yes, oh yes' chuckled McBowen to himself. 'It's a licence to print money.'

His imposing oak door suddenly burst open and a sweating, red faced technician fell in.

'Mr. McBowen, sir. We've got a serious problem!'

On the new estate, against a backdrop of cranes, Moldo-crete shuttering and queues of mixer-lorries, Sheila was gassing over the new Moldo-crete fence, to her neighbour, Lucille.

'Well, as I was saying to Janice, it's all very well my Terry coming home and chucking all his work clothes on the floor but it's me 'as to get them clean. I tell you that Moldo-crete dust gets everywhere an all. I'm forever dusting an a hoovering the place. God knows all the drains must be full of the stuff as well!'

Lucille tutted. 'Gerry's just the same. Comes back covered in the stuff. I make him stand in the front garden and whack him with the carpet beater.'

A huge mixer rumbled past. 'Bet that's going to the new road junction they're building' said Sheila. 'Terry reckons they're pouring hundreds of tons of the stuff into it.'

A flushed technician at the company lab tried to explain to McBowan again, slowly.

'We've just discovered that the ingredients in Moldo-crete… over time… and in certain hot conditions…can break down to form a new chemical structure. One that is more explosive than dynamite.'

McBowan went white and sat down.

The technician bit his lip.

'And that's not the worst of it.'

McBowan closed his eyes.

On a small hill overlooking the main railway line, Greg was in charge of capping off the old mine heads. For weeks they'd been pouring Moldo-crete down the shafts to seal them. He turned to his jib operator.

'Such a shame shutting these mines down. My mate on the Board reckons there's still millions of tons of coal down there.'

The jib handler shrugged.

'All the same to me mate. I had to cap off a load of half full oil tanks, just down the line before this job.'

'Yeah,' replied Greg 'since they set up that new gas works made out of Moldo-crete over the hill, no one's interested in anything else.'

'That's right mate. Mind you, now that that new explosives factory constructed from Moldo-crete is open, at least there's plenty of work around.'

The technician took a deep breath and quickly consulted some notes.

'OK, from our initial experiment it also looks like that if a sample of

Moldo-crete does ignite, it sets off a chain reaction with any other Moldo-crete in the area, regardless if that Moldo-crete has reached its critical breakdown phase.'

Shaun McBowan looked up to the ceiling.

The technician put his head to one side and whispered.

'Er, how many thousands of tons have we produced, sir?'

Shaun McBowan was about to answer when they both heard a distant rumble.

Nick took the tray of drinks back to the team, leaving George to pour himself a double Scotch. Pete was just finishing off the story.

'Luckily for Moldo-crete their exhibition layout was still under construction when it went bang over a weekend. Nothing was ever found of the layout or indeed the shed that contained it, apart from a small section of roof deposited in a nearby tree.'

Colin rolled his eyes and turned to Stew.

'Just save you the trouble of mentioning you have the news clipping in your 'scrapbook'.'

'Oh! But I do Colin. The investigators believed it was one of the most intense explosions they ever had to study.'

'So why have I never heard of Moldo-crete then?' asked Adrian, taking a gulp of bitter.

'Because they made it up?' suggested Colin.

'Because' said Nick, holding up his JD and coke, 'the army came in and bought them out. Very interested in a mouldable, lightweight explosive. The modeler's loss was the military's gain.' He put on a dreamy face. 'Imagine what mischief you could get up to with a little Moldo-crete at your disposal.'

Pete laughed. 'Legend has it that there's a crate of the stuff in pre-production packaging samples out there somewhere. So… maybe one day.'

Colin shook his head. 'I still don't understand this list. What you described was an industrial accident.'

Pete shrugged. 'Oh no, an entire model railway was vaporised. That has to go on the list. It's the law.'

Stew chipped in. 'I thought it was quite an appropriate story considering Nick's built a nuclear bunker on our layout.'

Colin gave Nick a suspicious sideways glance.

'Well' said Pete, 'I think we know all we need to. Let's spend the next couple of weeks making sure we do absolutely everything we can to make the final at Potton… ours.'

Ken pulled up into TRACK's small car park and gently turned off the engine. Captain Hargraves had ordered him over at short notice to discuss, well, Ken wasn't sure what. Hargraves had merely said 'Some chapters require no heading', one of his stock phrases that apparently everyone used to say. Ken suspected he just made them up, especially the ones that sounded deep but were in fact 'shallow as a puddle', another of his phrases, which had irritatingly stuck like 'Flanders mud to a mule'. Ken slapped himself on the cheek. He took a long, deep breath, closed his eyes, visualized his calm place, held it a precious few seconds and reached for the door handle.

Ken had to wait a few moments outside his office as his secretary said he was on a very important, she coughed theatrically and winked, international call. He nodded in acknowledgement and absentmindedly looked round the enclosed space that served as a waiting room. Lots of framed photos of a young Hargraves in uniform, pictures of trains and several glass cabinets with a variety of miscellaneous cups and medals recounting a life of service, model railways and badminton. A sudden guffaw escaped from under the Captain's door, followed by a descending round of indecipherable mutterings, hoo-hahs and goodbyes. There was a short pause and the door opened.

'Kenneth, dear boy, do come in.'

Ken raised himself up and entered Hargraves' office.

'Extraordinary weather for this time of year' said an expectant Hargraves.

'Yes' said Ken with just a hint of irritation, 'a fish landed on my head the other day.'

'Excellent! Our security is still working. Cup of tea perhaps?' Before Ken could reply he bellowed out to the secretary. 'Tea!' Hargraves sat down and pointed Ken to a small wooden chair. 'Now Ken, I bet you want to know why you're here?'

Ken squirmed slightly in his chair, he never knew why he was there, even when told why he was there.

'As you know, several of the regional finals are coming up and I would like you to go specifically to the South East one. I'm, shall we say, very interested in the outcome.'

'Any particular reason why sir?'

Hargraves spluttered a little. 'Well, for operational reasons of safety and integrity it would be inopportune for you to know too much.'

Ken momentarily closed his eyes. 'I don't really know anything sir.'

'Well good, very good. Let's leave it at that then.' He tapped the table dramatically. 'If you were to be captured and interrogated they would learn nothing Ken. Nothing.'

Ken realized at this juncture that pursuing this conversation would be pointless. He changed tack. 'How was your trip to Hong Kong sir?'

'Absolutely splendid Ken. Met up with that old rogue Philip, you know my old far eastern counterpart from the war. Gosh, he has a damned good life out there. Took me out to some pretty crazy bars and the casinos Ken. Honestly, if it moves, they'll bet on it, made some interesting new contacts too.' Hargraves stopped, seemed to mentally go over what he'd just said, frowned slightly and smiled at Ken. 'Well, it was wonderful to catch up. Er, did you get my postcard?'

'Yes, yes I did.' He remembered the creased picture of a tram. 'How is the Major by the way? Is he happy with the progression of the regionals?'

Hargraves glanced to one side and reached for his pipe, which he preceded to fiddle with while talking. 'The Major is taking a wide view of the current competition and how it may help the next phase, that is to say the Nationals. In so much as that regard he is, indeed, happy.' He put the pipe to his mouth, sucked a little and took it back out. 'Although, I have to say, in the context of the Nationals, the upcoming regional finals are somewhat important.'

Ken frowned. 'How so?'

'Oh I couldn't possibly, I mean the Major couldn't possibly say. It's all a little touch and go, feely-feely. Monkey up, monkey down, monkey go to church.

'I see.' Ken didn't. 'Er, so how do I proceed?'

Hargraves nodded, as if receiving instructions. 'All will be clear when you return to your car. Now I do believe this meeting is over. Wonderful to see you again Ken and I thank you for your diligence in collating all the information from the regionals.'

Ken stood up and shook Hargraves' outstretched hand. 'I shall no doubt be in contact shortly.' As he closed the office door the secretary hurried over with a cup of tea.

'So sorry it's late.' She handed the cup and saucer to Ken.

Ken was about to hand it back but took a sip instead. 'Have you seen the Major recently?' he said in as innocent a manor as possible.

There was a stifled snigger. 'What Major Catastrophe? Major Roadworks?'

She started laughing. 'Major Stare.'

Ken cocked his head to one side. 'You've never seen him, have you?'

'Nope.

'What, never?'

'Nope. I don't think he actually exits.' She started to laugh again. 'Unless he represents a major flaw in the organization.'

Ken couldn't help a crooked grin slip out.

The secretary pointed towards Hargraves' door. 'That said I have overhead him talking to the Major but I always suspected he was talking to himself. He is a very strange man. I'm sure you're aware of this.'

Ken finished off the tea and placed the bone china down onto the secretary's desk.

'Hmm, well I better be going, lovely to talk to you.'

As he turned the secretary whispered after him in a voice about to collapse into hysterics: 'I've placed your secret -' she paused to wipe a tear, '- secret mission envelope in your glove compartment.' She snorted. 'It's the gold one with 'TOP SECRET' typed on the front.'

Ken felt another small part of him die.

CHAPTER TWENTY-FIVE: GARETH

Barely five days later, on a bright, blue-skied Autumnal afternoon, Nick made an arranged visit to Gareth's. As he walked down the path he noted with relief that Chris had returned the Sherman topiary as promised and replanted it, with apparently little loss of shape. It did appear, however, to be pointing the wrong way. He knocked at the door, not quite sure what to expect. A shadow emerged from the depths of the house and slowly became more defined as it ambled towards the stained glass panel set into the front door. The door opened.

'Alright Nick? Admiring the Sherman?'

'Admiring the fact that it's there and in one piece. Wasn't it pointing the other way originally?'

'Yeah, but I prefer it that way round. Hey, you went to all that trouble to dig it up, might as well get it replanted where I want it.'

Nick laughed. 'Very positive Gareth. I like it.'

Gareth ushered him in. 'Cup of tea Nick?'

'Good idea. Milk and two sugars please.'

Nick was led down an airy parquet-floored hallway to a large kitchen, with a stripped pine table. He sat down in a beautifully aged Georgian Windsor chair and took in the décor. 'This is a really smart place you've got here. I have to say that I thought the type of person who had topiary tanks in his front garden might not be so bothered about the interior.'

Gareth stuck the designer Italian kettle on and grinned.

'Must be the gay in me.'

Nick smiled and nodded. 'How's that all working out for you then?'

Gareth took a couple of mugs from a little wooden mug tree and placed them next to the kettle. He shrugged.

'Not thinking about it, not because I don't want to think about it, I just don't need to. It doesn't worry me like before. I feel...release.'

Nick laughed. 'See, you should have just had a chat with me before and saved us all a load of wasted time.'

Gareth chuckled and poured the boiling water to make the tea. He placed Nick's mug down on a marble coaster and sat down opposite, on a rather splendid Regency carver.

'So, what's Fishplate up to? Getting ready for the final?'

Nick took a quick sip of tea.

'Yeah, it's the usual. Lots of frantic model making, train practice and Pete running around trying to look useful.'

Gareth nodded. 'You've got a team though. Must be nice to have a close group supporting you.'

Nick closed his eyes and smiled. 'Yeah, I suppose. It can also be a pain in the arse.'

'Any news on the saboteur?'

Nick snorted. 'Nothing solid.' He paused. 'When we met at the pub.' He deliberately stared at Gareth. 'You talked about a common connection... and you mentioned Justine.'

Gareth nodded submissively and ran his finger around the mug.

'Well, alright, don't interrupt.'

Nick placed his hands on the table and motioned him to continue.

'I was up in Coventry on an insurance thing and I remember being angry about stuff and I was thinking of my next move against you and there was a railway exhibition going on next door to my hotel.' Gareth instinctively raised a hand to stop Nick chipping in. 'I was wandering around and quite literally bumped into this guy. Long story short, we got talking and unbelievably he knew Justine and mentioned she'd just joined a club and was going away for a break with you and maybe I should join them if I was so interested in model railways.' Gareth started to raise his hand again.

'No! Fuck off Gareth. You will let me interrupt.'

Gareth rolled his eyes. 'Go on.'

'Bollocks.'

'Is that a question?'

'There is no way you just 'bumped' into this guy. What was his business there?'

Gareth shrugged 'Construction? He was on a site down the road, said he had a meeting in the hotel lobby later.'

Nick snorted. 'So he was just wasting time then?'

'No, I don't think so. It looked like he was scoping the place out, he was very engaged in what was going on, kept stooping down to check angles and stuff.'

'So he could have been a saboteur?'

Gareth started laughing 'Yes.'

'It's not fucking funny.'

'Oh yes it is. It really is.'

Nick shook his head and let out a silent scream. 'What was his name?'

Gareth stopped laughing but carried on grinning manically. 'No idea.'

'His link to Justine?'

'I don't know, he didn't say. Actually that was a bit strange.' He grinned at Nick. 'Maybe he was an ex, he did have some sort of rascal, devil may care bit of rough going for him.'

'Stop, stop, fucking stop.' Nick put his hands to his face. 'No more.'

Gareth took a polite sip of tea. 'Complicated old thing this model railway business.'

'Gareth?'

'Yes Nick.'

'In future?'

'Yes.'

'Could you please, please, fucking please, mention these small details… a little sooner. Thank you.'

Gareth suppressed a fresh surge of laughter. He got up and walked over to the Welsh dresser. He pulled open a richly patinated drawer and took out a small box.

'Little present for you. Help take your mind off things.'

Nick carefully opened the delicate cardboard flaps to reveal Monty.

'I tidied him up a little' said Gareth. 'Poor chap looked a bit scuffed after being shot down and captured.'

Nick couldn't help grinning and nodded his approval.

'Looks great Gareth. Must have been odd, working on something without a gun.'

Gareth snorted. 'Well, I bet it was weird working on something with lots of guns. That Lancaster didn't build itself.'

'Actually quite enjoyed it, Gareth. Even enjoyed adding a load of bullet holes to your Messerschmitts.'

'It was a little more than bullet holes. I found one that looked like you'd stamped on it.'

'Yeah, I was running out of time… lucky for you Monty

didn't shoot more down.' Nick picked up the little figure and turned him slowly round in his fingers.

'What's so special about Monty?' asked Gareth.

Nick put the tiny station master carefully back in the box and finished off his tea.

'My dad built me a model of a Lancaster as a birthday present and Monty was the pilot. The plane got wrecked when we moved house, but I managed to save Monty and when I remodeled Lower Didsbury station on our present layout, I made him the stationmaster.'

'So he was actually a pilot then?'

'Yes. It always makes me smile when I see him on the platform, reminds me of dad.'

'And you risked him on a mission to my garage?'

'Yep. The only model up to it, apart from Hancock perhaps.'

Gareth shrugged his shoulders.

'Hancock worked out you liked Tiger tanks.'

'I always seem to under estimate how mental you really are. I never stood a chance, did I?'

It was Nick's turn to shrug before turning to point at a large black and white framed photo that hung above an oak sideboard. 'Have to ask Gareth, is that rakish figure in the Austin Cambridge your dad?'

Gareth half closed his eyes and nodded gently. 'He loved that car, loved it to death.'

Gareth suddenly jumped up.

'Hey, want another cup of tea? I've got something to show you in the garage.'

'My mum warned me about people like you.'

'Oh fuck off, you'll like it and I bet you'll use it on your layout.'

Nick chewed his lower lip.

'Intriguing Gareth. Very intriguing.'

CHAPTER TWENTY-SIX: FAT BOB AND PETE

Fat Bob needed to speak to Pete urgently. So urgently that it required the eating of pie and chips at Bob's local that evening. Pete had agreed, more for the fact of a pint of Guinness than the pie and chips.

Autumn was beginning to take hold as Pete arrived at The Iron Duke. He brushed the accumulation of drizzle from his freshly cropped hair and walked through to the lounge. Fat Bob greeted him with a wave of a chubby hand and immediately got stuck back into his plate of food. Pete smiled and got himself a pint before joining Bob.

'Alright Pete?' said Bob, barely looking up from his trough.

'Very well Bob. That looks… looked tasty.'

Bob crammed the last of his pie into the capacious cavern that served as a mouth and washed it all down with a slush of lager. He let out a delicate belch and wiped his mouth with a paper serviette.

'So Pete, I suppose you can guess why I needed to talk?'

Pete nodded slowly. 'One word, sabotage?'

'Exactly' said Bob pushing his plate to the far end of the table. 'I think we know how they got us.'

'Go on' said Pete.

Bob fumbled in his pocket and brought out a little paper bag. He opened it for Pete to see.

'Lemon Sherbets?' frowned Pete.

Bob looked into the bag, apologised, offered Pete one and put them back in his pocket. After more puffing he produced another little bag and opened it.

Pete peered in. 'It's empty.'

314

'For God's sake!' muttered Bob and shook it out. A very fine tangle of what looked like artificial spider web tumbled out.

Pete stared at the transparent, tangled mess.

'What the hell is that?'

Bob folded his arms.

'That Pete, is very, very, fine nylon line.' He paused. 'We had four derailments and one motor fail due to that shit.'

Pete picked it up and tried to tease a couple of ends apart.

'God, it's really strong!'

'Yep. That was the problem. It either wound round the wheels and jammed them or put so much strain on the motors that they burnt out. Trouble was it's so fine it's almost impossible to spot.'

Pete winced.

'So this stuff could be dropped onto the line very easily?'

'Yep' sighed Bob.

'Bugger' replied Pete and took a long gulp of Guinness.

Bob curled up his hand into a fist.

'Only way to prevent it is to catch the prat doing it and batter him.'

Pete assumed Bob meant beat up, but it wasn't beyond the realms of possibility that Bob could deep fry the saboteur in a flour based mixture and consume him with a squirt of lemon and plate of chips. He took another mouthful of Guinness. 'Don't suppose you have any idea what said prat might look like?'

Bob shrugged. 'Graham thought he might have worn a hat.'

Pete groaned and rolled his eyes.

CHAPTER TWENTY-SEVEN: THE NIGHT BEFORE

Colin looked in despair across the control board. Lights flashed, things beeped, the odd spark arced between power levers. He could hear Nick shouting at him.

'You wanker, you've killed all my models!'

Colin tried to reply but every time he opened his mouth a plastic cow jumped in and savaged his tongue. He tried to regain order on the layout but whenever he touched a control it caused a derailment. There were dead trains everywhere. Why wasn't Stew helping? He tried to find Stew. Now he found himself in a wood, the trees crowded around, blocking his progress. Colin sat down, he could still hear in the distance Nick shouting at him. There was a rustle from above, Stew was perched on a branch grooming his feathers. Adrian was sat next to him taking wagons from a leather hat and eating them.

'Stop eating my rolling stock' shouted Colin. A plastic cow jumped in his mouth and bit his tongue.

'Stop it you mad cow!' bellowed Nick.

Colin received a slap to the head. The trees dissolved away to be replaced by a brooding, dangerous, invisible entity.

'What did you just call me?'

'What? Shit. A dream… thank fuck. Sorry… er what did I say?'

There was an angry silence and even though it was pitch black in the bedroom Colin knew she was glaring at him.

'Sorry love, bad dream.'

The immense hall was filled to capacity. Row upon row of

expectant fans stood shoulder to shoulder murmuring in rhythmic waves, anticipation crackled through the air. The attention of everyone's gaze - a small table in the middle of a grand wooden stage. Upon the table, in the exact centre, something draped with a black silk cloth. A blast of trumpets and an explosion of light heralded the arrival of the legend.

Nick entered the hall and walked slowly towards the table, glancing at banks of silenced, adoring disciples. He reached the table and stood to one side, his right hand hovered above the silk cloth. Time stood still, the earth ceased to rotate, Nick lifted the shroud to reveal the most awesome, unbelievable, model of a light industrial unit (ready to let).

The crowd went berserk, ticker-tape fell from the sky, his name echoed across the vast space. Nick sucked in the glory but suddenly the cheering ceased. A darkness fell across the small table. Justine materialised in a flash of blue light and held forth to the shocked masses a model of a chicken hut, complete with brooding hens. Nick staggered back, catching the light industrial unit and knocking it to the floor, where it shattered into a thousand tiny shards. He started to sink, dissolving into the wooden floor, drowning in floorboards.

Nick gasped and snapped upright.

Justine rolled over.

'You ok?'

Nick blinked.

'Yes… fine, just a dream… you're not building a chicken shed are you?'

But Justine was already asleep.

Stew woke up feeling refreshed and from the gentle burble of Radio Four that wafted up from the kitchen, deduced

Margaret was already awake and preparing breakfast. He rolled carefully out of bed and did some light stretching until he felt safe enough to put on his socks. They were followed by his lucky trousers and his light blue driver's shirt coupled to a tan waistcoat, into which he tucked his station master's timepiece. He put on LMS slippers and trotted downstairs. Margaret had laid out the table and he sat down in his place. Her head popped round the frame of the kitchen doorway.

'Morning dear. Could I interest you in a small bowl of cereal?'

'Lovely dear.'

A few minutes later.

'Two slices of brown and a tea?'

'Lovely dear.'

'Marmalade?'

'Lovely dear.'

A few minutes later.

'How would you like your artichokes in garlic dear?'

'What?'

'Your pasta with rabbit shavings dear?'

'Pardon?'

'Your badger casserole dear?'

Stew woke up in a cold sweat. What a nightmare, he always had toast first.

Adrian never dreamed except during the day, usually when he'd just finished explaining how to make a wooden spice rack for the three hundredth time.

Deep inside Pete's head he was pursuing the saboteur. The shadowy figure, never fully defined and always just out of reach had successfully evaded him, but now Pete renewed his efforts. He bounded up some stairs, flung himself round a corner and charged down a long straight corridor. The saboteur, tantalisingly close, his flapping overcoat almost within reach. Pete lunged and grabbed air, he slipped and fell just as the figure leapt down a hole in the floor. Pete scrambled up and dived headlong through the hole. Now he was flying, below him the saboteur was hopping across a meadow, Pete swooped towards him. Time seemed to drag, his arms stretched out, fingers extended. The saboteur started to slow but he couldn't quite get a hold…

'Alright John, how much you want for that old Marina there?'

Pete landed in the field and turned to the voice. A bloke that looked like someone was bent over, tapping the glass of an orange Marina.

'Smells a bit' said the voice.

Pete flashed a look at the saboteur, he was still there, just out of reach but not moving. Pete returned to the geezer.

'A monkey.'

'A monkey? Bit steep ain't it? What about a camel?'

Pete frowned, he needed close to a monkey to make any profit.

'What about a chinchilla and I'll throw in a gallon of petrol?'

The blokey geezer man puffed out his gills and reached into a bucket next to him.

'What about a frog and two sticklebacks?'

Pete needed to catch the saboteur.

'OK. How about we settle on a perfumed otter and call it quits.'

The geezer grinned.

'Nice one mate' and disappeared in a puff of lemon sherbet scented smoke.

Nick suddenly appeared.

'I don't want to alarm you but the alarm's going.'

'What? Where did you come from?'

'The alarm's going' repeated Nick.

Pete opened his eyes and reached out to turn off the alarm. He rubbed his eyes and grumbled.

'Stupid Marinas, never could get good money for them.'

CHAPTER TWENTY-EIGHT: ONCE MORE UNTO THE BREACH

Stew was the first to get to Potton, having packed his Montego estate up the night before. He quite liked the idea of a walk around the quiet town to stretch his legs and mentally settle before meeting up with the rest of Fishplate for a pre-match fry up at 'The Full Monty.'

Colin, meanwhile, was feeling boisterous, even Helen was paying attention to him despite her perception that he'd called her an irritating cow or something during the night.

'So what do you win again?' she said, slowly stirring her tea.

'Some big shiny cup and a chance at the nationals' replied Colin.

Helen sipped her tea thoughtfully.

'I don't think anyone in this family has ever won any sort of shiny cup before.'

Colin chugged the last of tea down.

'The years of shame and failure end here. I will bring pride and glory back to our bloodline once again.'

'What do you mean, once again?'

'Turn of phrase my lovely… although I did win that colouring competition.'

'It was for seven to eight year olds.'

'Pride and glory Helen. Pride and glory. Prepare the mantelpiece.'

'We don't have one' smiled Helen.

'Make one then, woman. Right I'm ready… Get to Potton,

fry up, win the competition, return home triumphant. That's the plan.'

Helen walked up to him and gave him a hug. She whispered in his ear.

'Tell you what, if you win, I'll wear that stupid outfit you bought as a joke.'

Colin grinned.

'The Princess Leia with matching bun accessories.'

Helen sighed.

'Yes.'

'It wasn't a joke.'

'Out.'

Colin was half-way down the street before he realised he needed the car. He had to win, he was on a promise.

Nick and Justine got to the greasy spoon first and managed to bag the biggest table. Pete arrived shortly afterwards and joined them with a steaming sugary tea.

'I never thought back in May that we'd be sitting here having a pre-final breakfast.'

Nick nodded. 'Feels good though doesn't it?'

Pete smiled and eased back into the orange plastic chair. 'Certainly does and I want to try and enjoy every moment of it.'

Justine put her mug of tea down and moved a hand slowly towards Nick. He gently grasped it and winked at her, before looking back at Pete.

'I know this may sound presumptuous, but have you dared to think what we'll do if we get to the nationals?'

Pete shook his head. 'Nope, don't want to jinx anything.'

Justine looked deep into his eyes. 'I think you have Mr Fletcher.'

Pete glanced down at his tea and squinted, before grunting and shaking his head. 'OK, alright, maybe.'

Nick raised an eyebrow. 'OK maybe what?'

Pete shook his head again and shrugged. 'Perhaps a completely new layout, maybe a different gauge… I don't know, something like that, maybe.'

Nick and Justine looked at each other in shock.

'Please not fucking N gauge' groaned Nick.

Pete smiled. 'Hey, you asked. I don't know, but we're not there yet. Let's just get today out of the way, ok?'

Justine removed her hand from Nick's grip and took a delicate sip of tea while exchanging a silent moment with him.

The sticky door of the café suddenly rattled open and Colin bundled in, followed slowly by Stew.

'There you are' laughed Colin, as he clocked them. 'Found this strange little fella walking round the square.'

Stew picked up a nearby serviette, wiped down one of the plastic chairs and sat down next to Pete.

'I was stretching my legs and admiring the architecture.'

'Course you were' fussed Justine and gave him a warm smile.

Colin plonked himself down and grabbed a sauce-stained menu.

'Fry ups all round?'

There was a collective nod.

'What about Adrian?' said Stew.

Colin shrugged. 'We'll get his in anyway' and went to order

from the green Formica-topped counter.

Stew looked around the table. 'It's all very exciting isn't it? I hardly slept a wink.'

Pete folded his arms. 'Enjoy the moment Stew, remember these times. Everything could be different tomorrow.'

Stew laughed nervously. 'Do you think we'll get in the paper?'

Nick rolled his eyes. 'Christ yes. Might even make page six, next to anonymous local in dispute with the council over unfilled pot holes or some other shit. You'll definitely be fending the women off with a sharp stick.'

Stew bit his lip and looked concerned. 'Might have to get a new tie.'

Colin returned to the table and plonked down a couple of sloshing mugs. He slid one towards Stew and dropped a couple of stained sugar cubes into his before taking a noisy slurp. 'Nice day for it.'

Justine wiped a finger over the steamed-up window to create a 'v'.

Pete raised his mug. 'Amen to that.'

Before long, six plates of slippery, fried food were being passed along the table and a momentary silence prevailed as they all tucked in.

Stew set about his food in an orderly fashion, a bit of bacon, a snip of sausage with a little dab of mustard, one mushroom (halved), a section of egg and then back to the start.

Pete was from a similar school of thought although he involved his toast in the proceedings, while Stew would attend strictly to his toast afterwards.

Nick simply ate from the front of his plate to the back but

ignored the fried tomatoes.

Justine was typically more playful, creating a recognisable picture of 'Hadley's Hope' using egg and ketchup.

Colin however, was a bulldozer and ploughed rampantly through everything, pausing occasionally to top up with HP. His excuse being that at home, there was rarely anything other than soggy cornflakes and Lego on offer.

The sixth plate of slowly congealing fat became an increasing worry as the other five plates rapidly cleared.

'It's unusual for Adrian to be late for anything' remarked Stew, as he carefully dabbed the corners of his mouth.

'True,' added Colin, 'if anything his general puppy keenness gets him everywhere early.'

Pete ran his tongue over his teeth and took a last slurp of tea.

'Well, there's plenty of time yet. Let's get those boards set up and take it from there.'

Ken Bruce pushed his English breakfast to one side and took a polite sip of coffee, replacing the small cup gently into its saucer. He absentmindedly looked around the cosy dining room of the small hotel he'd booked into yesterday evening, courtesy of Captain Hargraves. Through the window he could just make out the roofline of Potton Town Hall above the terrace of shops and houses opposite. A youth, untidily jammed into a tight uniform, came over to his table.

'Are you finished sir?'

'Yes, thank you' replied Ken.

'Could I get you anything else sir?'

'Perhaps a top up of coffee in a moment, thank you.'

The youth cleared his plate away and disappeared through

a door to the kitchen. A brief sound of frying, clattering metal and Radio One escaped, before the heavy door swung shut.

Ken Bruce looked around again. An elderly couple were fastidiously buttering their toast in the far corner. Behind him a businessman leafed through the pink pages of the Financial Times, his shirt an almost identical colour. Some visitors from Germany carefully absorbed all that the Potton Tourist Board leaflet could impart. Ken reached into the warm inner pocket of his jacket and took out a folded gold envelope. On the front in a precisely typed style, were the words 'TOP SECRET to be opened on the morning of the final'. Ken couldn't help but snort derisibly. At least he didn't have to go through a daft code word farce. What had that last one been? 'My regulator has jammed – try using a crowbar'. Ken closed his eyes and shook his head. Using a spare butter knife, he carefully opened the waiting envelope and unfolded the paper within. He read and carefully re-read the contents before folding the message and placing it back in the envelope. A curious set of instructions. Ken was beginning to wonder if he wasn't in some way being manipulated in support of an agenda known only to Hargraves or possibly the Major, if he actually existed. It was curious that whenever he was asked to specifically observe a designated club they invariably won. Ken rubbed his forehead. He was supposed to be the Vice President, well, today he was going to start acting like it. Bugger the instructions. Anyway he had some of his own hunches to follow, starting with the judges.

The kitchen door swung open and the youth approached with a fresh pot of coffee. Ken quickly tucked the envelope back in his pocket and smiled.

Pete and Nick surveyed the team's location, having just locked-in the final board of the layout.

'I quite like these corner positions,' commented Pete 'much easier to control the space.'

Nick nodded. 'Sure, but I don't like being this close to the main mezzanine walkway.'

Pete looked up and was sure he saw a head immediately pop back into the shadows. He scratched his chin.

'Yeah, I see what you mean. We need to stay sharp for this one.'

Nick pointed back down the hall.

'Harbour Town are near the entrance and there should be a load of trade stands and other club layouts in-between, so we're quite isolated in many ways.'

Pete exhaled deeply. 'Could be good or bad.'

Stew and Colin ambled over.

'Are we ready to rock?' said Colin.

Nick smiled sarcastically. 'Yes, you can start playing trains.'

Stew let out a little cough. 'What about Adrian?'

Pete moaned. 'Christ, forgot that. There's a phone box near the car park, I'll try him.'

'Oi! What about the tea?' shouted Colin as Pete walked off.

'Nick can sort it out' Pete shouted back, shaking his head.

Colin smiled at Nick and was about to open his mouth, but Nick cut him off.

'Yes I know, two sugars for you, one for Stew.'

Colin gave him a thumbs up and started to unpack trains.

Nick looked about to see where Justine had got to. He spotted her reading from a marble plinth set into the east wall. He sidled up to her.

'Fancy helping get some tea?'

She smiled.

'It's strangely nostalgic being back here, where we first met.'

Nick laughed.

'C'mon let's see if our table's still in the café.'

Pete walked out to the car park and straight into Adrian. 'Where the hell have you been?' barked Pete.

'Sorry mate, went out to my car to find some git had slashed the tyres.'

Pete shook his head. 'Christ, bad luck.'

Adrian nodded. 'I know. It's not that unusual for teachers to get their cars vandalized by kids, but I do woodwork for God's sake. Who the hell gets a grievance over making sewing boxes and egg timers?'

Pete screwed up his face. 'Don't think… it could be you-know-who?'

Adrian screwed up his face to mimic Pete.

'I did wonder that, bit of a coincidence otherwise. Anyway, are we set up yet?'

Pete bundled him into the town hall. 'Yes, they're probably about ready to run some practice trains. Have you eaten?'

Adrian looked him forlornly in the eyes.

'I bet you had an epic fry up, didn't you?'

Pete patted him on the back.

'Yes we did mate, it was indeed epic. Look, get settled in and I'll try and rustle something up from the tea room for you.' Pete left Adrian with Colin and Stew and headed up the stairs.

Ken Bruce nodded at the receptionist and walked out into

the fresh early morning air. He'd heard that the judges liked to meet up at Green's café and he harboured a theory that they might be behind some of the alleged 'irregularities'. This whole business with supposed attempts to manipulate the regionals had been blown out of all proportion. Derailments happened and teams got upset but a systematic, criminal organization involved in model railway subversion seemed unlikely to him. Hargraves, he suspected was up to something and Ken knew from tedious past conversations that he still hankered after his wartime position. Perhaps he was in some strange way trying to reconcile his role in the defeat of National Socialism with the realities of running a model railway society. Green's café was coming up ahead of him, he checked the time – 9:34 – and hovered outside to see if he could spot anyone of note through the condensation-smeared windows, one of which had a large 'v' written on it. He quickly concluded the targets were not yet present, unless this criminal gang was fronted by an elderly gentleman in a long raincoat and a plastic Sainsbury's bag. Ken pushed open the door and walked in. He chose a small table in a secluded corner where he could quietly observe any comings and goings. A short, rotund fellow in a stripy, grease stained apron shuffled over to the table.

'Yes mate?'

Ken smiled congenially at the café's patron.

'Cup of tea please.'

'Mug of tea' nodded the owner. 'And to eat?'

Although Ken had just eaten, he bizarrely had an immediate craving for toast.

'Some brown toast please.'

'Two rounds of white.'

'Er, brown would be lovely' smiled Ken.

There was a slightly irritated sigh.

'Tell you what mate, I'll leave it in the toaster a little longer, definitely be brown then.' The owner shuffled off.

Ken rolled his eyes and reached for a discarded paper on a nearby chair. This could be a long wait.

The upstairs tea room in Potton town hall was still relatively empty apart from a couple of guys near the counter and a smattering of trade standers taking it easy before the public were admitted.

Nick and Justine were happily settled at 'their' table reminiscing.

'I was so nervous waiting for you to turn up' confessed Nick. 'Felt like I'd sat there all my life waiting for, that moment.'

Justine smiled. 'Lucky your model making was up to scratch then' she teased.

 Nick nodded. 'I knew it would be, I was just praying you hadn't found me too weird in the few moments we had on the spinner.'

Justine laughed. 'Your weirdness drew me in. I wanted to find out more.'

'Even inspector Hancock didn't faze you.'

'No chance, it attracted me, made your weirdness even more compatible.' Justine paused and then whispered. 'Actually I never told you why I was really there that day.'

Nick copped Pete entering the room.

'What was that? Hang on Pete's coming over. Seem to remember him interrupting us the first time.'

'Alright chaps?' said Pete, as he sat down next to them.

Justine sighed. 'Déjà vu?'

'I'll stick to tea thanks' said Pete. 'Hey! I found Adrian.' He clicked his tongue and looked across to the counter. 'What do you think he'd like for breakfast?'

The door of Green's café opened and four officious looking men marched in. The lead looked round before pointing to a window table. Ken lowered his red top slightly to get a better look. They were definitely model railway judges. Something about the plethora of waistcoats, clipped moustaches and gold pocket watches perhaps gave it away.

The café's patron grumped over.

'Wot you lot dressed up for eh?'

Mr Blue waistcoat (with gold trim) observed him professionally before replying.

'We are here to help officiate at The Grand Final of the SE Regionals. Do you model?'

There was in reply a face used when treading in something brown and smelly, followed by some sort of primal grunt, a very brief moment of what might have looked like 'thought' to the casual observer but was in reality a wormhole into intellectual oblivion, another grunt and then:

'So, you want some nosh then?'

There was an audible huff from the judges before the Blue trimmed waistcoat ordered fry ups all round with extra toast for the British Racing Green trimmed waistcoat.

Ken Bruce did a mental snort and thought 'Hope he likes 'brown' toast' before having another sip of tea and settling down to listen in on their conversation. Precisely fifteen minutes later Ken left the café, muttering heavily to himself. *'That's a small part of my life I'll never get back. At what point does talking about the correct way to install a fishplate become interesting? It certainly wasn't the third time. Christ!'* Ken stopped and took a deep breath. '*Still, at least I know they don't have anything to do with supposed sabotage. That would require, at the minimum, some sort of creativity*' He glanced back at the café and then spotted a phone box a short way down the street. He decided to phone Hargraves and confirm that he had read his instructions and would proceed to the venue. On arriving at the somewhat shabby looking phone box, he realised there was someone already there, holding up a crumpled red diary and having what sounded like a tricky conversation. Ken stood a polite distance back and fumbled in his pockets for some change. As he did so, odd words escaped from the grimy booth that piqued his interest. Words such as 'exhibition', 'final', 'money' and 'target.' Ken scuffled a little closer. This actually might be something. He strained his ears at the conversation leaking through the cast iron door and began to comprehend the odd sentence and phrase.

'A few hours.'

'Harbour Town and Smooth Fishplate… I know but…'

'Yes, they're in place.'

'The syndicate should know better.'

'No, because I don't want to go to prison, not for that anyway.'

There was a long pause. Ken felt it wise to back off slightly. The door suddenly swung open and a short guy in a green bomber jacket walked swiftly out. Ken tried to nod in as brief and as casual a manner as he could muster, before entering the booth. He quickly picked up the receiver and angled himself to watch where the guy went. He was naturally amused when the bomber jacket disappeared into Green's café.

Back at the exhibition, team Fishplate had finally all gathered together at their layout. The warm up trains had been run, tea had been drunk and a cold soggy breakfast substitute sausage roll had been nibbled. Colin looked out from his cab across the large hall before looking to Pete.

'Any chance we'll get a normal, human judge for the final?' Pete nodded in acknowledgement.

'I may have omitted to mention that we'll get two judges for the final. One to inspect the creative side of the layout and one to check the timetable.'

'Finally!' exclaimed Nick. 'They're actually devoting a bit of time to the details.' He patted Justine on the knee. Justine gave him a knowing nod.

Adrian cocked his head at Nick. 'I see we've got Monty back on the platform and he's looking spruced up. I really missed him last time out.' Nick winked back.

'Hopefully he'll be a good omen for you because you're going to need all the luck you can get today.'

'Really?'

'Yep.'

'Why?'

Nick sighed. 'The saboteur, remember? He's going to have to make a move today. This is it. We dealt with Gareth, but we know nothing about this other twat and what they're capable of.'

Pete interrupted - 'True, but just on an optimistic note, they could go after Harbour Town instead. You never know this could be the easiest victory yet.'

Colin laughed sarcastically. 'If there's any sabotage about I guarantee it's going to stick to us like shit on a blanket. Tell you what though?'

'What?' smirked Nick.

'I'm going to take whatever gets thrown at us and fucking deal with it.'

Nick's eyes narrowed. 'You're on a promise, aren't you?'

Colin turned his head away. 'Might be.'

'Not the Star Wars outfit?'

'Maybe.'

Nick laughed. 'Christ, you might not get a chance like this for years.'

'Yes… exactly' replied Colin.

'What Star Wars outfit?' whispered Justine.

Stew looked confused. 'Like Darth Vader?'

Colin's head jerked back. 'Stew! Hush. I really, really don't need that image in my head.'

Pete felt he needed to steer the conversation back to the immediate reality.

'Look guys, this is the final. You can see the place is getting pretty crammed with spectators, not just down here but also up there.' Everyone glanced up at the mezzanine level, where a line of the public was already leaning against the sturdy railings looking down at them and occasionally pointing at something.

'Just like school' muttered Colin and Adrian in unison.

Pete continued. 'There's going to be little chance of stopping someone up to no good. Too much cover and you can bet whatever they do is going to be subtle. For all I know they've already got to us.'

Stew looked guiltily around the layout.

'Well, I moved that key if that's your concern.'

'Which concrete animal is it now then?' smirked Nick.

'It's with Percy.'

'Percy?' Nick shook his head.

'Yes,' said Stew, 'it's a -'

'Don't tell us!' laughed Nick.

Pete suddenly looked concerned.

'You did check the rolling stock Stew?'

'Yes, of course. Twice.'

Pete nodded. 'Ok, ok, look, we just have to get on with the timetable. Obviously I'm going to attempt some sort of security role.' Nick and Colin exchanged a patronising glance. 'And let me tell you I really want to win this thing. Which means I will beat the living crap out of anyone I catch trying to fuck things up.'

Colin did a little fist pump. 'Yeah, give 'em one from me too!'

Stew raised his hand. 'What if it's a woman, I mean a lady, lady girl?'

Nick looked at Justine. 'Well, Justine gets to beat the crap out of them.'

Justine looked startled. 'A girl? No, I mean I'd rather hit a bloke, a man bloke.'

Pete folded his arms. 'OK, we've got nearly an hour before the judges turn up. I'm going for a snoop round. Everyone else just relax but not too much, y'know. Stay sharp but relaxed. You know what I mean.'

There was a collective silence.

Pete sighed. 'Ok?'

Colin saluted him Benny Hill style. 'Yes boss.'

Pete decided that was good enough and left. As he disappeared toward the entrance Colin stood up and stretched.

'Well, I'm with Pete. I really want to win this. Never thought I could feel this competitive.'

Stew chuckled. 'Well, it's very exciting and I feel, er, a little bit nervous actually.'

Colin affected a serious face. 'Do not get nervous Stew, stay excited but do not get nervous. Remember what I told you last time?'

Stew winced. 'Something about a Brontosaurus?'

'Oh for fuck's sake' muttered Colin. 'No, you're a motherfucking T-Rex, remember?'

Nick shook his head. 'How did you become a teacher exactly?' He mimicked Colin. 'Now Timothy, if you feel nervous about any of the questions in this exam, especially the ones about Romans and fractions, just remember… you're a motherfucking T-Rex.'

Everyone laughed including Colin, who pointed at Nick. 'So what are you and Justine going to be up to?'

Nick pulled a wonky face. 'Not sure. The usual probably. Wander around, make sarky comments, discover something useful and inevitably save the day.' He beckoned Justine away.

Colin watched them go and turned to Stew and Adrian. 'Right, that's the excess baggage gone, let's have a proper team talk.'

It suddenly occurred to Ken Bruce, in a terrible wave of crushing reality that the bomber jacket may have gone to the café to have a little chat with the judges, now that he had his instructions. Ken moved to a discreet vantage point to observe the café a while longer. He was pretty sure there wasn't anyone in the café other than the judges when he was there, but maybe someone entered when he was outside the phone box. He really needed someone else to be involved because if there wasn't, it looked like a huge coincidence that all the judges happened to be in there. He bit his lip. Hargraves' instructions to get to the venue and stay there were looking suspiciously like a simple way of keeping him away from this hotbed of subversion. The café door opened, four judges walked slowly out, checked their pocket watches and strode off in the direction of the Town Hall. Ken took the option to stay put and wait a little longer to see if the bomber jacket might also leave.

Nick decided to go and have a look at Harbour Town and possibly wind up Angie. He'd mentioned the idea to Justine, but she quickly remembered she needed some stuff from Boots, 'Y'know, girls' stuff' and had disappeared.

With about forty minutes to go before the judges turned up the atmosphere was beginning to liven up. Nick recognised faces from previous rounds and had to keep reminding himself that this was the final and he was actually one of the finalists. There was a light screen of people around Harbour Town but a rope cordon was keeping them a yard back. He eased himself toward the left of the layout and spotted Angie bending over an engine shed fiddling with something. He dipped under the rope and coughed politely. There was a chilly exhale of breath and without looking up she ordered Nick back behind the rope. Nick coughed again.

'Angie, it's me, your old mate Nick.' He couldn't help thinking that if a grizzly donned some old blue overalls and a cap, the resemblance would be uncanny. Angie straightened up and turned to him, a small tube of superglue in her right paw.

'Hi there,' beamed Nick, 'have you lost some weight? Ready for the kick off?' Angie adjusted her cap and scowled at him.

'You see that rope?'

Nick looked behind him and nodded.

'Just pop yourself behind it for me.'

Nick shrugged and moved back.

'What you want Nick?'

Nick wore a hurt expression.

'Just thought I'd pay a little visit, see how things are. You confident? The layout's looking grand. A few new models I see.'

Angie screwed up her face.

'More confident with that rope there and two judges to look out for us.'

Nick sighed.

'Still think Fishplate are somehow involved in, er, how shall I put it? Trickery?'

'Something is definitely going on with your crew. I hear all sorts of stuff involving plots with expanding foam, stuffed rodents and topiary and you or your bunch always seem to be connected, especially that... girl you let in.'

'Justine?'

'Whatever her name is. She's been seen buying goods in Johnsons Building Supplies. Not the sort of stuff you might normally need for a model railway either.'

Nick choked in surprise.

'Er, well, there is life outside this activity you know.' It didn't sound convincing.

'Didn't know that did you?' smirked Angie. 'Didn't know your girlie was up to something did you?' She thrust her hands into the front pouch of her overalls in triumph.

Nick frowned and turned away, which was a shame because he missed the slow dawning of realisation that rose upon Angie's face when she felt the warmth of escaping superglue weld both her hands into the denim pocket.

Ken Bruce checked his watch. The judges had left over thirty minutes ago and no one of note had entered or left the café. He was about to call time when the café door rattled open and Bomber Jacket strode out followed by a gangly youth in drainpipes and what looked like a tennis top. There was a brief exchange in which Bomber pointed up the street, Drainpipe shrugged, Bomber pointed again, Drainpipe shrugged with attitude, Bomber slapped Drainpipe on the back of the head and pointed up the street, Drainpipe walked up the street, Bomber walked in the opposite direction shaking his head and having some sort of imaginary argument.

Ken decided to follow Bomber, he was clearly in charge. But in charge of what?

Eleven o'clock was nearly upon the grand finale. Pete stood dead centre of the Fishplate layout awaiting the judges. A veneer of spectators hung at a nervous distance and murmured like a herd of farm animals. And just like cows they readily parted as two judges strode through their ranks and up to Pete. He nodded to them as respectfully as he could manage and handed over the timetable.

The judge in a blue waistcoat (gold trim) stepped forward to accept the document.

'Hello Mr Fletcher. I'm Mr Shaw and this gentleman is Mr Hampton.' The green waistcoat (silver braid) nodded. Mr Shaw fixed the timetable to his clipboard and started to go through the running order. Pete sniffed and waited for the inevitable questions concerning some of their schedule. Surprisingly Mr Shaw almost made it to the end without comment until the nuclear bunker special stopped his gently nodding head.

Mr Shaw scratched his chin thoughtfully and looked up.

Pete caught his eye and smiled.

'The nuclear bunker special,' began Mr Shaw. 'I get the point of it. It's most innovative in fact. What I'm a tad concerned about are the asterisks at the end.' He quickly slipped into confusion. 'Or should that be asteriski?' Mr Shaw beckoned Mr Hampton over. There was a low exchange of muttering before Mr Hampton stood back. 'Right, as I was saying, I'm a little concerned about the.' Pause. 'Asterisks.'

Pete frowned. 'The asterisks?'

'Yes,' nodded Mr Shaw slowly, 'the plural of asterisk. One of the asterisks reveals that there will be a small nuclear explosion as the finale.'

Pete waived his hand dismissively. 'It's just a little bang and a puff of smoke, we thought it might be a little closing entertainment.'

Mr Shaw half smiled. 'Well, the creative element will be judged by my colleague,' he glanced at Mr Hampton, who winked and clicked his shoes together, 'but for my part I will expect this nuclear explosion to occur after the train is safely underground.' He chuckled to himself. 'If the explosion occurs before then I will fail you on that part of the time table. Can't have the nuclear bunker special destroyed by a nuclear bomb because it's not running on time.'

Pete nodded. 'Absolutely.' Pete had no idea what Nick had prepared as a nuclear finale and frankly if they'd actually made it to that point in the timetable he wouldn't care.

'The other asterisk of note talks of breakdown cover?' continued Mr Shaw.

Pete nodded while raising a finger to his cheek and tapping it.

'Yes, that is a little strange. Er, during our timetable we sometimes run out a recovery train, to, erm, provide a little extra random entertainment value. Sort of keeps everyone on their toes. What you need to know is that we don't always use it. Er, that is to say it's not a scheduled thing, as such.' Pete smiled cheesily at Mr Shaw. If he accepted this little manoeuvre it'd be a miracle.

Mr Shaw screwed up one eye and pulled a strange face. 'OK then, we can accept that.'

Pete grinned and gave a thumbs up. The old asterisk ploy had worked beautifully, just as it always did in the second-hand car trade. I mean if you had to sell anything made by British Leyland you needed a lot of asterisks to cover your arse and this guy had only questioned a couple.

Mr Shaw took a step back and Mr Hampton came forward. He coughed slightly and addressed Pete.

'As you know TRACK are placing a greater emphasis on the creative side of our hobby and so for the final they are devoting one judge to concentrate solely on that. I will inspect your layout in the next half hour and mark it before also allocating marks on the creative nature of your time table.'

Pete nodded. 'Good. I guarantee you're going to be busy.'

Mr Hampton nodded back and turned to start investigating the layout.

Pete shuffled to the back of the layout where Colin, Stew and Adrian were huddled. Colin spoke first in a low whisper. 'What's the score boss?'

Pete squatted down. 'I think we may have a half decent pair of judges. Which makes a nice change.' He looked at his team. 'So far, so good. Anyone know where Nick and Justine are?'

Stew piped up. 'I saw Nick heading upstairs. He looked a little upset actually.'

Bomber was walking with haste and purpose along the quiet residential street. Yellow brick Victorian terraces crowded either side held back by mature limes that were in full shed. Their leaves gathered in deep piles between the densely parked cars and it was at one of these that Bomber stopped and rummaged around in his pocket.

Ken tucked instinctively behind the cracked bark of one of the limes. Bomber pulled out a set of keys, checked around and opened the boot of a rusty orange Marina. Ken couldn't quite see what he did but Bomber now had a small rucksack hanging from his right shoulder and was walking at pace again towards the Town Hall. Ken let him gain more distance and then stepped out to follow. By the time Bomber rounded the final corner that took him to the edge of the Town Hall car park, Ken was a good thirty meters behind. He decided to up his pace a little and affect what could almost be called a jog. Sadly, his canter was almost immediately ended outside Boots, when he blundered into a young lady exiting the store. Ken managed to remain on his feet, but his victim fell to one side, spilling the contents of her carrier bag. He momentarily watched Bomber reach the entrance to the exhibition before he knelt down to help up the woman.

'I'm so sorry' he stumbled. 'Was in a bit of a rush but that's no excuse. Are you ok?'

Justine got slowly to her feet with the aid of Ken's outstretched hand.

'No problem' she groaned. 'Got a train to catch or something?'

Ken laughed. 'No, just, er, keen to get to that model railway thing, you know, the final.'

'Yes, I know, I'm with one of the finalists.'

Ken bent down and picked up some nail varnish remover.

'Thanks' said Justine, as she popped it back in the bag.

'Which club?' enquired Ken.

'Smooth Fishplate' answered Justine.

'Ah, very good. What do you think your chances are?'

Justine shrugged and smiled.

'If it was a level playing field, I'd say pretty good.' She clutched her Boots carrier again and started to walk off. 'I better get going. It all kicks off in ten minutes.'

Ken called out after her.

'Good luck, might see you later.' He watched her scuttle across the car park. A few thoughts occupied his mind. What did she mean by level playing field? And she didn't strike him as the sort of girl that wore nail varnish.

11 o'clock suddenly appeared as though late for an urgent appointment. There was a shrill whistle and the grand final of the SE Regionals finally got under way. Justine eventually found Nick in the tea room, hunched over a cold cup of tea.

'Are you ok? You look a little pissed off.'

Nick shook his head. 'No. I don't think so. Well I might be.'

Justine raised her eyebrows and pulled out a chair to sit down.

'Oh great, nice timing to get all complicated. Shouldn't we be doing something to help win?'

'Why are you buying things in a builder's merchant?'

'Where did that come from?'

Nick frowned. 'I got talking to Angie and she said -'

'And she should mind her own business.'

'OK, so what were you doing there?'

'If you must know I was buying some stuff so I could make Dad something for his birthday, but apparently I'm not allowed to do that.' Justine folded her arms and did a good impression of a sulk.

'Well why didn't you tell me? Why the secrecy.' Justine needed this conversation to be over, there were far more important issues at stake. She decided to deploy the only excuse that would kill the topic and get Nick back on the competition and away from awkward questions.

She sighed theatrically. 'If you really must know I was getting materials for a surprise. For you, you idiot.'

Nick felt stupid in the special way men feel stupid when they spoil a surprise meant for them. 'Crap, I'm so sorry, I, er…'

'Should have kept quiet and trusted me?'

'Yes, exactly that.' Nick got out his wallet and placed Inspector Hancock on the table. 'I made the mistake of not consulting this little fella.'

Justine smirked. 'Yes, you should always consult small plastic figures before jumping to some sort of conclusion. And I don't want to know what you thought I might be up to.' She gave Nick her special stern stare, with extra stern.

'But –'

'What?'

'Just one question?'

Justine screwed up her eyes and breathed out heavily.

'Go on.'

'Angie said you were buying things that you wouldn't normally use on a model railway.'

There was an angry silence. Nick knew that whatever Justine was thinking and was about to say would need a careful answer.

'You are such a moron sometimes' sighed Justine. 'When did you ever buy materials that were specifically designed solely for model railways? I remember you going into a specialist tobacconist so you could buy a certain type of Russian matchstick because it was made of a certain type of wood that you needed to make window frames from.' She paused to think. 'Angie doesn't know what I need, so she should just shut up.' Justine unfolded and refolded her arms.

'I absolutely agree' nodded Nick.

'About which bit?'

'That I am a moron.'

Justine laughed. 'Indeed. Now, can we go and check out how our team are doing? And you can carry that Boots bag for me. Give you a chance to check out what I've purchased and its relevance to model making.' In the back of her mind Justine was thinking she was now going to have to make a 'surprise' present for Nick.

Nick reached over and took the carrier. He had a quick glance in. No need to ask about the varnish remover, he used it all the time. As they exited the tea room a small voice from his wallet cried out. 'Be careful I caught a glimpse of something!' He ignored Hancock and diligently followed Justine's lovely bottom down the stairs.

Monty 'The Moustache' Rawlins gazed down the line towards Greenvale with what one might call a proud expression on his face. To be honest it looked like his normal expression, but Monty knew the difference. Today was a big day for Lower Didsbury. The busiest timetable ever devised was underway and he couldn't help but feel immense satisfaction that his humble little station would see much of the action taking place on the network. It strangely brought back fresh memories of his final mission in 'Lucky Sexpot', of his brief incarceration and eventual triumphal return. He lived for those

*pivotal moments of history. Perhaps today would be one of those such
moments. Another through freight train thundered past the platform
and he watched it disappear down the line and into the far tunnel
mouth. Almost instantly a commuter train emerged from the same
tunnel mouth and pulled hard up the slight incline until slowly
coming to a halt on the opposite platform. Monty checked the
timetable. Everything was running smoothly and bang on time.
'Everyone pulling together, just like the war' thought Monty.*

*All over the local area there was a general feeling that something was
up, for good or bad. But for most it was still business as usual.*

*Janet had already missed one connection because her mother would
just not finish the phone conversation she was having on the station
platform. Christ! Now she was wittering on about the bloody wisteria
that grew over her porch. A man waiting to use the phone huffed
loudly. Janet couldn't help noticing his ruffled appearance, he actually
looked like he'd been literally dragged through a hedge backwards.
Anyway, there were plenty of trains around today, he'd just have to
wait until mother had stopped talking.*

*Dennis had idled his new, old, repainted Ford tractor down, while
waiting to cross the rails but there seemed to be no end to the rail
traffic today. In the end he turned the engine off and day dreamed of
aluminium trailers.*

*Stevo and Ginge were in the beer garden. They drank heavily from
their pints. Trains made them nervous and there seemed to be lots of
trains on the move today. Stevo rubbed his neck instinctively and
realised that months of therapy had done nothing for him. Only
alcohol numbed the memories. 'Fancy another one mate?'*

*Ginge met his eyes and nodded. It was going to be a long old day.
They really ought to find another pub a little further away from the
line.*

*In the Greenvale station carpark Mr Mouncey tutted loudly to
himself. Some idiot had parked over the allotted white parking line
by several inches. He noted the car's manufacturer, a Ford, how
typical. He jotted down the reg and started to write a ticket. Another
mixed freight train trundled slowly past the nearby platform before*

gaining speed. Mouncey watched it go, there was definitely lots going on today and he'd also noticed a part of the car park near the siding had developed what looked like regular splits in the tarmac. He had of course coned it off, but it troubled him. This car park seemed to have a life of its own. These concerns immediately vanished when he suddenly spied Margaret Spencer trying to park her battered old Vauxhall in the space between his office (shed for cones) and his brand-new Triumph, the trouble being, there was no space.

Pete looked down from the mezzanine at Smooth Fishplate. The lads seemed to be holding up well with the extreme timetable, if anything things seemed to be going more smoothly than at any other point in the competition. He scanned the crowd watching below, which was about two people deep. Nothing suspicious going on yet but how would you know? He looked along the line of the mezzanine, which itself was almost fully lined with people. There were several hobby types with cameras sporting huge zoom lenses, the distinctive noise of the shutter going off surprisingly loud in the voluminous hall. Just then a flicker of movement caught his attention on the opposite side of the mezzanine. There wasn't such a good view from that side and consequently less people, and someone, with a red baseball cap, was rummaging around in a rucksack. After all the investigations, witness accounts and general rumours were taken into account, the only thing Pete could reliably be suspicious of was hats, even baseball caps, which he assumed counted as a hat. He cupped his eyes with his right hand and squinted to try and get a better look. The guy in the red cap seemed to look in his direction and pause, just for a fraction of a second, before fumbling with something and quickly zipping up the rucksack and heading back down the mezzanine, toward the main stairs. Pete was off in a middle-aged flash, which involved lots of apologies, 'excuse me-s', involuntary groans and a complete lack of success, in that the red cap made it to the stairs first and disappeared down them. Pete stood, frustrated, his foot dangling over the top step. He pulled back and instead made his way to where the red cap had been. He took the view in. It was a nothing view. Pete leant forward against the railing and then bent over with his elbows firmly supporting his heavy face via the polished teak balustrade. He let out a heavy sigh and casually observed the people milling below in the central area, reserved mainly for trade stands and exhibiting club layouts. Almost immediately he clocked onto a shortish, neatly dressed chap, who looked strangely aloof. He had a slightly bewildered air but seemed to be seeking something or someone. Pete tucked in from the edge slightly and kept his eyes glued to him.

Ken Bruce was feeling a tad directionless. He was hoping to catch sight of Bomber again but the number of spectators and people milling around was a little disorientating, plus he had an increasingly urgent desire to go to the toilet, unsurprising since all he'd done this morning was drink tea and coffee. He decided to make his way over to see Fishplate and then use the ground floor toilets at that end of the hall.

Pete watched his quarry go over to Fishplate and briefly observe the operations before stepping lively away and heading towards the back of the hall. The only thing at the back of the hall were the toilets. He paused momentarily, dismissed some cautionary internal dialogue and headed to the staircase, again.

'I like holding hands' chirped Justine randomly, as she and Nick negotiated their way down the stairs from the tea room.

Nick squeezed her hand in reply. They reached the mezzanine and Justine guided Nick around a corner and towards the front of the hall, where Harbour Town were located. As they passed above Smooth Fishplate Nick noticed Pete bolt out from below, look round and head back towards the toilet. He let go of Justine's hand to alert her. 'Looks like Pete's getting into his security role.'

Justine stopped so they could both peer down onto their layout.

'Everything looks like it's going well' commented Nick. 'Won't last long' he added.

Justine sighed. 'I haven't really seen the layout from this height. If you squint your eyes it's like looking down from a plane.' She moved her head in a slow looping movement, her gaze transfixed.

Nick watched her and felt strangely contented. His emotional reverie lasted almost ten seconds before Justine stopped her looping trance and commented that he'd forgotten to glue the rusty TV aerials to the pet shop roof line.

Nick grunted, 'Bollocks! C'mon, let's go and see if we can spot any mistakes on Harbour Town.'

Justine giggled. 'OK, but let's stay up here so I can rain down a few death stares at Angie.'

Nick tutted. 'Still scared of her, eh? Don't worry, she's like a dog, never looks up.'

Ken pushed open the door to the gent's toilets and stepped in. To his left was a row of three urinals and, contravening every law of urinal etiquette, was a portly man, occupying the middle one. Ken naturally decided to use one of the old-fashioned stalls to the right. He eased the wooden door open and walked in, closing it with a satisfying clump. The Victorian stall was surprisingly roomy and as Ken went about his business he couldn't but help notice a slight metallic glint coming from behind a large cast iron pipe in one corner. After flushing and zipping himself up, he leant down and investigated. The glint came from a buckle that was attached to a – he pulled at the buckle – to a rucksack. The same rucksack Bomber had and judging by its shape, he stuck his hand in, yes, there was his bomber jacket. Ken put the rucksack back and stood up, he opened the door and walked over to the sinks. So, what had been in the rucksack? And could he recognise Bomber without his bomber? Such important questions were instantly put on hold when the gent's door flew open and Pete came flying in, immediately losing his footing on the tiles and ending up sprawled on the floor under the hand drier.

Adrian flexed his fingers, took a few quick breaths and started to assemble another train. So far, the fiddle yard had been operating perfectly, the siding extensions had allowed him to pre-assemble more train combinations and the resultant efficiency had allowed them to run a larger timetable. He finished coupling up the last iron ore wagon.

'Hey Colin, the ore tail's ready, still want Sooty to be the engine?'

Colin clicked his tongue. 'One second. Stew I'm bringing out that scrap train, be careful on this one, it's quite heavy.'

'Indeedy' replied Stew.

'Adrian?'

'Yes boss.'

'OK, let's run old Sooty, we need his weight for that load plus he's got the torque.'

Adrian laughed. 'I love it when you talk torque to me.'

'I hope that's not a musical pun' retorted Colin.

'Commuter special coming over to your control, Colin. In three, two, one.' Stew turned briefly to Adrian. 'One more hour to go, keep it up, you're doing grand.'

Justine put her arm round Nick and nestled her head into his grey jumper.

'Nick?' she half whispered, 'Do you think all the models in Harbour Town have funny little lives, like our creations?'

Nick gave a knowing smile. 'I'd like to think so. Angie has a few personality problems but she's definitely one of the most creative model makers I've ever met.'

Justine gave Nick a gentle pinch.

'Oi!'

Justine smiled. 'So, do you think she gives them their own special back stories?'

Nick paused. 'Er, possibly? I've never really thought about Angie that deeply.'

Justine frowned. 'Do the Daleks have a back story?'

'Of course.'

Justine paused, grinned and bit her lip. 'In brief?'

Nick took a deep breath. 'OK. Dalek one. Fed up with being a Dalek. Wants to travel and meet interesting people. Told Davros to fuck off and can be seen heading to the travel agents. Dalek two. Loves being a Dalek, wants to take exterminating to a new level. Denied love at an early age, sent to boarding school, abused by a young C3PO. Hates almost everything apart from, obviously, exterminating. Shown modelled out of sight in a garage adding an extra-large sink plunger to his weapons array. Dalek three. Has a gambling problem and owes various people money, including Davros. Davros thinks he borrowed the cash to build a conservatory. Dalek three actually blew it all at the gee-gees on a horse called Steptoe. At the moment he is hiding behind a pillar box near the bank waiting for the bullion van. The bullion van won't turn up because Dalek seven is currently holding the driver hostage in an attempt to extort money from the bank, having learned of Dalek three's plan. Dalek seven also owes Davros money due to his addiction for drugs and cheap hookers. Dalek four. Currently submerged in the duck pond because –'

'Stop… please.' Justine wiped the tears from her eyes. 'Tell me the rest another time when I'm in a bad mood, its gold.'

Nick pulled her close and lightly kissed her cheek. 'No one else would find that funny.'

Justine chuckled. 'Good. That stuff's just for us.' She paused. 'But I do wonder what sort of life the inhabitants of Harbour Town might have?'

'Guess you'll have to ask Angie about that.' Nick shrugged and they both stared down at her kingdom.

The bay was calm. It nearly always was. Young Greg was sat on an upturned fish crate mending nets. He paused momentarily as another tourist train pulled out from the harbour station, it was the twelfth in the last half hour. He couldn't remember it ever being quite this busy. His large powerful hands methodically went about their business, freeing his mind to wander. It was a day like this five years ago that he left home fed up with his overbearing parents and their plans for him, when he eventually told his dad that he'd decided to become a fisherman. His dad freaked and cut him out of his will. 'Well, fuck him' said Greg to a watching seagull. 'I'm doing alright.'

Up the hill from the harbour front, just as the town gave way to the verdant green pasture of Barrow's dairy farm, was Tom's small stone cottage. Tom himself could be seen propped up by the front window always staring out and down towards the seafront. Local legend had it that after falling out with his dad's choice of career for him, Tom never once set foot in Harbour Town. His father ran a small accountancy firm there and every year Tom would symbolically burn a giant wicker ledger in protest at his father's intransigence. No one knew what Tom actually did for a living, including his dad, but as Tom often said. 'Tain't out a snuffs as worth a mig tin tut mid 'o' the plut.'

The Mayor of Harbour Town stood admiring the view from the war memorial down the narrow high street towards the shore. Half way down he could make out the wonderful model shop that his adopted daughter ran. She was an utter genius within the field of model making and he felt a deep sense of pride that he had rescued her from her natural parents who were, it had to be said, a complete pair of ignorant, selfish, small minded, visionless, mean, tyrannical, unimaginative, bone headed, uncompromising, conventional, unloving, why bother having a child, wanted a boy anyway, they'll be sorry when I'm dead pair of human beings. 'Yes!' exclaimed the Mayor, holding back the tears. 'I'm so, so, so very proud of my adopted daughter. Thank God I got them away from her parents. What a waste trying to force her to go to secretarial school. Imagine the loss to the world of models.' He looked around sheepishly hoping no one had heard his little outburst. It was so hard keeping it in sometimes when your chest was so swollen with pride.

Ken Bruce leant over and offered Pete his hand. Pete accepted it with a slight air of suspicion and pulled himself up. They stared at each other for slightly longer than would normally be considered polite although considering Pete's informal entrance, all etiquette was null and void. Ken was the first to speak. 'I believe I've met you before,' he paused, 'at some model club do for this region.'

Pete brushed out his finest Millets checked shirt. 'Yes, I think so, yes, you're Mr Bruce. Captain Hargraves' man.'

Ken nodded. They stood in silence.

'What's going on?' they asked in unison. Ken smiled. 'You

first.'

Pete shook his head quickly. 'Right, er, I'm Peter Fletcher by the way, President of Smooth Fishplate. And I was wondering what you were up to, because someone's out to do us today. And I can't have that and I'm trying to protect my lads. And?'

Ken mustered his serious face. This Peter chap was obviously a little on edge. A couple of men entered the toilets and Ken took the opportunity to usher Peter away to a quieter area at the back of the hall. 'Look,' said Ken. 'I've been sent here to observe and that's all.' He waggled his head slightly. 'But 'observing' can mean many things. Look, from what I've seen, I think something is up.'

Pete frowned. 'Like what exactly?'

'Well I can't really go into much more at the present moment.' Ken looked at his shoes.

'I see' exclaimed Pete. 'So, what if we get put out through no fault of our own then?'

Ken squirmed uncomfortably. 'I won't do anything about it. I have my orders.'

Pete folded his arms in a slightly aggressive manor, it was all he could think of.

Ken shrugged and held out two apologetic hands. 'Look, I'm here. I'll be looking around, let's hope that between the two of us we can deter any wrongdoing.'

Pete rolled his eyes. 'Well if that's all you're offering, I guess, er, that's all you're offering.'

Ken nodded and turned towards the main hall. 'After you.'

It was at about this time that Colin detected just the merest whiff of electrical distress coming from the layout and a couple of seconds later Stew whispered urgently that Sooty was beginning to struggle.

Colin took a deep breath. 'OK Stew, how soon till Sooty comes under my control?'

'About thirty seconds, but his speed's falling and I'm running out of voltage.'

Colin brought a mixed freight into Greenvale and isolated it into a siding. 'OK, guys, we're going to have to use the big button.'

'Christ' murmured Stew.

Adrian let out a low whistle. 'That's my job isn't it?'

'Yeah' said Colin.

Adrian rubbed his hands together. 'Ok, ok. Remember the drill, remember the drill.'

'Get on with it' muttered Colin impatiently.

'Right, right.' Adrian cracked his fingers. 'Cover plate removed. Actuating voltage control. In five, four…'

Colin whispered urgently to Stew. 'Keep all your trains grounded until I bring Sooty in.'

'…Two, one.' There was a very quiet little click.

While nothing appeared to have happened, the reality was that the voltage being supplied to the tracks had just doubled. Sooty started to speed up in line with an increasingly urgent electrical smell. Colin was manfully toggling the controls, coaxing the brave engine on to the safety of the fiddle yard. If he could just get it out of sight they'd be fine, no drama and no loss of points.

Mr Shaw, the timetable judge, was beginning to take a keen interest in the progress of Sooty, he clearly detected a problem.

Sooty started slowing again and Colin thought he could see something… thread, or fine plastic binding up the wheels. He whispered to Adrian. 'Can we knock out any more voltage?'

Adrian breathed out heavily. 'All I can do is temporarily isolate all power to boards one to five, which should give you a few more volts.'

'Do it.'

Sooty temporarily stopped slowing which was all Colin needed to finally get the mortally wounded engine off the main line and to the safety of Adrian and the fiddle yard.

'Adrian, reinstate the normal circuits and dump that extra voltage, Stew, we're going to have to run a slightly faster table to catch up. OK?' Colin temporarily closed his eyes and thought of the Princess Leia outfit. 'C'mon we can do this.'

A few seconds later Pete turned up. 'What's that smell?'

'That my friend is the smell of sabotage. By the way, we got through it. Weren't you supposed to be stopping that sort of nonsense?' hissed Colin.

'Fuck' whispered Pete back. He paused. 'If it's any consolation TRACK are here… investigating.'

'Investigating my arse more like' replied Colin.

There was a slight cough from the back of the layout. 'You'd really like that, wouldn't you?'

'Ah, Nick. And what have you been doing exactly?' muttered Colin.

'Watching Harbour Town.'

Colin accelerated a passenger train away from platform two at Greenvale. 'Standby Stew, inbound passenger.' He half turned toward Nick. 'And?'

Nick smiled. 'Nothing doing. All going smooth and by the numbers over yonder at Harbour Town. I've left Justine there to keep an eye out.'

Stew eased a heavily laden timber train out onto the main

line and gently rolled it past the Lower Didsbury station. 'Timber inbound to Greenvale.'

'Got it' replied Colin.

Pete crouched down. 'Ok, the plan is this. I'll stay here and attempt to do something useful. Nick, wander around and cause something to happen.'

'That's one desperate plan' laughed Nick

'Well, it's worked for us before. Now get.'

Ken looked down from the mezzanine at Fishplate. There was clearly some sort of discussion going on. Poor guys. What he couldn't quite understand was how someone could usefully sabotage a model railway in such a public space. Clearly the tactics being used were more sophisticated and the prize suitably larger than he had at first suspected. And as for that bomber guy, where was he? Ken stood back from the edge and gazed upward to the balcony on the top floor, outside the tearoom. There were a few people standing near the edge, but their backs were turned to the hall. He was about to look away when a single figure appeared. An arm reached out with a clenched fist, the fist opened, the arm withdrew and the figure disappeared again. Some sort of slowly dispersing cloud was falling gently towards Fishplate.

The mighty class 55 Deltic was beginning the final station pass before delivering its massive load of coal to Dukes End power station. Monty stood proud on the Lower Didsbury platform awaiting the traditional blast from its twin air horns, which always prompted a crisp salute from him. Meanwhile just up the line at the road crossing Dennis was awakened from his gentle snooze by the rapidly escalating rumble coming up the tracks. He yawned, fumbled around for a turnip and started his old ford tractor up.

Stevo and Ginge looked nervously at each other over their empty pint glasses. They could both hear 'Hadley's Hope' beginning its pass. The glasses began to shake and dance around on the old trestle table.

'Your turn mate' said Ginge

'Yeah, alright. Same again then?' replied Stevo.

'And crisps.'

Stevo grimaced. 'Don't fucking mention crisps, you know its bad luck.' He was about to remind Ginge what happened last time plain crisps were ordered when a very distinct clang came from the direction of the line.

'What the fuck was that?' hissed Colin.

There was the merest of pauses before Stew whispered back. 'Hadley's rear bogies skipped the track.'

'Shit. Shit, shit, shit! Slow it down quick.'

Silence, other than the horrendous squeal from a protesting train.

The protesting squeal began to quicken.

Colin craned his neck round and screamed in a whisper 'Are you speeding up?'

Stew was muttering 'Motherfucking T-Rex' repeatedly under his breath.

Dennis braced himself for impact. There was a paralysing shriek and a shock wave of grit, ballast and trackside vegetation that whipped about his neck and almost blew him off the tractor. He slowly opened his eyes, checked his legs were still attached and gazed back towards Ermintrude. 'You a rite thar me old gal?'

Ermintrude lowed back nonchalantly.

Monty squinted up the line. 'Hadley's Hope' seemed to be rolling up the track at an alarming rate and that sound was clearly not a regulation noise. He resisted the urge to dive for cover but couldn't help blinking slightly as several hundred tons of train thundered past, plaining several inches from the platform edging stones. Actually, it was rather quite exhilarating.

Colin looked on, transfixed, as Stew kept on the power. How the fuck Hadley's hadn't crashed was anyone's guess but the crunch point was now upon them in the form of multiple turnouts. Stew accelerated through the points and by a sheer miracle the trailing unguided bogey rode up over the first rail and reset itself on the tracks. Stew immediately reduced the power and took 'Hadley's Hope' through the tunnel towards the safety of the fiddle yard.

'You jammy bastard' muttered Colin.

Stew breathed out and rubbed his chin. 'I know. I know.' He scrunched up a trembling right fist. 'You know what I did there Colin?'

Colin eyed him. 'What?'

'I went for it!'

Colin laughed. 'Yes you did Stew, yes you did. Now let's keep this motherfucking timetable going.'

Pete had witnessed the whole event in slow motion and seemed to be recovering in slow motion also. Eventually he gathered himself and stood up in a meaningful way with his arms folded. He muttered something about 'sorting it out' and disappeared into the crowd. Colin watched him go and slowly shook his head. 'Security's off to the toilet again.'

Nick had taken on Pete's plan and wandered off to see if anything might occur. In reality he had gone straight back to see if Justine had noticed anything at Harbour Town.

Justine smiled as he approached along the mezzanine. 'A quick question for you my love.'

'Hit me.'

'Do you think Gareth would turn up to this event?'

'Where the fuck did that come from?' Nick spread out his arms.

'Seriously. Would he turn up?'

Nick shrugged. 'Maybe, I don't know why though, says he's done with us and I believe him.'

Justine nodded. 'Yes, I believe that too… but –'

'But?'

'But I saw this guy wearing a blue baseball cap and I got the strangest feeling.'

Nick stared at her.

Justine pulled a stupid face. 'That's all.'

Nick was about to say something funny and sarcastic but was luckily interrupted by a sudden crash and immediate pandemonium in the trade stand area. They both moved close to the edge to see what had occurred. Someone appeared to be rolling around on the floor attached to a trade spinner.

'That looks remarkably like the spinner we met at' mused Nick.

Justine smiled. 'Yeah and if I hadn't started talking to you, I bet that was your next move.'

'Oh ha-ha. What is occurring down there? Oh, hang on, it is the one, that's the same guy. He's not going to tolerate this shit.'

A highly agitated geezer grabbed the sprawling youth on the floor and yanked him up. It looked like for all the world that he was about to 'lay one on him' but instead the geezer snorted and shoved the youth to one side, before picking up the spinner and checking the little plastic bags of modelling delight were in the right order. The youth for his part looked strangely calm considering he'd been thrashing about on the floor like a trapped weasel just seconds before. He brushed himself down, looked up the hall towards Fishplate, made a strange hand gesture and then quickly exited the hall.

Justine turned to look at Nick. 'Bit odd? And that tennis top really didn't suit him. Bet that's what got caught in the spinner, one of those stupid pockets. Nick?'

Nick was staring wildly into space. Justine instantly recognised something big had happened.

'Crap, oh crappy crap' whispered Nick. 'I think we've just been fucked.' He ran off toward Fishplate, shouting back to Justine to keep watching.

Colin had allowed himself a few moments to follow the gazes of the on-lookers as some sort of disturbance broke out in the hall. He'd asked Adrian to stand up and have a quick look, which had generated no more insight into what was going on and so he'd just shrugged and got back to moving a line of wagons along a siding.

'Got the Green Vale special coming over to you and expecting the school run from you as my next inbound.'

Colin grunted acknowledgment to Stew, parked the wagons and awaited the Green Vale special. A few seconds later it emerged slowly from the tunnel and he brought it in under his control towards the lengthy platform two. He noticed the tiny plastic bar straddling the track just shy of the platform a split second too late. With a gentle pop the diesel simply and cleanly left the track and wedged itself into the platform. Two carriages rolled over and ended up on their roofs on the opposite track. In the space of an exhaled breath Fishplate were, to use one of Colin's more sophisticated phrases, buffer fucked.

'Oi! Come back here.' Pete crashed through another door in demented pursuit of Bomber. He didn't of course know he was chasing Bomber, but he did know that he'd most definitely seen the bastard up to something and the fact that Bomber had taken off confirmed to Pete that this was his man, this was the saboteur. Following wheezily behind came Ken Bruce, who due to his slightly delayed entry into the chase kept finding the doors closing irritably in front of him.

Bomber charged against the final obstacle, pushing hard on the bar of the emergency exit. The heavy door slowed him up allowing Pete to gain some precious meters but now Bomber had the street in which to get his legs going. Pete cursed as he watched his quarry start to open up a growing lead, the fried breakfast from earlier sent a small reminder to his mouth that if he carried on in this manner it might have to jump ship. Ken Bruce tumbled through the emergency exit just in time to see which way the chase was headed. He paused and then came to a complete standstill. Ken was cerebral not physical. It occurred to him that he knew where Bomber's car was and that was surely where he was headed. The fact that Bomber was headed in completely the opposite direction only confirmed that he was going to dump angry Mr Fletcher and then double back. Ken wasn't entirely sure how he was going to handle Bomber but he at least had the element of surprise. Ken retied his left shoelace and headed back to the carpark and the short walk to the rather ugly orange Marina.

Nick pushed through two rows of gawping spectators to get to Fishplate. Colin had just finished righting the train and sending it on its way. Mr Shaw the judge was rapidly scribbling things down and no doubt deducting vast amounts of points. Nick ducked under the boards and positioned himself in a small space behind Colin. 'What happened?'

Colin carried on moving a small shunter across the main line. 'Small derailment. I mean nothing major but bad all the same.'

Nick frowned. 'Sabotage. Classic stuff really. Big diversion, do the deed, get the hell out. How did the derail happen?'

Colin parked the shunter. 'Adrian, can you form up two mixed freight tails. Cheers.' He momentarily reached down and passed a small plastic part to Nick.

Nick turned the object around in his hands. 'Sneaky bastard. He's used an old plastic axle with a rectangular plate of… looks like ABS, stuck in the middle.' He held the axle closer and squinted.

'Yep' replied Colin. 'Acts like an anchor. Stops the train pushing the object forward. Makes it go over instead.'

Nick suddenly felt very sick and had to kneel down. Colin peered down at him. 'You ok? You've gone pasty mate.'

Nick staggered to his feet and stumbled away.

Pete started to slow up. His lungs were burning, a stitch was pushing against his rib cage and he was pretty sure that the swarm of bright lights fluttering around his peripheral vision was not a good sign. He'd lost sight of the guy anyway. Pete flopped down onto a nearby bench and wiped the sweat that was seeping out of his hairline. 'So close, just like that bloody dream' he muttered to himself. An old lady walked slowly past him pushing a chequered shopping basket on wheels. She gave him a disapproving look and tutted loudly to an imagined audience. Pete watched her trundle on before raising himself up and getting his bearings. He wasn't entirely sure where he was, but the chase had definitely taken two major right turns. Pete wearily reasoned that turning right at the end of the long street he was presently in would probably take him back in the general direction of the Town Hall. He looked at his watch. Twenty minutes left. Probably wasn't even going to get back for the grand finale. 'Oh fucking hell!' he shouted to himself.

Hank Nutsure, the chief safety officer for Harbour Town, was sat at his desk pondering the day's list of inspections. Through the large single pain of ultra, heat treated safety glass that sat resolutely in a steel reinforced frame he had a grand view of the viaduct that took rail traffic away from Harbour Town and off towards Clacton. The road under the viaduct heading down the hill was running freely and he had a satisfying feeling that today would mark another record day since the last accident, which hadn't had anything to do with him anyway because he hadn't been in charge then. He looked back down at the list. Item number three sparked his curiosity; 'check the points on the heavy recovery wagon siding'.

Hank wrinkled his nose and looked back through the window. He could see the recovery wagon over to the right and the points were right outside his office.

'Should be a quick job. Wonder why that's on the agenda though?' he said to both himself and his lucky cactus that sat quietly on a window ledge above the main radiator. The cactus continued to offer nothing, so he returned to his list. Item number one was the usual guff about replacing bulbs on the stretch of track approaching the viaduct. His boss had once had a dream about a train plunging off said viaduct and was in a state of almost permanent paranoia about anything to do with the signalling, especially the brightness of all the red lights. Hank glanced across the room to the large metal cupboard sitting squarely against the far wall, the contents of which were entirely composed of red and green signal bulbs. His extra-lucky pine cone hung from the handle, he would have preferred a rabbit's foot but was unfortunately a vegetarian. Hank sighed and was just about to

look at item two on the agenda when there was a gut-wrenching squeal that caused Hank to spin back round to the window just in time to witness a light goods train smash headlong into the back of the heavy recovery wagon, which in turn rolled forward through the buffers and retired itself in a straddling position across the main line. Hank couldn't be sure but amid the wreckage he thought he could see a compressed version of his lucky Austin Cambridge.

In the enquiry that followed it was deemed that Mr Hank Nutsure could in no way be blamed for the sequence of unlikely events that had led to the incident. The failure of a red light signal had allowed a train to enter a section of track too soon, not in itself a problem unless there was an Austin Cambridge parked across the rails. The Austin was there because a faulty handbrake had allowed it to roll through a safety fence (Item two, check safety fence integrity), the resulting low speed collision had caused the nearest points to fail and hence directed the train into the recovery wagon siding. Of course, the irony of the chief safety officer's car, in effect causing a crash that put out of action the main means of clearing up the resultant mess was not lost on the members of the inquiry. Mr Nutsure never again applied for any role involving safety, which instantly made him a disappointment with his third-generation safety operative parents. Since the incident he has also parted company with his lucky cactus.

Ken Bruce approached the orange Marina, there was no one in sight and the street was leafily silent. He took up a comfortable leaning position against a warm yellow brick wall and attempted to work out what his next move might be. He didn't have long to think however as, like a bee returning to its hive, Bomber appeared round a corner and began to advance steadily toward the car. Ken tried to casually observe him. Bomber looked smaller, almost weaselly. He had a somewhat stooped, animal manor to him and an easy physical confidence. Ken instinctively wrung his hands and felt the softness and weakness in them. He had no idea what to do. Bomber was now a mere ten meters away. Ken had to act.

'Er, excuse me sir.'

Bomber slowed slightly and looked behind him. Seeing no one, he stopped and looked Ken straight in the eyes. 'Yes mate?'

'I need to talk to you about the model railway exhibition.'

Bomber squinted and seemed to look at Ken anew. 'Have I seen you somewhere before?'

'Well, I was at the aforementioned exhibition.'

Bomber sniffed the air and looked slyly to one side, before focusing on Ken's shoes. 'You were hanging outside the phone box weren't you mate? I recognise those poncey shoes.' Bomber moved closer toward Ken, uncomfortably close.

'I, er, needed to use the phone' stammered Ken.

Bomber stuck out a thick finger and jabbed it repeatedly against Ken's forehead. 'So what's your game then?'

Being repeatedly poked in the forehead felt like the most awful assault Ken had ever had to endure. He couldn't think right, he didn't know what to do. Why was this man so needlessly aggressive? How dare he? He just wanted to ask him a few questions.

'Stop it!' cried Ken.

'Or what?' taunted Bomber in a mocking childlike voice.

'Or.'

'Or you're going to cry?' sneered Bomber.

Ken felt the fingers in his right hand contracting, his arm swung back and forward, the fingers opened and he delivered a slap to the side of Bomber's shaven head. Ken reeled back in shock and instinctively held up his trembling hand to his mouth as he tried to contemplate what had just happened.

Bomber rubbed a hand over the side of his head and

frowned at Ken, his mouth ajar. 'Did you just slap me, you little prat?' He took a step back while shaking his head and paused before gazing malevolently at Ken. 'Well that wasn't a slap mate. That was a tickle. This is a fucking slap.' His arm moved slowly back. Ken closed his eyes.

Nick made it to the mezzanine and stumbled towards Justine as she looked down at Harbour Town. He grabbed her by the shoulder and thrust the small plastic axle into her hand. 'I think we've got a major problem.'

Justine briefly examined the axle. 'What damage did it do?'

'A derail, not too bad but very heavily in the not good department.'

Justine butted in quickly. 'As long as it wasn't as bad as the utter cluster that just hit Harbour Town.' She smiled and almost immediately felt a little ashamed.

'What, they've fucked up?'

'Oh big time.'

'Trumpets, gold tassels?'

'Dancing girls, five tier cake and a guest appearance by Angela Rippon.'

Nick beamed. 'Fucking excellent. Oh hang on! Now I'm confused.'

'Why?'

'Well, that axle required some thought and a degree of craftsmanship. I was getting round to the idea that Gareth might have done some sort of double cross on us. You thought he might have been here, it just smelt a bit Garethy.'

Justine frowned. 'Well I reckon someone did Harbour. Maybe Gareth was here and helping us.' She paused. 'Maybe he fancies you,' she delicately stroked his thigh, 'big boy.'

Pete was ambling along a strange road, hopeful that it would take him toward the exhibition. He figured he had about fifteen minutes before their grand finale and the ultimate conclusion of all their recent endeavours. Optimistically, he figured that chasing the saboteur away may have given them the level playing field in which to win. Pessimistically, he wondered whether anything he ever did made any difference whatsoever and tomorrow he was going to have to go to work and sell second hand fucking cars all day. He sighed and looked up from his shoes, ahead were a couple of guys blocking the pavement, he instinctively thought about crossing over but realised with a dizzying dose of reality thwacking him in the face, that it was Ken and the saboteur. And Pete wasn't the only one to have just been thwacked in the face either. He started to run towards them.

Bomber opened up his palm, arched his elbow and was just about to slap Ken into next Tuesday, when he was roughly bounced off his feet by a bundle of aggrieved middle-aged energy.

Ken opened one eye slowly and the other quickly, he looked around and then down to witness Pete scrabbling away at Bomber like some sort of angry, fat rodent. Bomber seemed to be thinking about what he should do next, the expression on his face seemed to indicate that this whole situation was a little embarrassing for him. He clenched a fist, jabbed Pete viciously in the ribs, bent a knee and rolled him off to one side before springing to his feet and advancing towards Ken, who put up his fists instinctively to protect his face but ended up looking ridiculous. Bomber thought about thumping him but decided to just get in his car and leave, he turned and almost reached the door handle when something landed on his back. It was Ken, acting like some sort of mentally disturbed tree-hugging koala.

'Oh what the fuck is this?' screamed Bomber and tried to grab Ken. Pete had managed to get to his feet and stood holding his side in some degree of pain. He stumbled toward Bomber, tripped on a kerb stone and fell forward, head butting him in the stomach. There was a muffled groan as Bomber bent over, tipping Ken from his back and ending up sprawled on top of Pete. Ken scrabbled to his knees and for some reason decided to then try and hold on to Bomber's trainers. This really aggravated Bomber, who kicked out at Ken, hitting him squarely in the face with his size nine Nike Vandals. Ken screamed and fell on to his back holding the bridge of his nose. Pete attempted to get an arm round Bomber's neck but was rewarded with an elbow to the crotch that made his head swim and his body double up in further agony. Bomber rose slowly and tidied himself up. He looked down at Ken, said quietly 'Stay down you muppet' and kicked him in the ribs. Ken retracted up into a small, whimpering ball.

Bomber then turned his attention to Pete, bending down he whispered in his ear, 'It's not personal mate, it's just business' and thumped him hard against the side of his thigh. Feeling satisfied that no one was in any state to stop him getting in his car, Bomber straightened up, took one last, hard look at Pete and walked slowly to the back of his car. He calmly opened up the boot and reached in to retrieve something.

It was at this point in his life that Pete had his first out of body experience. He watched himself spring, fat-antelope like, to his feet and thrust forward to ram Bomber squarely in the small of his back. Pete nodded in appreciation at himself as Bomber catapulted briefly forward, before his bald head connected satisfyingly with the boot latch. There was a sort of 'crump' noise, what sounded suspiciously like a fart, and Bomber slumped neatly into the beckoning void of the old Marina's boot. Pete grinned, this was brilliant,

like watching an episode of Minder. He started to hum the
theme tune but was rudely interrupted by reality sucking
him back into his vacant body. Pete instinctively gripped
the car to stop himself fainting as the pain from his injuries
flooded back. He looked down into the boot, Bomber
appeared to be curled up unconscious, the merest hint of
surprise set into his ratty little face. Anger instantly flared
up and Pete slammed the car boot shut before his brain
reminded him to open it up and retrieve the car keys from
the limp Bomber. Pete clunked the lid down and locked it,
automatically checking it had indeed locked. It was
beginning to dawn on him that he'd sold this car at some
point, something was trying to make sense but doing it in a
way that somehow made less sense. A childlike moan
interrupted Pete's confusion and he turned painfully in the
direction of the noise. He could just make out Ken's shoe
protruding from under a tall privet hedge. He shambled
over and bent down.

'You alright there?'

There was a little scrabbly noise and Ken's head emerged.
'Please tell me he's gone.'

Pete frowned. 'You didn't see what just happened?'

'What?'

'Er, he left, er left his car and left. Just left. Not here,
anymore, no.'

There was a wheeze and Ken crawled out, glanced
nervously around and propped himself up against a low
yellow brick wall. Pete nodded and joined him, wincing at
the effort. A lazy breeze wafted past the fight scene, a dog
barked in the distance and an old lady with a shopping cart
moved slowly round them, tutting loudly. Pete rolled his
neck slightly and began rubbing his thigh, the pavement
began to feel quite comfortable from this new perspective.
He wiped his dusty face and turned to Ken. 'Well, that
could have gone better.'

Ken started a smile and stopped abruptly when it began to hurt too much. 'Yes… I suppose. He's a very angry individual, isn't he?'

'He's a fucking dickhead, is what he is' retorted Pete.

'Surprisingly strong for such a lithe chap' winced Ken and decided to readjust himself with much effort into a more comfortable position closer to Pete, who stretched out his arm and then reached into a pocket to fish out a small crumpled packet of Bensons. He offered the pack to Ken.

'No thanks, gave up years ago.'

Pete shrugged, flinched at the pain it produced and fished out a cigarette. It fell apart in his fingers. 'Bollocks.'

Ken attempted a chuckle, which ended in a stifled cough. 'Still, there was one good thing to come out of all this.'

'And that would be?'

Ken reached into his jacket and pulled out a small red diary. 'This!'

There were now only five minutes left before the final whistle. The bulk of spectators had shifted towards Fishplate, feeding off the rumour of a spectacular finale, a rarity in the world of model railway competitions. Colin and Stew had managed to bring the timetable back in line after the crash and were nicely poised to initiate the nuclear bunker special. Adrian had the train lined up, which was the smallest unit they were going to run, comprising of just a short six-wheel diesel and two stripped down carriages painted matt black. Adrian's finger was also hovering above the ridiculously large nuclear initiation button. Pressing this would set off the siren and commence the four-minute countdown to the 'explosion.' Nick had, for his own amusement, Sellotaped a scrap of paper below the button that read 'Don't Panic!'

A quiet calm had settled over the team. Colin checked his watch. 'Stew, are your lines clear of traffic?'

'Absolutely' replied Stew. 'I'm ready to bring in the prize.'

Colin grinned, 'OK then' and turned to Adrian. 'Release the Kraken.'

'Er…'

'Press the button Adrian, press the button.'

Grinning like a four year old, Adrian slid back the protective plastic cover, paused for dramatic effect and depressed the shiny red button.

There was an immediate nothing. Adrian looked alarmed and was about to press the button again but was stopped by Colin, who whispered that it was a Nick trait to build in a dramatic pause. Sure enough after a slightly longer than necessary silence a loud klaxon suddenly blared out, causing a ripple of shocked excitement to pass over the spectators and also to set off a couple of toddlers crying. Stew took his cue and set the special in motion, bringing it out of the fiddle yard and on to his section of track. To create a feeling of seriousness and expectation, Nick had set flashing red lights into the carriage roofs. The crowd 'oohed' in appreciation and edged nervously closer to the layout. Stew advanced the special down the line and past Lower Didsbury, he smiled and gave a wave of his hand before saying to Colin. 'Special entering tunnel to Greenvale, coming under your control.' And with that Stew had contributed his last to the competition. He turned to watch Colin take over and noticed that Nick and Justine had managed to tuck themselves into the small space next to Adrian. He winked at them.

'I have control of the special, bringing it into platform two, Greenvale.' Colin eased off the power and the nuclear special slowed to a stop, just before the turnout that would take it forward along a short stretch of straight track, round a tight bend and onto a section of line opposite the car park that terminated at some buffers. Team Fishplate (minus Pete) collectively held their breath and looked to Colin's hand that hovered imperiously above the controls. They waited. They waited a little more. Some of them needed to let go of their breath. Nick, naturally, was the first to make a suggestive noise. It was a small cough and could very accurately be interpreted as 'Colin, get a fucking move on.'

Colin remained static, apart from his lips that twitched rapidly as though he were thinking aloud, in silence.

Justine decided something needed to be said. 'Colin? Are you ok? You've gone a little pale.'

Nick helpfully added 'Get a move on mate, that nuclear bomb's not hanging around for you.'

Colin turned slowly to look at Stew and whispered. 'There's a small section of rail missing.'

Stew frowned, got up from his cab and leaned over towards Colin. Colin nodded very slightly in the direction of the trouble. Stew squinted, paused and then swore delicately under his breath.

By now it was clear, not only to Fishplate but also the crowd that something was wrong. Colin convened an emergency huddle meeting. The continuing klaxon sound effect was not helpful.

'OK, small gap on one side of the track between the train and the bunker… any ideas?'

Adrian raised the obvious question. 'Can't we lift the train over by hand?'

Nick answered impatiently. 'Lose too many points, it's in the time table.'

'Could we just activate the bunker anyway and pretend stopping the train here was part of the plan?' suggested

Stew.

Justine shook her head. 'We're supposed to drive the train into the bunker and then it all disappears underground. Anything less…'

'Is crap' added Nick.

Colin released a short angry grunt. 'How long till the bomb goes off?'

'Three minutes' replied Nick.

'Can you turn it off?'

Nick winced. 'Not really.'

Colin closed his eyes. 'OK, ok, only thing to do is back train up. Accelerate as fast as possible through that tight curve and hope that the centrifugal force against the back rail lifts the wheels above the gap on the inner rail and then hope to hell that I can stop the train before it hits the buffers.'

There was a short silence, punctuated rudely by the klaxon.

Nick tilted his head to one side. 'You make an act of desperate madness sound like a carefully thought out plan.'

Colin smiled. 'I'll take that as a go.'

'Yep, go for it mate' nodded Nick.

The rest of Fishplate murmured their consent, not that they had a choice at this point.

Colin took in a deep lungful of air and reversed the diesel slowly a foot or so. The crowd watched on excitedly, whispers and random pointing running through the huddled mass. Colin exhaled, glanced back at Stew and then went for it. The nuclear special was short, it was light and the diesel reliable, designed for heavy haulage. It accelerated rapidly, Colin kept the power on max as the diesel rammed into the tight curve, its momentum tilting it up against the outer rail. The whole train began to lift to one side but just as a complete tip over looked likely Colin cut the power and the diesel and its two carriages fell back onto the rail, the last bogie on the rear carriage just clipping the missing section of track. Colin's fingers moved as a blur to throw the reverse switch and power up again to bring the train to a dead stop before the buffers. It worked. He powered down and put the direction switch to neutral. The whole manoeuvre had lasted mere seconds. The crowd responded with broken clapping and the odd un-English type 'whoop'. Colin turned to look at his teammates only to find them looking incredulous. 'Oh great, you didn't think I could do it, did you?' There was a general shaking of heads. 'Fucking typical' muttered Colin. 'OK Adrian, get that bunker up.'

Adrian pressed the 'Up' button on the bunker control panel. Almost immediately the entire car park began to rise slowly. The lucky members of the transfixed crowd next to the scene inched forward to see more. With a satisfying clunk the concrete bunker locked into place, a curiously military piece of construction wearing a provincial town car park as a hat. The buffers holding back the diesel had vanished into the air and been replaced by a dangerously narrow looking set of rails leading into the darkened bunker interior. Of course, Colin had practised this part several times but every time it always looked like the entrance was too small. He turned briefly to look at the team. This was his last move of the competition and he felt strangely emotional. Nick caught his eye, Colin gazed at him with moist eyes. Nick mouthed back. 'You've got thirty seconds left you plonker.'

Colin shook his head and gently rolled the diesel into the bunker. Adrian hit the down button and the whole beautifully modelled nuclear survival bunker slid gracefully back under the car park. At some point the klaxon had stopped, Colin couldn't exactly say when it stopped but the silence felt weird, almost oppressive. It didn't last.

There was a nerve shattering bang that elicited shrieks followed by almost instantaneous howls of laughter. One of the judges dropped a clipboard and Adrian started to cough as a mushroom-shaped cloud of greyish thick smoke billowed up from the back of the layout.

It was at this point that Pete turned up, he hustled past the crowd and clambered under the boards to join the team. 'Please tell me that explosion was deliberate' he said, nodding his head.

There was a brief pause, broken by sporadic clapping from the crowd as it slowly dispersed. 'What the fuck happened to you? And. What the fuck happened to you?' asked Nick.

Colin took a closer look at Pete. 'Same question as Nick.'

Pete sniffed and ran a grazed-up hand through his messy hair. A small twig fell out. 'Well… I had a little moment with the saboteur. Man-to-man you might say.'

Nick caught Justine's eye. She looked away and reached up to Pete's face. 'Are you ok?'

Pete grinned manically. 'Absolutely fine, absolutely fucking fine. How did it end up?'

Adrian laughed. 'As usual Pete, it ended in an explosion and a cloud of smoke.'

Pete stood up and immediately spotted Ken Bruce, who had hobbled in just after him. Ken was in the process of talking to the four judges, he gave Pete a short nod and began to lead them up to the café.

'What now then?' shrugged Colin.

Pete turned from watching Ken disappearing up the stairs. 'We wait, they judge and I reckon in about half an hour we bloody better find out we're the winners or by God someone's off to the car crusher.'

There followed a slightly confused silence.

CHAPTER TWENTY-NINE: JUDGEMENT

In the final analysis there was very little Ken could add to the results submitted by the judges. Everything was correctly filled out, with absolutely no evidence of coercion, doctoring or buggering around. The judges had simply and competently recorded what was set before them. There was a decision, it would be final and Ken felt, given the general circumstances, it was fair. He sighed, not everyone was going to be happy but then there was always going to be a loser. Ken heaved himself up from the company of the judges and gently touched the large silver-plated trophy that sat imperiously in the middle of the tea-stained table. He turned to Mr Shaw.

'Mr Shaw, as lead judge you may continue your excellent work and award the winning club. I thank you for your diligence and patience on this.' He paused and brushed off some errant moss still clinging to the side of his jacket. 'I think I may stay up here and er, write a report for Captain Hargraves.'

Ken moved to a smaller side table and tried to make himself comfortable as the judges filed past him. The ache in his ribs was beginning to ease a little and he allowed himself a small experimental cough to settle his nerves. As the last judge left the café, he slipped his hand into the silk lined internal pocket of his jacket and removed the small red diary that had become, to his thinking, the real prize of the day.

George was contentedly fussing around his bar. This had been an exciting day for him because earlier, a new, salted nut hanging display had arrived. Sam Fox had finally relinquished her role to a pouting Linda Lusardi. He was pretty sure there were slightly fewer packets of nuts than the last Sam Fox edition, but he put this down to a smaller surface area, a notion often confirmed by the Sun. In further exciting developments the brewery had sent out some desperately needed new beer mats to promote their new bitter, 'Badger Snout'. George wasn't sure what the design of an overly aggressive Badger in a baseball cap meant, but it was colourful and at least the bitter wasn't half bad. He was just about to have a go at a persistent stain near the front of the bar when he was rudely interrupted by the arrival of Smooth Fishplate.

Pete marched triumphantly towards him and raised his arm as if a general addressing his troops.

'George my good man, we return to The Watertower and Tender as conquering heroes.'

George could feel he was in for an evening of 'tedium and trains', a phrase he'd invented to amuse himself whenever 'that lot' turned up, another phrase he oft used. He attempted to look professionally interested.

'Is it that railway competition thing then?'

'Absolutely. We've only gone and won it.' Pete lowered his arm and leant nonchalantly against the bar.

George couldn't help but notice Pete's somewhat battered appearance.

'What's with all the bruising? Is that a bit of privet?' He pointed accusingly at Pete's shirt.

Pete just scoffed and brushed the piece of hedge off.

'When you play against the big boys, things can turn rough.' He nodded and winked in the direction of Fishplate, who were settling down at their regular spot. George sighed and started to put together their usual order, it was going to be another long, incomprehensible evening.

Colin pushed the ash tray and a couple of empty pints

from the centre of the table and placed the large shiny trophy reverently down. There was a brief silence before he raised a clenched fist and stared triumphantly at everyone.

'Yes! Yes, yes, yes, yes, we fucking did it! I can't believe it. I just cannot believe we won. We always fuck it up at some point or someone else fucks it up for us.' He dropped down heavily onto a chair next to Stew and continued to grin maniacally at the cup. Stew pointed at the trophy base and turned to look at Nick.

'I think they've misspelt our name.'

Nick moved in closer and examined the freshly engraved plate before smirking and returning to his seat.

'Yep, we're all going to be remembered as team Fishpleat.'

There was a collective groan.

'Ah well, back to business as usual' laughed Nick.

Pete arrived with a precariously balanced drinks tray and carefully slid it onto the table next to the trophy.

'God, I still can't believe we actually did it.' He started to pass round the drinks. 'What a day, feels like all the crap was actually worth it this time.' He slid half a mild towards Stew. 'Is that a different tie?'

'Indeed' replied Stew, pleased that someone had noticed. 'I bought it just in case we won. It's my victory tie.'

'So what if we didn't win?' enquired Nick.

'Well obviously I kept the receipt.'

'Obviously' said Nick, shaking his head.

Pete finished passing out the drinks and plonked himself down before carefully buffing a small section of the trophy with the edge of his sleeve. Everyone watched him in amused silence which prompted Colin to ask an obvious question.

'So Pete, Mr President, Sir. How exactly are we going to divide out this gorgeous silvery object?'

Pete carried on buffing, his eyes shining with a degree of mania not normally apparent. Nick began to chuckle.

'Oh Peter?' he whispered, 'You can leave the precious alone now.'

Colin piled in straight away. 'We wants it my love. We wants the precious.'

'Tricksy Pete. Tricksy thieving Pete. The precious belongs to us. It's our precious. False Peter. False tricksy thieving second hand car salesman.' Nick made a pretend grab for the handle, which had the effect of breaking Pete's reverie.

'What? Oh! Hey! Oh, very funny. It's been a long day alright?' He stopped buffing and took a long sup on his Guinness. 'Sorry, what was the question Frodo?'

'Very good.' retorted Colin. 'How are we going to share the precious out then?'

Pete sniffed and glanced at the enquiring faces. 'Well, we've got it for two years. Who wants it?'

Everyone but Nick raised their hand. Justine jabbed Nick in the ribs. 'What!'

'Seriously?' said Nick shrugging his shoulders. 'I don't need a trophy to massage my ego. I know we're the best. Let the desperados have it' and then in a cheesy, barely audible, Barry White-style whisper. 'You're the only prize I want.'

Justine wrinkled up her nose, beamed and lowered her hand.

Pete frowned, 'Ok then, well, that's two years divided by four. Six months each.'

There was a general contented murmur. 'But as President, I get it for the first innings.'

Everyone essentially nodded their approval.

'So where's it going then Pete?' asked Nick, in a fairly disinterested manner.

'My office, just behind the desk.'

Nick harrumphed. 'I'm sure it'll look lovely amongst all those 'motoring' calendars and dusty pictures of old crap cars.'

Pete ignored him, took a hefty swig of Guinness and pointed at Stew. 'What about you?'

Stew folded his arms and dipped his head. 'Oh, I have an empty glass trophy case all ready.'

Colin shook his head. 'Christ! You're an optimist.'

Stew clasped his hands together. 'No Colin, I'm just prepared, although it has been barren some twelve years.'

Colin rolled his eyes and carried on shaking his head. Justine wagged her finger at him. 'Well, what about you then?'

'Simple. The lounge mantel piece.'

Nick rumpled his face. 'Have you moved recently?'

'No.'

'You don't have a mantelpiece… idiot boy.'

'So I've got six months to make one.'

Nick smirked. 'Knowing your DIY skills, you might need longer.'

'And' added Pete 'that's assuming you get it next.'

'Good point, well made Peter' said Nick earnestly.

Colin flicked one of Stew's peanuts at him. 'Stop stirring.'

Adrian let out a polite cough and raised his hand.

'For God's sake Adrian! Just butt in, like everyone else' suggested Nick.

'Point taken. Er, chest of drawers at the foot of my bed. I still have a few questions about what happened today.'

Nick closed his eyes and smiled. 'You don't know the half of it' and glanced sideways at Justine.

'So who is the saboteur?' Adrian nearly screamed. 'Someone here knows' and he looked directly at Pete.

Pete raised his eyebrows and smiled dangerously. 'You want to know who the saboteur is?'

Adrian backed up slightly. 'Well, er, yes please.'

'Tell you what' exclaimed Pete, standing up and knocking over his empty pint glass, 'I think we all need to know.' He looked down at the assembled and grinned. 'Back in a mo.'

They all watched him leave in concerned silence.

Colin piped up. 'Anyone else think he's acting a little weirdly?'

Nick shrugged. 'Give the lad a break, he's won the regionals and been beaten up all at the same time. It's quite the experience.'

Justine necked her drink and pointed at Colin. 'Who do you think it was then?'

Colin closed his eyes and very visibly gritted his teeth. 'Look, don't take this the wrong way but I thought the saboteur was you.' He risked opening his eyes again.

Justine was clearly attempting to compose herself before answering but Nick couldn't help intervening.

'Well Colin, so did I. It's so fucking obvious really. Attractive bird turns up, things start going wrong. Bloody weird if no one at some point went. 'Half a mo! This is all a bit odd."

Stew started nodding. 'I have to confess I did harbour a similar line of thought.'

'Well, cheers, Stew. Very noble of you' laughed Nick

sarcastically.

'And me' ventured Adrian.

'You as well?' Nick rolled his eyes. 'Oh very nice, well guess who I was suspicious of?'

Colin rubbed his hands together. 'This should be good. C'mon Nick, lay it down.'

Nick screwed up his face. 'I accuse Mr. Tanktop, with the fiddly brushes, in his bungalow.'

There followed an impressive silence, only broken by Stew, gently putting down his packet of KP. Colin shook his head. 'What on God's green earth would make you suspect Stew? I mean look at him.'

Stew's mouth had dropped a little, exposing a half chewed nut to the world.

Nick adopted a shrewd look and theatrically rose. He looked around the table before rubbing his chin thoughtfully. 'I first became suspicious at Dewesbury, scene of the first derailment. Why would Stew swap cabs with Colin? Perhaps -' Nick waived his hand nonchalantly, '- he thought it would be a good chance to test out his derailment block and let the blame fall on Colin.'

Colin moved in closer and squinted quizzically at Stew. 'You old rogue.'

Stew looked perplexed and started to nervously fiddle with his tie.

Nick continued. 'My suspicion grew when the alleged started to feed us all that Agatha Christie psycho-babble. It was all clearly a foil to distract us from his nefarious activities. And -' Nick paused. '- And what the fuck was all that stuff about a concrete frog or whatever. Quite possibly the worst cover story ever. I put it to you Stew that you sabotaged the wagons with foam.' He started to laugh.

'Knew you couldn't keep it up' remarked Colin.

Nick patted Stew lightly on the head. 'Course it wasn't you! You're about as devious as a piece of cheese!'

Colin slurped down some bitter, belched and pointed at Adrian. 'He's the really dodgy one, after Justine that is.'

'What?' moaned Adrian.

'Yeah! 'Oh hi. I'm the new woodwork teacher, would you like some free railway stuff, sure I can build some new sidings. Oh my car got vandalized, I bet you had a lovely breakfast." Colin stood up and waved a soggy beer mat at the accused. 'I put it to you sir that you're a vegetarian and not to be trusted and that… oh fuck it! Nope, that's all I've got.'

Adrian shook his head vigorously. 'You can accuse me of many things but I'm not a vegetarian.'

Pete suddenly made an appearance, muttered something about a minor complication, ran to the bar, ran back, checked who needed a drink and ran back to the bar again.

George watched Pete frantically scanning the selection of crisps. 'Everything alright?' There was no answer. 'I would recommend the ready salted, covers all occasions.'

Pete finally made a decision. 'Right George, I need three salt n vinegar, three plain, two cheese and onion, two tangy beef and one of those.' He pointed to a large bag of pork scratchings. 'Oh! And a round of drinks, same again. Oh! And a pair of scissors and some Sellotape.'

George shook his head and looked mournfully at Linda Lusardi. 'No nuts then?'

'Not now George.'

Pete grabbed the crisps and headed off. George watched him go and muttered. 'I'll bring the drinks over then.'

Captain Hargraves read carefully through the compiled results of the Regionals, a satisfied cloak of contentment slowly enveloping his entire being. Yes, this had been a most satisfactory competition and bode well for the Nationals that would take place next year. He felt sure the Major would be entirely happy with the direction of play that events were taking, a direction that he had, shall we say, nudged a little.

Hargraves reached for his pipe and the small pouch of tobacco that sat patiently at the side of his sprawling desk and was just about to settle down for a decent puff when the phone impertinently rang.

He huffed irritably and lifted the receiver. 'Captain Hargraves.'

'Good evening sir, Ken Bruce here, just checking the results were in order.'

Hargraves sniffed.

'Yes, they were all more or less fine. All in order. Very good. I have been meaning to…' Hargraves trailed off as if suddenly distracted.

Ken prompted him. 'Meaning to?'

'Ah, yes, meaning to talk to you about the goings on in Potton. I need a meeting with you tout suite, chop chop.'

Ken smirked to himself.

'Let me just check my diary.'

There was a brief silence before a second phone started ringing in Hargraves office, eliciting an immediate string of 'dams, buggeries and knickers.'

Hargraves spluttered into the first phone.

'I'll have to phone you back Ken, emergency. You understand.'

Ken let the line go dead and carefully reset the phone with

his right hand. He then passed the second receiver over from his left hand and sat grinning as he listened to Hargraves for a second time.

'Hello, hello. Captain Hargraves here. Can you hear me? Who is this? Who is this?'

Ken put the second phone down and underlined the number in the little red diary. He drew a long breath, forgot the pain this currently induced, winced and then muttered to an empty hotel room. 'Well my Captain Hargraves that answers one question and opens up a whole lot more.' He ran his finger down the list of nameless numbers in the diary and chuckled. Chuckling was at least pain free. He picked up the first phone again and began to dial.

Captain Hargraves sat frowning at his clenched fist. He didn't like his top-secret phone ringing when there was no one on the other end. If nothing else, it was a bugger to get it back into its hidey hole behind the bust of Winston Churchill. In a reflex action he reached for the small locked top drawer of his desk and took out an ornate box. He carefully removed the faded walnut lid and unwrapped a tiny object. A carefully painted lead figure stood staring across the stained green leather of his writing surface. Hargraves moved closer and smiled reassuringly to himself. The Major would calm him down.

'Pete, please mate, I can't eat any more crisps.' Colin pushed the half bag of cheese and onion away.

Pete grabbed the wrapper, tipped the remaining contents onto the table and proceeded to add it to the strange construction that he'd built.

Justine jabbed Nick in the ribs and silently mouthed at him. 'Has he gone mental?'

Nick shrugged and helped Pete Sellotape a final bag on. 'Looks marvellous Pete, any reason why we've built a large tea cosy?'

Pete grabbed the crisp bag cosy and the scissors and jumped up. As he headed out the door he shouted. 'Back in a mo.'

Stew double checked he'd gone before talking. 'So sorry I couldn't help with the crisps, I'm more of a nut man.'

Colin shook his head. 'Stew, the only nut man round here is our dear Peter. I think he's finally gone loco.'

Adrian chuckled. 'Loco! Very funny.'

Justine appeared genuinely concerned. 'Shouldn't someone go out and see if he's ok?'

Everyone stared at her in disbelief.

'What? I'm concerned.'

Nick took it upon himself to translate. 'Justine, my love, no one in here, is going out there, to check on a mentally disturbed man, with a pair of sharp scissors and a tea cosy made from crisp packets... in the dark.'

Life in Lower Didsbury had quickly returned to normal after the climatic events that had unfolded. The 'nuclear explosion' had proved to be an exercise and the apparent existence of a secret nuclear bunker under the carpark at Greenvale had been dismissed as mass hysteria by local officials. Mr Mouncey had begged to differ on this account and had been quickly transferred to a more remote car parking location. The inhabitants of the small Welsh town of Llwunbaddiel never knew what hit them. Another prominent local figure to disappear was Monty 'The Moustache' Rawlins. It was widely assumed he'd been promoted to run a larger station. His replacement was no less as impressive as Monty, sporting a huge beard, false leg and a distinguished career in the Royal Navy.

'Does anybody here know what's going on? I foolishly thought we were celebrating winning a large shiny trophy.' Colin swept his hand theatrically toward the cup.

Adrian let out a large sigh. 'It's my fault, I just wanted to know some more about the saboteur.'

The pub doors banged open and two figures stumbled in.

'Oh my dear fucking hell!' gasped Nick. 'He's really gone and done it this time.'

'At least we know what the tea cosy's for' remarked Colin.

Pete bundled Bomber toward the table and forced him to sit in the corner of the oak settle and then dropped heavily onto the bench himself, jamming Bomber in.

'Adrian, you wanted to know who the saboteur is. Well, here he is!' Pete slapped Bomber heavily in the stomach which elicited a groan and some incomprehensible expletives.

Nick pushed in closer. 'Erm, Pete, just quickly, y'know, before the police are called, is he securely taped up?'

Pete nodded expansively. 'Fully duck taped up, hands, bit of leg, mouth of course and the piece de resistance, the head containment device.' He poked Bomber in the face. There was a slight crunch from an errant bit of crisp trapped in the cosy.

Colin cleared his throat. 'I think this has gone so far one way I'm not sure where to begin. So I won't.' He scrutinized Bomber. 'He's not that big is he?'

There were some more mumbled expletives from the corner.

'Also, did you deliberately put the salt and vinegar packets where the eyes are? Seems unnecessarily cruel.' Colin paused. 'I approve.'

George ambled over. 'Is everything alright over here?

Thought I heard -' he caught site of Bomber. His immediate thought was. 'Oh Christ there's another one of 'em.' George steeled himself. 'Can I get your mate anything?' He nodded toward the corner.'

Pete laughed a little too loudly for comfort. 'Yes indeed George. Could you please get a screwdriver.'

George let out a long disapproving sigh. 'Look, gentlemen, you know my policy vis-a-vis cocktails.'

Everyone looked confusingly at Pete and then back at George.

Pete snorted. 'No George, a screwdriver for screws.'

George smiled, nodded and headed back. To be honest he hadn't got a clue how to make a screwdriver. He was almost at the bar when he suddenly stopped, had a moment of clarity and rushed back to Fishplate. 'Would that be a flat head or a Philips?' He looked visibly pleased with himself.

Pete dipped his head thoughtfully. 'I'm not sure.' He motioned at Nick. 'What do you think would hurt the most?'

Nick shrugged. 'Not the obvious topic of conversation I was looking forward to, but since you ask. 'He paused. 'I would say the flathead, easier to get under the nails.'

Justine dug her own nails into him. 'Nick!'

Pete nodded approvingly. 'Good thinking. George, a flat head if you please.'

George grunted and headed off.

Stew finally spoke. 'I really think we should all pause to think about what happens next. I'm most uncomfortable with,' he pointed at Bomber, 'this.'

Justine nodded slowly. 'I have to agree. Have you any suggestions Stew?'

'Well.'

'Here we go' muttered Nick.

'Well, I really think we should contact the police. I'm sure they would understand the situation and take the appropriate action.'

Colin and Nick burst out laughing.

Colin looked to Nick. 'After you.'

Nick took a deep breath. 'Ok Stew. This guy allegedly derails a train, remember it's a toy train. This is an important point. For this 'crime' he is physically run down and assaulted while trying to escape. During said assault he is somehow knocked unconscious.' Nick and Colin both stared at each other and mouthed 'how?' Nick continued. 'This poor man is then bound up with tape and locked in the boot of his own car' he looked at Pete for confirmation. Pete nodded. 'For a period of -' he looked at Pete again. Pete held up five fingers, while trying not to laugh. 'Christ! Ok then. After being incarcerated for five long hours he is taken to a pub, dressed in crisp bags and tortured with a screwdriver. Have I missed anything?'

'A flat head screwdriver?' snorted Colin.

'Good point. Sorry! Bad joke' laughed Nick.

Stew coughed. 'Well he did break into my inner sanctum.'

There was a collective groan. Colin put his arm round Stew. 'That was Gareth, this is someone else.'

Stew put his hand to his mouth. 'Of course, oops. Gareth was Luke Vader... with the pants, wasn't he?'

'Christ!' Groaned Colin. 'No more nuts for you Stew.

Nick rapped the table. 'The point is, we can't go to the police.'

There was a reflective silence.

George turned up with the screwdriver just as Nick

suggested they contact Big Chris and feed Bomber through his German shredder. This had the effect of George returning tout suite to the safety of his bar and of a renewed bout of mumbling from Bomber.

'What did he just say?' queried Adrian. 'Sounded like. 'Mushin I'm a lorry.'''

'More like 'Cushion and some porridge,'' ventured Colin.

'Must sheen up Norwich?' said Nick.

'Blaspheme I'm horrid' suggested Justine. 'Makes more sense.'

Stew had been quietly examining the screwdriver. 'I tell you what, this is an absolutely beautiful antique screwdriver. Sycamore handle, hand forged, maker's mark. Could be worth a bob or two.' He held it up for the rest to see.

It seemed to jolt Pete into action. He sat bolt upright, looked at Bomber anew and addressed everyone. 'Ok, enough.' He grabbed the screwdriver off Stew and prodded his victim teasingly in the thigh. 'Right, this is what's going to happen.' He put his face close up to Bomber's. 'I'm going to remove your head covering, so we can all stare disapprovingly at you. Once everyone has seen adequately the shit that tried to ruin all our hard work, all our hopes, all the teamwork, all that fucking effort… I will take you outside, undo the tape, hand your car keys back and walk away. I expect you to do the same. If you nod your head in agreement, I promise that this beautiful antique, sycamore screwdriver will be returned unused to the bar and absolutely no more harm will befall you.' The rest of Fishplate mumbled agreement. Pete whispered approximately into Bomber's ear (Cheese and Onion) in a tone full of furious intent.' Remember, it's not business mate, it's very, very fucking personal.'

Pete drew back and started to tap the table gently with the

screwdriver. Team Fishplate looked on in silence.

At first there was no reaction from Bomber, his head was slightly dipped as though thinking and only the sound of breath through a ready salted bag could be discerned. Then the merest of head movement, which grew rapidly to, what could be described as a nodding motion.

Pete smiled. 'A sensible conclusion. Ok then. Time to reveal our friend.' He slipped his hand behind Bomber's neck and slowly peeled off a strip of tape which elicited a string of muffled expletives. The crisp bag cosy became loose and Pete reached to get a grip on the top. 'Here we go then.' Pete pulled off the head covering.

What happened in the next five seconds was a frequent topic of conversation in subsequent Fishplate meetings. Interpretation of events varied depending on viewpoint but some things were agreed upon. Bomber turned to look at Justine and tried to shout something. Justine definitely screamed 'You bastard, so it was you' and reached for the heavy glass ashtray. At this point there was some sort of scuffle in which Nick spilt his drink, Stew fell off his chair and Adrian said something like 'Cheese.' Justine picked up the ashtray and swung it at Bomber. Pete dived to his right while shouting 'I said stare at him,' Stew tried to get up but banged his head on the underside of the table, Adrian started to point at something while Nick raised his hand to shield himself from the ashtray flashing past his face. The sound of said ashtray connecting with Bomber's jaw ended that fateful five seconds and would forever be a point of discussion. It was the 'clunk' (for the sake of argument) that ultimately led to George calling in the police.

PC Collings was there pretty quickly and after securing all the witnesses made the fateful error of talking to Stew first. It was observed by all that he ceased taking notes very shortly after 'model train' was mentioned and was already packing up to leave once 'crisp cosy' was referred to. Because of Justine's relationship to Bomber it was classified as a 'domestic' and since Bomber was still alive, PC Collings thought it best everyone should just go home and put it down to 'experience'.

Peter Fletcher, President of The Smooth Fishplate model railway club, now representing the SE region in the Nationals said later of the episode. 'Oh well, turned out nice again… Trophy looks good there, doesn't it?'

THE END

A BRIEF GLOSSARY OF TERMS

Fiddle yard: A set of sidings where trains can depart or terminate. It is hidden from the viewer and gives the impression of the existence of a much larger rail network in operation.

Fishplate: A piece of metal for joining rail lengths together.

Smooth Fishplate: As above but, smooth baby!

Gauge: The distance between the rails on the track. Smooth Fishplate runs a OO gauge layout or 16.5mm. This gauge is perhaps the best known and most popular in this country. It is however utterly illogical and stupid since OO works to a scale of 76:1 or 4mm to one foot which means that the gauge doesn't match the modelling scale (brilliant). The rest of the planet uses HO which uses the same gauge (16.5mm) but a more accurate scale of 87:1 or 3.5mm to one foot. If none of this makes any sense, ask Nick about it. He can explain it all with a heavy use of expletives and sarcasm.

Pedant: Someone who knows all this detail and suspects the author also knows this and perhaps a whole lot more but remains unable to suspend his disbelief for the duration of the book.